DREAM LOVER

Brianne felt as if she were floating between wakefulness and a delicious state of sleep, filled with erotic
dreams. It was as though she had returned to her earlier
dream, the one that continued to elude her. Every nerve
ending was sending signals to her brain as a phantom
lover caressed her, and lips that demanded a response
took possession of her own.

She wanted him.

It mattered little that he didn't as yet have a face or a
name. She wanted that fulfillment that had always been
just out of reach. It would be all right this time—she just
knew it. Desire and a passion that she had never come
close to experiencing began to take over.

She felt his wide shoulders and sensed the strength
that lay within them as she ran her hands down a smooth,
muscled back. Then, all at once, she realized that she was
no longer dreaming, that she was awake, and about to
come face to face with her mystery lover . . .

TIMELESS PASSION

Constance O'Day-Flannery

ZEBRA BOOKS
KENSINGTON PUBLISHING CORP.

To My Husband, Bill . . . for being the first to believe in me, and giving me the time to believe in myself.
and
Frank, Pat, Ginny, Chris, Don and Maryanne . . . my brothers and sisters by birth . . . my valued friends by choice.

ACKNOWLEDGEMENT AND SPECIAL THANKS

Dale Rose-Fountain, Anne O'Day, Hilari Cohen and Adele Leone . . . for their individual talent and combined encouragement.

ZEBRA BOOKS

are published by

Kensington Publishing Corp.
475 Park Avenue South
New York, NY 10016

First printing: June 1986

Printed in the United States of America

Prologue

Philadelphia 1986

"One drink. You'd think I'd just asked you to check into the Marriott."

"Don't disappoint me, Alex. We may not always agree, but at least I've respected your intelligence." Brianne Quinlan resisted stuffing the papers they had been discussing into her attaché case and instead placed them carefully inside it.

Alex Walker looked at the small, attractive woman as she left her desk and reached for her coat. He sighed as he leaned against the doorway into her office. What was it about this woman that kept bringing him back here, making a fool of himself? He watched as she put her arms into the expensive gray raincoat, not missing the way the material of her dress stretched across her full breasts. He'd worked with her for a year and a half and knew her to be a witty, intelligent woman with a keen eye for organization; but never once in all that time had he seen, or even heard, of her being involved with a man. He'd watched her turn down a fleet of men, and hated himself for joining their ranks.

Possibly Alex found her so irresistible because she was such an enigma. Or perhaps it was because Brianne

Quinlan never seemed to acknowledge the startling effect she had on men. Not quite five foot three, she looked at least five years younger than her twenty-six years. Auburn hair framed a delicate face and fell below her shoulders in a mass of loose curls. Her complexion was almost flawless, marred only by the rosy blush, brought about by either anger or embarrassment, that would creep up her neck to settle on her high cheekbones. It wasn't either of those emotions that Brianne felt as she picked up her briefcase. It was more annoyance. She'd been through this before with Alex. She turned off the overhead lights in her corner office and looked at the tall blond man who continued to stand just outside the door.

Not wanting to make an enemy, Brianne merely smiled and quietly said good night.

As she walked through the deserted office, she could feel his eyes following her the short distance to the elevator.

"Know what they call you? The Ice Maiden."

She stopped walking when she heard the nickname, then inhaled deeply and took the few steps more to the elevator. As she pressed the down button she heard him remark, "I'm starting to believe it's true. What's wrong with you, anyway? One drink."

Brianne entered the elevator but held its heavy steel door with her hand from closing automatically. "Go home, Alex," she said in a tired voice. "It's been a long day."

She removed her hand and the door slowly blocked her from his vision, thus preventing him from seeing the humiliation that clouded over her deep emerald green eyes.

Alex continued to stare at the closed elevator for a few seconds. Shrugging his shoulders, he turned and walked toward his office. It had been worth a shot, he thought. What the hell, he might as well go home to his wife.

Forty minutes later Brianne kicked off her heels and gratefully dug her toes into the soft yellow carpet beneath her feet. Eyeing the canopied bed with longing, she made a face before turning to her closet. Two years ago, when she took the job as group supervisor for a major insurance company, she knew that it wouldn't be easy. But then no one told her about the eight to twelve hours of unpaid overtime she would sometimes be required to put in each week. Granted, her income had allowed her to live quite comfortably, but she was tired of listening to complaints and excuses from those under her, and particularly tired of pacifying those above her. Why was it that she was expected to either perform miracles or fall flat on her face? Where was the happy medium?

Taking out a padded hanger, she carefully hung up the Evan-Picone dress and brought out the deep green sweatsuit. The sharp contrast between her work clothes and those she worked out in never failed to amuse her—from designers' during the day to J. C. Penney's at night. Quickly slipping into the sweatsuit, she ignored the bed that silently beckoned to her, and hurried into the living room before she changed her mind and answered its compelling siren's song to rest for just a little while. Ha! A little while. Brianne knew if she gave in she'd wake up tomorrow morning, still clad in the sweatsuit.

Reaching the stereo, she picked up the familiar tape and pushed the cassette in. A creature of habit, she then hurried into the kitchen and hastily put out the ingredients for her dinner—another cheese omelet. Running back into the living room, she made it just as the heavy bass of the drums began.

Standing in front of the machine, Brianne put her hands on her hips and rolled her head completely around in a circle, stretching her neck and feeling the tension slip away. Five times each way. By the time the horns joined in, she was on her second set and ready for the petulant voice to really begin her exercises. God, the guy could sing, and Brianne loved this song in particular. It wasn't the words or anything meaningful, it was just that he made her want to move. And move she did, in earnest, as Michael Jackson sang to her about a shallow woman named Billie Jean.

Lifting her leg in unison to the chorus, she counted off . . . seven, eight, nine . . . "she says I am the one . . ."

As the song finished, Brianne felt better and waited a few seconds for the next one to begin. She had taped eight songs together to form the cassette and at its conclusion, both she and the driving music were finished. Collapsing onto the rug, she waited for Handel's *Water Music* to begin, bringing her back down and relaxing her heartbeat until it was almost normal.

Stepping out of the shower, she wrapped herself in a fluffy white terrycloth robe and let it absorb the moisture from her body. She unpinned her long, thick hair and brushed it until it shone copper in the harsh bathroom light, then, grabbing Lancôme's Fluide Douceur, she left the small bath for the warm comfort of her bedroom. Absently she hung the robe on a hook attached to the back of her closet, and beginning at her ankles, sprayed her body with the silkening dry oil treatment. Using long, gliding strokes, she smoothed the delicious oil into her skin. Inhaling its delicate fragrance, she reflected that she wasn't doing too badly for a lady of twenty-six. Looking down at her body, she decided it wasn't exactly a great one, but it definitely was not too bad either. In a few years she'd begin to pay for her love of laughter when the lines around her green eyes deepened, but Brianne wasn't disappointed. For now, for her height, she was holding her own. Oh, she'd never have a classical shape, especially now, when it was more fashionable to look like an adolescent boy, but she had done the best she could with the body she'd inherited from her mother—ample bust, small waist and hips, and almost average height. There had been a time a few years ago when she was self-conscious of her breasts and had walked around for months with her shoulders hunched over in an attempt to make them look smaller. But not anymore. She was who she was . . . and it had taken her a lifetime to like the woman who stared back at her each morning in the mirror.

Finishing with the oil, she slipped the nightgown over her head and padded barefoot into the kitchen to prepare her dinner. Glancing at the clock, she shock her head in disgust. Nine twenty-three. What kind of person had dinner at that hour? She knew the answer. A person alone.

"Your own fault, Brianne," she admonished herself aloud. She had received plenty of offers from the men at work and the constant flow of salesmen that passed through her office, but she refused them all, without exception. It wasn't that she was better than the other women that did accept, it just wasn't her policy to mix business with her social life. Besides, most of them were married anyway . . . like Alex. And thinking of him, she clenched her teeth together. How she wished she were more like Corrie and possessed her freedom of vocabulary.

Corrie was one of the resident bag ladies at Penn Center. Each morning she greeted Brianne loudly as she got off the train and made her way through the terminal. Corrie had an opinion on everything and colored each sentence with a thundering four-letter adjective. It didn't matter if she was describing the weather or her aching feet, Corrie went for the shock value. When Brianne first saw the other woman, she was appalled by her language and living conditions and had called a few social agencies to see if they could help. The woman was absent for less than a week before she reappeared, cursing the do-gooders of the city. Now Brianne gave her a smile, returned her greeting in a much less crude way, and minded her own business.

Standing in front of her stove, she shook her head. Corrie wouldn't have had any problem telling Alex what to do with his one drink, and she found herself chuckling as she pictured the scene between them. Yes, Corrie would have done better. She might have told him which part of his anatomy would have to freeze off before the Ice Maiden would accept his offer. She would have scolded, denounced, and reminded him of his wife waiting at home. And thinking of the shy woman she had met a few times at office parties, Brianne took a deep breath and turned off the gas flames. The old standards she had grown up with just didn't exist anymore. With few exceptions, marriage and fidelity no longer went hand in hand, and she only knew she didn't want or need that kind of complication in her life.

Sliding the golden omelet onto her plate, she poured herself a glass of chilled white wine and sat down to eat her dinner. She dismissed the unpleasant incident with Alex from her mind and looked around the kitchen, admiring her work. Last weekend she had spent the two precious days off wallpapering it in a miniature blue print. She loved decorating her home and slowly the townhouse was becoming a reflection of her tastes. Eclectic, the professionals would term it, but to her it was a delightful combination of the soft, soothing pastels of her traditional furniture mixed with the deep, rich woods of antiques. A large, dreamy pastel drawing graced her living room wall with tastefully framed museum posters. Silk flowers vied for room along with a growing collection

10

of plants and two Ficus trees.

She just loved it. Loved seeing her mother's silver tea service resting on her buffet table, her grandmother's hand-crocheted lace canopy atop her poster bed.

It was home . . . hers.

Occasionally a frightening thought occurred to her: that she loved it too much, that she liked living alone, perhaps didn't make more of an effort to find someone because she didn't want the intrusion. Just as in the past, she brushed away the suggestion. She was too busy now to look for Mr. Right. She didn't know who he was, or if he even existed except in her mind. Her friends said her standards were too high, but she just knew the gentle, faceless lover of her dreams was out there someplace . . . waiting.

Sometimes the loneliness was almost overwhelming and she would silently berate herself for constantly turning down offers. It was at those times that she would accept, only to find that before the evening was over she would again be disappointed. She didn't know where this fantasy man was, but she knew for certain he would find her, and she was willing to be patient.

The insistent ringing of the telephone saved her from further self-analysis and brought her back to reality. Grabbing her glass of wine, she raced into the living room to answer it.

"Hello?" she asked deliberately. She was always a little hesitant when it rang after ten, afraid it might be bad news.

"Hi, Bri. Take you away from anything?"

Unconsciously exhaling in relief, she sat down on the sofa and cradled the receiver by her ear. Smiling in anticipation of her younger sister's reaction, she answered, "Actually, Morganna, I have a gorgeous set of Norwegian twins waiting to ravish me in the bedroom. Do you think this will take long?"

11

"Sounds exciting. I knew I shouldn't have left the North. I don't think you could find a decent Norwegian in all of New Orleans—must be the climate."

Brianne listened to her sister's light, breathy laugh as she spoke, but sensed her heart wasn't in the normal easy teasing of their relationship.

"What is it?" she asked. "Don't tell me you've finally made me an aunt."

"Sorry, I'm still in a holding pattern." Morganna sounded down and out.

"Okay, today is Monday. That means you've seen Dr. Crandall. What did he have to say?"

Morganna answered with all the frustration of a woman who has been pregnant too long. "The same thing he's been saying for the past two weeks—I can go any time. It's obvious all his talents are in obstetrics, his predictions aren't worth a plug nickel. He did have one new thing to say, though. If I don't go into labor on my own by Thursday, he's going to induce me."

Brianne's eyebrows came together. "Induce you?"

"Actually, he's going to induce the baby into meeting the outside world. He'll give me a drug, Petosin or something like that, and supposedly labor begins shortly after the injection. Can't say I'm thrilled at the prospect. I've heard it makes for shorter labor, but the pain is more intense."

Brianne looked about the room as she sipped her wine. Suddenly she made a decision. "Listen, I was going to come as soon as you had the baby, so what would you think if I came earlier?"

Morganna's voice sounded almost cheerful. "You're serious? What about work? Can you manage it?"

Brianne laughed. "Are you kidding? Everyone knows I was going to take three weeks off as soon as you delivered. It will just be a little earlier than they expected. Believe me, they're prepared. Ken Seagram is

12

just itching to take over the department, so I'll give the gentleman the opportunity. Besides, they owe me the time. I'll call Larry Huber at home tonight and set everything in motion."

"Bri, are you sure? I'm all right, really, just feeling a little sorry for myself."

Brianne rolled her eyes back. "Don't do this to me, Morganna. I'm coming! Truth is, I need it too. I've never been to New Orleans, never seen your home, except in pictures. This way I can be with you on Thursday. Big sister lending moral support and all that."

Morganna sounded more like her normal, cheerful self, and Brianne could visualize the happy smile on her face. "This is terrific! Charles will meet you at the airport. Call me back when you have your flight number."

"I'm not going to fly down," Brianne stated abruptly. "I'm going to drive. The car's almost new and I've never taken it on a long trip. As a matter of fact," she said as plans started materializing in her head, "I think I'll leave tonight. Well, tomorrow morning, actually. It's the best time to drive. When I get tired, I'll pull over and find a motel, sleep for a couple of hours, and then get back on the road. With any luck, I should get there by Wednesday evening."

The concern came through the wire. "Oh Bri, why go through all that when you could get on a plane and be here in a couple of hours?"

"Because it's an adventure, Morganna, something I'd enjoy. Now stop being silly and let me get started. I want to call Larry before he's asleep. I promise I'll call you tomorrow night and check in with you."

"If you're sure . . . just be careful."

Brianne grinned as she said, "I'll be careful, I promise. Won't take the car over eighty miles an hour or pull over at any truck stops, unless some fabulous man in an

13

eighteen-wheeler insists."

Morganna groaned, "Oh God! I'm not worried about a trucker, you're too hard to please when it comes to men. But that car is a different story."

"Will you please stop it?" Brianne insisted. "When have you ever known me not to be careful? For God's sake, my whole life has been careful. This time won't be any different. Now do me a favor, Mrs. Barrington. You've waited this long, see if you can hold out until I get there. Tell that baby to wait for his aunt." Brianne's voice became serious as she whispered, "I love you, Morganna. See you Wednesday."

The young, self-sufficient wife of one of New Orleans's leading attorneys sounded like a very young girl as she answered in a tiny voice, one that Brianne had been familiar with since childhood, "I love you too. And Bri? Thanks."

Brianne smiled as she dialed her boss's number. She and Morganna still reached for each other when they were down, just as they had done as children. Some things never change, she mused, and obviously the Quinlan girls' dependence on each other, even long distance, was one of them.

Brianne threw her bags into the back seat, put the key into the ignition of her new Mustang GLC, and checked her watch. One forty-seven. She was almost forty-five minutes ahead of schedule.

She went over in her mind everything she had done, checking off a mental list. Work was taken care of, clothes were packed—both casual and a few dressier outfits, she'd be there for the christening—and her makeup was in the overnight case. She had watered the plants and slipped a note under Mrs. Hanraty's door asking the kindly widow neighbor to look after them in

14

her absence. Anything she'd forgotten would have to take care of itself.

Taking a deep breath, Brianne turned the key and listened to the powerful roar of the V8 engine. Confident in the machine and her ability to control it, she maneuvered the stick shift into reverse and her excitement grew as she drove to the electronic machine at her bank. There she would be able to withdraw the money for this trip. With a limit of three hundred dollars, she planned to use her credit cards to gas the car and charge the motels. The cash was for anything unexpected.

Fifteen minutes later, she was on Interstate 95, and even though she knew it was crazy to start a long trip on the spur of the moment, she nevertheless was happy and excited. It was so unlike her to do something like this. Usually she was conservative in her way of life, and, passing a large truck—one that had to have at least eighteen wheels—she smiled thinking of her conversation with Morganna. Without the slightest interest in its driver, she happily pursed her lips and started to whistle Dixie as she headed south.

Two nights later, the last thing she wanted to hear was Dixie or anything remotely pertaining to the South. What had been a relaxing, easy trip, especially through the Blue Ridge Mountains, had turned into a disaster outside of New Orleans when she missed the turnoff for the Ponchartrain Causeway. Twice she had tried to get back, but failed. That one stupid mistake meant she'd have to go around the lake and come into New Orleans from the opposite direction. What she hadn't counted on was the size of it. She'd seen oceans that seemed smaller. To compound her error, she followed something called the Bonnet Carré Spillway and wound up on the other side of the Mississippi. True to form, when she messed up she did it big.

With her patience reaching its limit, she stopped and was reassured by an older man, who spoke to her as though she should have known better, that if she followed Route 18 it would take her to Route 90. And Route 90 would take her back across the Mississippi, by way of the Huey Long Bridge. Then if she could manage to stay on 90, it would take her right into New Orleans.

He seemed a bit suspicious as he looked at her car and the Pennsylvania license plate and she bit her lip in vexation, but still thanked him politely as she tried to memorize his directions.

Pleased to have found Route 18, Brianne leaned back against the soft leather seat and exhaled loudly in an effort to expel some of the tension. Turning the radio back on, she went through the stations but was unsuccessful in locating anything but country music. Having listened to it through three states, she switched the selector to tape and pushed in the first cassette she laid her hands on in the dark.

Billy Joel. Northeastern music. Her music.

Brianne estimated she was about thirty-five miles out of New Orleans and with any kind of luck, she should arrive at the ancestral home of the Barringtons in forty-five minutes or so. Wait until she told Morganna and Charles about driving through almost a quarter of the United States without getting lost, only to have it happen at their back door, so to speak. All that was separating them at the time was a massive lake!

She shook her head at her own stupidity, but knew she'd laugh about it later tonight over drinks with her brother-in-law and sister.

Brianne saw headlights in the distance, her eyes riveting to them because of the lonely, dark stretch of road. Returning her eyes to the asphalt in front of her,

16

she continued to hum along with the music, tapping her nail on the steering wheel.

Squinting her eyes as the lights came closer, she stretched her neck closer to the windshield.

"Damn!"

He did it again. Must be drunk, swerving into her lane like that!

The headlights abruptly veered into the correct lane and Brianne relaxed slightly, still anxious to pass by the other car. About a hundred yards away she'd see his rear lights in her mirror and unconsciously she tightened her grip on the steering wheel as the distance between the two cars closed.

Suddenly, unbelievably, the lights were in front of her! *Not in his lane, but in hers!* An onset of terror, the feeling of her heart dropping to her stomach occurred as the other car's headlights blinded her with their stark intensity. Without thinking and with no time for logical alternatives, Brianne gut reacted and she pulled the wheel sharply to her right.

She had no time to be grateful for missing the car as she fought to gain control of her own powerful automobile that she had sent careening down an embankment.

It happened so quickly, in a matter of seconds, that only one thought flashed through her mind—she couldn't remember a single prayer!

Brianne knew she was going to hit the tree and tried to brace herself for the impact. But because she had not used her seatbelt, she was sent into the windshield as the huge trunk of the tree melded into her engine.

Brianne's eyes slowly opened, then abruptly closed as if the effort were too much. She heard the motor running and felt something smooth against her cheek.

The window. Her face was pressed up against the window. Why? Confused, she reopened her eyes and it

17

came back to her in a terrifying flash. The drunk driver. She'd had an accident! Lifting her head, she tried to sit up straight and felt a sharp pain in her temple.

Sucking in her breath, she shut off the ignition and blessed the peaceful quiet that immediately followed. She knew she shouldn't stay in the car; she had to find help. Her head hurt and she knew it had to be taken care of.

Dear God, she silently pleaded, make it stop throbbing!

Such a simple thing as opening the car door took all her strength and seemed a colossal feat. Stumbling from the car, she looked in the direction she had come. The other driver hadn't even stopped! Even though she could no longer see the highway, from the dead silence that surrounded her she knew the drunk had kept right on going.

Wanting to cry but unable to, she suddenly began to shake uncontrollably, and looking into the darkness she felt cold, chilled to the bone. Wasn't it supposed to be warm down here in June? Brianne knew she was in shock, knew she had to find help soon. She saw the headlights of her car shining into the woods and bracing herself against the fender, using it as a support, she eased her way to them. Perhaps there was a house out here somewhere.

Too late, Brianne saw that the tree only grew at the edge of another hill. Trying desperately, she clawed at the smooth, silver gray metal of the fender in a hopeless attempt to stop herself from sliding down it. She felt sick as the ground gave way under her and she cried out in panic as she fell. Down into the unknown, her already abused body was forced to endure more.

She wasn't sure if she had blacked out again or if her mind had just shut down, not letting her feel the pain of the fall. She lay on the soft, damp earth and closed her eyes.

In her mind, in the distance, was a bright light attracting her to its warmth. And beyond it she could see

18

her mother and father as they had looked when she was a child. Both were smiling, and her dad was holding out his hand to her. She wanted to reach him, knowing it was urgent that she do so. He would take care of everything—just as he had always done.

But they started to fade away.

No! Her mind screamed silently at them to come back, but they were gone as gently as they had come.

In her desolation she shivered again with the unbelievable cold that had taken over her and opened her eyes. Stars were shining through the tree limbs, and the sounds around her were more acute. The crickets, the frogs, and the rustling of leaves mingled harmoniously, creating a symphony of nature just for her.

It was all unreal and for a few timeless seconds, she let the peacefulness wash over her. Then, as she felt herself slipping back, she closed her eyes and willingly gave herself over to the comforting darkness.

Later, after she'd rested, she'd think about what she should do.

But not now. There'd be time later . . .

Chapter 1

"Madam? Are you aware that you're trespassing?"

Brianne's eyelids fluttered open at the sound of an annoyed human voice. The sun was shining into her face, and she could only make out the silhouette of a tall man holding the reins of a very large horse.

Stumbling to her feet, she ignored the pain as she absently brushed the hair back from her face. "Thank God you found me!" she exclaimed in relief. "I had an accident last night and fell down the hill as I was trying to find help."

He removed his broad hat and tapped it against his leg as though impatient with her. From his stance, she felt obliged to reinforce her gratitude. "I can't tell you how relieved I am that you discovered me out here. Perhaps you could direct me back to the main highway? I could get help from there."

He made her nervous, just staring at her like that. Why didn't he say anything?

Bringing the horse with him, he came closer into the shade of the trees, and Brianne could see he was much taller than she had first realized, and well dressed, in dark brown pants tucked into high riding boots and a crisp white shirt opened at the throat. She took all this in a matter of seconds, but resisted the impulse to brush off the debris that clung to her jeans. She had good reason to look terrible, after the night she had just spent.

When he finally spoke he startled her so, with his rich, deep voice, that she jumped like a frightened kitten.

"You happen to be on Briarfawn, Miss . . . ?"

"Oh, I'm sorry. My name is Brianne Quinlan. Look, I am sorry if you think I'm trespassing, but I can assure you . . ."

"As I was saying, Miss Quinlan," he rudely interrupted, "you are on Briarfawn, my family's plantation, and there is no highway that you speak of, only a small road that is seldom used. Are you quite sure you did not travel by boat and miss the return trip due to an indulgence in childish pranks?"

Brianne merely blinked at him for a few moments, trying to make sense out of what he said. "Boat? I told you I had an accident. And what do you mean by childish pranks?"

All right, so she was trespassing, but this man was positively obtuse, or a little unhinged. How many times did she have to explain?

"Come now, Miss Quinlan, we both know I was to expect my new overseer late yesterday, recommended by Stephan, of course, and he hired you to show up in his place. From your accent I can tell you aren't familiar with the area, so you became lost and missed the returning boat. Don't worry, I'll not tell Stephan you failed in your mission. In fact, the symbolism would be quite amusing at any other time."

Astonished, Brianne stared at him while stuttering, "Are you mad? How can you possibly think I would impersonate your . . . your *overseer?* I don't know any Stephan and I've never heard of this Briarfawn. All I want is to get out of here and find my way into New Orleans."

Suddenly, she was filled with apprehension as she watched him tie the reins from the black horse to a branch. As he walked up to her his eyes, which were a startling shade of blue, turned slightly darker, contrasting sharply with his tanned face and dark brown hair. "If I were you, I would not speak lightly of being deranged, considering your appearance," he said, coming closer to her.

She could see a muscle working below his cheekbone as though he were fighting to control his temper, and her skin prickled as instinct told her something was wrong with this man. Could he really be insane? He certainly was irrational. His mannerisms were out of place and his speech too formal. Maybe his family kept him out here in the country, away from people, so he wouldn't harm anyone. With the way her luck was running, anything could be possible . . . and now she had made him angry with her.

Obviously the quicker she put an end to this conversation, the better. "Listen, I don't want to cause any trouble. I apologize again for being on your property, but I think now that it's daylight I can find my own way."

Turning her back on him, she looked at the hill before her. Funny, from the fall she took, she thought it would have been higher. And where was the tree she had hit last night? Confused but determined to get away from the hostile stranger, Brianne started to climb the short incline, wincing as her ankle throbbed in unison with her head. She was forced to drag her foot behind her, making her gait resemble Walter Brennan's. What difference did it make? The whole encounter was a comedy of errors anyway. His overseer! There had to be a good laugh in this somewhere. Maybe when she was safely with her sister, she'd be able to find it.

"Wait!" He shouted at her in a loud voice that seemed to bounce off the surrounding bushes.

Brianne felt the adrenaline start rushing through her veins, and she broke into a hobbled run as she heard him begin to follow her. Desperately she tried to reach the top of the hill, her only thoughts of escaping the unbalanced man whom she considered to be a threat.

Almost to the top, she looked beyond the ridge and was stunned. Water! What . . . ? Before her was a muddy river of some kind. Where was her car? Or even the highway?

She heard him yell after her and frantically searched for a means of escape, but she was boxed in by the water in front of her and the man behind.

Beginning to panic, she quickly decided on the water as her only option. Hesitating for a fraction of a second too long, she felt an iron grip on her upper arm. Then something even more frightening than the menacing stranger happened. Her last thoughts were of Morganna and the child she might never see, forcing her vision to darken like miniature tunnels as the ground came up to meet her.

"God!" Ryan was barely able to keep the woman from hitting her head as she went limp before him. This habit some women had of fainting when confronted was damned annoying. Gathering the stranger in his arms, he looked at her as her hair fell back from her face. From the look of the bruise on her temple, which had swelled to the size of an egg, she must have been telling the truth about having had an accident. Probably happened when she fell last night in the dark. Stupid thing to be doing, wandering around out here at night. Mindful of the leg she'd been favoring, he carefully picked her up and, silently grateful for his stature, began the slow descent.

Placing her on the soft ground as he reached the cover of the trees, he left her to unhook the canteen of water from his saddle. He soaked his linen handkerchief with the still, cool liquid and knelt down beside her as he wiped her face.

Looking closely at the woman in front of him, he realized that with the dirt washed from her, she was almost pretty. Skin that had glowed in anger minutes ago was now pale, and light brown hair, which the sun highlighted in copper, framed fine features. As his gaze lowered to her body, he was surprised to find generous breasts on such a small frame.

Cursing himself as he felt the familiar tightening below his belt, Ryan abruptly stood and began pacing next to her.

"Damn Stephan and his practical jokes!"

This one had gone too far, he thought with growing anger. Not only had the girl been hurt, but he'd lost valuable time in hiring an overseer for Briarfawn. After three long years of backbreaking work the plantation was finally self-sufficient, and with a competent overseer it would remain so until he returned from Virginia. He had finally made up his mind to marry Caroline Daniels, cousin to his best friend. Not that he actually loved her— but he understood her. He knew she needed a strong hand to restrain her selfish nature, but he could afford to be indulgent as long as she gave him the son and heir he wanted.

With thoughts of the lusty blonde Caroline still on his mind, he stopped and looked at the woman at his feet.

This kind of trouble he didn't need. Stooping, he re-applied cool water to her face, gently running the cloth across her high cheekbones and smooth brow. Unconsciously he studied her lips, noticing how well shaped and defined they were—full, ripe and partially opened. Then foolishly, without thought and acting on an inner instinct, he bent his head and kissed them lightly, giving in to the inviting temptation.

Fragile lids fanned by long, dark lashes snapped open and eyes the color of the dark green forest itself stared back at him.

"Who *are* you?" she breathed.

Every bone in her body had felt jarred until Brianne sensed the soft brush of lips upon her own. It was so pleasant and warming that she had felt sorry when the kiss ended. Trying to recapture it and failing, she opened her eyes, only to be held prisoner by the bluest ones she had ever seen. The face before her was undeniably handsome. With his lips parted in an almost amused half grin, she could see even white teeth and the beginning of a slight cleft in his chin. Lashes a woman would envy circled his eyes and a stray lock of dark brown hair fell over a brow that, surprisingly, looked intelligent. At any other time his appearance would have made her look twice in appreciation, but the face still belonged to the man she had tried to escape, and his manner disturbed her more now than before.

Cocking one eyebrow as he looked down on her, he said smoothly, "Ryan Barrington at your service, Madam. Now if you can sit up, perhaps we can see to that bruise at your temple."

Brianne's hand flew to her head. Feeling the hard knot, she inhaled sharply with pain as she tried to rise. He extended a ringless hand to help her, and much as she hated to, she accepted it, seeing no other way to get to her feet. Their eyes met briefly and she could feel herself blush, remembering how she had felt when he kissed her.

"I must apologize for that," the stranger laughed lightly. "It was unfair of me to take advantage of you in your state."

Good Lord, it was as though he could read her mind. Uncomfortable with that thought, she dismissed his apology and stated, "I just want to contact my family in

26

New Orleans."

She still didn't trust him and had no intention of entering into a discussion that could only embarrass her.

Rising, she let out a gasp as she tried to put her weight on her leg.

"It seems you've sprained that ankle. Here, lean on me until we reach Raven." He indicated the large horse still waiting patiently.

As his arm encircled her shoulders she noticed how tall and muscular he actually was and felt dwarfed next to him. The difference in size made the short walk awkward, and after a few yards he stopped to unleash an oath and Brianne found herself abruptly swept up into his arms.

"It seemed much easier to carry you," he muttered, and Brianne was forced to put her arms around his neck to keep from falling. She was at a loss for words. No one had ever carried her except her father, and this man did so with ease.

Reaching the horse, he gently placed her next to it and looked into her face. "Do you think you can stand if you lean against him?"

Nodding, Brianne placed a hand against the leather saddle and watched as he picked up his hat, put it on, and came back to stand in front of her.

"Can you ride?"

"I'm afraid I never learned." She had always preferred to admire the sleek animals at a distance, their size making her timid.

"Never mind." Impatiently, without asking, he picked her up again, this time to place her on the back of the huge mount.

"Raven can carry us both," he stated, and without giving her a chance to reply he swung himself up behind her.

Brianne thought of little else than the man, so close to her that she had to concentrate to keep her back away from his chest. He had a clean, citrusy smell to him, mixed with the faint scents of leather and tobacco. Angry with herself for even noticing it, she again straightened her back. Who could he be? And where was he taking her? More important, why was she letting him, without any questions?

Jolted, she remembered. Oh God! Had he really said his last name was Barrington? All she needed was to discover that this man was some distant relative of Charles, Morganna's husband. Fine way to meet the extended family. No sense wondering about it, she might as well find out. He couldn't be any more upset with her than he already was.

Turning her face halfway, she asked, "Did you say your name was Barrington?" And silently prayed, as she waited for his answer, that she had misunderstood him.

But Ryan was engrossed in his own thoughts. Thoughts that had begun when he put his arms around the woman to grasp the reins and keep her still, her nervousness being easily communicated to Raven.

She was lovely, no doubt about that, and once she was dressed in proper clothes, instead of the man's trousers she had worn as part of the joke, she would probably be stunning.

With her unbound hair so close to his face, Ryan's thoughts darkened. This couldn't have happened at a worse time, and with Samuel Murdock staying at Briarfawn, along with his wife, he'd have to come up with a plausible story when he rode up to the house carrying this woman. Samuel, his godfather, was a good man and Ryan enjoyed his company, but he was ruled by his wife Catherine, a kind woman afflicted with very high moral standards who vowed that a good example was the best teacher. Poor Samuel didn't stand a chance in her company and lived in fear that tales might reach her ears of his conduct in her absence.

28

How was he to explain this Brianne Quinlan . . . to them, of all people? Samuel might see the humor in the situation, but Catherine? Never.

Damn Stephan again! Ryan silently cursed his best friend. It was only two weeks ago when they were dining at the St. Charles Hotel in New Orleans, and their discussion came back to him now with a sharp clarity. It was then Ryan had told Stephan of his intention to marry Caroline and his need for a temporary overseer. Not that Nathen, his negro foreman who had worked at his side these past years, couldn't handle the job . . . but his neighbors would be uneasy with an unsupervised plantation that was home for close to two hundred negroes.

Stephan had hotly disagreed with his choice of a wife. Knowing that there was no love lost between the cousins, Ryan had tried to explain. "I'm aware of Caroline's nature. She's willful, petty, and spoiled, but I find I now desire a family, and Caroline has already proved to be an excellent bed partner. I certainly have no illusions of being the first, but I intend to keep her very busy until she is carrying my child. After that, she may indulge her every whim. Think of it, Stephan, we shall be related. I know you don't care for Caroline, but I also know you'll do your best to get along with her. I've made my choice. Besides," Ryan had added, "it's the child I want."

Stephan had slowly shaken his head. "Ryan, we have been friends for many years and although half the mothers in this city will breathe a sigh of relief, and the other half will be furious they missed the chance at the Barrington money, I cannot approve of Caroline as your wife. But since your mind is set and I cannot dissuade you, I'll look for someone to attend to Briarfawn while you make the biggest mistake of your life in Virginia."

Later that night, at an infamous New Orleans brothel, each of them with a woman under his arm, Stephan had

29

laughingly looked up at Ryan as he started up the stairs with a curvaceous redhead. Although slightly drunk at the time, Ryan now recalled Stephan's words . . . words that had first come back to him when he had initially seen the woman lying beneath the hill. With that trouble-making look in his eye, Stephan had muttered something about "What you need, Ryan, is a good woman to oversee *you*, not your people. Forget about going to Virginia and look closer to home."

Feeling the woman in front of him shift, Ryan was brought back to the present. She had turned to him and he was treated to a profile that again stirred the desire he had earlier overcome. It was the purity of it that infuriated him.

Feeling she had no right to look so innocent, he asked her shortly, "You said something?"

"Yes, I asked if your last name was Barrington." As he nodded in the affirmative, Brianne groaned. If it were up to her she wouldn't say another word to him, but this involved Morganna and her brother-in-law's family. She decided it would be best to be honest now and avoid later embarrassment.

"My sister Morganna is married to Charles Barrington of New Orleans. Would you be related?"

"There is no Charles Barrington living in New Orleans that I know of, and if there were, he certainly wouldn't be a relation. The only Barringtons in Louisiana are myself and my brother Gavin. With Gavin away, you are looking at the only one in residence." What scheme was she hatching now? Ryan wondered. Now that her first plan had failed, did she intend to make trouble? If it was money she wanted, he would give her something. Although it was against his better judgment, he would do anything to avoid difficulty when the Murdocks were visiting.

Brianne breathed a sigh of relief. At least he didn't

30

know Charles, and he must be a recluse if he had never heard of the Barringtons of New Orleans. Maybe it was a common name in the South, but even Brianne had been impressed with the Barringtons' graciousness and quiet dignity when they had traveled north for Morganna's small, informal wedding.

She noticed they were approaching a large field and saw a good number of black people working in it. When they neared, faces would look up and nod or smile and a few said, "Mornin', Misser Barrington, suh."

Forgetting her decision not to speak to him, she asked out of curiosity, "Are these all your workers?"

If she was assessing his holdings, he would let her know the extent of his wealth and how very little of it she might expect.

"These are some of my people. There are more in the south field, at the mill, and of course there are the house servants. However, you should know that I prize everything I own and loath parting with even a small part of it. I'm sure Stephan will compensate you for the trouble you've had, although you did bring it upon yourself. If you hadn't run off like a frightened animal, you wouldn't have fainted at the levee."

Brianne could hardly believe her ears. This guy was incredible! She spent a good deal of time trying to gain control of her temper, but it was useless. She was too angry now.

"If you hadn't frightened me, I wouldn't have run away! And as far as acting like an animal—I would say that description fits you, considering your actions after I fainted."

Now that she had started, she couldn't have stopped even if she wanted to, which she didn't. The man was really offensive. He was right. He couldn't be any relation to the Barringtons she knew, he was so pompous and overbearing.

31

Turning from the waist so she could face him, she let loose. "And, you speak about these people as though you own them, and considering the way they're dressed, they probably feel as though you do. How can you possibly defend this?" she asked with a wave of her hand.

Ryan looked into her face as it came alive with indignation. "Where are you from, Miss Quinlan?"

"Philadelphia. What difference does that make?"

Ryan considered her answer for a moment and then referred back to her original question. "For your information, I do own them—at least those who have not yet bought their freedom with the wages I pay them."

He was so tired of justifying his convictions. He had come to expect it from those Southerners who bled both the land and their slaves dry. They refused to understand that with a little dignity a man will work harder and longer and avoid any trouble that would interfere with his future freedom. It always gave him a certain amount of happiness to recall the freedom parties, as the negroes called them, where he would present one with his bought papers of freedom. He thought of it as an investment in the future, but more than that, it was positive proof that his way could work. Most decided to stay on at Briarfawn, but those who wished to leave were welcome to remain until they had the means to move on. It had cost him a lot in acquaintances and money to follow his beliefs, but he was rewarded with one of the finest plantations in Louisiana.

Now this woman, this person masquerading as a male, in a man named Calvin Klein's trousers, would dispute everything he had worked for. By God, he'd not have it!

Angrily he asked, "What's wrong with their clothes? Believe me, Madam, I have traveled north, even to your home city of Philadelphia, and I would be ashamed to clothe another human being, be he of color or not, as I have seen in our northern states. Since you are obviously

32

an abolitionist, I would think you could appreciate working within the system."

Abruptly, he looked out into the field. "Celia, please come here a moment."

Stunned by his words, Brianne watched as a young girl in her teens came to stand before them.

"Yes suh, Misser Barrington," she greeted him with a shy smile, but her eyes looked over Brianne in open curiosity and remained on her jeans.

Barrington interrupted her staring. "Celia, this is Miss Quinlan. She was injured on Briarfawn. Find Nathen and have him tell Mattie to prepare for us." They both watched as the girl ran off across the field.

Turning back to the woman, Ryan said forcefully, "Look, I don't want to argue with you. I have guests and I won't humiliate either one of us by telling the truth about your reasons for being here. If you're smart, you'll keep your mouth closed and let me do the talking."

Brianne's mouth was most certainly opened now as she gaped at him. Finding her voice, she fumed, "I don't believe you! You have the nerve to tell me to keep *my* mouth shut when every time you open yours, you've proved just how unstable you are! I have sat here and listened to this . . . this myth you've created for yourself. Where do you think you are? You swagger through this place like some outdated version of Rhett Butler. I don't know how you got these people to act and dress the part, but don't expect me to *Massah* you! First I'm impersonating your overseer, and now I'm an abolitionist! My God, you really are insane!"

"Shut your mouth!" he hissed through clenched teeth. "You're becoming hysterical!" Looking around he saw that work had stopped and they were being watched. More quietly he continued, "I know exactly where I am and who I am. You're the one with all the wrong answers."

33

Her chest was heaving from her outburst and her eyes were filling with tears as she tried to reason with him. "Listen, Mr. Barrington, you can keep your vision of the Old South. All I want is to return to the real world. You remember, that's the one with telephones that you use to call cabs. If you can manage to find your way to that one, I'll gladly be out of your fantasy."

His eyes narrowed as he looked closely into her face. "And where exactly is this real world that you speak of?"

Exasperated, her patience having long given way to frustration, Brianne practically yelled, "I don't know. It's in reality—the 1980s. Certainly not here, in your personal version of the 1800s!"

During this last outcry she had unknowingly grabbed the front of his shirt. Seeing her thin digital watch at her wrist, she said urgently, "Look at this . . . I have proof!"

Smugly she pushed the watch into his face, hoping she might see a spark of reason in his eyes. Instead, she watched them narrow suspiciously.

"What is this thing you wear?" he asked, with confusion plainly written over his handsome face.

Brianne's eyes widened. "A watch. Don't you even know a watch when you see one?" she asked in disbelief. "Just look at the numbers," she urged.

He glanced down at her hand. "It says nine twenty-two. Am I to assume that is the correct time?"

Impatiently she went on, "Wait! Now push the little button on the side."

He indulged her. As soon as his tanned finger depressed the tiny piece of gold, the digits immediately changed. His whole body tensed and he pulled his finger back quickly. "This is no watch. I have never seen another of its kind," he observed hesitantly.

If she weren't so desperate, Brianne could have giggled at his childish wonder. "Believe me, Mr. Barrington, it's a watch. What does it say?"

"It reads six-two."

Excited, she said, "That's right. The sixth month, the second day. Though really it should say six-three, but never mind. Now push it again. The year will appear next."

He looked into her eyes briefly, as if judging her sanity, before he again touched the watch. The numbers 1 9 8 6 flashed at him. His lower jaw dropped in amazement before he recovered and flung her hand away, saying, "Enough of this! It's a very good trick, quite ingenious, but I don't find it amusing."

She heard him make a clicking noise with his mouth and the horse started again. The man was hopelessly lost in the past. Uselessly, she waved her arm at him. "How can you argue with that?"

He brought the horse up sharply and Brianne had to grab the pommel to keep her balance.

"How can you argue with this, Madam? Look around you. It is April 11, 1856 . . . and the entire world will tell you so."

Chapter 2

The eyes that stared back at him were frightened. Ryan could see that she was fighting back tears, and in spite of everything he had to admire her. When she turned away from him, she began to breathe deeply as she stared off into space.

Soon she pleaded in a broken voice, "Please, no more games. I'm exhausted. I don't have the energy for this." She pressed the palm of her hand to her head as though in pain.

As much as he was inclined, Ryan couldn't afford to comfort her. If they were to get through the excitement their arrival was bound to cause, she would need her wits about her.

In a deceptively stern voice he commanded her attention. "Stop crying and listen to me. We're almost there. Look!" he pointed to his home in the distance. "Now this is what we'll tell them. I found you this morn—"

Brianne looked up as though defeated, and turning her head in the direction of his outstretched arm, her small body suddenly became stiff before him. He stopped speaking when unbelievably, without any warning, the woman's whole body seemed to soften and she slowly

37

toppled onto Raven's neck.

"Christ!" He caught her about the waist and brought her back against his chest. She was unnaturally pale and the bruise at her temple was an ugly shade of purple, all the more pronounced because of her color. Cursing himself for losing his temper when the girl was injured and needed medical care, he drove his heels into the horse's sides.

Mattie and both the Murdocks were on the porch waiting for him when they saw the cloud of dust. Realizing that the speed at which they were traveling meant urgency, Catherine turned to the housekeeper. "Ryan would never push Raven that hard unless the woman was seriously hurt. Quickly, tell Mary to prepare the yellow room."

As Mattie nodded and hurried into the house, Catherine called after her, "And bring your medicine kit. We don't know what to expect."

Samuel and Nathen came running toward him as Ryan reached the house.

"What happened?" Samuel asked as he steadied Raven, whose sides were blowing from the run.

Not answering his godfather, Ryan nodded to his foreman. When Nathen reached up to take the unconscious girl, Ryan saw the watch on her wrist, and feeling like a thief, slipped it off before releasing her to the others.

Catherine, meeting them in the entry hall, repeated the question, "What happened?"

"It's her head."

Not waiting for Ryan to finish, she commanded them, "Bring her upstairs. Mattie has the yellow room ready."

They all followed Nathen into the bedroom and watched as he gently placed her down on the feather mattress.

"Is it just her head?" Catherine came closer. "Is there

anything broken?"

"I don't think so," Ryan said uncertainly as he watched Catherine brush the hair away from the wound and start issuing orders.

"Mary, bring me the towels and water. Mattie, your bag, please."

Samuel, who had remained silently at the doorway watching the flurry of activity, approached Ryan. "Who is she? What happened to her?"

"Her name is Brianne Quinlan. I found her by the levee, behind the north field. There's a hill back there. I thought she was asleep, but she must have been unconscious. When she came around she didn't remember anything except her name."

He was surprised at how easily the lie came, since it wasn't anything near his original story. Feeling guilty, he added, "Check her ankle. She had trouble standing."

"Can't do nothin' with you standin' here," Mattie pronounced. "You jus' be grateful you found her when you did. No tellin' how long that poor chile been layin' out there."

"Samuel, take him downstairs," Catherine ordered. "We have work to do."

For once Ryan was relieved to be cast out of a room, even if it was in his own house. He sure as hell could use a drink.

"Well, Miz Catherine, what d'you think?" the housekeeper asked after the men had left.

"I don't know quite what to think, Mattie," Catherine replied as she washed the young woman's head. "First let's take care of this wound."

The older woman took the cotton cloth and again dipped it into the basin of water Mary had brought. "The skin is hardly broken," she observed. "It's the swelling

39

I'm worried about."

After they had tended to her as best they could, Catherine added, "We won't know the extent of the damage until she wakes up. Let's look at the ankle."

Catherine's horrified eyes met Mattie's amused ones across the bed. "Was wonderin' when you'd notice them," Mattie said, then chuckled as she nodded to the pants.

Catherine unconsciously fingered her own gray silk gown and thought of her filled closets. If she had one vice, it was beautiful clothes. How could she have missed seeing those dreadful things? "Mattie, she must have been in desperate trouble to be forced to wear men's trousers," she said charitably. "Help me get them off and we'll wrap that ankle."

Once they had removed Brianne's designer jeans, Catherine held them out to Mary. Looking at them with distaste, she said, "Take them out back and burn them, along with this shirt. It's ruined anyway." Without mentioning them, she included the strange undergarments along with the shirt, and then turned back to the housekeeper. "Mattie, go to my room and bring back a nightgown. I don't care which one. We'll bathe her first and then make her comfortable."

Satisfied that she had done everything possible, Catherine told Mattie to stay with the girl. She was going to go downstairs and ask Lizzie to make a light broth, but more important, she wanted to see Ryan. She loved that boy as though he were her own, and something told her there was more to this than finding a stranger in need. It was as if he felt responsible.

When Ryan had first come downstairs after being led out of the girl's room by Samuel, he was met by Aaron, his manservant, who shared high rank with Mattie on the

40

plantation. Before the valet opened the door leading into his study, Ryan stopped him. "Aaron, do you have the time?"

The man reached into his pocket and brought out the fob watch given to him two years ago at Christmas by his employer. "It's comin' on eleven thirty-five, suh."

"Thank you, Aaron." Then, knowing his godfather's love of horses, he turned and asked, "Samuel, would you check on Raven for me?" Samuel would gladly go and be kept busy for some time.

With the door shut behind him, Ryan walked straight over to the liquor cabinet and poured himself a good portion of bourbon. Lifting the glass to his lips, he finished it in one swallow. He then brought out the watch that seemed to be burning a hole in his pocket, and taking a deep breath, looked down at it.

"Hah! Nine twenty-two." He pushed the small button and saw the same numbers come up that he had read earlier. "I knew it was a trick!" he said out loud as he quickly replaced the watch in his pocket, embarrassed at even checking.

When Samuel returned to the study he saw Ryan refilling his drink. "Pour me one, son, before Catherine comes down. It looks like it's going to be that kind of a day."

Taking the glass from Ryan, he voiced, "What a shame, she appears to be quite lovely. If she can't remember where she's from, what do you intend to do with her?"

"There doesn't seem much I can do until she comes around. Maybe she'll remember something and we can dispatch with her."

It was totally unlike Ryan to be so ungracious, Samuel thought, as he watched him sit down heavily in the leather wing chair opposite the desk. Bringing his drink, Samuel Murdock sat down in its twin next to Ryan but

41

said nothing, eyeing his godson, who seemed to be very absorbed in the rug beneath his feet.

Ryan didn't know how he was going to get out of this one. By coming up with the amnesia story, he had complicated matters. It would have been much easier to give his original version, tend her wound, and send her on to Stephan with something for her trouble.

When she had collapsed, though, after seeing his home in the distance, he had been frightened, and all thoughts had escaped him except getting her back to Briarfawn.

In the bedroom, with everyone asking what had happened and the girl with a head injury, it had seemed logical at the time to say she had no memory rather than explaining the hoax Stephan had perpetrated and the girl's ridiculous story of being from the next century.

Jesus! That was laughable! Even a child could come up with a better one than that. Stephan had gone through a lot of trouble to do this and later, when his anger lessened, it would be interesting to find out how he had got the watch to change numbers.

Finishing his second bourbon, Ryan deduced his only hope was that the woman upstairs didn't wake up while Catherine was in the room. Somehow he had to warn Miss Quinlan to remain silent. If Samuel's wife were to hear the truth of it, all hell would break loose.

"No! Oh God, please, no! Let me be dreaming!" Brianne whimpered as she looked into the face of the black woman.

"Shh . . . don't be scared, honey. You had a bad fall. Misser Barrington brought you here. I'm Mattie. I take care of him and his home, Briarfawn. That's where you are, chile. Now you jus' lie still and rest. I'll tell them you woke up."

The woman straightened and smiled kindly into

Brianne's startled face, then left quickly in spite of her large size, her floor-length skirt swaying behind her.

Brianne stared at the closed door for a few confused seconds, then, as it all came back to her, she looked about the bedroom. If she weren't so frightened, she would have appreciated the care someone had taken to furnish it, but that wasn't important to her now. She was looking for her clothes. Not seeing them, she decided to rise and search the large wardrobe.

Just get into the jeans, she thought, and get out of here before that woman comes back with "them," one of whom she was sure was Barrington. What a disturbed man! But she had to admit he had brought her here, and the woman named Mattie seemed kind and genuinely concerned.

With difficulty she threw her legs over the side of the high bed, noticing that one ankle was bandaged. Moving her body over to the side until her one good leg touched the floor, she tried to stand, using the draped poster as a lever.

The pain exploded behind her eyes as she stood upright, and grabbing her head, Brianne managed to throw most of her body back onto the bed when she fell. Panting, she kept her head flat on the mattress and waited for the spasm to subside into a dull ache while with her foot she felt for a bed stool, anything to lift herself back up onto the bed. Someone had wrapped a cloth around the top of her head. It felt like a vise crushing her temples, and in her frustration she ripped it off.

It was then she heard the door open.

"Lordy, Miz Brianne! What you tryin' to do to yourself? You can't be gettin' out of bed!" The woman named Mattie raced over to her side, and Brianne saw that she was followed by an older couple and the lunatic, Barrington.

43

Within seconds the same strong arms she remembered encircled her as he lifted her effortlessly. Before placing her back on the bed, while he still held her, he lowered his head and whispered into her ear, "You have amnesia!"

Tucking her in, he looked into her astonished eyes and said aloud, "There now, try and stay put. You're in no condition to walk until Catherine says so." He indicated the older woman dressed in a long gown of gray silk trimmed with white lace.

The woman, holding a tray, came up to her and smiled. "Hello Brianne. May I call you by your first name? We haven't been properly introduced yet. I'm Catherine Murdock and this is my husband Samuel, Ryan's godfather." She nodded to the portly man, who smiled at Brianne from beneath a huge white mustache.

Brianne stared at them for a few moments, unable to find her voice. They all played the part well, right down to the clothes. What kind of place had she been brought to? Barrington must have already told them she had amnesia, for they acted as though they were walking on eggs. She glanced at the tall stranger who had fabricated this lie and was momentarily gratified by his uneasy expression.

Looking at the couple who, except for their clothes, appeared reasonably normal, she smiled weakly. "How do you do? My name is Brianne Quinlan. Thank you for taking care of me, but I have family in New Orleans who must be very worried. If I could only reach my sister, I'm sure her husband would make some arrangements to come and get me."

She looked over the heads of the couple and smiled sweetly at Barrington. So much for amnesia, she thought with satisfaction.

"That's wonderful! What is your sister's name? We'll send a message to her at once." The woman named Catherine looked delighted with this information as she placed the tray she was carrying onto the night table.

44

"Her name is Morganna B—" How could she say Barrington? It sounded crazy, even to her. If they already thought her to be confused because of her head injury, surely saying that last name would convince them of it. Over the woman's head she caught Barrington's eyes warning her to go along with his story, then watched miserably as Catherine's expression changed from hopefulness to pity.

"Don't you worry, dear," she said, patting Brianne's shoulder. "It will all come back to you eventually. Do you think you'd like to try some broth? Lizzy, Ryan's cook, is famous for her skills in the kitchen."

Brianne gritted her teeth in frustration but managed to return the woman's smile. "I'm sure it's delicious, and I am hungry. Thank you." She remembered she hadn't eaten since yesterday, and then only lightly.

The tray was placed on her lap as Catherine said, "We'll leave you now, dear. Mattie will return for the tray later." Placing a soft hand on Brianne's cheek, she added, "Don't be too upset, Brianne. Whatever happened, you're safe with us here."

As the door closed behind all of them, Brianne knew she wouldn't feel safe until she reached New Orleans. She was probably an aunt by now, and by damn she was going to get into the city to see that baby.

Taking her first spoonful of the consomme, she thought of Barrington and his manipulations to have everything, including her, changed to suit him. He must be schizophrenic. And hadn't his breath smelled of liquor when he'd ordered her to lie about the loss of memory? She didn't remember smelling it this morning. Brianne smiled wryly at the thought of his being upset enough to drink so early in the day. Or maybe it wasn't unusual.

Taking another spoonful of the deliciously light soup, she looked up at the ceiling. No one was going to believe this . . .

Chapter 3

Not having had the chance to talk with the girl in private since Catherine had again cleared the room, Ryan now found himself back in the study contemplating his third drink—and it was barely mid-afternoon. Miss Brianne Quinlan, whoever she was, was interfering in his life, and that was something he deeply resented.

He hadn't been prepared, though, when they entered the room earlier, for the sight of the woman half out of bed and clinging to the sheets in obvious pain. Losing no time, he had raced to her side and picked her up, managing to whisper her affliction into her ear. He had experienced a few moments of apprehension when she began to speak and continued in her invention about a sister in New Orleans, but as she was about to reveal the last name he had caught her eye in warning and Catherine, assuming she was at a loss, had covered for her forgetfulness.

Pacing the floor in front of his oversized desk, he brooded over the problem. Nothing was going right, and there was too much yet to be done if he was to leave for Virginia by next week. His first priority, though, was to get rid of the troublesome girl upstairs. He would wait until Catherine was occupied with dinner preparation and then go up and talk to the Quinlan woman. He'd settle this once and for all, and then get on with his plans.

Throughout the rest of the afternoon and into dinner, Catherine had thwarted every attempt Ryan had made to get into the girl's room.

Finally, at dinner that night, he had had enough. "Catherine, I have always respected your wishes, but I think this time I am right. I am, after all, the one who found her, and if I could speak to her in private, reminding her of the surroundings where she was located, perhaps something would sound familiar and trigger the return of her memory."

Catherine sat listening to him across the long expanse of cherry table laid with Sèvres china and Irish crystal that even she would be proud to display. She was, however, at the end of her patience with Ryan. He had closeted himself in his study, drinking no doubt, for most of the afternoon. He'd only emerged long enough to try and annoy the poor child upstairs. Samuel had told her of Ryan's impatience to be rid of the girl, and Catherine was incensed by his lack of hospitality.

"Enough of this, Ryan! Mattie has been with Miss Quinlan all day and she does not show any signs of her memory returning tonight. Before dinner I checked her myself, and the poor thing almost resorted to tears when I tried to find out about her past. She's totally drained, and Mattie is going to dose her tea with laudanum to insure a good night's sleep."

When Ryan attempted to speak, she held up her hand. "I absolutely forbid you to see her tonight, especially in your condition. Let her rest. Speak with her tomorrow, if you must."

Despite the constant worry she knew she must be causing Morganna and Charles, Brianne felt very pampered by the care given to her. She was snuggled into a soft feather bed, wearing an oversized nightgown of cream silk. If it weren't so maddening she would have liked to enjoy the sensation of slipping for a night into the charm of the Old South. She had read a few novels on antebellum New Orleans, and Barrington had this place down pat. It was definitely a plantation, and a working one from the evidence of the field. He must have a small town in his employ to keep up this charade, for despite the lack of modern conveniences, like electricity and telephones, this was not one of those places that was restored and kept as a museum for tourists.

She looked about the bedroom. It was decorated for the era Barrington was pretending to live in, and she assumed the people she had seen were dressed for that period too. Brianne thought about Catherine and Mattie and the care and attention they had willingly given her, and she found herself liking them, even if they were mesmerized by Barrington.

"This is jus' what you need," Mattie proclaimed when she handed Brianne the tea. "At the end of the day, my poor bones needs somethin' soothin'—and from the looks of them bruises on your legs, you could use it too. It'll make you feel real warm, and you'll sleep like a chile."

Brianne sipped the tea as Mattie filled in the time by telling her about the house servants—from Aaron, and she spoke this name with respect, who was Barrington's manservant or butler, down to someone named Mary, who was one of the housemaids.

Brianne knew she'd never remember so many names, and since she would have no need to, didn't bother to concentrate. It was becoming difficult just keeping her eyes open.

49

She smiled at the woman before her. Mattie seemed so practical and down to earth that it was hard to understand why she went along with Barrington's game.

Wanting to know but afraid to insult her, Brianne merely said, "Mattie, thanks for being so kind to me today. I know I've been sleeping on and off all afternoon, but I can't seem to stay awake. I'm sorry."

"Don't you be sorry 'bout nothin', Miz Brianne. That's jus' the laud'num I put in the tea." Blowing out the candle, she added, "Don't you be worried, neither. Miz Catherine's room is right down the hall and she'll hear you if you need her. You jus' sleep real good now."

Mattie's voice seemed to be coming from across the room, and soon Brianne heard the door close softly.

Suddenly, her eyes snapped open. Laud'num! My God, that's opium! Mattie didn't seem like the type to drug her. Maybe it was just a sleeping potion, as she said. After all, if she were in a hospital she would probably be given a sedative to sleep. However, Brianne was convinced her sleep wouldn't be "real good," as Mattie said. She just hoped it wouldn't be filled with nightmarish flashes of the past twenty-four hours.

She simply had to get to Morganna. Somebody must have found the car by now, and there was identification all over it—on her luggage, in her purse, and in the glove compartment. The one thing Morganna didn't need right now was her disappearance. She would contact her sister tomorrow and reassure her that she was all right.

As her eyes started to close, she thought how unreal it all seemed. And imagine her fainting! Why, she'd never done that before in her life.

When Catherine announced she was retiring, Ryan stood on unsteady feet to bid her good night. He knew he had drunk too much, and again resented the girl upstairs as the cause.

Samuel, following his wife from the drawing room, paused, saying, "Ryan, have Aaron put you to bed. Whatever it is that's bothering you about the girl, there's nothing to be done about it tonight."

Ryan's deep blue eyes narrowed as he watched the couple leave. For Christ's sake, he was being treated like a child in his own house—told when to go to bed and what rooms were off limits to him! Everyone was so concerned about the chit lying abed—mustn't upset her. What about him? He had every right to feel angry. She was the one in the wrong. What kind of woman would go along with a prank like that? And where did Stephan find her? Probably some actress, or more than likely a lady of the evening making some extra money.

With his thoughts traveling in that vein, it was inevitable he would again remember her soft curves. From the first time he had picked her up at the levee to this afternoon when he had held her in the silky nightdress, she had stirred him.

Damn! It had been almost two weeks since he had had a woman, and the sensation in his groin was almost painful.

Hell! Stephan had probably paid her already. She was right here, in his own house, and if nothing else he would get his chance to speak with her. With little sober thought he left the room and started up the stairs, intent on satisfying the hungering craving he had for the woman. After all, it was what she was paid for . . .

Very quietly, he eased the door open. He could barely make out her form on the bed. Walking slowly over to the window, he opened the drapes so the moon would illuminate the room.

She didn't seem real, surrounded as she was by a soft beam of light. She was sleeping on her side, with one leg thrown out over the cover, and her gown had shifted up

51

to her waist, treating Ryan to a view of her long flank.

Looking up, he saw her hair fanned out on the pillow as though the wind had blown it so, and her face looked peaceful and innocent.

For a fleeting second he almost wished that were her true personality.

He already knew her nature was anything but peaceful—but as far as being innocent? He'd soon find that out!

He stood gazing down at her for a full minute, enchanted by the beautiful picture she presented. Wanting to make sure she was tangible, he reached out his hand and gently ran it over her exposed hip, down to her thigh.

With a soft, drawn-out sigh, she turned over onto her back. Not needing any more proof that she was real, he started to unbutton his shirt as he walked around the bed to the unoccupied side.

Easing himself onto the mattress next to her, he studied her profile. Even in sleep, her chin had an insolent curve to it. With his index finger he traced its outline and was pleased when she breathed deeply and turned her head slightly toward him, exposing more of her neck. Lowering his own head, he feathered the side of her face with soft kisses as his hand reached down and under her gown to lightly capture her breast.

He had wanted to do that since this morning, and gasped audibly in surprise at the pleasure it gave him.

Brianne felt she was floating between wakefulness and a delicious state of sleep, filled with erotic dreams. It was as though she had returned to that earlier dream, the one that had eluded her that morning. Every nerve ending was sending signals to her brain as a phantom lover caressed her skin and lips that demanded a response took possession of her own.

She wanted him.

It mattered little that he didn't have a face or name. She wanted that fulfillment that had always been just out of reach. It would be all right this time—she just knew it, as desire and a passion she had never come close to experiencing before took over.

She felt the wide shoulders and sensed the strength that lay within them as she ran her hands down a smooth, muscled back.

Dizzy, knowing all of this was caused by the drug given to her earlier, she gave in to it. She wanted the dream to reach its natural conclusion, wanted the lover to be inside her. Easing him with her hands, she let him know it too.

This dream lover teased her, entering her slowly, inch by inch, and her frustration was almost unbearable until she felt the full length of him.

Slowly he moved, and Brianne heard herself moan out loud. It was so right . . .

Rolling her head back and forth on the pillow, she started to silently shed bitter tears. Why was it happening now, in a dream? Wasn't she capable of this as normal people were? Or did she need a strong drug, like opium, to induce it? And was her life so empty that she could not attach a face to the body that was stirring up these new sensations?

Suddenly, it was very important that this visionary lover not remain nameless. She tried to think of someone, men she had been attracted to once, but all their faces faded away and only one appeared clear in her mind. It was the same face she had seen this morning, bending over her, kissing her lips and restoring their warmth . . . Barrington, with his piercing blue eyes smiling into her own. So great was her need now as the lover's pace increased that Brianne gave full vent to her imagination and let the newly named lover take her with him. She moved her hips in unison with his and gasped

53

with pleasure as liquid fire ran softly up her legs to settle in a churning inferno where their bodies were joined together. It was happening, she was so close . . . every muscle in her bruised body straining to reach the ultimate plateau as her breathing quickened and her heart began a frenzied beat inside her chest. The fleeting thought occurred to her that she might be dying, but she dismissed it quickly and gave in to her inflamed body, for she had never felt so alive as now. Delicious rivers of passion washed over her and she was soaring toward completion when she felt a long, warm rush of breath against her cheek, and cruelly the hot pressure of the lover was removed from her feverish body.

She wanted to scream at the dream's unfairness, to bring it back to ease her seething subconscious, but it was not to be. She could not recall the wild passionate thoughts on their own, nor the sweet fullness while the lover was within her. It was gone, and she was left to taste bitter frustration. She was never to be complete, and the tears of her failure fell silently past her ears to gather on the pillow beneath her head.

Time had little meaning as she willed her mind to release its erotic thoughts and become blank, and finally, mercifully, her cooled body began to relax and she was once more returned to the peacefulness of deep sleep.

Catherine was never to know what caused her to awaken with the sudden urge to check on the young guest down the hall. She was bone weary from the unexpected excitement the young woman's appearance had caused. As she gathered her robe about her, she again sighed at the thought of amnesia. She knew almost nothing about the strange malady, and there was less than two weeks left before she and Samuel sailed for Europe. Brianne's past might be a mystery to her, but one thing Catherine knew for certain, her background was quality. Watching and listening to her during the day had assured Catherine of that, and as she opened the young woman's bedroom door, she silently prayed that she could effect a reunion for Brianne and her family in such a short time.

Since she carried no candle, Catherine's eyes were already accustomed to the dark as she came closer to the bed. Vaguely she took notice of the deep snoring and was surprised that such a resounding noise could come from so small a woman. The closer she came, the stronger the uneasy feeling in her stomach grew until she stood at the side of the bed and gasped in horror at the naked form of her husband's godson. Confusion, wild and accusing, made her slightly dizzy as she reached out her hand to his shoulder.

"Ryan!" she whispered frantically. "Get up . . . get up!"

Ryan's groan was loud and drunken.

She glanced over his body to Brianne. Her nightgown was raised to her shoulders and she whimpered in her sleep. Outrage coursed through Catherine as she raised her voice in near hysteria.

"Samuel!"

Alarms went off inside Brianne and her subconscious screamed at her to open her eyes. They felt as though heavy weights were attached to their lids, and she fought against them. When she was finally successful, she blinked a few times in disbelief. Samuel came rushing into the room, light held high above his head, and stared at her. Then his unbelieving eyes turned to Catherine, who stood at the opposite side of the bed, and then back again to Brianne. She felt the cool air on her breasts and was mortified to see that her nightgown had exposed them. As she maneuvered the wide shift down to her waist, she became aware that she was not alone in the bed. Snapping her head to her side, she saw the lunatic Barrington, asleep . . . and practically nude.

This couldn't be real! It had to be an effect of the drug. Isn't that what opium does—make you have strange dreams? She desperately wanted to believe that but couldn't dismiss the noise of his snoring, nor the astonished and outraged looks of the older couple who now were at her side.

Catherine tentatively reached out a hand to her, and memories of the dream came back in a shameful rush. It was no dream! Barrington was here . . . in her bed! And thoughts of what she had done, and what she had wished to be done to her, made her shake with humiliation. She groped for Catherine's outstretched hand and broke into tears. "Catherine . . . my God!"

Catherine's sturdy arms enveloped her and Samuel whispered over his wife's shoulder, "Brianne, I must know. Did he . . . ah, that is . . . Are you injured? Should we send for a doctor?"

Her face pressed against the older woman's breasts, Brianne shook her head and sobbed, "No! Just get him out! Please . . . get him out of here!"

Catherine's thin thread of patience finally broke and she turned her head to her husband. "You can see just what he's done, now get him *out!*"

Samuel moved with the quickness of a man half his age as he attempted to shake Ryan from his drunken stupor.

"Go away . . . iss too early," Ryan slurred, as he felt his shoulder shaken by some unknown person.

"Good God, man! Wake up!"

Shaking his head as if to clear it, Ryan reluctantly opened his heavy lids to see his godfather's red face, and when he met his eyes, Samuel flicked a glance to the other side of the bed. Following the line of his vision, Ryan turned his head to see the Quinlan woman sobbing into Catherine's chest as his godfather's wife glared at him, disgust clearly written on her face.

Christ! What the hell was going on? Just as his

confused mind began to function, guilty memories crept in. He remembered coming in here, drunk though he was, and beginning to make love to the woman across from him. He vaguely remembered her urging him on, then, just as confusing, he thought he had felt tears on her cheeks at the same time. After that he wasn't sure what happened, except that at some time during the night he must have passed out.

If it were possible that any color was left in his face, he could actually feel it drain as he looked into Catherine's eyes. "Catherine . . ." He attempted to explain, but couldn't bring forth the words, nor in his heart was he sure if there was any way of explaining his actions.

"Ryan, just leave this room," Catherine said with exaggerated patience. "I have nothing to say to you . . . not now."

Samuel grabbed an extra blanket from the chair and wrapped it around Ryan's shoulders, saying, "Come along. You have quite a bit of explaining to do."

Cloaked in the blanket, with Samuel leading him by the arm, Ryan turned at the doorway and looked back for a few seconds toward the bed.

As if she felt his silent plea, the woman glanced over in his direction and Ryan felt sick to his stomach as he looked back into Brianne's tortured eyes.

"I'm sorry," he whispered hoarsely.

Catherine turned to the poor child on the bed, and putting her arms around the other woman, attempted to console her. "Shh, hush now . . . it's all right. He's gone, and I'm going to stay with you all night. Are you injured in any way? Did he hurt you?"

Shaking her head, Brianne clung to her and felt a small measure of security.

Enveloping the trembling form once more into her arms, Catherine rocked her, and gently rubbing the child's back, swore that Ryan would pay for this—the ageless sisterhood of women prevailing over her love of the man she had once cherished as a son.

Tying the sash on his robe, Ryan sat down in the large overstuffed chair in his room. He made a point of not looking at Samuel, sitting on the edge of the bed opposite him.

He could never remember being so humiliated or more ashamed of himself . . . and he couldn't blame the drink entirely. He had to be honest with himself now, and admit he had wanted the Quinlan woman from the beginning. What was it about her that drove him beyond normal behavior?

He had never taken a woman without her consent. It mattered little that she had encouraged him in the beginning, or that she was no innocent virgin—that much of it he remembered. What did matter was that for the first time in his life he had forced himself on a woman, and it left a bitter, rancid taste in his mouth.

God! That Catherine should have been the one to find him so! The disgust in her voice made him shudder, but he would never forget the look on Brianne's face. He had seen that same look of sheer terror on wounded animals. For him to have caused such a reaction was unbearable.

He had no excuses or explanations. He would not tell them why he had assumed that the girl would be willing. He owed her that much. Remaining silent, he did not answer his godfather's questions, but continued to hold his forehead in his hand, thinking painful thoughts . . .

Honor had always been important to him. It was more than just an attribute associated with Southern gentlemen. To him it was a way of life.

His father, the second son of a wealthy landowner from South Carolina, had not had much to leave him at his death. What he did leave, though, was priceless beyond value . . . a legacy of pride and honor.

When Ryan's father was disowned for falling in love and marrying the lovely Kathleen Ryan, daughter of an Irish immigrant, Travis Barrington took his dark-haired bride and left his home forever. He knew there was no future for him there; his older brother was being groomed to succeed his father. Travis never achieved the greatness of his father, nor came close to giving his family the way of life he had known, but what he did secure for them was a happy and loving home in Charleston, where he earned a comfortable living as a broker in the busy seaport.

What had all been so carefree and normal came to an abrupt halt when Travis was killed in an accident at the wharves. The once cheerful and spirited Kathleen could not function without her husband, nor comprehend life alone.

Ryan had barely turned thirteen when he watched his mother give up on life. Looking back now, he realized that it wasn't selfishness, to want to leave him and his younger brother Gavin, so much as a firm belief from her Irish upbringing—that her Travis was just waiting for her to join him.

Within a year Kathleen was with her husband, and with Samuel's help Ryan sold everything they possessed to install Gavin in a boarding school. He would not go to his father's family for help, and at fourteen, alone and naive, Ryan made his start in life on the very docks that had ended his father's.

By seventeen he was a man in appearance and attitude, his open and trusting outlook forgotten in the realities of the world. Working with a singular determination, he had begun to make his way up the ladder of success and by twenty-nine, with the help and guidance of his godfather, Ryan had enough investments and capital to begin his dream. His home.

As much as he had wanted Briarfawn on sight, he had given the previous owners sixty days to come up with the necessary money to retain it. He had been more than generous in his offer, for he never wanted it said that he obtained his home dishonorably. He wanted it to be a haven his parents would have been proud of, and with honor, dignity, and pride in ownership, he had worked hard these past three years to make it so.

Catherine and Samuel Murdock had always been close to his family and were substitute parents for the ones he had lost when he was so young. They had cared for him, worried over his adventures and misadventures, and lovingly advised him over the years. He valued their opinion more than any other's, including his own brother's. It didn't matter that they weren't really related and had no actual hold over him; Ryan couldn't bear to have disappointed them . . . especially in this way. That was why tonight hurt so much. In the span of a few hours he had brought dishonor to the memory of his parents; to the Murdocks, who loved him and had always believed in him; to Briarfawn, the place in which he hoped to recreate the warmth of his own childhood; and finally, but most painful of all . . . to himself.

When the crying had subsided and only an occasional whimper came from her, Brianne looked up at the woman who still held her. For all that her loyalties might lie with Barrington, she had quickly come to her aid tonight, and Brianne was grateful. She felt protected with Catherine near and couldn't understand why this sensitive woman was involved with a person like Barrington. He was a dangerous man. She couldn't bear to think about her own actions while she was in a drugged state, for it was too embarrassing to recall the acute surge of sensuality that had overtaken her and the way her body had wildly responded to his.

Why did he think he had the right to come into her room? Had he ordered her drugged? Never wanting to face him again, she looked upward. "Catherine, you must help me get away! You must admit it's impossible for me to remain here now!"

Catherine looked down at her and brushed the hair back from her face, informing her of the plan she had already worked out.

"We'll leave here first thing in the morning, Brianne, after I have talked to Ryan. I can't understand why he would have done something so abominable. Believe me, I know him, and this isn't like him at all."

She took a deep breath before continuing. "However, I've seen with my own eyes, God help me, what he's capable of, and by this time tomorrow, you'll be asleep in my own home in New Orleans. Carla, one of the house servants here, is also an excellent seamstress and has been altering one of my gowns for you."

"Catherine, thank you for your generous offer, but you see, I remembered . . . my sister lives on Prytania Street, by a cemetery. If you could only get me there, I'll be all right. And I can wear my own clothes, there's no need for you to ruin one of your gowns."

Catherine's face registered her surprise. "The Garden District? Our home is there! Of course we'll take you to your sister's. Do you remember her last name yet? I only ask because I'm familiar with most of the district's residents, and perhaps I could be of help in explaining the situation."

As Brianne shook her head, Catherine thought to add, "And I'd be most happy to give you a simple gown, since it was I who ordered Mary to burn what you were wearing when you came to us. They were ruined, and most unsuitable, my dear."

Brianne decided not to make an issue about the

clothes. It didn't matter what she wore, as long as she left this house. She would ask Charles to help her find out what had happened to the car and collect her luggage once she was safely in Morganna's home.

She had little choice but to trust Catherine, and silently prayed that this gracious woman wouldn't disappoint her.

Chapter 4

Catherine was up and dressed at dawn. From the aroma drifting upstairs, she knew Lizzy was already busy preparing breakfast. While Mattie took her place watching over Brianne, Catherine descended the stairs thinking about her decisions and the lives they would affect. It seemed to her the only possible answer.

She entered the drawing room and sat in a lovely brocaded chair to await the men.

Upstairs, Ryan prepared for the inevitable confrontation with Catherine. Not sleeping the entire night, together with his mental anguish, had taken its toll. Looking into the mirror as he shaved, he was not pleased with its answering reflection. His eyes were ringed with dark circles and his skin had an unhealthy hue.

Ryan had always been satisfied with his appearance, although never aware of the extraordinary good looks that attracted the fairer sex. To himself, he was merely a wonderful combination of his parents' best features— and worst. He had his father's looks and coloring and hopefully his honest nature, and his mother's eyes, humor, stubbornness, and—unfortunately—her quick Irish temper.

Sighing, Ryan turned away from the mirror and

started to dress, knowing already he would accept the consequences of his actions last night. He would protect Brianne's already tarnished reputation from further blemish, since it was he who had deceived the Murdocks, not her. Her only deception involved Stephan and the insane story of her origins.

Feeling somewhat better, he left the room to brave Catherine, who must surely be lying in wait for him.

"Would you care for coffee, Samuel?" Catherine asked her husband, who had joined her. "I told Lizzie to hold breakfast until we are finished with our discussion."

As she poured the strong chicory-flavored brew, Ryan entered the drawing room, and nodding in his direction she asked the same question of him, explaining the delayed meal service.

Accepting the cup, Ryan straightforwardly stated his position. "Catherine, Samuel, I have no excuses. Nor can I justify my behavior. I can only offer my sincere apology for involving both of you. It grieves me that you have been witnesses to a dark side of my nature I hadn't known existed until last night."

Catherine thought he looked terrible, and understandably so. It was obvious he also had not slept.

Withholding any shred of sympathy, she began. "Ryan, there is no defense for what transpired in this house last night. Setting aside my own reactions, I have a moral obligation to Brianne. I gave her my word yesterday that she would be safe here at Briarfawn, and I personally will never forgive myself for leaving her. Dear God, Ryan, she was injured, confused and alone, depending on strangers for comfort and help. To think that we could have abused her trust!"

Seeing Ryan meant to give no defense or explanation for his actions, Catherine straightened her shoulders.

Looking him directly in the eye, she continued, "I have come to some decisions and will brook no interference. Brianne has remembered her sister's street in New Orleans. We will leave this morning for her family's home. When we reach there, I will explain the situation as delicately as possible and state that you wish to set things right. If I obtain their permission . . . you, Ryan, will marry Miss Brianne Quinlan—as soon as possible."

Ryan stared at her in shock, his lower jaw falling open. He looked to his godfather for help, but finding none, returned to the woman before him. "Surely you can't be serious, Catherine! I don't even know her, and I'm sure she wouldn't agree to this either!"

"I would say you *know* her very well, Ryan. I haven't talked to Brianne yet about this. I plan to tell her on the way to the city. Think about it. It's the only honorable thing to do."

Ryan was desperate. He hadn't been prepared for this! "Catherine, please listen to me. I am to leave for Virginia in less than two weeks. Caroline's family is expecting me. You are aware I was going to ask Caroline to be my wife?"

Catherine shot him a look of impatience. "Caroline! Bah! She isn't suitable for you, and you know it. The only reason you're considering her is because of her family, and your haste to start a family of your own. Let me ask you something, Ryan—have you given any thought to the possibility that because of last night, the woman upstairs might be carrying your child? No? Well, just think about it while we are in New Orleans."

Ryan had no answer for her—at least none delicate enough for her ears. Miss Brianne Quinlan was definitely not the type of woman he had envisioned for a wife. Damn! It didn't matter who she was if she was pregnant, but it would take a matter of weeks to find out, and by that time Catherine would have him married off.

He could easily delay his trip to Virginia for a month

or so. No one knew of his actual reasons for coming, other than a social visit. Caroline might have suspicions, but nothing had ever been definite. Ryan made sure of that.

Straightening his back, Ryan looked into the determined hazel eyes that until last night had always been soft with love.

"Catherine, I will await your word from New Orleans. You are right; if Brianne is carrying my child, I will do the honorable thing."

As Catherine nodded her approval, he bowed slightly and walked with a false calm out of the drawing room, furious that he had no way of remembering if there had been time to accomplish the possible deed.

Mattie awakened Brianne with strong, hot coffee and warm buttered croissants, announcing that her bath would be ready in a few moments. Brianne had barely oriented herself and was sipping the coffee when the door opened and a small fleet of servants entered, carrying a large enameled tub and pails of steaming water. One of them set up a lovely Chinese screen at the base of it and Mattie said with a smile, "Bet you sure lookin' forward to this, Miz Brianne, after yesterday."

Not knowing exactly what Mattie was referring to, Brianne blushed deeply. As she glanced up, though, she felt reassured by the housekeeper's open expression.

"Mattie, bless your heart. I've dreamed of soaking in a hot tub for days. If it's all right with you, I think I'll eat later. Right now, that water is more inviting."

With Mattie's sturdy frame supporting her, Brianne rose, and testing her ankle, found she could walk if she rested most of her weight on her left foot.

After pouring a delicious jasmine oil into the water, Mattie remained with her, bustling about the room while Brianne luxuriated in the warm, scented bath. After last night it felt marvelous to relax in the light of day and let the tensions ease slowly out of her body. She tried not to think about the previous night and concentrate only on today and reaching her sister.

There was a soft knock on the door and she tensed until hearing Mattie exclaim, "Jus' right for her! She sure gonna look pretty in it!"

Coming around the screen, the housekeeper held out a beautiful yellow gown with fine gold braiding at the neckline and sleeves.

"It's beautiful! This can't be the dress Catherine meant to lend me."

"This is it, Miz Brianne. You should see them dresses Miz Catherine has—she ain't never gonna miss this one. She gave it to Carla herself yesterday and told her to start fixin' it up for you. There's shoes and everything you need to be dressed proper again."

Brianne watched as Mattie looked at her with pity and surmised the woman probably hadn't seen too many women in jeans around here lately.

Although it was awkward, she washed her hair with Mattie's help, then rose as the woman rinsed her off with fresh warm water and wrapped her in a long length of fleecy cotton.

Seated on a chair by the window, Brianne got her first real glimpse of Briarfawn as Mattie dried her hair. In the distance she could see neat, orderly fields and closer to the house, adults and children alike were busy attending chores. On the green lawn below her, a small boy was laughing at the antics of two puppies.

"That's Jimmie, Carla's youngest," Mattie announced. "He sure loves animals, that one. Always bringin' home strays, like that one over there. Brung her in 'bout Christmas, and Misser Barrington says he can keep her, long as he looks after the dog. Jimmie was pleased as can be when she dropped her litter a month ago. Misser

Barrington, he says Jim got one over on him—seein' as how he got five dogs, 'stead of the one."

Brianne stood abruptly. She didn't like hearing the warmth in Mattie's voice when she spoke of her employer. She didn't want to think about him at all.

"Mattie, why don't I try on the dress and see if it fits?" She tried walking by herself and found the warm bath had done wonders for her muscles.

Reaching the bed, Brianne couldn't believe her eyes. On the mattress were underwear, starched slips, actual hoops, and one particular item she couldn't identify. Picking it up, she saw it looked suspiciously like an antique version of a corset.

Looking directly at the woman, she protested, "I can't possibly wear all this. I wouldn't be able to breathe if I did."

"Why, Miz Catherine'd be shocked if you was to get dressed without 'em," Mattie pronounced as she removed Brianne's towel and held out the underwear to step into.

Not wanting to be unkind to the two women who had cared for her, and especially not wanting to alienate Catherine and hurt her feelings, Brianne allowed herself to be dressed in the silky undergarments, but couldn't suppress a groan when Mattie pulled the long strings to cinch in her waist.

"Can see why you'd be upset, Miz Brianne. I don't think you need this, and that gown might not fit if you was to use it."

To Brianne's immense relief, Mattie untied the corset and took it off. So grateful was she that the constricting garment was removed, she donned the hoops without a murmur.

Mattie wanted to call the young girl Mary back in to dress her hair on top of her head, but Brianne insisted that she wear it down, and tied it back behind her ears with a satin ribbon that matched the dress. Without a curling iron to tame the wild curls that always came after she washed it, Brianne soon gave up trying to control them. Satisfied that she had at least managed to conceal part of the bruise at her temple, she left the mirror and sat down to eat the remaining cooled breakfast, clad in her slips and the ridiculous hoop.

Between bites, she watched the servants return to remove the tub and was torn between wanting to offer to help them and her guilt at the unexpected pleasure the pampering gave her.

When the room was cleared, Mattie held out the gown to her and Brianne rose with anticipation. She couldn't wait to try it on.

Looking back into the mirror, she caught her breath at her own reflection. She looked almost beautiful, and much younger, with her hair falling naturally and the complete absence of any makeup. She was reminded of her Prom night, although her mother would never have allowed her to leave the house showing so much cleavage. Her breasts were practically falling out of the dress. She only hoped she didn't have to bend over in this!

Pulling at the bodice in hope of raising it, she heard "I knew it! I jus' knew it! You sure is one beautiful lady."

Turning, she saw Mattie grinning from ear to ear, and smiling herself, asked, "It is a beautiful dress, isn't it?"

"It ain't the dress, Miz Brianne . . . it's you. And no use you tuggin' at it like that, it ain't gonna go nowheres 'cept how it's made. You look jus' fine."

Afraid she might tear it, Brianne gave up trying to cover herself. "Thank you, Mattie. Would it be possible to see Carla again?"

The efficient housekeeper left with a pleased expression on her face, and Brianne turned back to the mirror. Although she might look like a complete fool, arriving in New Orleans dressed like this, right at this moment she was fulfilling a girlish fantasy. Wishing that her ankle weren't tender, she would have liked to pretend she was at a dress ball and whirl around the room, seeing the skirt float out in a circle about her. Contenting herself with just looking, she mused over the fact that she had never felt more feminine, even if the dress was more confining than slacks. And thinking of them, she again regretted their loss, along with a good silk blouse and a fairly new pair of espadrilles Mattie had said were ruined with mud.

A short knock brought Carla and Mattie into the bedroom. The seamstress stood before her with her eyes downcast and Brianne came closer to her. "Carla, I want to thank you for altering this dress for me. You did a wonderful job without knowing my measurements. I only hope you didn't stay up the entire night doing it."

The young woman had expected to be brought to task for some imperfection that her tired eyes had missed in the flickering candle light that burned until dawn. She looked up at the pretty white woman who was so unlike the others she had labored for.

"No mam. It didn't take that long, and Miz Catherine, she helped with the measurements. I'm glad it fits so good, we was only guessin' at 'em."

Brianne ran her hands over the wide skirt. "Well, you're a very talented woman and should be pleased with your efforts—the dress is perfect, thank you again. By the way"—Brianne felt uncomfortable at the girl's subservient manner—"I saw your son Jimmie this morning outside my window. He's a very handsome boy, you must be proud of him."

Carla's face lit up. "Yes mam, I surely am. He's a good boy, and thank you for askin' 'bout him." She briskly curtsied and left the room, hurrying downstairs to inform the rest of the staff of the kind angel Misser Barrington had brought home.

With the help of Mattie's supporting arm, Brianne descended the wide stairs and saw the Murdocks entering the beautiful square foyer from a side room.

Catherine had a very pleased expression on her face as she glanced up. "Brianne, my dear, you do look lovely!"

Waiting until the young woman reached the bottom step, she put her hand on Brianne's arm and said softly, "We'll be leaving in a few minutes. As soon as our trunks are loaded, we'll be off."

Samuel came forward and bowed deeply for a man his age. "You are a vision, Miss Quinlan. I shall be the envy of the city when I arrive with two such enchanting women."

Brianne smiled nervously at his exaggerated compliments. She knew both of them were trying hard to make this exodus from Barrington's home as painless as possible. "Thank you both so much for all your help. And Catherine, the dress is beautiful. I'm just sorry it had to be altered to fit me."

"Nonsense, my dear, the color is much too young for me. I really don't know why I even bought it—probably trying to recapture my youth. I'm just glad you like it."

Catherine was very happy with her choice of a dress. It really was too youthful for a maturing woman.

Ryan eventually left the dining room after an uncomfortable breakfast with the Murdocks. Entering the foyer, he stopped short as he looked at the friendly scene before him. All conversation ended, however, when his presence was noticed.

Brianne moved closer to Catherine as though for

protection from him, and he almost winced as she did so.

Samuel turned and tried to include him in the group. "We'll be leaving, Ryan. You've done wonders with Briarfawn since our last visit, and have good reason to be proud of it. Remember, son, when Raven sires a foal, I have first option. I've already spoken to Nathen about it."

Ryan knew Samuel was uncomfortable because he was rambling on about horseflesh, something he never did in front of women.

Smiling slightly at his godfather, he answered, "Samuel, Catherine, thank you for coming. You know this home, and its *stable*," this last he directed to Samuel, "is always open to you. I'm very grateful that you could spend some time here before you sail abroad."

Looking at Catherine, he said, "Please contact me after you reach New Orleans, as to your plans."

He turned his attention to Brianne. Her eyes had flown to the floor when he entered, and remained there. Now he willed her to lift her face so he could see them. "Miss Quinlan, I wish you good fortune when you reach New Orleans, and hope you find your relatives there. The Murdocks are respectable people and they will assist you any way they can."

Was he baiting her? Trying to insinuate that *she* wasn't respectable? How dare he!

Deciding he wasn't worthy of a reply, she fought to regain her composure and purposefully unfurled the rim of the straw hat she had absently rolled in vexation.

Looking up defiantly into his eyes, she merely gave him a short nod and walked straight out of his house to wait on the porch for the others.

Thank God, thought Ryan as he watched her leave. He had provoked her on purpose—he wanted to make sure she looked up at him. Her eyes had haunted him throughout the remaining night, and he needed to replace the terror he had found there earlier with anything—even animosity. With her eyes flashing her suppressed fury and her cheeks flaming with color, she had nodded to him and then tossed those riotous curls, marching out of his house as though he were beneath her notice.

She had looked magnificent in her anger, though, and he had to admit—she had spirit.

Samuel also had admired Brianne's fearless attitude as he joined her on the veranda. Over the years he had tutored Ryan in the complex ways of business and human nature, and the younger man had far surpassed him. His business interests were so vast that Samuel could only guess at their value, and although he would never verbally admit it, both he and Ryan knew it was a matter of the teacher becoming the student.

But in human nature? There Samuel still had the edge, and as he looked at the straight back of Miss Quinlan as she left the porch for the carriage, he thought perhaps his godson had finally met his match.

Chapter 5

As the carriage suddenly started, Brianne turned and looked back at the house. Reluctantly she acknowledged its beauty. It was just the setting Barrington needed—a graceful mansion from the past. Four immense white columns stood proudly, like sentinels guarding the front. The house itself was two stories of light pink brick under a slate roof that was interrupted by numerous chimneys. The porch ran the complete width of the house and was filled with cane furniture and a profusion of plants. Funny that she hadn't noticed them while she was on it . . . but then she had been almost blind with rage at the time.

She could scarcely believe the arrogance of a man like Barrington. He actually had the nerve to imply that *she* wasn't fit company for the Murdocks!

Thank God she was out of that place. For all its beauty, it still contained a seriously deranged man. Her only regret was Mattie. She still didn't feel right about leaving her with him, even if the woman seemed content to be there.

Brianne was glad she had said her goodbyes to the housekeeper privately, while they were still in the bedroom. Instinctively she had thrown her arms around

75

the large woman, saying, "You've been so sweet to me. I'll never forget you."

Surprised, Mattie had hugged her back. "It's been the easiest thing to do, honey. Dry them eyes, now, you jus' come back and see me. You're one fine lady, Miz Brianne. You take care of yourself."

"Brianne, dear," Catherine gently intruded, bringing her back to the present, "why don't you put on your hat? The sun can be brutal on your fair skin. When we reach the boat, you can relax under the awning. We should make New Orleans by early afternoon . . ."

Once aboard the craft, Brianne didn't see how they would reach the town by nightfall. It seemed as though everything and everybody moved at a gradual pace, as if she were the only one anxious to get to the city. When Samuel informed her that they weren't even on the Mississippi yet, but a bayou that ran into the mighty river, it only added to her frustration.

The pace picked up when they reached the muddy Mississippi, and feeling that they were going to make it after all, Brianne began to relax.

Catherine settled herself beside the younger woman under the canvas and removed her hat. She used the flowered creation for fanning her face and without looking at her companion, broke the serenity of the scene.

"You must know I'm concerned about you. Can we be frank with each other?"

Brianne nodded, open dread showing on her face.

Taking a deep breath, Catherine continued, "Neither of us wants to dwell on last night, but the fact is, it happened—and not facing it won't make it easier for you, you must know that. Please listen to me before you comment. Ryan's behavior toward you was criminal and your family could create a scandal by seeking retribution, as is their right.

"I hope that you will believe me when I tell you that Ryan Barrington, until last night, was one of the most admirable men I have known. He has always been kind and generous with friends and strangers alike— honorable in his dealings, honest to a fault sometimes, and much sought out in business for his intelligence. If all this sounds as though I think he's perfect, I know his shortcomings too. He's stubborn and quick-tempered, and has too much pride for his own good."

Despite Brianne's stiff posture, Catherine strove to make her understand. "I'm not trying to excuse him for his conduct, I just wanted you to know the Barrington name is one of the most respected in the state, and Ryan alone achieved that. After talking with him this morning, I've convinced him to do the right thing by you. I'll explain all this to your family when we reach New Orleans, and abide by their decision."

Brianne had tolerated the woman's recital of Barrington's virtues, knowing the affection she had for him, but during the last part of Catherine's speech her own eyes had narrowed. "And what exactly do you mean by saying he has agreed to do the *right* thing by me?"

"Why, by marrying you, dear, of course."

Brianne felt as though someone had slapped her. Her cheeks were burning and her eyes turned a dangerously dark shade of green.

"There is no need for Mr. Barrington to do anything for me. I never want to set eyes on him again. He's the most unstable person I have ever met, and he's been offensive from the first time I saw him. I would never consider marrying him, no matter what his name was . . . or what it stood for!"

"Brianne . . ."

"Please, Catherine, hear me out. I am a grown woman

77

and will make my own decisions about my life. Thank Mr. Ryan Barrington, model citizen, for his obligatory offer, but tell him I'd rather marry that horse he rides. When I do marry, Catherine, it will be for love . . . not a guilty conscience."

Catherine listened as Brianne vented her anger, then patiently said, "You have every right to feel the way you do. I have one last thing to say on the subject, though. I ask you, as I did Ryan this morning, what if the two of you are not the only ones involved? What if you are carrying his child? Please think about that, as I know Ryan is doing."

Catherine was right in her assumption that Ryan was deep in thought. One question kept running through his mind . . .

Who was she . . . really?

Only one person could answer that, and Ryan was waiting for him. He had sent an urgent message to Stephan asking him to come to Briarfawn immediately. This was all his doing, and he had better be able to supply the correct responses. Until such time as he could get his hands on Stephan, he thought about Miss Brianne Quinlan.

She was most certainly beautiful. He had known she would be once she was dressed in feminine clothes, although he had to admit the trousers had shown off her legs nicely. It was her face, though, that Ryan found most appealing. All her emotions were revealed in it. When she had left this morning in a huff, he almost regretted not to have met her under normal conditions until he realized that in her business he would probably have had to stand in line for the favor.

A knock on the door startled him, for he knew Stephan couldn't have traveled the four miles separating their homes this soon.

Aaron entered and announced that a Mr. Wilcox was waiting in the foyer to see him.

"Did he say what it was about, Aaron?" Although the name nagged at the back of his mind, Ryan wasn't in the right frame of mind to see anyone except Stephan. His throbbing head and queasy stomach were a constant reminder of last night's overindulgence.

"Yes suh, Misser Barrington, he says he's the new overseer . . ." Aaron said the last word as though it were a curse.

Jumping up, Ryan nearly ran to the foyer. A man in his middle years, dressed in clean, worn clothes, was clutching a hat and looking about nervously.

He sighted Ryan and extended his hand. "Henry Wilcox, sir. I must apologize for arriving late. My wife took sick on the journey here, and since we have family in Biloxi, I detoured there to leave her and the children with relatives."

As Ryan continued to stare, Wilcox cleared his throat and continued, "I know you were expecting me before this, and I'm sorry for putting you out like that. Mr. Daniels said you were anxious to leave on a trip next week, so I can get started right now if you like."

Ryan had always considered himself a good judge of character, at least with men, and every instinct told him that this one was telling the truth. And if he was, then what about Brianne? Or were they both to have arrived at the same time? It would have been just as good a game for him to have to make the choice between a beautiful woman and this weathered man who stood before him waiting patiently for an answer.

"Mr. Wilcox, I'm sorry your wife is ill, but there is no need to rush into work yet. As it happens, I've had to postpone my trip for a few weeks, so no harm was done." It was hard to keep from groaning when he said that. "I'm waiting for Mr. Daniels now to confer on a business matter. If you haven't eaten yet, I'll have Aaron show you into the kitchen. Lizzy, our cook, will fix you something. Afterwards, please feel free to relax until Mr. Daniels and I have concluded our business.''

The overseer looked confused, but thanked him and left with the servant as Ryan dropped to a chair in the foyer.

Where was Stephan? How many more pieces of this puzzle would fall into his lap before a clear picture could emerge? What was going on?

The front door slammed open and a frantic Stephan burst into the hall. "Ryan, what's wrong? My God, you look terrible! What's happened?''

"Calm down, Stephan. And don't shout! I don't think my head can take much more. Let's go into the study where we can talk in private.''

When the doors were shut behind them, Stephan threw his hat onto a chair and complained, "Why did you send that message? Damn it, it sounded like a life and death situation. What the hell's wrong with you? You knew I'd race over here hellbent, and now I've probably ruined a good horse in the bargain.''

"Right now I don't give a damn about your horse,'' Ryan growled. "My entire future is threatened because of you, and I want some answers now! The first of which is . . . who the hell is this Brianne Quinlan you sent over here to make a fool of me?''

Ryan watched Stephan's brown eyes widen in surprise. "I've never heard of her. And why would I send her to you?''

"You know damn well why. I haven't forgotten the night at Delphina's when you said I needed a woman, not an overseer. Henry Wilcox didn't arrive until this morning. When your substitute got lost and then hurt in the woods yesterday, I was forced to bring her here.

What were you thinking? You knew the Murdocks were staying here, and the embarrassment she would cause. Up until now all your little capers were innocent, but this time people were hurt."

Stephan leaned forward in his chair and faced Ryan, evidence of his growing anger showing clearly on his face. "Now you listen to me. I tell you again, I've never heard of the woman. I did not send her here in place of the overseer. I engaged a Mr. Henry Wilcox, out of Mississippi, as you requested—period. The fact that he arrived late is not of my doing. Give me some credit, Ryan—signing your name on dance cards and leaving you to face some irate mother is not the same as this kind of deception you have accused me of. Have I ever lied to you in the past? Have I? Well, I'm not lying now, either. You've put together a group of circumstances and assumed I'm to blame. I'm the one that should be angry."

Getting up, he went to the window and looked out. "I can see how it must have been embarrassing with Catherine here, but how does this threaten your future?"

Ryan didn't answer him. Nothing was clear anymore. He was sure—positive, in fact—that it was Stephan who was behind this. He looked at his friend's broad back and thought back to the past.

When the two of them were together, they were a formidable duo. Opposite in coloring and slightly shorter than Ryan, Stephan garnered his fair share of attention, and neither considered the other as competition. Stephen Daniels captured the ladies' hearts with ease, and Ryan felt his bad boy image helped. Whereas Ryan had always tried to stay within the bounds of propriety, Stephan took a certain pleasure in flaunting it. On more than one occasion Ryan had been the brunt of his jokes. Rather than resenting it, Ryan, who had never had the time to be young and carefree, usually enjoyed Stephan's jovial personality.

81

But he was right; he had never lied to Ryan, or tried to deny his guilt when found out. In fact, he had always derived a certain pleasure at the completion of his pranks.

Something was very wrong here, and Ryan wasn't sure he wanted to find out what it was.

Outside the door they could hear a commotion. Stephan cast him a questioning glance, and rising, Ryan thought with irritation that the one thing he didn't need right now was another problem.

Throwing open the study door, he saw Mattie shaking her head at the young housegirl, Mary, who stood wringing her apron as she cried into it.

"Mattie, what's going on out here?"

"I didn't want to bother you and Misser Stephan, but Mary here won't stop this cryin' and she said she done somethin' terrible to Miz Brianne, and you'll think she's bad and maybe won't let her buy her papers. Chile won't tell me, says she have to see you."

Exasperated, Ryan turned to the young woman. "Mary, stop that crying and tell me what you've done. Miss Brianne was all right when she left this morning, so it can't be that terrible."

Mary turned frightened eyes up to him. "I wasn't takin' it, I swear! I jus' forgot! When Miz Catherine told me to burn them clothes, I took 'em out back jus' like she says. And when I was 'bout to throw 'em into that fire, they felt heavy, like somethin' was in 'em. So I looked, and that's when I found this."

Holding out her hand, she gave him two keys that were attached by a short chain to a round metal object. The keys had the word *Ford* at the top, and the round disc looked like embossed pewter. Looking at it more closely, he saw that it was a coin of some kind and at its center was the likeness of Independence Hall in Philadelphia. Inscribed around the edge were the words "America's

Bicentennial 1776–1976."

What the hell . . . ? Dumbfounded, he turned it over and saw the initials "B. Q." and "Insurance Company of America."

Was she telling the truth? Had she really had an accident, and was only lost? And if that were so . . . then what had he done?

Looking again at the front of the coin, he held it up closer to the light. It couldn't possibly be correct. 1776 to 1976? This was ridiculous! Another trick of some kind!

Aware that both women were staring at him expectantly, Ryan pocketed the keys, telling Mary not to be upset. He knew it was a mistake and would see that Miss Brianne got them back.

Rejoining Stephan, he sat down next to him. "I owe you an apology, my friend. You were right. I was looking for someone on whom to place the blame for my own actions. You see, unfortunately, I became drunk last night and made a complete fool of myself." Sheepishly he added, "Sorry I made you rush over here, but I hope you'll forgive me my rash accusations and stay for dinner."

Stephan smiled. "Forgiven." Then, with relish, "I'm just glad to see you're human, like the rest of us, and occasionally make mistakes. Ordinarily I'd accept your invitation, just for the opportunity of seeing you suffer through a hangover, but I left a team of workmen at the new barn. I want to be sure the roof goes on as I designed it. Some other time when you're up to it we'll dine, and then you can explain what the hell took place here."

Picking up his hat, he placed a hand on Ryan's shoulder and laughed. "Life is strange, isn't it? There I am, only a few short miles away, alone and in dire need of female companionship. And here you are . . . ready to give up your wandering ways and settle down to a questionable life with my *sweet* cousin. And where does

83

the poor woman show up? Here, under the watchful eyes of dear Catherine! Strange, don't you think?"

As Ryan gave him a baleful look, Stephan smirked, then quickly added, "Now if you'll lend me a fresh horse, I'll be off."

Ryan still had Henry Wilcox to deal with. Wanting to be done with it, he sent Aaron to find the man.

Entering the study a short time later, Wilcox eyed the tall man behind the desk whose reputation as first a sea captain and now plantation owner was widely known. It was one of the reasons he had agreed to such a short stay of employment.

Ryan invited him to sit down and although he felt foolish, decided to be honest with the overseer.

"I'm sorry to have kept you waiting. Since my trip has been delayed, I see no reason for you not to rejoin your wife. The timing was unfortunate, but my plans were changed only this morning. If you could leave the address where you can be reached, I'll contact you if I decide to resume my journey. Again, I apologize, and please accept this for your trouble."

Ryan handed him a pouch containing half the agreed amount for his three weeks of employment had he stayed. Wilcox felt the bag as if weighing it.

"You realize, Mr. Barrington, that I have a permanent position waiting for me in Mississippi? I did tell Mr. Daniels I was to start there in five weeks."

Rising, Ryan shook the man's hand. "I am aware of that, and I'll be in contact soon if I should still need you."

Ryan walked with him to the door. "I hope you find your wife improved and I wish you good fortune, Mr. Wilcox."

Moments later, Ryan attempted to relax in the quiet of

his study. Sitting at his desk, he leaned forward and massaged his aching temples. Nothing was going as planned, and he wasn't used to that. Once he had an objective in mind, he set all his energies in motion to accomplish it. This time he'd been cut off at the knees and when he attempted to rise and get on with his plans, some unforeseen circumstance knocked him right back down.

Perhaps he wasn't meant to go to Virginia after all. As much as he hated to admit it, Catherine was right. It wasn't Caroline he wanted, so much as her family name. He was realistic enough to know the joining of the Barrington and Daniels lines would one day prove very advantageous to the next generation.

Picturing Caroline in his mind, he compared her to Brianne. Both were strong-willed and proud. But he had seen a look of vulnerability in the Northerner he had never seen in the woman he had planned to make his wife.

Reaching into his pocket, he withdrew the keys. Turning them over and over in his hands, he thought of how many times she had asked, even pleaded, to be taken back. But to where?

He refused to think about the possibilities. He unlocked the desk drawer where he kept his valuables and took out the watch. Pushing the buttons, he read the same numbers as yesterday. It hadn't changed. He stared at the two puzzling articles for some time before reaching a decision.

He wouldn't wait for Catherine to send for him. He would leave tomorrow morning for New Orleans and return the watch and keys personally.

That was where all the answers lay . . . with the woman who had suddenly come into his life and turned it upside down.

Chapter 6

Brianne took little pleasure in the Mississippi. Grateful to be nearing her destination, she wiped the perspiration from her brow and determined not to think anymore about Catherine's conversation. It was too hot anyway, for June or even April—if she were to believe the lunatic Barrington's time. Every boat they passed, the people were dressed as strangely as she, or more so. It must be some sort of carnival, she thought, like Mardi Gras . . . though she knew it couldn't be that, since it was always celebrated before Lent, in February. This must just be another day of celebration that she had never heard of. Not too surprising, since she had never been to Louisiana before.

Samuel had told her they were to dock at the Washington Avenue Wharf, and from there ride directly to Prytania Street. Brianne could just imagine Charles's face, if he was at home, when the door opened. She must look ludicrous, even if everything she was wearing was pretty and new.

Approaching the docking area, after what seemed like hours on the water, she could see it was a hive of activity. Men of all races were busy loading and directing cargo on and off ships. It was strange that all of them were huge sailing vessels, nothing modern in sight. Perhaps the Historical Society that Morganna was involved with was preserving the Old World atmosphere in this part of the city.

It didn't seem right, though, that a city as large and famous as New Orleans wouldn't have trucks to transport the goods coming from the ships. Everything was horsedrawn in flatbed wagons and being carted to large wooden warehouses that lined the area. Although everyone was in costume, the same as she, they seemed too busy to be taking part in a holiday. Something was very strange, and in the back of her mind there was a terrible foreboding that she tried to bury.

Once they were docked Samuel escorted them to a commercial carriage, and on settling the arrangements for their luggage, gave the driver Brianne's sister's street.

Catherine questioned her gently. "Have you never visited your sister before?"

"No, this is the first time I've been south. Morganna has been married for two years, but our visiting had always been done up north. She's pregnant with her first child. In fact, she's probably already had the baby. That's the reason I've come—to help her."

As they left the dock area and drove into the city, Brianne noticed women who loitered on the streets. The outfits they wore were gaudy and garish in color, and their faces actually looked painted with makeup. If she hadn't known better she would have sworn they were pretending to be prostitutes, from the postures they assumed as strangely dressed men walked past them. She didn't mean to, but she stared in open curiosity.

Catherine placed a hand on her arm, drawing her attention. "I know you're shocked, my dear, but it's best to ignore them. I'm told they populate every port around the globe, and unfortunately New Orleans is no exception."

Brianne suppressed a giggle. Even the prostitutes were dressed for the occasion.

The carriage left the taverns, inns, and shops and approached tree-lined streets with a progression of lovely houses. The further they traveled, the larger the homes were. They passed streets with names like Magazine and Camp and Chestnut. Catherine told her that the one after next was Prytania, and Brianne's pulse started to race. In a few minutes she would be at Morganna's home! The houses were magnificent, more like mansions, one more beautiful than the next.

Morganna had sent pictures, but nothing could do it justice except seeing it in person. She almost missed recognizing it because the coloring was different and the shrubbery was changed. In the photographs the house was more stately and all the landscaping seemed more mature, almost overgrown. It was still imposing this way, though, with the large white columns and the stone drive leading up to it.

Catherine looked puzzled when she announced, "This is it! This is my sister's house! Oh, isn't it beautiful?"

As she excitedly pointed it out, the driver turned into the approach.

A look of concern passed between the Murdocks, and Samuel asked, "Are you quite sure this is the house?"

Brianne was so impatient she wanted to jump down and race to the door. "Of course I'm sure! I should know my own sister's home. Besides, I've seen pictures, and this is it!"

Catherine tried to be gentle with her. "Brianne dear, I think you've made a mistake. This is the home of Emily and Carl Howard. They're friends of ours, and we've visited here many times. Emily couldn't be your sister, and she's too far up in years to give birth to a child. It must be another home that is similar to this one."

Brianne hadn't come this far or gone through so much

to be put off now that Morganna's and Charles's home was in sight. "I'm telling you, this is the house! If you won't take me, I'll get out and walk—but I'm going there. I'll prove to you I'm right as soon as the door opens."

Seeing no way to avoid an embarrassing situation, Catherine motioned for the driver to continue, hoping that Emily would be patient with the poor girl.

Brianne pulled the rope, ringing a bell somewhere within the house, and waited for someone, hopefully Charles, to answer. She was more than a little disappointed when an elderly black man opened the carved wooden door and greeted them.

"Miz Murdock, mam, come right on in." He then bowed to Samuel. "Suh, can I take your hat? Miz Emily be with you in a minute. Please wait in here, while I go up and tell her you come visitin'."

The man indicated a room off the foyer with the door already open, and Brianne was about to follow his direction when she heard Samuel.

"Thank you, George, I think we'll wait right here. And since we won't be staying long, I'll just keep my hat."

The man George bowed again and slipped away, presumably to announce them. Brianne looked about the entry hall for something that she would recognize from Morganna and her eyes were drawn to the huge winding staircase that dominated the room. Satisfaction lit her face when she remembered the picture her sister had sent her. Morganna was dressed in a formal gown and Charles in evening clothes, and they were posed on those very stairs. They had both looked so happy, and Morganna's accompanying letter had been filled with an exciting account of her first Governor's Ball.

An older woman dressed in a floor-length mauve gown was descending those steps now. "Catherine, Samuel!

90

How nice . . . when did you get back? And what are you doing standing there in the hall?"

Catherine came forward. "Emily dear, I'm sorry if we've interrupted your afternoon. We've just returned, and Brianne, a distant cousin of mine whom we haven't seen since she was a baby, remarked on the beauty of your home. It was an impulse, I know, but I wanted you to meet her."

Catherine brought her forward to stand in front of the woman. "Brianne, may I present Mrs. Emily Howard, my very dear friend."

"Brianne, how very nice to meet you. And Catherine, I do hope you don't lose any friends when you present her—those with daughters will be green with envy."

Brianne didn't concentrate on the woman's greeting. What had made Catherine say she was her cousin? If she thought that would keep her from finding out about her sister's family, she was surely mistaken.

"Mrs. Howard, it's very nice to meet you too. This home is quite lovely; have you lived here long?"

"Why yes, for about eight years. Why do you ask?"

Brianne decided the time had come to be straightforward and shock them all. "My sister Morganna, married to Charles Barrington, lives in this house. I don't understand what's going on, or why you say you live here, unless you're a relative of Charles's. Please don't think me rude, it's just that I must find my sister and her family. I'm sure they're terribly worried about me. If you know anything about them or the name of the hospital where she's had her baby, please tell me!"

She was on the verge of tears when she finished. Why was she thwarted at every turn?

Emily Howard looked from Brianne to Catherine with shock plainly written on her face. Even Catherine was taken back when she heard the name of Brianne's sister. The poor thing was grasping at straws. Barrington was probably the first name that had entered her tortured mind.

Knowing there was going to be a scene, she took action. "Samuel, please take Emily into the drawing room and explain Brianne's accident. Emily, I'll be in shortly."

Catherine led Brianne to a chair that lined the wall of the foyer and when the drawing room door had been shut, she softly spoke. "Brianne, look at me. I know you've been through a great deal in the last few days and I wish that there was some way I could ease the pain that you're now feeling, but there isn't. I can only try to help you, and be truthful with you."

She placed an aged hand against Brianne's soft young cheek. "This is the home of Emily Howard, and she has lived here for a very long time. No one by the name of Morganna lives here, and never has. And if she did, she would never have gone to the hospital to deliver her child. Anyone with means has her children at home in her room, attended by her private physician and surrounded by those close to her. No one would willingly go through the horrors of the hospital, Brianne. Certainly we'll search further for her, but her last name *can't* be Barrington. Child, the only Barrington of New Orleans is Ryan . . . and you must know he's not married."

Catherine patted her hand. "We will begin our quest tomorrow, dear. You'll come home with us and rest— you've had far too much excitement for one day. Don't worry, Samuel has contacts throughout the city and I'm sure he'll be able to find your sister for you. Right now, I must speak to Emily. Imagine her confusion! Will you be all right for a few moments?"

Brianne tried very hard to concentrate on Catherine's speech, but all the words sounded as though they were coming through an echo chamber, and her hands were beginning to shake. In a small voice she asked, "Catherine, why did you say I was your cousin?"

"It seemed the best way to explain you at the time, and until you can find your own family I'd be pleased if you would think of yourself as part of mine. Besides, you'll soon find out that down here the term 'cousin' is applied very loosely. It isn't always a blood relation."

Catherine was very worried about Brianne when she left her. She appeared so lost, and it was obvious she was fighting for self-control.

When she entered the drawing room, Samuel and Emily both rose.

"Emily, I'm so sorry if we've upset you. I take it Samuel has explained the reason for Brianne's confusion? I've heard that with head injuries such as hers, loss of memory is not unusual. I only pray it's temporary."

Seeing Emily's tightly held hands, Catherine was afraid of the impression Brianne had made and knew she must try to correct it. "She's such a sweet young woman that she must have been very distraught to speak to you so. I think of her as a frightened child, and when she insisted that this was her sister's home, I counted on your friendship to help me gently show her that she was mistaken."

Emily Howard had always championed the underdog, and this situation tugged at her heart. "Of course, Catherine, you may count on me. How can I help? The poor child must be so bewildered. Imagine not remembering your past . . . she must feel so alone right now. Would you like me to speak with her?"

Catherine had been holding her breath, and slowly she let it out. Thank God Brianne had chosen the home of such a good person. "How very kind of you, Emily. I knew I could rely on your charitable nature. Perhaps it would be best if you spoke to her briefly—it might put her mind at ease."

Soon after Catherine had left her alone in the hall, Brianne rose, intending to explore the rooms leading off the entry hall. Staying clear of the drawing room, she opened the door opposite it. Obviously it was a library, and quickly she looked about for clues as to the inhabitants of this house. A large oil painting hung on one wall portraying a younger Mrs. Howard sitting on a bench outside the home. Surrounding her were three teenage children, all boys, dressed in old-fashioned clothes. The paneled walls were lined with books, and picking one out, she read the title: *Iliad and the Odyssey* by Homer. Opening the leather-bound book, she searched for the publication date. Her eyes riveted to the print, "Limited Special Edition for Harcourt Publishers, London, England, 1837."

Feeling ill, she looked about the room and felt transported back to another time. For all the old books and furnishings, there was no musty odor to indicate age. Everything was clean and well cared for. Seeing nothing to connect this room with her sister, she replaced the old volume and returned to the foyer.

She had to find something to prove she was right. This was Morganna's home!

Unsure which room to search next, she was startled when a black woman approached her. "Are you all right, miz? Maybe you should sit down, you don't look real good—I'll get Miz Emily."

"Please!" Unthinking, Brianne grabbed the woman's arm and pleaded with her. "Please, tell me the name of the owners of this house! Do you know my sister Morganna Barrington? Is this her house?"

The woman looked frightened by her actions and stared back at her.

"Please tell me! I have to know!" Brianne was becoming hysterical, and although she knew it, she was unable to control the mounting panic.

"You lost, miz? This here house belongs to Mista Howard." She pulled her arm free and backed away from Brianne with eyes as round as saucers. "I'd best get Miz Emily."

She thinks I'm crazy, Brianne realized. They all think I am! She fell back into the chair and stared into space. Maybe she was losing her mind. None of this could really be happening—Morganna's home taken over by strangers, everyone living as though in the last century. None of this was real. If only she could be dreaming and wake up from this nightmare.

Where are you, Morganna? she thought miserably. What's happened to *both* of us?

Accompanied by the Murdocks, Emily Howard found Brianne leaning her head back against the wall and staring off into space with anguished eyes. It was a pitiful sight, and in sympathy Emily went to her, kneeling in front of the woman.

"My dear, I'm sorry this isn't your sister's home. It is a lovely house, though, and perhaps when you have more time I can take you through it. I would love to have you see the entire house. For now, I'll just thank you for the compliment of wanting to come and meet me. Since you'll be staying with Catherine for awhile, may I come and visit with you? I'd like to be your friend, Brianne."

Brianne slowly looked down into the kind face of the real owner of this house. "Thank you, Mrs. Howard, I'd like that. I'm sorry for all the trouble I've caused."

Her voice was merely a whisper when she spoke to the woman who had faithfully stayed by her side since last night. "I'm so tired, Catherine . . . could we possibly leave for your home now?"

Brianne's mind barely registered the view from the

carriage, her thoughts were in such turmoil. Barrington had said this was the nineteenth century, and she had laughed at him. He had said, Ask anyone—the whole world would prove it. Dear God! Could he possibly be right? Had something happened in those woods, or had she simply dreamed this whole thing?

She had never asked Catherine about the date, thinking she would go along with Barrington to pacify him, but this was different. The entire city was involved.

I'm afraid, she thought. She couldn't believe she was frightened to ask Catherine, who had been so protective, what year it was! Her heart was pounding against her chest and the palms of her cotton gloves were damp. She looked over to the woman sitting next to her, and Catherine smiled with affection.

Taking a deep breath, she said fearfully, "You've been very good to me, both of you have, and I do appreciate it. Now I'm asking that you also be absolutely truthful with me. Be a friend, Catherine, tell me the truth . . . what is the date?"

"I've always been honest with you, Brianne, as hard as it's been, like in Emily's home. This time what you ask is much easier. It's April 12th, dear, 1856."

Brianne could feel the numbness set in. Her face was frozen in fear, and neither of the Murdocks could get an answer from her to their anxious questions.

Realizing she was being led out of the carriage and into another large house, Brianne walked on stiff, numb legs. She could barely feel the ground beneath them. Everything was in a haze and her eyes felt glazed over in shock.

Catherine wasted no time in settling Brianne into the room next to her own, all the while wondering why the date could bring about such a reaction. Every servant within earshot was given a job to perform and in a matter of minutes Catherine, with the help of her personal maid

Letty, was putting Brianne into the soft bed.

It was a large, sunny room decorated with a female in mind, but the sunshine wasn't in accord with the atmosphere inside the chamber.

"Draw the drapes, Letty. Only let in enough light to see. Sarah, bring that basin over here."

As she began to sponge the girl's face with cool water, Brianne's hand came up and captured her own.

"Please, Catherine, don't. I just want to be left alone. Please . . ."

She uttered the last word while choking back tears, and Catherine gave in to her wishes. Grateful that Brianne was at least speaking, she cleared the room. Turning at the doorway, Catherine glanced back at the woman who at that moment looked more like a child in the large bed.

Pursing her lips at her own inability to be of help, she whispered to her, "I'll be right next door, Brianne, should you need me."

The silence was deafening as Brianne's thoughts seemed to bounce off the bedroom walls back at her. Could any of this be real? Or had she left reality back on that highway?

I'm not dreaming, she reaffirmed. She had seen and heard too much, and it was ludicrous now to believe everyone she made contact with was involved in some elaborate lie for her benefit.

Tears ran down her face as she thought about her sister Morganna, the only family she had left. First her father had died before her eyes of a heart attack when she was thirteen. And last year her mother had died peacefully in her sleep.

If somehow she had actually been transported 130 years back in time, then she was now truly all alone. Morganna didn't even exist yet.

No! She vehemently denied the possibility, yet the grief was overwhelming. Would she never see her sister

97

again? Was she never to hold the child that through Morganna was a part of her too? Flashes of her childhood ran through her memory . . .

They were two young girls, not yet burdened with the pressures of adolescence. Rather, they greeted each day bursting with energy and a carefree exuberance for life. One, dark-haired, with large serious green eyes showing confidence in her role as teacher, was running next to the bike yelling instructions. The other child, Morganna, blonde and slightly shorter, with panic marring her usually happy face, was screaming that she was afraid to turn the corner.

Brianne remembered the burning in her chest as she raced behind her sister, shouting encouragement. And finally, when they had successfully maneuvered the entire block, she too had shared in Morganna's sense of accomplishment.

Smiling, she reached back even further and pulled from the shelves of treasured memories other images . . .

Playing bakery with mud cookies they had carefully formed. Going door to door, selling potholders. Tree forts and magic places like Devil's Canyon, where a clearing in the woods was transformed into an enchanted forest that housed their private club. Here it was that they discussed the overwhelming mystery of sex, each trying to straighten the other out about the misconceptions they had formed from all-knowing friends.

Years later, Brianne had taught Morganna to apply makeup and they had collapsed onto the bed, laughing at their experiments. Borrowing clothes and hair rollers, and fights over the ownership of both. Whispered accounts when one would come in from a date. Sharing a room, and uncontrolled giggles late at night . . .

Each fragmented memory brought a sad smile.

When Brianne eventually left the suburbs to strike out on her own in Philadelphia, she missed the physical presence of her sister. And at times felt almost like the amputee who consciously knows a limb has been lost but continues to feel the sensations that no scalpel can sever.

It wasn't unusual for one to reach for the phone to make the necessary contact, when it would ring with a call from the other. There was a special bond between the two, and as they grew into women, it strengthened. They could almost sense when the one needed the other.

"Can you feel it now, Morganna?" she whispered aloud as tears clouded her vision. "I don't know what's happened to me, or to you either. What are you going through, trying to find me? I promise we'll be back together again, Morganna . . . someday. I don't know how or when, but I know it. Somehow, I'll get back."

She turned into her pillow and sobbed for the loss of her loved ones. Her mother, a woman she had greatly admired, dealing with the early death of her husband and continuing to strive for a full life with her children. Working outside the home and being successful at it, she had managed as a single parent to raise happy normal children in a turbulent era.

Her father, a tall, handsome man she proudly remembered. Blessed with the gift of patience—and he must have needed it, living with three females of differing personalities. He always came through for her, taking her friends everywhere . . .

Brianne suddenly sat up in bed and grabbing the other pillow, hugged it to herself as though to contain her pounding heart within her body.

It played across her mind like a scene in a movie . . .

It was the year before he died, and as always her friends could depend on Mr. Quinlan for a ride to the Junior High dance. In the back seat of her father's car, she and her classmates were discussing the death of a

99

friend's grandparent. Everyone was giving their opinion on the subject of death, and Brianne remembered expressing her fear of it and the terror she felt at nothingness, never to again see, or feel, or think . . . just nothing.

Her dad had listened to all of them in silence. Then, at a red light, he had turned and looked straight into her eyes. "Do you really believe we were put here to end up as nothing? Don't be so afraid of death, Bri. Dying is falling asleep in one world . . . and waking up in another."

Brianne now looked about the room fearfully.

"Daddy . . . ?" She called to him in a tiny voice that sounded strange, even to her.

For a very long time she stared about the dimly lit room, as though expecting an answer. Swallowing several times, she tried to rid her mouth of the acrid taste of panic.

Dear God, could she really have died? Did she no longer exist in the twentieth century?

She held her hands out in front of her, looking at them as if they could provide the answer. All they confirmed, as they shook uncontrollably, was that she was tottering on the brink of insanity.

Chapter 7

Ryan paced the beige carpet in his bedroom like a caged animal. He was too worked up to sleep, too confused by the events of the last twenty-four hours, and too haunted by a pair of green eyes. He kept seeing the woman's beautiful face. Yes, he grudgingly admitted, she was beautiful, even if she was stubborn, infuriating, and a consummate liar.

He pulled the sash tighter on his velvet robe as he pondered the mystery of Brianne Quinlan. Why was he so attracted to her when, compared to Caroline, Miss Quinlan had to come in second best. Or did she? He mentally pictured both women and was shocked to visualize the woman he had intended to marry as cold, almost too perfect. He recollected the only warmth Caroline showed was in bed, and then it was more a fever than a giving emotion. He had never seen her show compassion, never heard her argue for those less fortunate, as the strange Miss Quinlan had done.

Sitting on the edge of his bed, he stared across the room and reevaluated his opinion of Brianne Quinlan. Yes, she was stubborn, infuriatingly so, but she fought for what she believed in. He also had to admit that she hadn't lied about Stephan. But the story of her origins?

Yes, there she had lied, and it wasn't a very intelligent lie either. Even with her props, the watch and key chain, it was too farfetched.

Leaning back against a huge pillow, Ryan closed his eyes. It was all too confusing. He wanted to banish the small, green-eyed woman from his mind, but she refused to disappear. Annoyed with his over-active imagination, Ryan leaned forward and removed his robe. Throwing it on the foot of his bed, he extinguished the small bedside lamp, plunging himself and the room into darkness. Lying on his side, he buried his cheek into the pillow and concentrated on relaxing. If he was to rise before dawn and catch the first packet into New Orleans, he needed to sleep.

But she wouldn't leave him alone.

She quietly intruded, reminding him of another bed, just down the hallway from his room. Why had he gone to her? he anguished. She was no prostitute of Stephan's, and if she was an actress, she wasn't a very good one. Even though he was drunk, he remembered that she had welcomed him, putting up no resistance to his caresses. Damn it, he *couldn't* have imagined that!

Was it the drug Mattie had given her that had made her so provocative, so passionate? Or was it all a drunken man's dream? Still, he could feel himself grow warm just thinking about her astonishing softness. When had he blacked out? Was this warm, passionate woman only alive in his imagination? Who was she? Who *was* she?

The house had been quiet for nearly an hour when Brianne crept from the bed, careful not to make any noise. Hurriedly she put out the yellow gown, leaving the wide hoops and slips behind. This was her chance, she thought, as she struggled with the tiny hooks at the back of her dress. She had to find out for herself what had happened to her.

She must have been hysterical to have thought she might have died! Granted, everything was working against her, but she was a fighter, and the first rule of fighting was to protect yourself. Until she found out the truth, she couldn't begin the struggle of finding her way back to Morganna.

Impatient to leave, she cursed under her breath at the stupid hooks between her shoulders that were impossible to reach. Giving up, she grabbed the light shawl to cover her open back.

Carpeting, soft and thick, hid the sounds of her departure as she made her way down the stairs. After her eyes had adjusted to the faint light, she was able to see the front door at the bottom of the steps. Eager to be gone, Brianne carefully sidestepped a round table in the center of the entry hall where someone had placed a large floral arrangement.

Seeing it reminded her of Catherine.

She wished there were some way she could let the older woman know why she was leaving, but in her heart she knew it was hopeless. The Murdocks thought her to be unsound, thanks to Barrington, and the scene she had foolishly made at Emily Howard's had supported that.

Damn that man for interfering in her life!

Not having the time or inclination to search the house for paper and pen, Brianne walked to the large oak door. She put her hand on the latch, but hesitated before it.

This is it! Either I leave Catherine's protection and discover for myself what actually lies beyond the door, or turn around and accept what I've been told.

No! Never! Brianne's hand pressed down with determination.

Outside the smell of magnolias was heavy, and breathing in deeply, Brianne quietly left the sheltering care of the Murdocks.

*　　　*　　　*

It seemed to her she had walked a very long time before seeing a street sign. "Prytania?" Catherine lived on the same street as Morganna!

Well, she would just have to return later and explain everything, or maybe write her a note. Yes, it would be safer that way.

Once, a carriage made its way down the road and Brianne hurried into the trees until it passed. Upon leaving them, her hem caught in the underbrush and tore.

"Damn!" she swore aloud. This was ridiculous! Why was she hiding as though she were a criminal, not wanting to be recognized? She'd give anything for someone to admit knowing her. However, in all of New Orleans, the only people she knew were not where they were supposed to be. They weren't even in the correct century, if she were to believe the others. Well, she'd find all her answers soon.

Emotionally, she felt better by regaining her independence and making her own decisions again, but she couldn't quite shake off the guilt of leaving Catherine without explanation.

Catherine was the one person who bothered her.

Barrington she could write off as an unbalanced man suffering from delusions. Hopelessly lost in the past, he probably would have trouble functioning in the modern world. Emily Howard seemed nice enough, but the Murdocks had talked to her alone and could have told her what to say.

It was Catherine. She wasn't the type of person to successfully carry off such a deception. The woman's actions from the very beginning spoke for her character, and Brianne acknowledged that it was Catherine's admission of the date that had thrown her. The woman had no reason to lie about it. It was obvious from the way she had treated Barrington when they left his home that

Catherine was very angry, and she had made it clear where her sympathies lie. If she had gone along with him in the beginning, as Brianne had thought, then why now, when she had seen how dangerous he was, did she still support his story?

Of them all, it was Catherine whom she trusted, whom she wanted to prove wrong, and who had cast the terrible doubt that all of them might possibly be right.

The fragile shoes she wore were never meant for serious walking and Brianne could feel the beginning of blisters on her feet. Seeing another street sign a short distance away, she gritted her teeth and continued to walk toward it.

"Camp Street!" She turned around in the middle of the road and looked about her. How could she have become lost? She had made certain to remain on the same road. Discouraged by this new setback, she sat down on the grass and pulled the voluminous skirt back from her calves.

God! Her feet were killing her. She must have come well over a mile by now. Afraid to take the slippers off for fear of never getting them back on, she swore the very next thing that passed, be it car or horse-drawn carriage, she was going to stop it and ask for a ride. For all she knew, she was going around in circles.

Massaging her ankles, Brianne went over again in her mind the incredible events of the last twenty-four hours, and sooner than she expected she heard the sound of a horse. Turning, she saw a carriage approaching and screwed up her mouth. Naturally, it couldn't have been a car! That was too much to hope for. Well, she didn't care if it was Jean Lafitte himself, she was going to stop it!

Tired, bedraggled, and looking less like the fine lady Mattie had proclaimed her to be this morning, Brianne stood in the middle of the road, waving her arms.

She had a moment of fright when it seemed the horse

was about to collide with her, and imagined she felt the moist breath of the animal closing in on her until it finally came to a halt.

She let out her own breath and walked on shaky legs to the carriage. A small lantern was hung at the driver's seat, and by its light she could see a black man staring at her as if he had seen a ghost.

"Please excuse me for frightening you," she apologized, "but I'm trying to get into the city and I was wondering if you could give me a ride."

Before the startled man could find his voice, the side door of the vehicle opened and another man stepped out. Coming toward her, he took the lantern away from the driver and held it close to her face.

Squinting with the sudden light in her eyes, Brianne could see he was dark and attractively distinguished, appearing to be in his mid-forties.

"What's the problem, Madam? Are you lost? Hurt?"

Brianne attempted to smile. "No, I'm not hurt, but I do seem to be lost. I was telling your driver that I was trying to get into the city. You see, I was walking on Prytania Street and somehow wound up on this one, Camp. I don't know where I went wrong, but I do need to reach the city tonight. If that's where you're going, would it be possible for me to ride with you?"

She knew she was taking a chance, and it wasn't like her to be so forward. The man was looking her over from head to toe, and taking his time about it too. It wasn't insulting, for some strange reason, just an assessment, and with good cause. She herself never picked up strangers.

"May I ask where you are going so late at night?" He spoke with a slightly French accent.

Brianne was unsure of how to answer him; after all, he too appeared to be living in the past, dressed as he was in

106

dated evening clothes.

"I would like to go to the City Hall, or wherever they keep records. I have relatives living in New Orleans, but can't seem to locate them. If you would be good enough to drop me off there, I'd be most grateful."

He stared into her face longer than necessary and Brianne was beginning to feel uncomfortable when he suddenly turned from her and opened the carriage door. "I would be pleased to be of assistance, Miss . . . ?"

Accepting his outstretched hand, she stepped up into the coach. "Brianne Quinlan. And thank you for your help."

Once they were both seated and the rolling motion of the carriage began, he turned up the small lamp by the door and inclining his head, introduced himself. "Gregory Duville, at your service. This must be your first visit to our city, Miss Quinlan."

"Is it that obvious? From what I've seen of it this morning when I arrived, it was quite lovely—very exotic, with everyone dressed so strangely. Is there a festival being celebrated?"

Please let him say yes.

"Strangely? I'm afraid I don't know what you mean." He looked slightly insulted and continued, as though having to justify his city. "We in New Orleans are now a mixture of almost all nationalities, and I suppose some keep their native dress, but actually we are very cosmopolitan, embedded in tradition and culture. If you are planning to stay for any length of time you'll see for yourself, and I'm sure our city will not disappoint you."

He smiled slightly as though excusing her ignorance. "Now I could have understood your question if you had arrived some weeks ago, when the pre-Lenten carnival, Mardi Gras, took place. It's called Shrove Tuesday by some, and many festivities are held throughout the city."

While he was speaking, Brianne took in his appearance. His thick hair was graying at the temples, but it was attractive and softened his strong, lean face and clear brown eyes.

She was being foolish, and she scolded herself for daydreaming—she didn't even know the man!

"And by the way, Miss Quinlan, you were not lost. Prytania Street does turn into Camp, and in a few more blocks when we cross Canal Street, the main artery of the city, it will once again change. This time to Chartres— very confusing for a visitor, I'm sure. So you see, if you had continued on your own you would have come to the very center of the town and the building that you seek."

He appeared to be amused by her confusion and spoke to her with the condescending voice of an adult to a child. She was used to that. Because of her size people always thought her to be younger than her twenty-six years, especially men. Unlike other women, she felt it wasn't always flattering. She had worked hard to be taken seriously and normally in a situation like this would have come back with a biting reply, spoken naturally with a sweet smile. It rarely failed and usually she made her point.

But this wasn't the moment to be offended. She needed this ride and could afford to swallow her pride for it.

"I'm afraid that I couldn't have walked much further, Mr. Duville. It seems that I misjudged the distance, so I'm very grateful that you came by."

He was looking at her clothes, especially her ripped hem and soiled shoes, when his eyes suddenly shot right into hers.

"You must know the Presbytere, the Court House, will be closed this time of night, along with all other official buildings. Do you have any place to stay until morning?"

Now was the time to tell him Morganna's name, but something about the man made her hesitate from confiding in him. He acted just like the Murdocks, spoke with the same grammar, had the same polite demeanor.

She wasn't getting the reassurance that she wanted from him. He was a total stranger, there could be no way their meeting could have been arranged, and now there could be little doubt that he too would support the preposterous story that this was the mid–eighteen hundreds.

She was more determined than ever to check the city records and wouldn't be satisfied until she saw them with her own eyes.

"No, I don't have any place to stay right now, but I will come morning, as soon as I find out where my sister is."

His eyebrows came together. "The hotel may have a room for you. Please excuse the question, but seeing no reticule, I wondered if you had any funds?"

How stupid! It hadn't even occurred to her that she was without money. The only thing on her mind was successfully getting away from the Murdocks and reaching the heart of the city. At least she had accomplished the first and was on her way to achieving the second. She wasn't too worried. She had been on her own for the last six years and could take care of herself now.

"As a matter of fact, no. I don't. But I'll manage until morning."

His eyes widened and he looked at her incredulously. "Miss Quinlan, where will you go? What will you do until morning? Why not let me arrange a room for you? You cannot simply walk around New Orleans at this time of night!"

The city might be a puzzle to her, one that she would solve tomorrow morning, but the people, at least those that she had met so far, were certainly generous.

"Thank you, Mr. Duville, for your kind offer, but that won't be necessary. I'll be quite all right . . . really."

Shaking his head, he glanced out the window. "We're almost there. This large building we are passing is the Cabildo. It housed the Spanish Government. From there Spain ruled New Orleans and all of her territory west of the Mississippi River. The arrangements for the Louisiana Purchase took place there, something some of us will always regret."

Brianne enjoyed his recitation. She thought he was a great tour guide and she could tell by his voice that he enjoyed it too, until his last statement. She looked at him curiously until he directed her attention to the opposite window.

"This you must see during the daylight. Jackson Square, or Place d'Arms, as it was originally known. And flanking it are the Pontalba Buildings. They were completed a few years ago and are designed in the Renaissance style. The ironwork running the length of the galleries is exquisite."

As though suddenly aware of the way he was rambling on, Duville stopped and looking over to her, studied her face. When his eyes lowered to her breasts, Brianne pulled the shawl tighter in an attempt to shield herself.

Smiling at her actions, he rapped on the wall. "We have reached the Presbytere, that large building on the corner. Are you quite sure we cannot agree on an arrangement? In all good conscience, I couldn't just leave you here."

She might be at a disadvantage, but she wasn't naive. She had picked up the slight inflection in his voice when he said the word "arrangement."

Knowing she couldn't trust anyone, she opened the door herself and stepped out. When he looked like he was about to follow, she stopped him.

"Mr. Duville, again I must thank you for all your kindness and I appreciate your concern, but I'll be just fine. This is something I must do alone. If need be, I'll sit

110

in a hotel lobby until daylight, so please don't worry."

For a brief moment she saw a flicker of disappointment cross his face, and almost of its own volition her mouth opened. "I do have one last favor, though. Could you please tell me the date?"

It was a sadistic question, for before he spoke she already knew what he would say.

Again his eyebrows came together, and she could only guess that he thought her to be a very strange and willful woman.

"The date is April 12th," he answered in a confused voice.

"The year, Mr. Duville, what is the year?"

A disbelieving smile showed. "The year is 1856. Don't you know that?"

Brianne returned his smile with a sad one and slowly said, "I just wanted to hear you say it. Goodbye, and thank you for helping me."

Quickly, she shut the door and ran away from him before he tried to stop her. She slowed and caught her breath halfway down the street, then turned onto another. She could smell the river before her, and speeding up slightly she almost came to it.

Wasn't that amazing? she thought. You had to go up to the river. It was actually higher than the street.

She couldn't afford to get lost now, and she committed the street names to memory as she turned onto one called Decatur. Nothing must stop her from being at the Court House when it opened in the morning.

Across the street were blocks of quaint buildings divided into stalls.

This had to be the French Market. Excited that something she had read about existed, she crossed over to get a better view.

It was mostly deserted, but a few people were unloading vegetables. She loved being independent again, and stopped for a moment to breathe in the lingering scents that still permeated the air around her. It awakened her sleeping hunger, and she decided to ask the night workers when the market would be opened. Not that she had any money to buy anything, but she might be able to talk them into letting her work for her food.

About to walk up to them, she cried out in alarm when someone grabbed her arm.

Over her shoulder she saw one of the most repulsive faces she had ever laid eyes on. "Out lookin' for someone, gal? Ain't this your lucky night—you jus' found him!"

As he threw back his head and laughed at his own joke, Brianne gasped. His vile breath assaulted her and was enough to make her ill. He was grinning a monstrous smile that showed rotted teeth and was wearing filthy, outrageous clothing.

"Take your hands off me!" Brianne commanded. "You've made a mistake. I'm not looking for anyone, and that includes you."

He only grabbed her more tightly and turned her around. "I didn't make no mistake. If you're real good and that body gives what it promises, I might throw in a little somethin' extra. Even if you are a runt, it's been awhile since I had one as pretty as you."

His raspy voice sent chills up her spine. "Well, it's going to be awhile longer, mister, because if you don't release me this instant I'm going to scream to wake the dead. I'm sure those people up the street will hear me and come running."

Her heart was pounding at an alarming rate and she could feel the blood draining from her face.

He gave her a smug look and tightened his grip on her arms. "Where'd you think you are, girlie? Those peddlers ain't gonna do nothin', 'cept mind their own business. Nobody meddles with Sam Harkins, you'll soon learn that. Now let's get on with it."

The brute pulled her even closer, so that his mouth was inches away from her own, and Brianne felt sick when he began rubbing himself against her.

She was very frightened. She tried desperately to remember everything she had heard about self-defense and rape, but it all fled as instinct took over. She'd be damned if another man was going to use her. She'd fight this one.

Her heart was racing, but she fought to stay calm. She still had her voice and her nails, and most important, her knees. She hoped she maimed the bastard for life!

Willing her body to relax, she let him think his obscene movements were exciting her and soon could feel his grip lighten. Pulling her arms free, she surprised him with the speed of her hands as her nails raked his face, drawing rivulets of blood.

She was about to bring her knee up with all her strength when she was suddenly shoved out of the way.

Her legs became entangled in the long skirt and she landed face down on the ground. Looking up, Brianne saw a woman with bright red hair and a face that appeared almost comical with heavy, outlandish makeup.

"What the hell're you doing, pig?" she yelled down at Brianne. "This is my territory, and I'll cut that face of yours if I ever see you down here again. You got that?"

Coming closer, the woman snarled, "Now, for stealing from me I'm gonna take from you. Gimme that shawl! It still gets cold sometimes at night, though I hate to cover this up."

She turned to the man to let him get a better look at her breasts, which were overflowing her low-cut blouse. Harkins took a good look, but pointing to Brianne, yelled, "I want that bitch! I'll fix her so that no man'll ever look at her again."

He was wiping the blood from his face onto his shirt

113

sleeves when the woman went over to him. Spitting on her hem, she helped him clean his face.

"What did you want with her in the first place? Look at her! She doesn't know how to treat a man, probably won't know the first thing to do. Now take me, honey. I know how to do everything . . . and I do it real good too."

Forgetting his face, Harkins began fondling the woman, obviously influenced by her speech.

Everything happened so fast that Brianne couldn't believe she was witnessing this. She started to crawl away while the two were busy, when suddenly the woman whirled away from Harkins and shouted in her heavily accented Irish voice, "You heard me, slut! I want that shawl!"

Brianne would pay any price to get away from them and quickly took it off to give her. So eager was she to pacify the redhead that she almost didn't notice when the woman's expression changed.

She screwed up her mouth as though disgusted and rolling her eyes to the blackened sky, indicated Harkins with her head. Brianne was so startled by her change that she couldn't move.

Kneeling down to take the shawl from Brianne, she whispered, "Wait for me behind the vegetable stall . . . I'll give it back." She grabbed the wrap and muttered under her breath, "Sorry about this."

Without warning she brought back her arm and hit Brianne soundly on the face. Shrugging her shoulders, the woman stood up. "Let that be a warning. Learn the lesson well, girl. I could've let this bucko have a go at you, but I've got better plans for him. Now get the hell out of here!"

Brianne scrambled to her feet and took off as though the devil were at her heels, and he might have been, too, if not for the redheaded woman, whose mocking laughter followed her.

Reaching the stall, she ignored the curious faces and ran behind it. Leaning her back against the wooden frame, she slowly collapsed to the ground.

"This is too much!" she sobbed angrily. The tears ran freely down her face and she knew there was no stopping them, nor did she want to. It was small comfort, but she gave in to feeling sorry for herself. She had every right. She'd been separated from her family, stranded in time, or else she was the victim of a cruel mass deception. In her heart she knew the last wasn't true, and that struck terror through her.

"Oh God, get me out of here!" she cried, and putting her head into her hands, wept tears of abandonment.

Chapter 8

Brianne jumped when she felt the hand on her shoulder, and jerking her head up, she saw the prostitute who had taken Harkins's interest away from her.

The woman knelt down beside her. "Here's your shawl, honey. Did I hurt you? I had to make it look real."

Wiping her eyes, Brianne shook her head and looked behind the woman. "Is Harkins gone?"

She nodded. "He didn't want much . . . his kind never do. Likes to get rough and then go right to it. You took care of the first, and I handled the rest. Surprised me, though, and actually paid me," she said, holding out a coin.

Brianne noticed she had lost her heavy accent, and now spoke with only a faint lilt to her voice.

"What are you doing out here? This your first time?"

"It's a long story, but you're wrong about me, I'm not a . . ." Brianne struggled for a word that wouldn't be too insulting to her.

The woman laughed. "What? Whore? Prostitute? River dove, lady of the evening? Personally, I like the last one. I am a lady, believe it or not, and I do most of my work in the evening. I'm very choosy, and normally wouldn't have gone near a man like Harkins, but I followed you after you got out of that fancy rig, back up by the square. Since you were heading the way I was, I watched to see where you were going. Saw him grab you and could see you were scared. After you clawed him, I knew he'd beat you for that, so I stepped in. Name's Maureen Ahearn, by the way. You can call me Rena."

Brianne stopped sniffling and held out her hand. "Thanks for coming to my rescue," she said gratefully. "I'm Brianne Quinlan. You pack a mean right, Rena," she laughingly added as she rubbed her cheek.

"That was nothing. Grew up with three brothers and learned how to take care of myself, which is more than I can say for you. Where were you going? Have any place to stay for the night?" Rena stood up and held out a hand to Brianne.

Rising, she told the now familiar story. "I have to be at the Court House in the morning to look up something important. I thought I'd walk around and see part of the city until then. I can see now that was a foolish idea."

Rena shook her red curls. "It wasn't foolish, it was stupid! You want to sightsee, you do it in the daytime. It's dangerous down here at night if you don't know what you're doing." Rena looked down at the small woman in front of her and felt her heart constrict. She knew the fear. It was almost tangible. Rena had felt it herself, her first time. It never went away completely, but now she had learned to swallow it down before it paralyzed her. Seeing it again so close in the green-eyed woman made her want to forget the throngs of others that she couldn't possibly help and take in this one small, trembling stranger.

Her mind made up, she said, "My place isn't too far. Come home with me, and first thing in the morning you can be about your business."

The smaller woman's mouth opened in the beginnings of a protest. "I can't ask . . ."

118

Rena shook her head and pulling Brianne's arm, she said, "C'mon, I'll be sick if I soon don't wash that Harkins character off me."

Together they left the French Market, and again Brianne could only hope she was doing the right thing—following her instincts and a total stranger.

Rena kept Brianne in tow as they made their way to her room. Weaving in and out of the late-night faction and avoiding the clutches of rough-looking men, Rena led them past noisy taverns. At one called the Crouching Tiger, they turned onto a quieter street. It was more like an alley, Brianne thought, as they stopped in front of a rundown building.

"This is it," Rena proclaimed. "Not much to look at, but nobody will bother you here. Come along."

They went around back and climbed a long flight of stairs. At the top Rena paused at her door. "You are about to enter hallowed ground, Brianne," she said seriously. "No man has set foot here since I moved in, and that's the way I want to keep it."

Pulling a key out of her red and green drawstring purse, Rena unlocked the door and held it open.

Crossing the threshold, Brianne waited as the other woman struck a match and lit a hurricane lamp. As the light grew stronger, Brianne was surprised. Whatever she had expected to find, it certainly wasn't this.

Even though the apartment was sparsely furnished, it was immaculate. The bed had a pretty blue and white homemade quilt and the dresser and tables gleamed with polish. The wooden floor shone with wax amid multi-colored rag rugs.

Turning to Rena, Brianne said gratefully, "Your home is very nice. Thank you for letting me stay the night."

"I'm glad you like it. As I said before, it isn't much. But this room is mine, and here I can be myself. There's some bread and cheese in the cupboard over there, and some wine on the shelf next to it. Why not fix us something to eat? I can use the wine, and I'm sure you can do with a glass yourself. I'm going to wash and change out of this." She indicated her dress and left to set up a beige screen. Going to the door, Rena said she was getting water and would be back in a few minutes.

Alone, Brianne looked about the room. She couldn't believe that she was here. What would happen to her next? So much for being self-reliant. She couldn't even take care of herself for one night!

She kept repeating to herself, "tomorrow morning, tomorrow morning," as though the incantation would act as a magic charm to see her safely through. Going to the cupboard, Brianne found the food and discovered the bottle of white wine, three-quarters full. Taking the glasses and dishes out, she began to set the table, all the while conscious that she was performing these actions in the wrong century.

Rena quickly returned to the room carrying a large bucket of water. "There's a tablecloth and napkins in the bottom drawer of the dresser. While you're there, would you hand me the towels in the drawer above it?"

She took the water behind the screen and Brianne could hear her pouring it as she opened the bottom drawer. Carefully she lifted out the tablecloth and napkins. The napkins were beautiful. Linen, to match the cloth, they were embroidered with a fine stitching of flowers in one corner. She was still holding them when Rena came around the screen to get her towels.

"Like them?"

Brianne nodded. "They're lovely. The work on them is absolutely exquisite."

She looked inquiringly at this strange woman.

Rena smiled and winked at her. "There's just no end to my talents, is there?" Going to the dresser, she got out the towels herself and admonished Brianne, "Now set the table correctly."

Brianne went about resetting the table, and when finished she viewed it with a critical eye, not wanting to disappoint Rena.

What a puzzle she was. A prostitute who was so fastidious about her home and the proper setting of her table. Of course Brianne had never met one before, but it still seemed odd.

Shrugging her shoulders, she looked back at the table and satisfied that it was done correctly, sat in one of the chairs to wait for her hostess.

Brianne's mouth hung open. The woman who emerged from behind the screen was a stranger. Never would she have known it was Rena. The flaming red hair was pulled back into a neat bun and she wore a white cotton wrapper with pale green embroidery on the lapels. What had brought about her complete transformation was the lack of makeup. Her face had been scrubbed clean and a light dusting of freckles could be seen across the bridge of her nose. She had pretty blue eyes and a soft mouth that was now curving into an embarrassed smile.

Brianne thought she was delightful, and as Irish-looking as her name sounded.

"If you're going to keep that mouth open, at least fill it with food," she said to Brianne. "I don't know about you, but I'm starving."

Rena sat across from her and placed the napkin on her lap. When their eyes met, it was Brianne who spoke.

She uttered only a single word in wonderment. "Why?"

Rena swallowed the bread she was eating and poured wine for both of them. Looking directly at Brianne, she asked impatiently, "Why what? Why do I work at night? Why do I disguise myself? Why do I embroider napkins?

121

What? What exactly is it that you want to know?"

"I'm sorry, Rena. It's none of my business. I had no right to pry," and Brianne was embarrassed for doing just that.

"You're right. It isn't any of your business." She cut a thick slice of bread and a piece of cheese and put them on Brianne's plate.

"Look, everyone here has a story about what led them to this place, and mine's not very new or original."

Rena stared at her glass as though lost in her own thoughts, and somewhere in that mixture of pale yellow wine and candlelight she made her decision.

"I'm going to break one of my rules and tell you what you want to know. But only because you're so damn green, and seem innocent enough to get really hurt if you don't know what you're in for."

Brianne tried to explain that it wasn't necessary, and that she was sorry she'd brought the subject up in the first place, but Rena ignored her as she sipped her wine delicately and sat back in her chair.

"I came down from Maryland after my father threw me out and you can guess the reason why. Seems the handsome young merchant who ran after me for months failed to tell anyone he was already engaged, until after he got from me what he wanted. Lord! If I wasn't stupid enough to think he wanted to marry me. What a sweet talker he was," she said in a disillusioned voice.

"What I remembered, though, when I found myself alone, was the way he had talked about New Orleans—how exciting it was when he had visited the city with his father. Even after I grew to hate him I kept remembering the way he talked about it. How a person could make their way in New Orleans because it was growing and constantly changing, like from the Spanish to the French, then to the Americans."

"So you came here," Brianne volunteered.

"No, not then. Didn't have the money for it."

"Couldn't anyone have helped you? Your mother?"

Rena shook her head and smiled sadly. "My mother married down, she liked to tell us. Her people being better than my father's. She always said that even if a person was poor it was no excuse for laziness or sloppiness, so our clothes were mended many times but always spotless. She's the one who taught me how to embroider. She loved it. I think it took her away from that dismal little farm house and let her pretend she was back in her father's home in Ireland. She talked about it many times and was training me to be a lady's maid. I used to practice fixing her hair and serving her. I truly believe she lived for those lessons, pretending to be some grand lady."

For a few moments Rena remained silent, fingering the embroidered corner of the napkin, then shook her head as though clearing it of the memory of her mother. "Anyway, when I found myself on my own, I made my way to a city on the Chesapeake Bay. I worked there for over a year in a tavern, serving tables instead of high-born ladies, and eventually scraped enough to buy a one-way passage to the city of promise . . . New Orleans."

Brianne was fascinated that this woman could talk so openly about her life, and listened without interruption.

"That's when I found out I'm no sailor," Rena continued. "God, it was terrible! I never want to be on board a boat again. When we finally reached New Orleans, it truly looked like the Promised Land and I had all my grand ideas of finding work for some rich lady and never having to worry about where I was going to sleep, or where the next meal was going to come from. Didn't take me long to find out that New Orleans is the same as any other place, and sometimes worse."

She looked directly at Brianne and said bitterly, "It's one thing to be poor. But if you're poor *and* Irish, well then you're little better than the black people here. They

123

have names for us, not pretty ones either, and so the Irish band together and live in miserable poverty trying to scrape out a meager existence. What's amazing is more arrive every week. More pathetic creatures trying to find the Promised Land. I used to watch the ships come in. I wanted to stand at the dock and wave them off, tell them to go back, anywhere must be better. But I never did. Instead, I watched the light die in their eyes and the hope leave their souls.

"I soon realized my dreams were as foolish as those of the ones who came before me. All the better homes have negro servants, slaves that have been born in those homes and trained from the time they are children to serve their ladies. Nobody was going to pay me to be a fancy maid when they had slaves to do it for nothing.

"I didn't have much money left, so I went looking for work. I thought I would go back to serving tables again, and tried the taverns around the waterfront."

Rena again stared into her glass of wine. "It was in one of them that I was first asked, not too nicely either, to trade my body for money."

She squared her shoulders. "I don't know if you've ever been starving and desperate, Brianne, but I was. Enough to make me say yes. But I won't make any excuses for what I've done. Oh, I was scared at first, until I found a way to separate myself from it. My body does all the right things, but in my mind . . . I'm far away in some lovely house, a place of my own where everything is neat and clean and the sun shines on the waxed furniture."

She stopped short and looked at Brianne almost with embarrassment before adding, "Guess I'm no better than my mother, pretending to be something I'm not. When I've really become the very thing my father accused me of when he threw me out."

Brianne had listened enraptured throughout her story. Why, we're alike, she thought. Two women who found

124

themselves alone and in desperate circumstances. Just because Rena chose this way of surviving didn't give Brianne the right to pass judgment on her. She did what she had to.

"Didn't you ever try to contact your mother? Couldn't she have helped you? After all, it was over a year since you left home. Things must have gotten better."

Rena shook her head. "She'd never go against my father. I've written to her, but I think my father tears my letters up before she ever sees them."

She looked at Brianne and smiled. "Don't look so sad. I'm getting by. During the day I still look for work, but it seems at night is the only time I can find it."

Brianne couldn't help asking out of curiosity, "Don't they know, Rena, that you're just pretending? The men. Can't they tell that?"

Rena's soft mouth was curved at the corners when she looked up from her plate. "You really don't know much about men, do you?"

This time it was Brianne who had to look away. She toyed with her food and tried to sound casual when she answered, "Enough. I mean, I'm not totally naive. It's just that what experience I've had wasn't all that it's cracked up to be."

Brianne hated the blush that she could feel creeping up from her neck.

"It seldom is," Rena said laughingly. "How old are you?"

"Twenty-six. Why?"

"I'm four years younger than you, but I feel twenty years older. Listen, Brianne, I'll give you some free advice. From my 'experience,' as you call it, I've found out one very important thing . . . most men are all physical. They want a woman either to top off a good day, or to forget a lousy one. There's no pretending for men. It's all clearly there, or it isn't. That's one thing we

125

women have over them. Give them what they want to hear and feel, and their manly pride will have them thinking they just did you the biggest favor. Those men don't bother me, the ones that think only of themselves. It's that rare one, the one who tries to get through by taking his time and trying to please me . . . that's the one that's upsetting. Then it all seems wrong, and makes me think of that bastard in Maryland and how I mistook his careful seduction for love. Love! Hah! I don't even know if I believe in it. I think it only exists in the minds of women. That's what I mean when I say men are all physical. It's clear to me that they're all ruled from their waists down. But with a woman, it's got to be real for her up here," she said pointing to her head, "before it can be good anywhere else.

"Ah well," she sighed, reaching for her wine again. "Remember this wisdom comes through experience with a certain kind of man. So if you're still thinking about coming into this business, you'd—"

Brianne hurried to interrupt her. "No, I was never thinking about it. I have a good job in Philadelphia. I'm only here for a short time."

Rena gathered the plates in front of her. "Well, this isn't Philadelphia, so what are you going to do for money? How are you going to take care of yourself now? You're welcome to stay here until you can find something, but let me be honest with you. Respectable jobs aren't that easy to come by down here. Not for a woman. You can try all the shops, like I did, and maybe somebody's looking for a girl to sell hats or something, but just don't get discouraged too soon. You're not like me. When I came here I had no one to turn to, or even a place to get out of the night. You've got both. And besides, there's something different about you . . . you don't belong down here."

Brianne was touched by the generosity of the girl in

offering her home, and pitied her for the unfair way she had been treated by her family. No matter how little she now had, she was willing to share it with a stranger.

"What did you mean, Rena, when you said I was different?"

Eyes that had been open and friendly only moments before became hard as Rena gathered the dishes and took them to the makeshift sink.

Carrying the food to be put away, Brianne joined her. She waited silently until Rena turned and said to her, "Let's face it, you're a nice girl and I'm not. Most women would have walked on the other side of the street from me, not sat down at my table and talked—even if they were starving."

Brianne put the food down and faced her. "Look at me, Rena."

When the younger woman's eyes met hers, she said earnestly, "You *are* a nice girl! A lot of people wouldn't have bothered with me back at the market, nor have taken me in as you did. I don't blame you for the kind of life you were forced into. It isn't my place to do that. Who knows what I might have done in the same situation? I do know one thing, though—you're a special woman and you have talents you aren't using. Your needlework is extraordinary. You're also a bright and sensitive lady."

Touching the girl's arm, she said softly, "Rena, you don't belong here either."

Her new friend's eyes were starting to fill and Brianne quickly felt guilty. "I'm sorry. I didn't mean to sound like I was trying to reform you, or anything like that. It's just that I see the potential in you to be that lady's maid, or anything else you want to be."

Rena wiped her eyes. "Don't go apologizing now," she sniffled. "You just called me a lady. I haven't heard anybody say that to me, and mean it, for years. I don't think you're preaching, Brianne. I just don't think you understand the way it is down here. Just because you want it to be different doesn't mean it can happen. I'm trapped now. Nobody wants an ex-whore for a personal maid."

Putting an arm around Brianne's shoulder, she added, "Don't you go worrying about me. I think you have enough to worry about for yourself. Let's get ready for bed, and then you can tell me your life story—if you want to."

Brianne smiled back into the returned warmth of Rena's eyes and hoped the girl hadn't felt her muscles tighten from that last statement.

Chapter 9

Brianne turned her back as she undressed, and reaching for the worn cotton nightgown, she wondered just how much she could tell Rena. She did owe her some explanation, and perhaps it was time to confide in someone. The most Rena could do was think she was crazy and demand that she leave. But something about the younger woman made Brianne believe that she could trust her, and not be cast back out into the night. Probably Rena had seen so much of life in her short time that very little came as a shock anymore.

As Brianne fastened the last button, she turned and found Rena staring at her.

Smiling, she said, "You don't have to tell me a thing, Brianne. Let's just go to bed. Morning will come soon enough, and you'll want to be at the Court House early."

Rena placed the lamp on a small table beside the bed, and Brianne then helped her turn down the covers.

"Well, get in," Rena gently ordered. "It's a bit lumpy, but it's clean."

Brianne nodded and self-consciously pulled the sheet up over her. Rena turned the lamp down until a faint glow surrounded it, and following Brianne into the bed, gave a loud sigh of contentment as her head hit the pillow.

"Rena?" Brianne waited to hear her whispered answer.

"Hmm?" Obviously Rena wasn't one to push, for her voice sounded half asleep.

"Rena, I really do want to tell you about me. God knows I need someone to talk to, but I'm afraid of what you'll think.

"No—don't say anything," Brianne pleaded, as she felt Rena begin to sit up. "It isn't criminal or anything like that. It's more . . . unexplainable. Let me ask you one question. What year is it, Rena?"

"1856, why?"

Brianne took a deep breath and said, "What if I were to tell you it's June 4, 1986?"

Rena giggled. "I'd say you've had a tough night, honey, and what you need is some sleep to clear the cobwebs from your upper floor." She laughed again, but not hearing the same response from Brianne, stopped abruptly.

Sitting up, she increased the light within the glass globe and looked at the figure beside her. Brianne's face looked tortured, and Rena could sense she was about to cry. "You're serious, aren't you?"

Brianne nodded. "Completely! And I'm not insane either. Rena, I don't know how it happened or why, but I belong in the next century."

When Rena started to back away from her, she hurried to continue. "I tried to believe that everyone was acting and dressing so old-fashioned because of some carnival, or that it was them and not me who was misplaced. But after I came to New Orleans, in my heart I knew that something terrible had happened. Just listen to me, Rena, and let me tell it from the beginning before you say anything.

"My sister Morganna lives in New Orleans, and when

130

she telephoned me that she was about to have her baby, I got in the car and drove down here to be with her. I should have listened to her and flown but . . ." Brianne looked at Rena's open mouth and could have laughed if she weren't already so close to tears herself.

"All right, I can see I have a lot of explaining to do, but where do I begin? This will all sound crazy to you anyway."

Brianne ran a hand through her hair in frustration before beginning, "A telephone is a device that carries your voice through a wire over cities and countries, and even under oceans. It's like a telegraph, only you listen and talk into it. If I were in Philadelphia and you in New Orleans, we could have this same conversation at this same time. Ma Bell would shudder at such a simple explanation, but it's the best I can do. I've always taken it for granted as something that was simply there, but it is a marvelous invention when you think about it."

Rena didn't believe her, and she couldn't really blame her. Trying again, she reasoned, "Imagine if this happened to you, Rena. How would you go about explaining the telegraph or" and Brianne's eyes lit up with a sudden inspiration, "the railroad?"

Watching Rena take this in, she pressed on. "Remember, you'd be talking to people in the seventeen hundreds. How could you make them understand it was possible to send messages through wires instead of having them carried by hand, or make long trips by sitting in coaches that are attached together and pulled by a steam engine? *You* know it's possible, but you don't know enough about them to explain logically how they work."

Brianne looked into Rena's eyes and could read the confusion. The doubt was clearly there, but at least it had replaced the outright disbelief she had seen earlier.

"They wouldn't believe me," Rena stated after

131

some reflection.

Excited that she had gotten even that small admission, Brianne said, "Exactly! And who could blame them, when they're limited by the time in which they live?"

"Brianne, I still don't understand . . ."

"I'm not asking you to. I only ask that you open your mind to the possibility that what I'm saying might have happened."

Rena looked frustrated, but her frustration couldn't have matched Brianne's when the younger woman said, "All right, so someday you'll be able to talk into a telegraph wire and another person will answer. That's not altogether farfetched. But what about the rest? You drove your own railcar here, instead of flying? You're asking too much, Brianne!"

"No, you don't understand. Not a railcar. It's called an automobile. It doesn't run on steam, like the trains you're used to seeing. It has something to do with pistons and motors, and uses gasoline, that's oil from under the ground. I don't know how to make you understand. Look, when it was first invented it was called the horseless carriage. Try to imagine that."

Rena laughed at the picture presented to her. "A horseless carriage!"

Throwing back her head, she continued to laugh uproariously until she held up a hand to Brianne. "I needed this. I haven't laughed so hard in years." Giggling, she continued, "You're saying that you drove a horseless carriage from Philadelphia to New Orleans, instead of flying? What a marvelous place you must come from! Do people sprout wings at will? Because yours seem to be missing! Brianne, people can't *fly!* I don't care where you came from."

This time when she took in Rena's incredulous expression, she forgot her own troubles. Falling back onto the pillow, she joined in the blessed relief found in laughter.

"No—not people. Planes. The airplanes carry the people."

Listening to Rena's renewed snickering, Brianne gave up.

"I'm not even going to try and explain this one. Forget the plane. You're right, people can't fly, and I can't explain it to you anyway. It's enough to swallow that I talk through wires and drive a horseless carriage."

Rena held her sides as she valiantly tried to compose herself. "I'm sorry, but you have to admit this conversation is beyond belief."

Brianne nodded her head. "Oh Rena, it's true . . . all of it. I know how it must sound to you, but if you think what I've told you so far is unbelievable, wait until you hear the rest."

In the end Brianne was tired and emotionally drained. She didn't leave anything out, not even her own reaction to Barrington's lovemaking. Saying it aloud and trying to put everything into perspective only made it seem all the more hopeless.

Rena was a very good listener, though, never interrupting once, and Brianne saw understanding in her eyes for another female, alone in a man's world.

Almost afraid of her answer, Brianne asked, "Well?"

Sitting next to her, Rena looked stunned. "I don't know what to say! It's difficult to believe I'm in bed with someone who lived a hundred years from now, but the Irish in me has learned never to make light of the unexplainable."

Looking at the incredible woman beside her, she asked, "Brianne, if what you say is true, then how do you plan to get back?"

Leaning back against the headboard, Brianne stared

into the darkness across the room. "I don't know, Rena. But I can't bear the thought of never seeing my family again. My sister and her child are the only ones I have left."

She closed her eyes briefly. "There has to be a way. Or maybe it will just happen like it did before—I'll fall asleep in 1856 and wake up in 1986."

"What about this Catherine Murdock? Will she be able to help you? I've heard of her husband, and he's pretty important. Maybe they could help until you've figured out what to do."

Brianne shook her head. "I don't think so. Catherine wants me to marry Barrington. It seems to be her answer to everything.

"But that's really not fair," Brianne reflected. "She doesn't know where I came from. No one knows except you, Rena, and I'm not sure if even you believe what I've told you. But I'm grateful you haven't laughed again, or thrown me out. I wouldn't blame you if you had."

Rena extinguished the light completely and settled back into the bed. "I'm not sure what to believe, but I'll have a good guess where you are if I wake up and you're not here next to me."

"If only it would happen again," Brianne wished aloud as she lay back down. She knew she wouldn't sleep but would just keep going over everything in her mind, trying to find the key that would open the way for her return.

Rena shifted to her side and whispered, "Brianne, tell me more about 1986. It sounds like such an exciting time to live."

Brianne had to laugh because Rena sounded like a child asking for a bedtime story, knowing there wasn't any doubt she was about to hear a fantastic one.

"It *is* an exciting time, Rena. The part you'll like best is the freedom. Not just for blacks—for everyone, including women. Oh Rena," she said affectionately, "wait until you hear what's happened to women!"

Brianne awoke to brilliant sunlight and vendors in the alley singing sweet and long about their wares. Stretching, she turned to find the other side of the bed empty and Rena nowhere in sight.

Brianne thought back to last night and smiled. She and Rena, no longer tired, had talked for hours until the younger woman's unending string of questions and her own inability to provide answers had finally exhausted them both.

Giving one last luxuriant pull on her muscles, she slowly rose from the bed, all the while wondering where Rena had gone.

Brianne padded barefoot into the kitchen area intent on making coffee, and had no trouble in finding a coffee mill. She was not, however, as fortunate when it came to the knowledge of its operation. Realizing she was as out of place here as Rena would be in her world, Brianne decided to wait for the other woman's return.

She didn't have to wait long before the only door opened and Rena burst into the room impatiently.

"Good. You're up," she said, placing a heavy wooden bucket on the table. "I've brought water and you can get washed while I start the coffee."

Gone was the inquisitive young woman of last night whose reactions had alternated between fascination by the twentieth century and utter disbelief of its capabilities. In her place had returned the Rena she had first met, the worldly woman who knew how to take charge.

"I thought you wanted to get to the Presbytere early? You'll never make it standing around like you have all the time in the world. You don't, you know," she informed Brianne. "We both overslept. Guess I shouldn't have kept you up talking for half the night."

135

As she was efficiently grinding the beans for the coffee, Rena looked over her shoulder at Brianne. "What are you waiting for? The towels are on the commode."

Brianne felt a little embarrassed. "You wouldn't by any chance have a bathroom?" she asked.

At Rena's look of puzzlement she murmured, "I didn't think so," under her breath.

"A convenience?" she tried again.

Finally she was understood. Rena opened the door and pointed to a small building about twenty feet away from the bottom of the stairs. "Sorry, Brianne, I should have thought to tell you. If you mind using a communal one, I do have a chamber pot."

Brianne unconsciously chewed at the bottom of her lip. If there was one thing she sorely missed, it was a modern bathroom! Never, never would she get used to this! Knowing from the past two days how acutely embarrassing the other was, she opted for the outhouse.

Holding up the hem of the taller woman's robe, Brianne hurried back up the steps. She didn't need any prodding to rush. This was an important morning, and she just knew she'd find some kind of answer waiting for her at the Court House. What, she wasn't sure.

The delicious aroma of freshly brewed coffee filled the small room, and Brianne realized how hungry she was. Rena was already partially dressed and quickly scolded Brianne as she began to pour herself a cup.

"I'll pour the coffee. You get dressed. You probably won't have time for coffee anyway. It's well past ten o'clock now."

Washing her face, Brianne thought Rena was like a mother hen, watching out for her and nipping verbally if she fell behind. She was, however, very fortunate to have met her, and she knew it. Brianne cringed, thinking what might have happened to her if she had not.

"Aren't you dressed yet?" Rena demanded. "There are no horseless carriages here. You and I will be walking!"

Rather than being annoyed with Rena's persistent nagging, Brianne quickly reached for the yellow dress, which was beginning to show the abuse it had taken in the past twenty-four hours.

Once they had left the area Rena called the Irish Channel, New Orleans was truly a beautiful city with a charm all its own. Brianne marveled at the lovely, intricate ironwork that decorated the windows and balconies. She stared like a country hick newly come to the big city at the fabulous creations worn by the women they passed. Rena didn't seem to notice them. She was more concerned with keeping the hem of her one serviceable day gown free from any dirt.

When a carriage passed the dust would fly, and Brianne was grateful for the handkerchief Rena had given her. Using it to cover her mouth, as she had seen Rena do, she almost inhaled it as she gasped in surprise.

On the other side of the street, in front of the large Court House, was Gregory Duville.

Stopping with her, Rena turned in the direction of her startled gaze. "What's wrong? Do you recognize something?"

Brianne kept the hankie over her lower face and nodded. "The tall, dark-haired man in front of the Presbytere is Gregory Duville. It was his carriage you saw me leave last night."

Rena whistled slowly. "You certainly have been rubbing shoulders with some big names . . . the Murdocks, Barrington, and now Duville. But why are you so frightened? He has no say over you."

137

She pulled on Brianne's arm. "Take that handkerchief away from your face and go and conduct your business. If all those things you told me last night are true, about women controlling their own lives, then one man standing between you and the information you want shouldn't matter."

Rena was right, of course. A few days ago she would have thanked Duville for his kindness and then politely brushed him off. But this wasn't a few days ago, when everything was normal and she was in control of her life. This was a world where women were either protected or used, depending on their status. Obviously Mr. Duville thought she belonged in the first category, and was in need of protection.

Taking a deep breath and squaring her shoulders, Brianne crossed the street to meet with the man.

"Miss Quinlan! I'm so pleased to see you are all right. I must confess to spending the remainder of last night worrying about you." Gregory Duville was intrigued by this young woman and had indeed been preoccupied with thoughts of her, much to the displeasure of his octoroon mistress.

Brianne decided on a compromise in her attitude. It would include a little of the old world, but most certainly she would not give up the independence she had worked so hard to achieve.

"Mr. Duville. How nice of you to have met me this morning, but there was no need for you to do so, or to have been concerned about me. I managed to survive the night in the home of my friend, Miss Maureen Ahearn."

Brianne introduced the two, and after an uncomfortable pause, Duville nodded his head, saying, "Miss Ahearn."

Rena, on the other hand, seemed completely taken back. With her eyes fixed to the pavement, she bobbed a little curtsey.

Watching this exchange, Brianne became annoyed. Thinking her to be a lady, Duville had accorded her every courtesy to the point of being overbearing. But Rena, who although scrubbed clean and wearing a gown that had seen its better days, was barely given a civil greeting. Who did he think he was to treat someone like that—someone he didn't even know?

The devil in Brianne quickly came to the surface. "Rena is a distant relative of mine," she blurted out. If Catherine could do it, then so could she!

"Her father, poor soul, passed on last year. The Ahearn Shipping Lines, out of Charleston, you know. Well, as you must have heard, through no fault of his own the line fell on bad times. When her father died, Rena naturally came south to find her relatives.

"Please excuse me, Rena dear," Brianne said to her friend, whose eyes showed her astonishment, "for relating anything so personal."

She turned to Duville. "Now you can see how fortunate it was that I left your carriage last night. Otherwise Rena and I might not have met so quickly. Now we can combine forces and search for our family together."

There! Brianne thought. See what you can do with that.

Duville looked from Rena to Brianne, then back again to Rena who, thankfully, met his gaze.

This man's no fool, Brianne thought as she watched him take Rena's hand and bend over it. Either he believed her, which was doubtful, or was just playing along, too well bred to call her a liar.

It didn't matter. Seeing Rena's face light up as the man said, "A thousand pardons, Miss Ahearn. It is indeed a pleasure to meet you. Please accept my condolences on your father's passing," was enough.

Brianne gave Rena no chance to reply as she spoke up.

"Mr. Duville, we really must be going now. Thank you again for your concern, but as you can see, I'm perfectly fine."

Replacing his hat, Duville's eyes bore into Brianne's. "Until we meet again, Miss Quinlan. Miss Ahearn?"

Uncomfortable under his gaze, Brianne smiled hesitantly before placing a hand on Rena's back and guiding her toward the Court House.

Before the two women were far enough away for them to speak privately, from the corner of her eye Brianne saw a carriage pull to a quick stop.

The door was flung open and out stepped two men who came rapidly in their direction—one short and stocky, the other tall and lean. One was Samuel Murdock, the other . . . Ryan Barrington.

Chapter 10

Brianne couldn't react. She just froze, watching them come closer. Poor Samuel looked as though he hadn't slept, but Barrington's face was livid with anger.

Coming to stand in front of her, those blue eyes pierced her own with their visible fury. "Are you satisfied? Must you cause problems for everyone connected with you? Poor Catherine is beside herself with worry, and Samuel has been out searching the city since dawn."

Grabbing her upper arm, he demanded, "Have you nothing to say for yourself?"

Seeing this, Duville hotly interrupted. "Barrington, take your hands off her. I think you should explain yourself."

Ryan turned toward the Creole but kept a firm grip on Brianne. "Duville, this has nothing to do with you. Stay out of it."

The man persisted. "I will not stand by and watch you accost this young woman. You have obviously made a mistake. Miss Quinlan is new to our city, and the only family she has is Miss Ahearn here. Since she has no male relative present to stand up for her, I demand that you release her . . . now!"

Ryan gave him an evil smile. "There you are wrong, Duville. Miss Quinlan *has* a male to stand up for her, and one that will be a relative in a very short time. Me! Brianne and I are engaged to be married."

Those surrounding him gasped audibly at his last statement, and Duville turned a shocked face to Brianne. "Is this true, Miss Quinlan? Are you to marry him?"

Brianne was still in a state of shock herself over encountering Barrington. Just when she thought she had successfully dealt with Duville and would be free to do as she pleased, that hated face appeared, bringing with it ugly memories of the night he had come to her room. Her fear of him rose to the surface when she felt the increased pressure on her arm.

Looking at the expectant faces before her, Brianne knew some answer was anticipated; the problem was she hadn't heard the question. "I . . . ah . . . I'm sorry . . ."

Seeing her confusion, Samuel answered, "Gregory, Miss Quinlan has recently suffered a head injury at Briarfawn and is temporarily confused, so you can see why we are concerned. When it was discovered this morning that she was gone, and knowing she was unfamiliar with the city, naturally we were alarmed. Catherine is in quite a state, let me tell you."

A flicker of disappointment showed in Duville's eyes before he looked at Barrington. "Sorry to have intruded, Monsieur Barrington. Please excuse me, I'm already late for an appointment. Ladies?" and bowing to Brianne and Rena, turned and quickly left.

Brianne thought even Rena was looking at her differently, reminding her of the maid in the Howards' house. The servant had thought she was deranged, and she could see that same frightened look coming into her friend's eyes. When Samuel said, "Thank you, Miss Ahearn, we'll take care of Brianne now," she nodded sadly and turned away.

"Rena!" Shouting to her, Brianne pleaded. "Please, don't go! Don't leave me!"

Barrington jerked her around. "Stop that yelling," he demanded. "You're creating a scene, and people are watching us. Now get into the carriage quietly and we'll return to the Murdocks'."

Brianne pulled her arm free and turned back to the street. Rena was nowhere in sight.

He'd done it again! Damn him for interfering.

Spinning around toward him, she whispered, "If you don't want me to make a scene, then get away from me. Take your hand away, or I'll let them all know just what kind of *man* you really are, Mr. Barrington . . . and you know I'll do it!"

Ryan pulled his hand back as though it were burned. What he really wanted to do was slap her beautiful face for that insult. He wasn't sure what she would do, but this was one woman he wasn't taking any chances with.

Brianne was relieved to see her threat had worked. "Now, I'm going into that Court House, alone. I never want to see you again, so if you'd please get out of my way . . ." and with that she picked up her skirt and left the two of them staring after her.

Later, after asserting herself with the male clerks, Brianne had the information she needed.

It was as she had expected. The date was April 13th, 1856, and the only Barrington listed in the city was the one she despised. Sitting on a wooden bench inside the building, Brianne was deep in thought.

What was she to do? Where would she go? Rena was surely convinced she was in need of mental help— Samuel had seen to that. Brianne seriously doubted that she would take her in again. There was no one alive today that could help her.

So lost was she that she jumped when she felt the slight pressure on her arm.

"Did you find what you were looking for?" Samuel asked patiently.

Brianne closed her eyes and nodded.

"Brianne, we've all been under a strain the past few days," he said gently. "Why don't you come home with me now, and rest? I know it would mean a lot to Catherine if you did. She's so terribly worried about you."

Brianne looked up at the tired face of this dear man and made her decision. She would go with him. She had no means of support, nor anywhere else to go. If she had to wait out the time until she found a solution to her problems, she might as well be selfish and do it with people who cared about her.

"Samuel, thank you for wanting me back again, after all I've put you through. I do want to see Catherine and explain that I never meant to hurt her by leaving."

Standing up, she added, "I'd like the opportunity to apologize to both of you, and I'd be grateful for your hospitality again."

In the carriage returning to the Murdocks', Brianne kept her eyes averted and her mouth shut. Samuel hadn't told her that Barrington would be riding with them, and she could now feel his gaze upon her. It was so uncomfortable that if it weren't for Samuel's presence, she would have liked to tell him off again.

With relief, Brianne saw the Murdocks' home come into view. She might have to face Catherine and come up with a convincing story about her disappearance, but she'd finally be rid of Barrington . . . and not too soon to please her, either.

As soon as the front door opened, Brianne found

herself enveloped in Catherine's forgiving embrace. "Thank God they found you. You poor child! I don't even want to know why you left, I'm just grateful to have you back."

She led Brianne back up the stairs and into the bedroom the young woman had been so intent on leaving the night before.

"Are you all right?" Catherine asked, signs of worry creasing her brow.

Nodding, Brianne sat on the bed with Catherine. "I'm fine. Catherine, I'm sorry to have put you through this. I shouldn't have run away like that, without any word."

"Shh . . . it doesn't matter now."

"But it does," Brianne insisted. "You deserve an explanation. I was so confused last night, and thought I could find my sister alone. It wasn't a very smart thing to try, and you were right, I should have waited until this morning and let Samuel help me.

"I'm fine, though," she continued. "I met a very nice woman named Maureen Ahearn, and she looked after me until this morning, when Samuel found me. But it's good to be back. I'll try not to worry you again."

Catherine kissed her cheek. "We can only be grateful to this woman, Miss Ahearn. When I think of the harm that could have befallen you, Brianne . . ." She shuddered. "New Orleans is full of dangerous types that seem to come out of the woodwork at night. I was so worried, and prayed so hard for your safe return. I can't tell you how glad I was to see Ryan's face this morning."

Rising, Catherine went to the closet. "Samuel had been searching since we discovered you were missing, but I knew Ryan would find you. My dear, you should have seen him—he acted as though he were personally responsible for your disappearance."

Shaking her head, Catherine took out a lovely pink gown. Laying it on the bed, she used the narrow tapestry

145

bell pull hanging by the wall to summon a servant. "We altered this for you last night. I'll have Letty prepare a bath, then you can join us for lunch downstairs."

Coming over to Brianne, she hugged her again. "I'm so pleased you're back," she said happily. "Now don't keep us waiting too long, dear. Letty will help you dress."

Descending the stairs after a hurried bath, and dressed in such a beautiful gown, Brianne had to admit she felt better. There was something about dressing like this, she thought, in these gorgeous clothes, and having your hair fixed for you just to eat lunch, that made you feel special. And there was certainly something to be said for the civilized gentility of it all.

With a dreamy smile on her face, she entered the room Letty had indicated. She was, however, totally unprepared to see Barrington rise with Samuel as she came into the dining room.

Coming to her side, Catherine guided her to the chair Samuel had pulled out, the one opposite Barrington.

"Pink is your color, Brianne. Doesn't she look just beautiful?" Catherine asked the men.

Samuel gallantly complimented her while Barrington looked her over before nodding grudgingly.

Throughout the meal, the three discussed the Murdocks' impending trip to Europe. But while Samuel and Catherine tried to include her in the conversation, Brianne was too shocked by the news that they would be leaving to really join in. Besides, how could she be expected to contribute anything intelligent while Barrington sat across from her trying to catch her eye? She could see now how foolish she was not to have expected him to remain as the Murdocks' guest.

When the lunch was finally concluded the men excused themselves, leaving the women alone and

Catherine, toying with a crystal goblet, suddenly put it back on the table. Brianne recognized the action with a feeling of dread. Catherine had something on her mind.

Brianne had guessed correctly; without looking at her, Catherine began. "I'm going to come right to the point, Brianne. Ryan came here early this morning because he wished to speak with you. I think it would be in your best interests if you heard him out.

"Please." Catherine raised a finger, motioning for Brianne to hold her comments. "Samuel and I are leaving next week, and much as I'd like to remain here with you, I cannot. You *must* think about your future, dear. Besides, it won't hurt just to talk with him . . . will it?"

Her *future?* That was all Brianne could think about. What could Barrington possibly have to tell her that could change it?

"Catherine, you know how I dislike the man, and you above all must admit I have good reason. I doubt if we could talk together; all we seem to do is argue. Besides, I can't think of anything he might have to say to me that I'd care to hear. I think we've said it all."

Catherine rose and came to her side. "Please, Brianne, as a favor to me? Won't you hear what he has to say? He really is a good man. I don't think he ever meant to hurt you, and I know it must be very important for him to have come so early this morning."

She kissed Brianne's forehead and said, "He's waiting for you in Samuel's study," then left the younger woman to consider her words.

Brianne told herself it was only to please Catherine that she went to the study. Standing in the doorway, she saw Barrington looking out the window, deep in thought.

There was no denying it. Even though she could only see a partial profile, he was exceptional looking, and it irritated her to no end that she found him so. It wasn't just the way the sun caught the tips of his hair strands,

147

or, if he should turn, those piercing blue eyes that seemed to look through you. It was that, and something more. The way he carried himself, projecting strength and commanding attention from those around him. He was the kind of man that most women would want to know better.

Mentally shaking herself, Brianne remembered that happily, she was not like most women. What she knew of Ryan Barrington was quite enough. She couldn't blame him for everything that had happened to her, but she certainly had enough reasons to distrust him. He was, after all, the one who started this stupid charade about amnesia. Well, this is one confrontation where he won't come out on top, she vowed. He's used to the sweet, compliant females of the 1800s, but he's about to meet the woman of the future!

"Mr. Barrington?" Brianne quietly drew his attention as she strode into the room, closing the door after her. "I believe you wished to see me?"

His eyes were immediately drawn to the creamy mounds of flesh so tantalizingly exposed by her low-cut gown. Ryan was again struck by her fragile beauty and he ground his teeth in painful frustration, for it was obvious by the way she entered the room that she was prepared to do battle. Ever since he had left Briarfawn this morning, he had been consumed by guilt. Planning to ask her forgiveness, he also desperately needed some explanations. He had intended to be gentle and patient with her. But once he arrived and saw the furor she had again created, this time for the Murdocks, all his good intentions were thrown to the wind. Initially, when they had finally caught up with her, he had been furious. This one woman, above all, had the exasperating habit of making him lose his temper—first with her, and then with Duville.

Whatever had made him say they were to be married?

And to Duville, no less! With that man's connections, it would be told throughout the city by nightfall. When he checked into the hotel tonight, he wouldn't be surprised if the bell captain congratulated him.

What had he done? He had only meant to get rid of the Creole, not change the course of his life.

His eyes narrowed as he watched her come closer. Somehow, this woman and he must come to an agreement. He only hoped she'd stay calm long enough for them to do so.

"Miss Quinlan—Brianne," he amended. "Thank you for coming in to speak with me, why don't you sit down?"

He was trying . . .

But the woman looked him straight in the eyes and shook her head. "I'd rather stand, thank you."

She certainly wasn't going to give him an inch, that was obvious.

"Brianne, I came here this morning to apologize to you for my behavior while you were in my home. I don't really have any excuses, but I would like to tell what led to my mistaken assumption that you would not be totally averse to my attentions."

He ignored her raised eyebrows and continued, "A few weeks ago I had dinner with a good friend of mine, Stephan Daniels, who is known for his practical jokes. During that dinner, I told Stephan of my intention to travel to Virginia. The purpose of that trip was to possibly ask his cousin to be my wife. Although they're related, there is no love lost between the cousins, and Stephan tried to talk me out of it. Seeing that he couldn't, he agreed to find an overseer for the plantation in my absence. You see, I am not from New Orleans originally, and many of my neighbors are suspicious of the way I run Briarfawn."

Seeing her questioning look, he told her, "I pay my workers, and they use that money to buy their freedom. I

149

believe I told you this when we met. I have an overseer in my employ now—a very good one, Nathen. But he is a negro, and that too upsets the other owners.

"To get back to the point of this story, later that same night, after a few drinks, Stephan again tried to talk me out of going, saying what I needed to find was a good woman, not a good overseer."

Her slight smile was a good sign; at least she was listening and not interrupting.

"The morning I found you, I was expecting the overseer. Because you had no explanation of why you were there or how you had got there in the first place, along with the way you were dressed, I assumed you were lying to protect yourself and the money I thought Stephan had promised you.

"There are very few women who would have gone along with such a scheme, and those would have been of questionable reputation. I apologize for putting you in that category."

Clasping his hands behind his back, he squared his shoulders. "I know it is no excuse for what happened. But I drank very heavily that entire day and furthermore was annoyed with Catherine, who seemed to think you were some lost child. She wouldn't permit me to speak with you in private, and as the night wore on, my anger increased. I have never forced my attentions on a woman before. I'm very sorry you were hurt."

For a man as arrogant and self-assured as he was, Brianne knew it had cost him a great deal to give this explanation, and it was to his credit that he didn't spare himself. Given the age that she found herself in, and its attitudes toward women, she could see, perhaps, why he would mistake her for a loose woman in a scheme for the money. Still, he had come into her room and taken advantage of her while she was not herself. Never, never would she admit to him the emotions he had aroused.

That was what she could not easily forgive . . . or forget.

Finally sitting down, she asked him, "And what made you change your mind about me, Mr. Barrington?"

He picked up a porcelain figure and stared at it for a few moments. Seeming to come to a decision, he replaced it and turned to face her.

"First, the real overseer arrived soon after you left yesterday—he was delayed because of family illness. Then I saw Stephan. He had never heard of you, and swore to me that he had no part in you being at Briarfawn. And lastly, this . . ."

He reached inside his coat pocket and held out her car keys.

Brianne jumped up out of her chair and made a very unladylike grab for them. "It's the keys to my car!"

She hugged them to her chest as if they were priceless possessions. Her eyes turned wide with happiness as she asked, "Where did you find them?"

"They were in the pocket of the trousers you wore. One of the maids found them before they were burned. She didn't give them to me until after you had left. What does all the writing mean, Brianne?"

She turned the pewter disc over in her hands. She had forgotten what was on it. Years ago she had found it in an old desk at work, left behind by the previous owner.

So pleased was she to have it back, she forgot where she was. Looking not at him but at the precious link with reality, she said in a low voice, "The company I work for gave them out for the Bicentennial. It was a few years before I came there, but when I found it I thought it was attractive, and I've used it ever since."

His brows came together. "You still maintain that it is 1986?"

Brianne looked into his face, and sighing, sat down again. "No. I can no longer claim this is the twentieth century, and you are living in the past. *I* am the one who

151

was transported somehow into the past. But it's *your* past . . . not mine. This isn't my time. Look—I listened to what you had to say, now give me the same courtesy. What I am going to tell you is the truth, I swear it."

She told him the same story and got the same reactions as from Rena. Barrington, however, paced the room and interrupted numerous times with questions, demanding explanations for words or terms he didn't understand. Toward the end, when she had reached the point of his waking her, she felt as though she'd been on the witness stand.

"Look," she said, exhausted from his interrogation, "you must have had some doubts yourself when you saw the keys and they confirmed my story. You also read the date on my watch, when we met. By the way, what happened to it—my watch?"

Barrington ran his hand through his hair and again pulled something from the pocket of his tailored jacket.

"Here. I was keeping it for you . . . no, that's not true. I took it from you when you were unconscious. I wanted to find out how it worked and was going to ask Stephan to explain."

Brianne held it in the palm of her hand, and looking at it said softly, "This was a gift from my sister Morganna. I can't tell you what it means to have it back."

She pushed the tiny buttons on its side. "Something's wrong. It reads nine twenty-two, A.M., and the date is still June the second."

"I know."

She looked up at him, and their eyes met and held.

Something really is wrong . . . I can feel it, she thought. Why has it stopped on the date I woke up in the wrong century?

Fearfully, she asked, "What time was it when you found me?"

"Somewhere around eleven o'clock. I checked after I

152

brought you to my home, and it was eleven thirty-five exactly."

Brianne checked the watch again and tried to advance the time. It remained at nine twenty-two; the date would not change either.

Clenching it in her fist, she raised her eyes. "What happened to me out there? Why does the watch repeat the same time and date? It's as though time, as I knew it, hasn't continued since that morning?"

Barrington was again pacing the room. "This is ridiculous! Why are you asking me what happened?" He raised his voice. "I don't know what to make of you, or this story of being from the future."

He shook his head. "I don't believe I even said that! All I know is that you're *here*, now," he said, pointing to the floor. "You should be thinking about what you're going to do tomorrow, and next week when the Murdocks sail away and you're left alone."

He came to sit across from her. "Brianne, I know we haven't had the best of starts and I accept full responsibility for what happened. Therefore, if you are willing . . . we can be married. You will have security for your future, and I will at least have the knowledge that I did the honorable thing."

She wanted to laugh at him, but he was serious. He was sitting back now in the chair as though pleased with himself. Just when she was beginning to understand him a little, he had to say something so stupid. What a pompous ass! Marry him? And for no other reason than to save his conscience? He was a fool.

Or perhaps this is exactly how he wanted her to react. Then, when she refused him, he could always say he tried to do the right thing. I should really fix him, she thought, and say, Yes, thank you, Mr. Barrington, I'll marry you.

It would be worth it just to see his face. She would live in the lap of luxury until she could find a way to get back

153

to her own time. And in the process, complicate his plans to marry the woman in Virginia. It wasn't complete revenge for the way he had used and manipulated her, but it was a start.

Why not? How many other options were open to her? If she were alone in the eighties, she'd always be able to make a living and support herself, but here? She didn't want to end up like Rena, and forced to live that kind of life.

Composing herself, before she allowed any second thoughts, she sat up straighter and brought her head up to meet his stare.

"Thank you for your offer, Mr. Barrington . . . I accept."

His jaw dropped before he whispered, "You accept?"

Brianne afforded herself a smile before answering him. "That is correct. We can be married today, tomorrow, next week." She watched happily as he quickly brushed back the stray lock of hair from his forehead. "Now," she continued, "before I send Catherine in, for I'm sure the two of you can make all the arrangements, I have a provision to this marriage that you must agree to."

Standing up, it was her turn to pace the room. "Do you remember the woman today in front of the Court House? Her name is Maureen Ahearn. She took me in last night and was very kind to me. I'd like to repay her. When she came to New Orleans, she intended to find employment as a lady's maid, but wasn't successful. I would like you to hire her as my maid and companion."

Just what I need, Ryan thought. Another female to cause problems. "Brianne, there are women already trained for that at Briarfawn. If you want to repay her, we can think of another way. Perhaps a large gift of . . ."

"I will never condone slavery," Brianne heatedly interrupted. "And Rena doesn't want a gift, she needs a

154

job. Also, I introduced her to Mr. Duville as my long-lost cousin. And it wouldn't do to have her remain there in that place she calls the Irish Channel, while a member of her *family* is in residence at Briarfawn."

Ryan jumped up. "You what!" My God, the woman was unbelievable!

Defensively, Brianne answered, "I told him Rena was a distant cousin of mine from Charleston, and that her father's shipping lines went bankrupt when he died. You don't have to yell. I know it was wrong of me to lie like that, but the man was positively cruel when she was introduced to him without any background. So I made one up. Besides, I got the idea from Catherine. She introduced me to Emily Howard yesterday as her distant cousin."

He looked at the ceiling as though contemplating whether by sheer willpower he could make it fall on her head. As Brianne watched him clench his jaw, she thought she might as well tell him everything. How much angrier could he get?

"And I think you should know," she said hesitantly, "I've told Rena where I come from and everything that has happened since that morning you found me."

Barrington put both his hands into his pockets, as if restraining them. "It seems you've left me little choice in the matter. I will have someone collect Miss Ahearn this afternoon. Later, when we have more time, I'll expect you to tell me how you came to know Gregory Duville and Emily Howard and managed to spend the night in a slum, all in one short day.

"If you have no other demands, I suggest you send Catherine in. She'll be overjoyed at the news, I'm sure," he added dryly. How in the hell had he let this happen to him? he thought miserably.

Brianne gave him the directions to Rena's apartment

155

as best as she could remember, and then felt obliged to say, "Thank you, Mr. Barrington."

She mustered all her courage to stand before him. Wetting her lips first, she began, "Since this is no ordinary marriage, but more of a business arrangement, shall we shake on it?" Brianne knew it sounded silly, but she wanted him to know the status of this marriage.

Ryan's dark eyebrows lifted. "A business arrangement? For the woman, Brianne?"

As she nodded, his brows quickly lowered and almost met above his straight nose. "I think you had better explain this 'business arrangement' once again. This time, for all of the parties involved."

Brianne could feel herself coloring. It was so embarrassing. How could she tell him he must never make love to her, never touch her, for fear of how she would respond? He was too much man, too sure of himself, and if she allowed it he would devour her completely.

It was her turn to pace the room. Staring at a vertical bookcase, she drew a deep breath and said, "There will never be a repeat performance of what took place while I was at Briarfawn. You understand what I'm saying? This is to be a business arrangement, period. Do you agree?"

She stopped ambling about the room and waited for his answer. Not hearing any sound at all, she swallowed and slowly turned her head to him. Brianne didn't like the look in his eyes. As the old saying went, if looks could kill . . . Were that true, then she should be mortally wounded. He was more than upset. His eyes were like deep blue daggers, searching her body to find their mark. Even through his dark tan she could see a furious color turning his face a strange shade of red. Brianne was afraid to move; never had she seen such controlled anger. They

156

continued to stare at each other, neither willing to be the first to look away.

She knew she should speak, say some word to arrest his anger, and was about to speak when she saw in amazement his malevolent expression change to one of amusement. His whole body visibly relaxed as he said emphatically, "Agreed!"

Suspiciously, she came closer to him. "I'm serious about this, and I intend to hold you to it."

Ryan inclined his head to one side. "I know you will. You have my promise as a gentleman. There will never be a repeat performance of what took place at Briarfawn."

Brianne had no idea what he found so amusing, but she did have his promise, and now was the time to make amends. She came to stand in front of him. "Thank you for agreeing to everything. I promise I'll try to be the kind of wife you want. It won't be easy, but I'll try to fit in." She held out her hand. "Again I ask, Mr. Barrington, may we shake on this arrangement?"

Barrington seemed to think it was humorous, but he did accept her hand. Looking down at her with that infuriating smile on his face, he said, "Seeing as how we'll be married soon, don't you think you should try using my first name? . . . It's Ryan."

Brianne had heard about it but didn't quite believe until now: an electric sensation passed between them through their hands. Brianne could feel her own growing warm as it was cradled within his. The warm liquid crept up her arm, passed her racing heart, and settled in her lower abdomen, making her legs feel heavy, so heavy she was afraid her knees might buckle under her. It was crazy, frightening, and embarrassing to have it happen now, and with this particular man.

Knowing she must leave before she made a fool of herself, she forced her eyes to look into his. Seeing how they had turned into soft, questing blue orbs, she fought to control her breath and managed to say, "I'll tell Catherine you wished to see her."

Slipping her hand away from his, she turned to leave, only to pause at the doorway and face him again. She smiled almost shyly.

"Thank you, Ryan," she said quietly, ". . . for Rena."

Chapter 11

Brianne was glad they had given her a few minutes alone. She needed this time to mentally prepare herself. This certainly wasn't the way she had always imagined her wedding day was going to be. She had thought that when she eventually married, it would be to someone she was breathlessly in love with. Instead, she was entering into an "agreement" with someone she barely knew.

She hadn't the chance of getting to know him any better either, since she hadn't set eyes on him at all in the past week . . . though her nights continued to be plagued with unwanted visions of the man. She admitted to herself that his hold on her was strong, but it was just physical. He had done things to her when her senses were heightened by a powerful drug. Surely those reactions could not be duplicated without such a stimulant! But still her shame was great. That she could recall in an instant his tall, lean, provocative body was unbearable— Barrington, the manipulator of this deception she was forced to continue. And how like him to drop everything at her feet, instead of remaining.

The day after she had shocked him by accepting his proposal, Barrington took off for that plantation of his, leaving all the arrangements to Catherine and herself, and it irritated her to know his absence annoyed her, when she should have been relieved by it. All of his directives, though, were carried out in a frenzy. He had insisted that she be outfitted with an extensive wardrobe. Dressmakers and an entourage of assistants had descended on her every morning of the past week for selection of materials, fittings, choosing of accessories, and again more fittings. It made her yearn for the days when she had walked into a store and bought off the rack.

It wasn't all that bad, though, she reflected, as she thought about the beautiful clothes packed away in the carved chest by the bed. Never in her life had she imagined she would possess such magnificent garments. And why would she?

Her own life had been comfortable. She owned some designer clothes, only because she had found through trial and error that classical lines rarely go out of date. Some of her outfits were over five years old, but once she had determined her most flattering hemline, she needed only to add a few new accessories to create a totally different look.

The clothes carefully folded inside the chest were of a higher caliber. Whereas before she had thought herself lucky to find in a store an attractive dress that hundreds of other women would also wear, these had been painstakingly assembled just for her, from the sheer underwear and nightgowns that were made from the finest lawn and silk, with lace created by nuns, of all people, to the day dresses and gowns of every color of the rainbow. Everything was adorned with lace and ribbons or delicate silk embroidery. How they ever finished was beyond her, but Madame Fountaine, the couturière, told her she was being paid a handsome bonus to finish before the wedding. She said it had been necessary to employ twelve extra girls, since Monsieur Barrington did not wish to make another trip into New Orleans in the near future.

Well, Brianne thought, they had granted him his wish. She had eight gowns that were finished. Enough to keep her, Catherine said, until the rest were completed and sent by boat to Briarfawn. Brianne had insisted she didn't need so much, but Catherine was in her glory conferring with the dressmaker, saying she was only carrying out Ryan's orders.

Brianne walked over to the dressing table and looked into the large gilt mirror. She was right to have insisted that her wedding gown be of her own design. It *was* beautiful, and she secretly knew she never looked lovelier than she did today. Of course, she might be the only one to think so, but it didn't matter. This was a dress she had dreamed of for many years, and if nothing else about this day was the way she wanted it to be, at least she would walk down the aisle wearing the gown she wanted.

There had been protests from Madame Fountaine and gasps from Catherine, who insisted it was much too plain for a wedding. Brianne had gone along with all their suggestions concerning the rest of the clothes, but she had been determined to win out on two outfits.

One was this gown made of ivory silk. Her wedding gown. It was plain and shockingly straight in a time when hoops were the rage. A band of heavy cream lace comprised the high collar, with the same thick lace carried onto bishop sleeves that were snugly buttoned from elbow to wrist. The fitted bodice then fell to the floor in soft lines. The only adornment she wore was a beautiful small brooch of Catherine's, which she pinned to the center of the collar. The stone matched the flowers in her hair, which she had pulled back from her head and secured in curls at the nape of her neck. Surrounding them was a circlet of violets and baby's breath, the same flowers she was to carry in a small bouquet. Attached to

161

the flowers at her hair was her veil, floor-length and again plain, without frilly lace.

It was just perfect, even if no one else agreed. This was the way she wanted to look. Soft, without the starkness of white, and feminine, without the gauzy lace and ribbons that took away from the perfection of the gown.

The other article of clothing that had caused a minor outrage was her riding skirt. It seemed only sensible to her that if she was stuck here, and the only means of transportation was a horse, then she should at least be comfortable while learning to ride one. She knew she would have to overcome her fear of the animal, but sitting sideways on its back was not the way. She had insisted on a split skirt, like long gauchos, so she would be able to straddle the horse like a man, lessening her chances of falling off.

Catherine had shaken her head in despair, but Brianne had seen the dressmaker's eyes light with inspiration.

A soft knock and the whisper of her name brought a smile to Brianne's face.

Rena.

She was the one bright circumstance in her life, and had made the last week bearable. Sweet though Catherine was, it felt wonderful to have a friend closer in age.

Telling her to come in, Brianne turned to greet her.

Rena, dressed in a gown the color of dark copper and wearing a frilly bonnet to match, entered the room carrying a small box.

"Ahh . . ." She exhaled her breath in appreciation. "Brianne, you look beautiful! I wish I could have helped you dress."

"That's all right. Catherine insisted she and Letty do the honors. I think Catherine hoped if she were here, I might let her dress up the gown a little. She still thinks it's too plain—not festive enough, she says."

"You were right not to let them have their way about

162

the gown. This is your day, not theirs."

Rena suddenly remembered why she had come in. "Miss Catherine asked me to give this to you," she said, handing the box to her.

Opening it, Brianne saw it contained a man's wedding ring of plain gold. Closing the lid, she said, "You keep it, Rena, until we get to the church."

It was all becoming too real for her, and the time was closing in. In less than an hour she would be Mrs. Ryan Barrington, for better or worse, and she didn't want to think about the outcome.

Rena took the gold band out of the box and handed it to her. "Don't be silly. Why would I carry it? You're supposed to tie it to one of the ribbons on your bouquet. It's a tradition."

Brianne felt as though the ring were burning into the palm of her hand. They were both shaking badly and she was unable to complete the bow, dropping the ring to the floor.

Retrieving it, Rena said, "Here, I'll do it for you. I know you're nervous. Who wouldn't be, marrying a man like Mr. Barrington? And you hardly knowing him at all. But just remember what you told me. This is one of those marriages of convenience . . . though I can't imagine a man like him agreeing to that."

She finished attaching the ring and looked at Brianne's stricken face. "He can't be all that bad, Brianne. In fact, he seems pretty generous. Look at all those lovely clothes he bought for you, and for me too! Why, I never thought I'd be wearing such grand clothes. I told you how nice he was when he brought me here. Most rich folks would have looked down their noses, but not him. It was like a dream come true for me."

"Please, Rena, stop chattering!" Brianne pleaded. Everyone but her seemed to think the man was some kind of saint.

"I just wanted you to know that I'll always be grateful for this chance. And I won't make you sorry you asked for me. I'm going to learn how to behave like a proper lady. After all," Rena lifted her chin, "how else would the cousin and companion of Mrs. Barrington act?"

Brianne giggled nervously, remembering her exaggeration to Duville. "When you find out how a proper lady is supposed to act, let me know. I'm afraid I have some learning to do myself."

Rena leaned over and surprised her with a quick kiss on the cheek. "It's time. Everybody's waiting downstairs. And there's a beautiful coach outside, with flowers all over it, to take you to the church. Come along," she urged, "it'll be all right."

Brianne took one last look in the mirror and was startled by the fear she saw reflected in her own eyes. It wasn't too late. She could call the whole thing off; she wasn't being forced into this. But she knew she would go through with it. She had few other alternatives.

Besides, it wasn't like a *real* wedding. She and Barrington had an agreement, and she refused to agonize over her decision any longer. As always, she would try to make the best of the situation she found herself in.

Taking a deep breath, she faced the door and said with more confidence than she felt, "Come, Rena. We have a wedding to attend."

Catherine and Samuel waited for her by the front door, and turned as they heard her approach.

During the last week Brianne had been caught up in the excitement, the almost electrical surge of energy Catherine and her charges had generated as they planned this marriage, and now she could see the happiness in the older woman's face as she came forward and took her hands.

"It was well worth the wait, my dear. You look absolutely beautiful. I wouldn't be surprised if you set a new fashion with that gown. Lord knows how tired we all are of maneuvering these hoops."

Before Brianne could say anything, Samuel joined his wife, and smiling at Brianne, exclaimed, "Lovely, just lovely."

Taking her by the elbow, he led her to the open door. "Your carriage awaits, and we should hurry before Ryan thinks you've changed your mind. Come along, dear."

Due to the length of her veil, only Rena and she rode in the first carriage. Brianne had no idea how long it took to get to the church, but it couldn't be long enough. Although she had sworn she wouldn't, during the ride she asked herself the same questions that had haunted her this last week. How had she got herself into this, and was she doing the right thing? Marrying a man for revenge and security could only lead to trouble, but at least she would have Rena close by. She looked up, and two pairs of anxious eyes met. Each gave the other a tight, nervous smile in a silent communication of support.

Brianne would have been surprised to know that Ryan, waiting in the small vestibule of the church, was asking himself similar questions.

As always when he was upset, he began pacing the floor. He had only himself to blame for this, he thought. Ever since he had laid eyes on that woman, she had embroiled him in one calamity after another. And here he was, waiting to be joined to her for life! At least for his lifetime—who knew where she'd spend hers! To listen to her that day in the Murdocks' study, she honestly believed that at any time she'd wake up in the next century.

Good Lord, he thought. He was wedding an unbalanced woman. But even that might be preferable than to be wed to one who pops in and out of time! The disturbing part was that he almost believed her. The story she had made up was fantastic, to say the least, and she must possess a brilliant imagination to be able to weave a tale like that with such detail.

Oh, she was intelligent all right, and she had proved herself to be a noteworthy adversary that afternoon a week ago. He had been intrigued, infuriated, and finally amused by her. If nothing else, life with her would be a challenge, and definitely more interesting than marriage to the spoiled Caroline Daniels.

He could tell, that day in the study when Brianne had left him to find Catherine, that she had been very pleased with herself—thinking she had come out on top of their discussion and that he had given in to her demands. The one was easy enough. Maureen Ahearn seemed grateful and eager to please, and according to Catherine was working out well. He still had doubts as to how Miss Ahearn had supported herself until being rescued from her poverty by his future wife, but it was a small favor to grant. Besides, Brianne knew he didn't have any other choice after her deception of Duville.

However, even if he had agreed and shaken hands, no less, with her, he had no intention of remaining celibate throughout this marriage. She thought she had won and no doubt was smugly secure in believing he wouldn't come near her. Well, tonight he would shatter that security. All he wanted out of this marriage was a child. And by God, this time next spring there would be one!

The slapping of kid gloves against a hand caught Ryan's attention. Leaning against the wall stood his best man, and with exaggerated patience Stephan asked, "Are you quite through wearing out the good Father's rug? Because I've just been told your bride has arrived, and they want us out in front of the altar. Hurry up, old boy, I've been waiting all week to glimpse this woman who captured you, and whom you have magnanimously described as passable.

"Why don't you try smiling, Ryan?" he asked as he opened the vestibule door. "This is, after all, your wedding day and you didn't even have to travel all the way to Virginia to find your wife. She was right in your own backyard, so to speak."

Stephan's eyes sparkled with mischief, but being in no mood for his friend's humor, Ryan felt like wiping that smirk off his face.

Coming to the altar, he and Stephan joined the priest and waited. Ryan looked out at the small gathering of people who would witness this auspicious event. Seated in the second pew were Emily and Carl Howard. Besides the couple, the only other people in attendance were a beaming Catherine, seated next to the maid Rena.

The priest beside him gave a nod and Brianne, escorted by Samuel, made her way up the aisle. The closer she came, the faster Ryan's heart beat, and Stephan didn't help matters by whispering, *"Passable?* Shame on you, Ryan. She's an enchantress!"

Stephan was right, he thought. She was beautiful, breathtakingly so, her gown slimmer than the huge ones most women wore, so that Ryan could better remember just how enticing her figure was. She looked like someone out of a storybook, so soft, with delicate flowers surrounding her face . . . but all woman, nonetheless. Observing her face closely as she joined him at the altar, he was gratified to see she was as nervous as he.

Brianne wouldn't have described herself as nervous, more like someone fighting down panic. It had started when she set eyes on his tall form at the end of the long aisle. The awesome power of his magnetism held her prisoner, and yet Brianne's fear was almost overcome by

167

the unexpected and unwanted rush of desire that could no longer be denied. Dear God, she thought in despair, she had had enough sleepless nights to attest to that.

His expression, though, when he looked at her, was dark and forbidding and it was obvious he didn't want to be there any more than she. When she finally joined him he looked into her face as if expecting something, some admission of the undeniable attraction that existed between them. Quickly, Brianne lowered her eyes to the elaborate tie at his neck, her pride refusing to give him what he sought.

Samuel squeezed her elbow reassuringly before leaving her with Ryan, and she watched as he turned his attention to the priest.

Brianne tried to do the same, but for the life of her she couldn't seem to concentrate on what the cleric was saying. It was hard enough just to stand next to the man. She didn't dare look at him again for fear she'd see that mocking glare of his. Only this time he would be right. What they were doing was wrong . . . making a mockery out of marriage, and Brianne had the sudden impulse to turn and run.

Barrington must have sensed her need to flee, because very smoothly, without taking his eyes off the priest, he lifted a hand to her elbow and held her in an iron grip.

Brianne started to perspire, and her heart beat so loudly she was surprised the others could not hear it. As the priest droned on in Latin, Brianne knew real panic. She couldn't follow what was being said and didn't know what was expected of her. Barrington led her through the ceremony, with a slightly stronger pressure on her arm for kneeling and rising. She went along like a marionette in a sideshow, responding to his fingers like a puppet to its strings.

She had the uncanny sensation of standing outside her body and watching an absurd drama unfold. She felt sorry for the woman who played herself. She looked so frightened, seemed frozen to the spot, unable even to untie the ring that hung from the bouquet of flowers that she held. She watched with dismay as the frightened bride took the ring from the priest and clumsily placed it on the man's hand.

With the ring in place, Brianne looked up at the man before her and shivered. It was real, and happening to her! Whereas before she had been detached, she now stared in amazement at her own hand. There it was before her, the proof of her marriage. On her third finger was a heavy gold band.

Her head jerked up as she heard the priest speak in accented English, "Before God and man, I now pronounce you man and wife. What God has joined together, let no man put asunder."

No! Brianne mentally denied it. It couldn't have happened already. She couldn't be married to this stranger! She'd made a mistake and carried it too far. Why doesn't someone stand up and stop this? she cried silently. Her own vocal chords felt paralyzed and she was unable to speak.

Staring at the priest's robe, she heard him say softly, "You may kiss your bride, Monsieur Barrington."

Brianne looked up into Ryan's eyes and hoped he would just kiss her cheek, for the sake of the ceremony. Instead, he held her shoulders in his firm grip and stared into her eyes for the longest time, again searching for something. As the priest nervously cleared his throat, Brianne watched as Ryan's eyes darkened and his full lips came ever closer to take possession of her own. At first he was gentle, barely touching her, and she could savor the faint scent of mint that clung to his lips, but just as she relaxed, the pressure on her mouth increased and Brianne was jolted by it. As she opened her lips to protest she realized, too late, it was exactly what he

169

wanted. His tongue, darting hotly in and out of her mouth, explored its softness for a brief span before he ended the kiss by softly nibbling at her bottom lip for an instant. Brianne felt as though a hot tempest had blown into the cool church and robbed her of her breath. She knew she was trembling and felt certain that at any moment her knees would buckle from the astonishing assault on her mouth. Her hands clung to his upper arms for support and when he finally released her, she couldn't help noticing his satisfied expression.

That quickly brought her back to reality, and she wasn't sure whether to be embarrassed or insulted. Before she could react, the rest of their little wedding party rushed to congratulate them. Amid the well-wishers, Brianne ventured to glance at Ryan from the corner of her eye and was mortified that he should be watching her over the heads of the others, thereby catching her at it. He raised one eyebrow as though in question, and she blushed before turning her attention back to Catherine. She knew what he was silently asking, but even under torture she wouldn't admit that yes, she had secretly enjoyed the kiss.

It was with relief that she heard Catherine directing everyone into their carriages, to return to her house for the luncheon celebration.

Outside the church she stood silently next to Ryan waiting for the carriage to be brought up. For the first time she realized they would be alone for the ride back to the Murdocks', and she looked with longing as the others drove off.

He startled her as he put his hand on her back and asked, "I take it this is our carriage?"

Seeing the one decorated with flowers, she nodded.

"Catherine has certainly thought of everything, hasn't she?" Not really expecting an answer, Ryan then asked in a formal voice, "Shall we go? The others will be expecting us."

He reached behind and picked up the long veil, and taking her elbow once again, led her down the steps and assisted her into the vehicle.

They rode in silence, with Brianne pretending to be very absorbed in the passing scenery. Everything was a blur as she forced herself to remain calm and ignore the eyes she felt burning into her skin.

From out of nowhere he said, "You look lovely today, Brianne. Is that a new design from Europe? Madame Fountaine has outdone herself. I must remember to compliment her when next we visit her establishment."

Brianne jumped at the sound of his voice. "Oh . . . well, actually it's my own design."

She watched his brows arch in appreciation at her disclosure. She knew he was trying to make small talk and decided that since they'd done it, had actually married, she might as well live up to her side of the bargain. She too would try to be agreeable.

"Madame will be pleased you like it. She was quite upset when I refused to wear hoops today and discarded all her suggestions."

He smiled slightly, and she was encouraged. "I wanted this dress to be special. You see, women haven't worn hooped gowns like that for over a hundred years, and I wanted to wear something from when I . . ."

She watched as his expression turned from benign interest to that of annoyance.

He held up a hand to stop her from continuing. "Please, just for today, no more talk of you being from the future. It will be recorded, after all, in the church records that you, Brianne Marie Quinlan, were married in New Orleans in the year 1856. So for the remainder of today, could we just forget that you are a *visitor*, so to

171

speak, to this century? And there is no need to jump every time I speak to you," he added with irritation. "I'm not the ogre you seem to think I am, nor will I harm you. You have no reason to fear me," he said gruffly.

So much for getting along, she thought. Brianne decided it was best not to answer him at all, and returned to her view of the streets.

Chapter 12

As the carriage pulled up to the Murdocks', she and Ryan were met with a barrage of rice and more good wishes. She didn't need to look at the man she had just married to know the same tight polite smile she had seen at the church would again be back in place.

In the foyer, as Brianne brushed the rice from her hair, she felt her eyes begin to fill. If only this could have been a truly happy occasion, she thought dismally. She had waited all these years for the right man to enter her life, and now to find herself married to a stranger, one who was as ill-disposed to this marriage as she, was just plain unfair. She wiped the righteous tears away with the remaining rice and resolved that she would make an effort to act happy, at least for Catherine's sake. The woman was so pleased with herself, Brianne thought her smile was beginning to resemble a Cheshire cat's.

From out of nowhere, Ryan appeared at her side. Sliding an arm around her back, he whispered into her ear, "Are you all right, Madam? I hope our guests think they are tears of happiness. I wouldn't want the Howards or Stephan to think you are displeased with this wedding. Remember our agreement, my dear. I believe your exact words were 'I'll try to be the kind of wife you want,' and I most certainly do not want my wife openly miserable at her own wedding."

Brianne tried to disengage herself from his grip, but he only held her even tighter.

"I remember what I said. My eyes happen to be tearing because I was hit in the face with some rice, so don't concern yourself. I will play the part of the ecstatic bride, if that will make you happy. Now, will you please release me? There's no need for us to be this close."

Almost as if he had never heard her, Ryan turned, and maneuvering her with him, said, "Ah, here is Stephan."

He forced her forward and they stopped in front of the young man with light brown hair, ruddy cheeks, and devilish eyes who she had seen at the church.

"Stephan, I don't believe you have been formally introduced. May I present my wife. Brianne Barrington . . . my very good friend, Stephan Daniels."

Stephan was grinning from ear to ear. "It is indeed a pleasure, Mrs. Barrington. May I take this opportunity to kiss the lovely bride, and also to wish you every happiness?"

He looked at Ryan, who gave his consent, and proceeded to kiss her cheek very briefly before whispering to her, "Be patient with him."

Hearing her new name had given her a jolt, but since Ryan wished her to behave as though she were joyous, she recovered in time to say, "Stephan, thank you so much for your kind words," and deciding immediately that she liked this young man, added, "It truly is a pleasure to meet you also. I've heard so much about you from Ryan that I feel I know you already. Please, won't you call me Brianne?"

She gave Ryan a smug look and arched her brows questioningly, as though to ask, *Is this what you want? Am I playing the part correctly?*

He ignored her as Stephan answered, "I would be

delighted to call you by your given name, and since we'll be neighbors, I hope to have many opportunities to use it. I'm not sure what Ryan has told you of me, but don't believe more than half of it. He tends to exaggerate where my character is concerned."

Brianne gloated in the turn of conversation, because it gave her a rare chance to set the record straight. "Ryan has spoken to me in great length about you. Have no fear, Stephan, I form my own opinions."

From the expressions on both their faces, it was evident that her comment had hit its mark. Stephan looked surprised, and Ryan's face was proof of his annoyance at being reminded that he had blamed Stephan for his own mistakes.

She didn't like the look in his eyes, and thankfully Catherine came to her rescue, announcing the luncheon was to be served.

The seven were seated at a table offering delicacies Brianne had never before enjoyed. A delicious cream of broccoli soup flavored with wine, so thick it might have almost been a sauce, made Brianne comment that she would love to have the recipe.

Catherine laughed and said, "I obtained it from Lizzie, Ryan's own cook, last spring. You know, Brianne, you are in for a treat when you return to Briarfawn. Lizzie is known for her culinary skills."

Glancing at her new husband, and seeing that self-satisfied look once too often on his face, Brianne made no further comment on the meal.

She suffered through embarrassing toasts to her and Ryan's future together before talk at the table turned to the Murdocks' trip to Europe, which was to begin tomorrow. She was almost desolate, thinking about Catherine's impending departure. Brianne knew she had managed this far only because of the kindly woman's concern, and in truth she was the buffer between herself and Ryan. Without Catherine between them, Brianne was afraid of what the future might bring. Reflecting on this, she lost her appetite and merely rearranged her food on the beautiful Wedgwood plate in front of her.

All too quickly the meal was at an end, and Catherine asked for the ladies to be excused, leaving the gentlemen to their cigars and brandy. As Brianne's chair was pulled out for her, she rose, and met Ryan's eyes across the table. His held such an intensity that she was frightened, and she felt as though someone had knocked the breath from her lungs. She broke the magnetic pull of his eyes and left the room on stiff legs, thankful that theirs was a marriage in name only. Ryan Barrington was a man who would dominate any woman foolish enough to care for him. At least that was one thing Brianne didn't have to worry about.

Rena, who had preferred to wait in Brianne's room during the meal, rose as she and Catherine entered. Helping Brianne out of her gown, her red-haired friend commented, "It was a lovely wedding, wasn't it? And you were such a beautiful bride."

Turning around, she thought to add, "Miss Catherine, it was everything a woman could want."

Brianne quickly turned to the older woman. "Oh yes, Catherine, thank you for all the work you've done. It *was* beautiful, and very thoughtful of you. I just wish my family could have been there to see me wed . . . it would have meant so much."

Her eyes met Catherine's, and the dam of tears that she had held in check all morning broke forth. Sobbing, she reached out for Catherine, who quickly came and embraced her.

"Shh, it's all right," Catherine whispered against her hair. "Cry if you want to. Lord knows, you have a right.

It's just that everything has happened so fast, and you haven't had time to become accustomed to it all yet. And that, Brianne, is all you really need . . . time. You and Ryan need time together, to get to know each other and to understand that each of you is a fine person. I know you're upset because we're sailing in the morning and you and Ryan will leave shortly for Briarfawn alone, except for Rena, of course—but listen to me."

She held Brianne away from her and looked into her frightened face. "I have come to care for you in the last two weeks as though you were my own. I've worried endlessly about your welfare, and prayed deeply for you. Do you think I would be able to leave you if I were not certain of your happiness? You may not think so now, but I'm confident that you've done the right thing in marrying Ryan. He *is* a good man, and he'll make you a good husband. Now dry your eyes, dear, and bathe your face . . . your new life awaits you."

She kissed Brianne as her own mother might have, then turned to a teary-eyed Rena. "Pack this gown away, would you, dear," she asked. "And then have the trunk taken downstairs. I'll help Brianne dress for her journey to her new home."

They had all gathered as a group at the bottom of the stairs, with Ryan in the center, and heads lifted in unison as she descended, dressed in a wide gown the color of pale green apples. Brianne looked into the face of her husband. *Good God, he really was!* Because of his height, he towered over the heads of the others, but his presence alone would have commanded attention. What is running through his mind? she thought. She only hoped he couldn't read the fear in hers.

When she became level with him, he reached out to take her hand and led her down the rest of the steps.

177

"You look lovely, Mrs. Barrington," he complimented her.

Embarrassed, she murmured a quiet "Thank you," and wondered what he was up to.

Quickly saying goodbye to the others, Brianne sought out Catherine and walked to the door with her. Almost afraid to look at her for fear the tears would start again, she hugged this exceptional woman and whispered, "Thank you again, Catherine. Have a wonderful time in Europe."

The older woman returned Brianne's embrace and took both of her hands in her own. "Remember what I told you. Time—it's a healer and a mender. Allow yourself that. Mark my words, when next we meet you shall tell me I was right. Be happy, dear Brianne."

Adjusting the bow of the large hat Brianne wore, Catherine touched the girl's quivering chin and said, "Go now. Ryan is waiting."

Nodding, Brianne turned and walked toward him. Standing at the door to the carriage, Ryan held out his hand to her and she unwillingly met his eyes as she accepted it. Gone was the look of insolence she had seen reflected there throughout the day. Instead, he looked at her almost with compassion, and she cringed inwardly, knowing that he should pity her.

As she joined Rena in the carriage, she heard Stephan say, "You're a lucky man, Ryan. Don't forget that."

She watched Ryan shake his friend's hand and nod impatiently before giving Catherine a goodbye kiss. He then climbed up and sat opposite the women, closing the door behind him.

Brianne had an immediate feeling of isolation and she quickly looked back and waved to the small gathering, hoping that Catherine was right in her prediction about her future. Although she herself saw little to hope for.

*　　*　　*

The river was as muddy, and the bayou as brackish, as she remembered. The going was slow and the temperature and humidity made her feel listless. Brianne spent most of the afternoon assuring Rena that this trip down the complacent waters of the Mississippi would be nothing like her last voyage.

Exhausted from the busy morning and early afternoon, Brianne finally dozed off and Rena didn't have the heart to disturb her, even though she was sure this small vessel would never carry them safely to their destination.

Ryan watched his wife from the front of the boat. Let her sleep, he thought. She'll need it. Later tonight would prove to be difficult, of that he had no doubt, but he couldn't see prolonging the inevitable confrontation his announcement would create. He had let her have her way this past week and had told Catherine to spare no expense in preparing her to be his wife . . . and a wife in every sense was what he intended to have.

Ryan sighed audibly and putting his head back, closed his eyes. He too needed a short respite from the constant turmoil that seemed to plague him lately. This evening would be soon enough for the clashing of their two strong wills to resume.

They were met by two carriages as they approached the small dock at Briarfawn. One was to carry the three of them to Ryan's home, and the other was for their luggage, which was considerable.

As the stately house came into view, Rena let out a gasp. "Lord, Brianne, is this where we're going to live? Such a beautiful house! Imagine me living here!"

Ryan didn't give Brianne a chance to answer. "Thank you, Rena. I'm proud of Briarfawn, and glad to hear you share my appreciation of it."

If he had only given her a chance, Brianne thought, she would have agreed with Rena. It was a beautiful home, one she was now expected to share with this man. She looked over at him, but his eyes were fixed on the house and his expression vividly said just how much it meant to him.

As the carriage brought them closer to the wide porch, Brianne saw Mattie and a small group of people waiting with her. Among them she recognized Mary, the nervous maid, Carla, who had altered the gown she wore when she left this house two weeks ago, and standing beside her with a dog at his feet, Carla's son Jimmie, whom she remembered watching play below her window. There were two men and another woman Brianne didn't know, but it was Mattie who held her attention.

Standing in front of the others, the large woman clasped her hands together as though in prayer, and was grinning happily.

When the carriage stopped Mattie came forward, and as Ryan stepped down she exclaimed, "Congratulations, Misser Barrington. 'Bout time you settled down. And you couldn't have picked a better wife for yourself, either."

Brianne didn't wait for Ryan's help, but left the carriage on her own, saying as she stepped down, "Mattie! It's so good to see you again. I've missed you."

She hugged Ryan's housekeeper, then turned as Rena joined them. "Mattie, I'd like you to meet my good friend and companion, Rena Ahearn. She'll be staying here with us. I hope you'll make her feel as comfortable as you made me feel when I was here last."

The two women looked at each other, each with her own doubts, but it was Rena who spoke first. "Actually, Mattie, I'm here to serve your new mistress any way I can. I hope we can work together."

Ryan looked surprised when he heard the exchange, and gave a look of approval.

Rena didn't realize it then, but she had just won Mattie's unfailing loyalty. The black woman smiled and replied, "Welcome to Briarfawn, Miz Rena."

She then gave Ryan a look and said matter-of-factly,

"Seems like this family's gettin' bigger all the time. You sure been one busy man, Misser Barrington."

Ryan gave her an impatient look in return and said, "Why don't we all go inside? I'm sure the ladies would like to freshen up before dinner. You did prepare it, didn't you? Or have you been too busy thinking up clever things to say when I returned?"

Mattie chuckled. "Oh yes, suh, you'll be havin' somethin' to eat, only it wasn't me that made it. Lizzie wouldn't let me in that kitchen, and you know it. I jus' asked some of the people here so's you could introduce your new bride to them, is all."

Ryan was left with no choice but to do so, and Brianne tried to remember the names and faces for the future.

First was Nathen, the overseer, a tall, strong-looking man with intelligent eyes. Then Aaron, the manservant, who was older and kind-looking. Then finally she met the paragon of chefs, Lizzie. She was very polite and bowed slightly when Ryan said she was married to Aaron. She reacquainted herself with Carla and young Jimmie, who looked up at her with a sweet smile, and then again Mary, the shy young housemaid.

Brianne smiled at the gathering and said with sincerity, "I'd like to thank all of you for coming out to greet us when we arrived. It was a lovely homecoming."

Before leading her into the house, Ryan cleared his throat, and looking embarrassed added, "Yes, thank you. We both appreciate it."

Damn! He silently cursed as he followed Brianne up the stairs. Why did she always manage to say the right thing to everyone else except him?

While the men unloaded the carriage containing their luggage, Mattie took Brianne and Rena on a short tour of the ground floor. From the large, square foyer, you could

181

turn left into Ryan's study or right into a large drawing room. Brianne preferred to turn right and avoid the study, which she considered to be her husband's domain.

Standing at the double doors, she immediately fell in love with this room. She crossed the polished oak floor to the Aubusson carpet in colors of cream, pale green, and rose. Looking about the room, she was impressed. Handsome furniture was upholstered in shades of mauve, deep green, and ivory cream. An abundance of greenery from large plants was scattered about and hanging from long cords were landscape paintings in muted colors. It wasn't the sort of room she could picture the strong, masculine Ryan occupying, but she felt right at home in it. It soothed the senses and made her feel relaxed.

Reluctant to leave, she followed Mattie from it to see the dining room. Mattie was very proud of this particular room as she pointed out the fine china and silver. Crystal was stored in large glass-doored cabinets, and Mattie happily announced there was a service for forty-eight, should the need arise, implying with a nod that she and Ryan would be entertaining on that scale. God forbid!

Leading from the dining room was a long hallway they followed until they emerged in Lizzie's province, the kitchen. Brianne had already smelled the delicious aromas emanating from this room and remarked on them to Lizzie. "Whatever you're cooking, Lizzie, smells wonderful. Even in New Orleans, the people spoke of your talents and were envious of Ryan. I hope some day you'll allow me to watch you. I've never been very good in the kitchen myself."

It was a little white lie, but she had seen the distrust in the older woman's eyes when she walked into the room. And truthfully, unless she was preparing dinner for a group, Brianne didn't enjoy cooking.

Lizzie had her reservations about the new mistress.

182

Ever since she had heard Misser Barrington was to be married she had been upset, fearing what changes a wife would make. Not at all like Mattie, who went about humming for the last week, so pleased was *she* with the master's choice.

Now that Lizzie had met her, and it was clearly stated that this was her area to run, she softened toward the young woman. Letting her guard down, she decided she liked her too.

"Anytime you want, Miz Brianne, you come and visit."

Brianne gave her a friendly smile just as Mattie said, "Those men must have your trunks upstairs by now. Let me show you ladies to your rooms."

By the time they stopped at the doorway of the room Brianne had last occupied, Rena was in complete awe of her surroundings. Just as Brianne was about to enter, Mattie held out her hand, "No, Miz Brianne," she said. "This here room is for Miz Rena. Misser Barrington says you was to be put in the big bedroom down the hall."

Brianne was confused but quickly forgot, hearing the joy Rena expressed in the bedroom. "Oh, Brianne, this is too fine for me. Maybe something smaller . . . I've always dreamed of a room like this, but never thought it would come true."

Brianne quickly reassured her. "Nonsense. You heard Mattie. Ryan made these arrangements, so it's settled. This is your room."

They left Rena admiring her new bedroom and entered a room at the far end of the hall. Brianne stopped at the doorway, a little intimidated by the size of it.

It was dominated by a huge bed off to one side that was draped with a canopy of soft brown, and panels pulled back by beige satin ties. In fact, everything in the room ranged in varying shades of brown, from the dark reddish brown of the mahogany furniture to the copper and tan stripe of the sofa, which was on the other side of the room, away from the bed. Before the sofa in front of the fireplace was a table already set for two. On it was the only feminine thing in the room, a bowl of fresh pink flowers.

Turning to the housekeeper, she said, "I think we've made a mistake, Mattie. This can't be my room. Look! See, there's Ryan's bag next to my trunks. Maybe the men brought them into the wrong room."

Mattie chuckled. "Sure enough is his bag. Now Misser Barrington's gone out to check on the runnin' of this place and he said to tell you he'd be back in time for dinner," she nodded to the set table.

"I'll have Mary fix you a nice, cool bath while Miz Rena is seeing to your things. You want anything, chile, you jus' pull that rope over there, and I'll come running."

She left a bewildered Brianne in the middle of the room, but just before closing the door she turned around. "Maybe I'm out of place sayin' this, but I'm sure glad you married Misser Barrington. He's been one lonely man, workin' his heart out for this place and fixin' it up for a family someday. Everybody workin' in this house, he bought from someplace else. None of us was too pleased either, comin' so far south. But I wouldn't want to work anywhere's else. I'm a free woman of color, Miz Brianne, and I owe him. He's a good man, and he loves this place. I'm jus' glad he'll be sharin' it with you, and not some others I could mention."

She gave a satisfied nod and added, "There, I said it . . . and I'm glad. Now you relax, Miz, this here's your first night in your new home."

She shut the door and Brianne sat down on the sofa wondering about the curious things the housekeeper had said. They were obviously important to her, or she never would have mentioned them.

The water felt so cool and refreshing, she was glad Mattie had thought of it. Rinsing the scented soap from her body, she looked over at Rena, who was almost finished putting her clothes away.

"Rena, give me a minute and I'll help you with those."

It was uncomfortable having everyone wait on her.

Rena impatiently shook her red curls. "Brianne Marie Barrington—and that's your new name now, so don't screw up your face every time you hear it. Brianne," she started again, "you're the mistress of this house now, and you better get used to it. You are never to help me. It's the other way around, and unless you forget about the way it was, and start realizing the way it is, *today*, you're going to find yourself permanently between two worlds. Furthermore, if you don't let me earn my keep, I'll go back to where I came from."

Brianne sat up in the tub. "You wouldn't! You can't leave me here alone! You're the only one who believes in me, Rena."

She would do anything . . . anything, rather than lose her. "I'm sorry I tried to do your job and I promise I'll try to accept this new life. It's just that I've never had servants. I've always done for myself in the past, but I'll learn. I promise, only please don't say you might leave."

She was really frightened. Rena was so pigheaded that if she didn't feel she was paying her way, she just might go rather than accept charity.

"It's for your own good that you accept this," Rena answered. "Mr. Barrington's a good man. You've told me what happened," she rushed to continue when Brianne started to protest. "Both of you weren't yourselves that night. He was drunk and you'd been drugged. Each of you

185

thought the other to be a liar—but you can't fault him now. That story about his friend, Mr. Daniels, adds up. So why can't you give him a chance?"

Seeing Brianne's closed expression, she added, "This could be a good life for you, Brianne, if you'd just try."

Shutting the closet door, she said, "I'm finished here. I'll lay out this dressing gown for you on the bed. If there's nothing else you want right now, I'd like to start on my own things."

She stood before the tub like the proper maid her mother had taught her to be, and Brianne was too upset to do anything but nod.

As Rena closed the bedroom door after herself, Brianne sat back in the tub, dejected. Didn't Rena know that she had brought her here to be her friend, not a servant? Brianne sighed loudly, sadly realizing there was to be a small wall between them now, separating mistress and maid.

She must have remained in the water a long time, thinking about Rena, because her fingers were starting to pucker, and seeing a long, fluffy towel, she stepped out of the tub.

The dressing gown Rena had laid out was one of her favorites—champagne-colored satin, with a high neck and heavy, intricate lace beginning at the collar and shoulders and ending in a deep V between her breasts, and with tiny covered buttons from her neck to the floor. It was a real work of art and as she admired it, while trying to fasten all the buttons, she heard the door open.

With her head still down, she laughed, and then asked in a light voice, "Rena, it will take forever to do all these. Would you mind helping?"

"Since I just told your maid that you wouldn't be needing her for the rest of the night, I'd be more than happy to accommodate you."

Chapter 13

Spinning around, she saw him standing in front of the closed door with that damn grin on his face.

"What are you doing in here? Please, get out. I was told this is my room," she stated.

Shrugging his shoulders, Ryan walked to the closet and withdrew a dark brown velvet jacket and tan trousers, which he then draped over a chair. Ignoring the incredulous look on her face, he started to remove his clothes.

"What do you think you're doing?" she rasped out, her eyes wide with disbelief.

Turning to her as though forgetting she was in the room, he said, "Dear lady, what does it look like I'm doing? The bath water still looks fairly fresh, and I'd like to wash the grime of the field away."

Astounded, she walked toward him while unconsciously placing her hands on her hips. "Well, you can't do it in here! Mattie said this was to be *my* room, so kindly take your clothes and get out!"

He hadn't planned it this way, but when he walked in and saw the tub, he decided to use this opportunity to assert his rights.

Unbuttoning his shirt with one hand, he replied,

"Madam, allow me to correct you. This happens to be *our* room—the 'our' implying that it is to be shared by both of us. Now, I don't know what other wonderful inventions or customs you have in the twentieth century but here we are quite provincial . . . we like to remove our clothes before bathing. So if the sight of me upsets you, I suggest you turn around."

And with that statement, he began unbuttoning his trousers.

Speechless, Brianne spun around and walked toward the fireplace. Breathing heavily from anger, she placed both her hands on the mantel, realizing she was enraged enough to scream, or even throw something. She spied a large ornate urn and spent a few pleasant moments contemplating the damage it would do to him. She would love to wipe the ridiculous grin from his face. It was infuriating! she thought. After years of independence, to now find herself indebted to a man, *particularly this man*, was a bitter humiliation.

Hearing him enter the tub, Brianne was shocked by his sudden shout.

"Good God! What the hell is in this water?"

Turning, she saw him half rise out of it and look at the water below his waist as though it were contaminated.

Smiling, she walked a few feet in his direction. "Why dear sir, what does it smell like? It's only a little bath oil. I believe Mattie called it oil of gardenia. You see, it happens to be a provincial custom of *this* century to scent a lady's bath. You may very well smell like a flower shop, but no one will ever notice the grime of the field. You *did* say that was what you were washing away, didn't you?"

"Very good, Brianne. You've established that you have a certain wit, now either hand me a towel or be prepared. Either way, I'm getting out of this."

He remained half-raised, not letting the water touch any more of his upper body, as he waited for her decision.

I really should let him stay like that, she thought with satisfaction. Only she wouldn't have put it past him to pop out of the tub at any moment, and the last thing she wanted was to see him nude. Just the thought of it made her move quickly to hand him a towel.

"Thank you," he said as he wrapped it around him. "You could have told me before I got in, you know."

"And you could have told me about sharing this room!" she stated hotly.

"Touché! What say you we discuss this over dinner? It should be brought in shortly."

He left the tub and walked over to his clothes. With the towel still wrapped around his waist, he put on a crisp white shirt, then removed the towel and continued to dress.

While he did so, Brianne walked about the room as she lectured him. "This will never do, you realize that? It isn't part of the agreement. I must have my own bedroom, and I want privacy. You can't just barge in any time you want . . . Are you listening to me?"

"Yes, I've heard every word, and I still ask that we discuss this during dinner."

"We can discuss it right now."

"Ah, saved by the door," and without missing a stroke as he brushed his hair, Ryan bade whoever knocked to come in.

It was Mattie, wearing a silly smile as she looked at them both, and considering the way she was dressed, Brianne could just imagine what the housekeeper was thinking.

"Lizzie made your favorite, Misser Barrington, pompano papillote. I hope you like it, Miz Brianne." She directed the servants into the room and watched as they carefully placed the dishes onto the small table.

Brianne saw that this pompano, or whatever, was fish of some kind with a sauce over it. There was seasoned rice as a side dish and a large bowl of fruit. Aaron then entered the room carrying a large silver tray. On it were liquor decanters and crystal glasses.

The tub was removed and Mattie, standing at the doorway, asked, "Will there be anything else I can get for you tonight?"

Coming to stand beside his wife, Ryan answered for them both. "Thank you, Mattie, this is fine. Good night."

As the housekeeper shut the door, he pulled out a chair for Brianne, saying, "Your dinner, Madam."

Sitting opposite each other, two pairs of eyes reluctantly met and held, hers showing distrust and his, determination.

Grinning at her, Ryan asked, "Would you care for a drink? Wine perhaps?"

Cautiously, Brianne replied, "Yes, please. Brandy—a large one."

His eyebrows shot up. "Brandy?"

"Yes, brandy!" she answered indignantly. "Do you have some objection to that? Don't provincial ladies drink brandy?"

"Usually not, but I have no objections to you having it, if that's what you really want."

"Why, thank you. How indulgent of you."

Ignoring her sarcasm, he handed her the drink and sat back down to eat his dinner.

She watched his strong hands handle the silver cutlery with a refined ease and knew with a sinking feeling that she was powerless to make him leave this room. Frustrated, she threw back her head and swallowed half the drink. It burned her throat so badly that her eyes watered and she began to choke, momentarily losing the ability to speak.

Gasping for breath, she watched him laugh as he handed her a glass of water. "If you're going to drink brandy, then you should learn how to sip it. It's meant for after dinner, to cleanse the palate."

"I'll remember that," she whispered hoarsely. It grated on her nerves to hear him advise her how to drink.

She tasted the fish, which proved to be quite good, but before long a warm, comfortable feeling permeated her body and she ended up pushing the food around on her plate again.

Looking up, she ventured to observe, "I see that you're enjoying your dinner, but do you think we could now discuss the living arrangements?"

Ryan calmly put his fork down, and wiping his mouth with a napkin, replied, "Certainly. The living arrangements are as you see them. You and I are to share this room. Peacefully, I hope."

"You can't mean that! We have a bargain, a . . . a marriage of convenience. You *shook* on it," she protested.

Ryan sat back in his chair. The moment of truth had finally come and he wasn't optimistic about her reaction to his next words, but looking her straight in the eyes he said, "That is true. I did shake your hand and agree to a marriage of convenience. I find it convenient to have my wife sleep in this room."

Brianne stood up and cried bitterly, "You lied! You promised that we'd never . . . that you'd never again . . ."

Ryan stood, and taking her glass, refilled it. "What I promised, Brianne, was that there will never be a repeat performance of what took place when you were here last, and I will keep that promise. If you should ever again have the need for laudanum, and are not in control, I promise not to touch you."

Ryan placed the drink in front of her, and taking it, Brianne stormed over to the sofa. Slumping down into the soft cushions, she accused him, "You tricked me, Ryan Barrington. You *knew* what I meant, but you never had any intentions of fulfilling my wishes, did you?"

Ryan sat in one of the striped chairs and leaning toward her, asked softly, "Did you ever think about my wishes? Agreed, what I did to you was wrong, but I too had plans that in one night of insanity were wiped out. I've worked very hard here, Brianne, and was on the brink of seeing all my plans come to fruition. I had planned to marry and raise a family here. That's all I've ever wanted . . . a family as I once had before my parents' death. You might be pregnant now. This would be a fine place to raise children, Brianne."

He was looking at her earnestly, trying to determine her reaction, and Brianne felt something that she couldn't put into words. He was lonely, of that she was sure, and tired of his bachelor ways, but what he wanted was more a brood mare than a wife. It was the children that were important to him, not the woman who produced them. She decided then, since it was of such importance, that she would tell him the truth.

"You have a right to know . . . I'm definitely not pregnant."

He stared into her face for a long time before picking up both their glasses.

Returning to his chair, he pronounced, "I'm glad. I wouldn't want our child conceived in that way."

"What child?" she demanded. "You make it seem as though I've agreed to share your bed . . . I haven't!"

Looking at her coldly, he asked, "What do you intend to do then? Spend the rest of your life alone, isolated in some emotional cocoon? You are married to *me!* You are also twenty-six years old, and by your own admission your sister was your only family. Now you don't even have her. Is that the way you envisioned your life to be? Have you never thought what you would tell your daughter about life? Hearing your own child's laughter about you?"

At her closed expression, he decided to switch tactics. "Or is it the intimacy of marriage that frightens you? To put it bluntly, you, Brianne, are no innocent. I have not asked before how you lost your virginity, or if there was someone else in Philadelphia waiting for your return, but I think I have the right to do so now."

How dare he! She looked at him with something near hatred. He had come too close to her real feelings, and she resented that this man was the one to probe the open wounds of her mind. She had tried so hard to suppress the envy she felt at her younger sister's motherhood. Of course she would like to have a child someday, but she was unsure about a husband. Funny, both of them were alike there—each wanting the product, but not necessarily the co-producer.

True, her experience with men had not been totally satisfying, and she accepted full responsibility for that, but it was the thought of losing her identity and the independence she had fought so hard to gain that was frightening. Now this man with his antiquated ideals, who had taken her independence from her, wanted the rest of her as well.

Through clenched teeth she told him, "You have no right to ask that. Whatever I've done in my life, before being coerced into this *marriage*, is my business, not yours."

"I have every right!" he nearly shouted. "I am your husband! And as far as being forced into this marriage, when you knew your options were becoming my wife and mistress of Briarfawn, or returning to the streets and your own devices for survival, you made your decision quickly. We will both benefit from this marriage, Brianne, one way or the other."

She stormed away from him to the filled decanters. Pouring herself a second drink, she was filled with disgust. First with him, for tricking her into this marriage

193

and now prying into her life, but mostly with herself, for compromising her principles in favor of security. But above all, for not having the courage to slap his arrogant face and walk out of this house. Less than a month ago she would have done just that and felt righteous in her actions, but not now, and not here. Besides, there was nowhere else to go, she anguished. And with Catherine gone to Europe, there was no one to help her.

She'd just have to deal with him alone. Let him know that he hasn't been that clever. She knew she was becoming intoxicated, and he was quickly helping her to reach that state by constantly refilling her glass. However, if he thought it would aid him in maneuvering her into bed, he was sadly mistaken.

What he really wanted was a story to use as a balm for his injured ego. He had, after all, taken to wife a woman, in his mind, of questionable virtue. My God, how archaic!

Returning to the sofa, she pulled her legs up onto it and made herself comfortable. Holding her drink before her, she watched the play of amber and crystal before quietly asking, "Am I to understand you want to know how I lost my virginity, and what other relationships I've had?"

He inclined his head once, as though being very patient with her, and she reasoned that nothing could be worse than the actual truth. She had tried to bury it over the years, but it was always there, lurking in the recesses of her mind.

Well, you egotistical barbarian, she thought viciously, if it's a story you want I'm about to give you an earful. Only it won't be the one you're expecting. There will be no young maiden taken advantage of.

She began slowly. "First, you should know some background of the twentieth century and the moral codes, or lack of them, that exist during the period you're demanding answers to."

"I see. We're back in the twentieth century. You really have a wonderful imagination for a woman."

"Mr. Barrington," she spoke his name with a distinct lack of respect, "where I come from women are not confined to domestic life as they are here. We are bankers, politicians, senators, even Supreme Court judges. Why, there might even be a woman president in the twenty-first century."

At his barely concealed laughter, she pursed her lips together in anger. "I don't care if you don't believe me! It only matters that *I* believe it. That I know it's true."

"Brianne, all this is very interesting, but you *are* straying from the subject, aren't you?"

She gritted her teeth as she glared at him. "I don't even know why I bother, you'll never understand! And why should I? What do you know of me? What my life has been like? How hard I've worked to get where I am today, or was, until I met you?"

She looked directly at him and said impatiently, "You know nothing. You've living in the dark ages and judging me with obsolete standards."

Ryan closed his eyes momentarily. She really was pushing him to the limit. What he was asking wasn't so unreasonable; he had a right, as her husband, to know these things.

"Brianne, standards, out of date or not, are what we live by, and I'm asking out of more than curiosity. I think it would help if you just stuck to the truth."

She knew a blinding second of fear. But it was fear of herself. In that brief flash of emotions that surged through her body, she knew without a doubt she was capable of doing bodily harm. Had she a weapon in her hands, she knew she would have wielded it with a vicious satisfaction.

Its intensity passed quickly, but she turned on him with a malevolence that frightened her only slightly less.

"You pompous bastard! The truth? You want the truth? You won't like it."

Brianne leaned forward and said with a hardness of heart, "I lost my virginity on purpose! And with a man who was practically a stranger!"

Ryan hid his surprise well, except for the slight widening of his eyes.

Brianne laughed coldly. "I shocked you, didn't I?"

When he made no reply, she continued. "It's the truth—that's what you said you wanted. I don't give a good damn whether you believe me or not, but I'll tell you the rest, just so you know why I'm not going to go along with this *marriage*."

Ignoring the man, her eyes settled into the darkened room behind him, not really seeing anything but her past in front of her.

"You wouldn't know what it was like, growing up when I did . . . the pressures that are put on a young person. I don't suppose I was yet fourteen when I thought out this whole sex dilemma. *I* was the one taking all the risks, it would be *my* body that would never be the same afterwards. I would be the one who possibly became pregnant, while he would be free to walk away from it. Adding it all up, I decided that no man was worth all of that, and until I met that someone who warranted all the risks, I would remain a virgin."

The anger was gone now, and she was hardly aware to whom she spoke. She was saying it now for herself, hoping that recalling it aloud would shed some of the bitterness that had plagued her for years.

"You see, I was brought up in a religious home, attended religious schools and listened to all their lectures on sins of the body, so I felt assured I was making the right decision. I remained that way for the next seven years—frustrated and frightened. Twenty-one years old and a virgin, something unheard of at that time.

196

"I was supposed to be a grown-up and know what I wanted out of life. But by that time this prize I had guarded so well, my virginity, I no longer considered a virtue. It was more like a stone that hung around my neck, weighing me down, something to be rid of."

Ryan let her speak without interruption, sensing somehow that this recital was not meant so much for him but sprang from an inner need of her own.

"I chose well, I thought. And I prepared myself that night as a bride might have done. I wanted that evening to be special and something I'd always remember. Well, I got half my wish . . . I'll never forget it."

Brianne unconsciously cringed. "When we were together, I froze. I couldn't go through with it. I begged him to stop, told him I was sorry I had led him on, but he laughed. David wouldn't listen. He kept telling me I was a woman and it was time to start acting like one. Oh, he was patient for awhile, I'll give him that. But his patience came to an end."

Brianne held the fragile glass so tightly, Ryan was afraid it would break in her hands.

Closing her eyes, she said in a shaky voice, "It was terrible . . . I lay there for a few moments, stunned, and I kept thinking, Is that all there is? When I looked over at him asleep, I felt nothing. Not anger, or disgust . . . nothing. I just wanted to get away. I couldn't believe this was what people wrote songs about, or described in books with such silly descriptions as fireworks going off. It was none of that, just distasteful. I got dressed and left. He never contacted me again, and for that I was always grateful."

Ryan came over to sit next to her. He wanted to offer something to stop the tears that were silently sliding down her flushed cheeks. "Brianne," he said gently, taking one of her hands. "You don't have to say any more. I'm sorry I made you tell me that."

She pulled her hand away and laughed bitterly. "Wait," she protested, almost hysterically. "You haven't heard the rest. You wanted this sordid little tale, the truth, now listen to the rest. Don't you see? Saving myself all those years . . . and for what? Isn't it the ultimate irony? Don't you find all this amusing?"

She was laughing and crying at the same time, and Ryan had seen her anguish as she relived her past. He didn't think she was truly aware of him, or why he was even there. She was drunk, through his fault, and just saying her thoughts aloud. Taking the untouched drink from her hands, he wiped her face of tears and put his arms around her.

"No, it's not funny, Brianne. The man was a fool."

She stayed within the circle of his arms. It felt so nice to be held again by a man, without any pressure. Just comforting.

"I blamed him for a long time, but it wasn't his fault. I never should have built it up to be something so important. It never was important to anyone except me. I should have listened to my body and forgotten all the rest. It should have come naturally. I've tried, but it just isn't right. I panic. There must be something missing in me, or maybe I'm cold, like someone once told me. I've never made *love*, but whatever the reason, it just isn't worth the disappointment in the end anymore."

He sat, holding her in his arms, for a long time until she stopped crying and her breathing told him she had fallen asleep, or, more likely, passed out.

Thinking about what she had said infuriated him. The stupid fools! Didn't they know what she needed . . . what she was asking for?

Ryan lifted her up and brought her to their bed. Gently laying her down, he unbuttoned her collar and left her to see to the lamps.

Watching her sleep, he removed his clothes and

silently got in bed next to her. He looked down at this woman, his wife, sleeping soundly at his side. Even after drinking too much and crying half the night, she was still beautiful and looked innocent in her slumber. She practically *was* an innocent. In her own words she had never made love to a man, not really, and secretly he was pleased.

He had never been with a virgin before, always steering clear of them, never wanting to be trapped or feel regrets later. He now saw how potentially injurious it could be for some women to depend on men for their attitudes toward sex. And if one had been initiated by a selfish oaf, then distaste for the act was natural.

Forgoing his plans to assert his husbandly rights, he vowed to be patient with her. What Brianne needed was time, not lust. And in time perhaps she would stop her incredible stories about the future. He wanted to build a life with her, something that would be lasting.

She was wrong about herself, though. Nothing was missing in her, nor was she cold. Anyone with so much visible fire in her eyes must have smoldering embers inside, waiting to be fanned. All she needed was confidence in herself, and in him.

He pushed the hair away from those sleeping eyes and bent his head to softly kiss her temple. "You've been sorely used, my wife," he whispered. "But all that has ended. Beginning tomorrow I'll start to win you over, and give you the courtship you should have had."

Pulling the coverlet over them, Ryan took her into his arms and closed his own eyes.

Tomorrow would be the beginning of their life together.

Chapter 14

Brianne awoke to the sun stabbing into her eyes, and immediately shut them as the pain in her head began. Dear God! What had happened? She remembered waking briefly in the middle of the night with someone's arms around her. It felt so nice, she had pressed up against the broad chest, and the arms had tightened protectively about her. She also remembered not caring whether or not it was a dream, but feeling so content, falling back asleep.

But how had she gotten into bed in the first place? She knew she had drunk too much, and was angry with Ryan for breaking his word. She could almost hear the two of them arguing back and forth . . . God!

Horrified, Brianne's eyes snapped open. Had she really told him about David? She turned her face into the pillow, mortified that she had revealed anything so personal. She had never told another soul, not even her sister, about that embarrassing ordeal. What must he be thinking? Pulling the cover over her head and wanting to remain hidden that way forever, she heard the door open.

Brianne held her breath, waiting to hear something that would identify the person she could sense standing by her bed.

With relief she finally heard her name whispered. "Brianne? Are you awake?"

"Rena, thank God it's you!" Since her head was still throbbing, trying to sit up was difficult but she managed by shielding her eyes. "What time is it?" she asked weakly.

Rena placed the tray in front of her. "It's after eleven. Mr. Barrington said to let you sleep, but I was starting to get worried. What's wrong with you? Are you sick?"

Brianne's stomach turned over at the sight of the big breakfast Rena had brought. "Just take the food away, Rena, please. I can't eat anything!"

Her friend quickly removed the tray and placed it on the dresser. Turning to Brianne, she asked with concern, "What's the matter with you? Mattie told me this morning that when they took last night's dishes away, your plate was hardly touched. And I'll just bet you didn't eat anything at your wedding, either. If you're sick, we should send for a doctor."

Brianne shook her head slowly, to minimize the pain. "I may feel like I'm dying, but I'm not sick. I'm afraid it's only a well-deserved hangover."

"A hangover! I don't believe you!" Rena reprimanded. "Fine way to spend your wedding night—drunk! Don't you know these plantations thrive on gossip? There's a very strong slave grapevine. And if you don't get out there and show yourself, it'll soon be all over the parish and into New Orleans that the new mistress of Briarfawn is sickly, or worse yet, has a problem with the bottle!"

Brianne lay down and pulled the covers over her head as though they would shut out Rena's voice, which was starting to reverberate inside her head.

Her own muffled voice came through the blanket. "I think you're blowing this up out of proportion. But don't worry, I'll stay in this room. I feel so rotten, I couldn't get up anyway."

Rena reached over and pulled the cover off the bed in one swift motion. "Like hell you will! I'm going to get a nice hot bath up here and you're going to sweat it out of you. Then I'll fix something to settle your stomach. By this afternoon everyone on this plantation—and they're all dying to get a look at you—is going to say what a sweet, pretty, and *healthy* mistress they've got."

She stormed out of the room, slamming the door behind her.

Brianne turned her face back into the pillow, thinking how disappointed Rena's mother would be to know her daughter had turned into a red-haired witch. She didn't know exactly how a proper lady's maid was supposed to act, but she was sure Rena had forgotten some of her mother's more important lessons.

Rena was right, Brianne thought later as she stood next to Mattie greeting the people who worked the plantation. They all looked at her with open curiosity, and she knew that without Rena's lecture and that vile-tasting drink that had been forced down her, she would never have been able to stand in the hot sun to meet them.

There were too many to try and remember names, so she just smiled and every so often managed to say something trite like "How nice to meet you," or "How are you?"

Men, women, and children stopped their chores when she and Mattie walked by. All were polite, but she could read the distrust in many of the faces.

Later that afternoon, while she sipped weak tea in the tranquil living room, she thought how stupid she must have seemed asking those questions. What else would a slave answer but "Fine, mam"?

With so much to learn if she remained here for any

length of time, she decided that tomorrow she would inspect this place and its conditions, and make up her mind then. One thing was definite. She was not going to remain in this house and be pampered.

Feeling better, and wanting to do something positive, she made her way into the kitchen. Brianne felt her appetite return as she smelled the delicious aromas coming from the room.

Lizzie looked up from the large wooden table in the center of the room, where she was elbow-deep in flour. "Miz Brianne. Glad you came in. Makin' peach pies— Misser Barrington loves 'em. Want to sit a spell and watch?"

Brianne spied an apron on a hook by the back door and went to get it. "Actually, Lizzie, if you don't mind, I'd like to help. You see, I've found that I never really learn if I just watch. I have to get in and do it."

Lizzie nodded her approval. "Can understand that. Feel that way myself."

Brianne thanked her while looking about the room. "I didn't notice yesterday how large it is in here. You certainly take care of it well, Lizzie."

The room was painted a creamy white to the beamed ceiling, and had large-paned windows that were open to let the heat out from the huge fireplace. Since the fire was the center of activity, there were gleaming pots, copper ladles, and an assortment of cooking utensils hanging from its mantle.

What a comfortable kitchen, she thought. Her own family had loved to congregate at the kitchen table, and all important conferences had taken place there. Shaking her head to clear it from the past, Brianne tied her apron and announced to Lizzie that she was ready to learn.

It was an instructive afternoon, and Brianne helped in

every phase of cooking, from the pies to the soup they started next. Filé gumbo, Lizzie called it, a clear chicken broth with pieces of chicken, sausage, and oysters. The filé part, she learned, was powdered sassafras root that Lizzie would add just before serving, to thicken it.

The celebrated cook turned teacher as she took Brianne out back to her vegetable garden. There the new mistress of Briarfawn saw a wide variety of plants, including yams, red and green peppers, eggplant, and others she didn't know. Lizzie explained that mirliton was a vegetable pear and alligator pears were avocados. Along with them were plantains, starchy large bananas, and misshapen tomatoes with horny skins. She was told to wait until they ripened to a rich red and then hold them over a flame to loosen the skin. Then, Lizzie promised, she would taste something started in heaven.

Coming back into the kitchen, Brianne was very impressed. With the beef, pork, and fish to be found on the plantation, in the smokehouse or the nearby water, the place was really self-sufficient for food. To her, Briarfawn seemed like a little town unto itself.

Lizzie told Brianne she deserved a treat, and said they were going to make beignets. First, she started coffee and then began to make square fried doughnuts. As the efficient cook took them from the simmering oil, she hurriedly placed them on a cloth for Brianne to sprinkle with powdered sugar.

The mistress and servant worked amicably side by side and Brianne joked, "I'll have to wait to pass judgment on the tomatoes, Lizzie, but these must surely have started in heaven too."

As she reached to push back a strand of hair that was quickly escaping the pins Rena had used, she noticed Ryan smiling at them from the door leading into the dining room. Embarrassed to be caught looking messy, but mostly because of last night, Brianne looked down at

205

her work and gave it her utmost attention.

Ryan looked at the scene before him. With a white dusting of sugar over her face and into her hair, the new mistress looked more like a serving girl. He had searched the house for her and was at the point of thinking she had fled after last night when he met Mattie, and the housekeeper had directed him into Lizzie's kitchen. He had stood for a few moments watching the two of them working and laughing together and noticed that Brianne looked relaxed for the first time, and was obviously enjoying herself.

Realizing he had never heard her laugh before, and liking the sound of it, he came further into the kitchen and asked, "Couldn't wait for breakfast for these, eh, Lizzie?"

His cook smiled up at him. "Miz Brianne been here all afternoon learnin' and helpin'. Thought she deserved somethin' special. But don't you worry, I'll make 'em again in the mornin' if you want."

"Why don't I join you and have them now?" he addressed them both, as he came to the table where his wife was furiously sprinkling the sugar.

"Don't think I've forgotten your own weakness for beignets, Lizzie. If I pour the coffee, will you sit with us and take a break before dinner?"

"Yes, please, Lizzie. Come join us," Brianne chimed in. Although she thought it odd that a master would serve a slave, she saw that Lizzie wasn't in the least surprised.

Not wanting to be alone with Ryan, Brianne hoped that having Lizzie with them would divert his attention away from her.

The cook disappointed her, though, saying, "No, thank you both. I've got my dinner to see to, but you two enjoy it. I've got to find Mary. Sent her over two hours ago to find mushrooms, and that chile ain't back yet. If I know her, she's off in them woods dreamin' about that young buck Roscoe."

Brianne's hopes fell as she watched Lizzie walk out of the kitchen door, leaving the two of them alone. She kept her head lowered as she finished the last of the doughnuts.

Why doesn't he say anything? she thought. She certainly had given him enough ammunition against her last night. He seemed happy, though, since he'd come into the kitchen, and was actually pleasant while Lizzie was in the room. Of course, that was part of the agreement. To show, in front of others, that they were happily married.

She removed the sugar and the powder-laden cloth and brought everything over to the counter to be washed, leaving only the plate of doughnuts in front of her husband. Hesitantly Brianne brought a washcloth to the table to clean up the powdered sugar that she had spilled.

Ryan had already poured two cups of coffee and was sitting back in his chair watching her. As she wiped the space in front of him, he grabbed for her wrist. "You don't have to be frightened of me, Brianne. I have no intention of forcing anything on you, at least not immediately. So you can relax around me and stop thinking I'm going to attack you at any moment."

He released her hand and asked almost gently, "Did you have a pleasant day? Mattie said she was going to introduce you to those workers not out in the field. Did she?"

Nervously Brianne finished cleaning the table and returned to the sink, all the while wondering what his plan was. He was being civil, and actually sounded interested in her day. She herself wanted to end the hostilities between them, and if he was making an effort, whatever the reasons, then she too would try.

"Actually, it was quite interesting," she began in a pleasant voice. "I met a number of people, though I'm afraid I'll never remember all their names. And this afternoon I asked Lizzie if I could help her here in the kitchen."

Sitting down opposite him, she sipped the strong coffee.

"I'm sure she liked that. Lizzie isn't the tyrant everyone makes her out to be."

Brianne agreed. "From the way people talked about her and her abilities, I was almost afraid of her, but she's really very sweet and didn't seem to mind the intrusion. I'd like to spend some time with her whenever possible."

"I don't see why she would mind. This is your home, you're the mistress here, Brianne."

Brianne shook her head and a few more copper curls fell onto her neck. "There's so much I don't know about the running of a house this large, I just thought the kitchen was the best place to start. You see, I'd taken so much for granted before, never bothering to find out how things worked or how to repair them when they didn't. So now that I have the opportunity, I'd like to correct that."

Unsure of his reaction, she said, "Tomorrow, if you don't mind, I'd like to see the plantation—the fields, the workers' homes, as much as I'm able. Would you mind?"

Ryan knew she was struggling to keep up this conversation, and he could guess her reasons. How much of last night she remembered, he couldn't know. But he was certain she recalled enough to be embarrassed. Now was not the time to tell her he was sorry he had forced her to relive unpleasant memories.

In keeping with the mood she set, he said, "I'm pleased that you're interested in your new home, Brianne. Tomorrow morning, before the sun becomes too hot, I'd be happy to accompany you on a tour of Briarfawn. Right now, though, I think we'd better leave Lizzie's kitchen to her. I'm sure she's found the wandering Mary and is just waiting for us to clear out."

Grateful for an excuse to get away, Brianne nodded and started to leave the kitchen, only to have Ryan hold the door open and motion for her to go first. As he followed her up the stairs and into the bedroom, she wondered at his change of mood. Where was the sarcastic, domineering man of yesterday? Perhaps after what she had told him last night, he no longer cared to make her his wife in the true sense of the word. Maybe his sensibilities had been offended, and if that were the case, then she had something to be grateful for after all.

But somewhere, in the back of her subconscious, there was a nagging little annoyance that he should give up so easily.

Dinner that night was surprisingly pleasant. The food was delicious and the conversation amusing. Ryan purposefully steered away from anything controversial, either personal or concerning the outside world. Instead, he related stories about his childhood and told her a great deal about his brother Gavin.

It seemed her new brother-in-law was touring Europe before deciding on his course in life. From what Ryan told her about him, Gavin did not seem like the sort of person to settle down to the plantation life. A free spirit, Ryan called him. Always in trouble at school for mischievous pranks or wandering away for days following a pretty skirt, only to turn up later with no excuse, just a smile on his face.

It was obvious that Ryan thought the world of his younger brother, saying that he had a heart of gold, only lacked direction in life, and that once he found that, he would become a fine man.

Brianne wondered if he had allowed himself the same time to be carefree. Somehow she doubted it. He seemed driven with his own life plan, starting with this

209

plantation, which consumed so much of his time and interest, to marriage and the family that was so important to him. If only she knew him better, she would have liked to ask what the catalyst was that had started him on this course.

He knew what he wanted in life, and even though she wasn't in the design, he had married her instead of the woman from Virginia.

Ryan Barrington wasn't about to let her upset his plans. He had stated he wanted a family, and she had no doubt he was going to fulfill his wishes . . . sooner or later.

As they left the table and went into the drawing room for coffee, Brianne was acutely aware of his hand on her back. His entire presence bothered her. While they were eating, they had something to be occupied with besides themselves. Now it was just the two of them, alone.

Taking a seat in front of the fireplace, which had been lit to take away the dampness of the light rain, she looked at him as he withdrew a cigar from a leather humidor. Asking her permission to smoke, he murmured a small thank-you when she nodded her head, and once again she was reminded of just how handsome he was. Light gray pants clung to powerful thighs and were tucked into high black riding boots. A large, complicated black tie offset the snowy white shirt, over which he wore a sable-colored coat, tailored to fit his wide shoulders and narrow waist. All of it contrasted sharply with the tanned face and the dark brown hair shot through with gold.

Ryan made a very handsome picture, and unwittingly Brianne's mind strayed to the night he had come to her bed. Before she had known who he was, and that she was not dreaming, she had wanted him as she had never wanted anyone before. His hands and body had done things to her that had evoked a response she hadn't thought was possible.

Becoming extremely uncomfortable while watching him, Brianne turned back to the fire and wished for the "good old days" of television or radio, a book—something that would be a diversion from the way her thoughts were turning.

She couldn't find anything to fault him on, though; his behavior toward her was impeccable. In fact, she felt he was going out of his way to please her tonight. Her instincts told her he was up to something. This could just be another way of softening her up for his plans tonight. So far, he hadn't succeeded in any of his attempts. Last night he had tried being forceful and getting her drunk. All he had gotten in return was a distasteful story and a wife who passed out on him. Tonight he might be trying a different approach.

Ryan interrupted her contemplation. "Did I tell you, Brianne, that you look lovely tonight? That shade brings out the color in your cheeks."

He's up to something, all right, she thought! She had purposefully picked out the deep rose gown for exactly the reason he mentioned. She didn't want Ryan to think she had suffered any ill effects from last night's overindulgence. And for the same reason she had had Rena pull back her hair with a matching ribbon, to fall in wild curls down her back. She wanted to appear the picture of health.

Deciding not to fall into his manipulating scheme, she changed the subject. "Thank you, Ryan, but I think my color might also come from sitting in front of the fire. You know, as you were talking about Gavin, I wondered if you too had made a Grand Tour of Europe. It must be wonderful to take a year or two off from life and explore the world."

Ryan sat down opposite her with his coffee and cigar. "No, I didn't have a Grand Tour, at least not what you're thinking. I did see Europe, though. Not quite the way

211

Gavin is seeing it, but I did manage."

He smiled, saying, "You see, I started at the docks very young and after a few years was able to sign aboard a clipper trading in Europe. I didn't stay in the best places or meet the best people, but I did see the continent and I learned a great deal about life in those years."

"I can't picture you as a sailor. Why did you work at the docks when you were young? I just took for granted that this was the lifestyle you grew up in. Or did you have an adventurous nature, like your brother?" She asked the questions shyly, knowing she was becoming personal.

He took a deep breath and looked into the fire with a painful expression. "It wasn't from adventure but necessity that I took to the seas. By the time I was thirteen, both my parents had died. I had Gavin, and no relatives came running to rescue us, so I grew up very fast. The only way open to me was the docks."

She looked at his profile, highlighted by the fire, and saw with surprise that he looked tormented by his own memories. For some undefined reason, she wanted to comfort him.

"I'm sorry about your parents, Ryan. I didn't know. I too have lost. My father died when I was a teenager and my mother passed away last year, so I have some idea of what you went through."

Still watching the dancing flames, he barely nodded, and Brianne also studied them for a moment before continuing, "After my father died so suddenly, I remember being angry for a long time—at him for leaving us, and at God for taking him while he was still so young."

She smiled at her own memories. "You know, there were times when I would wake up in the mornings and see the sun shining through my bedroom window and think, thank God I woke from that nightmare! It was all a bad dream, and he's alive. For those few moments, before reality set in, I was allowed to be happy and life once more seemed carefree. Then I would remember, and the aching would begin again and stay with me."

Ryan looked at her, and they connected on a different level, as wounded children. "I know . . . until those times became fewer and fewer, and then they just disappeared altogether."

Surprised by his answer, Brianne quickly agreed. "That's right! There were times I would expect him to come home at dinnertime and I would begin to set the table to include him, only to catch myself, and then I just wanted to cry from the unfairness. But we didn't do that in our house—cry. My mom was so strong, and fought desperately to set our lives to order again. She held up for us children, and we in turn didn't want to add to her problems, so we tried never to let her see us cry. Looking back, I don't know if it was the right thing to do. Everyone was being strong for everyone else, afraid if they let their true anguish show, somehow the other's fortress of strength might crumble along with them."

Feeling embarrassed, Brianne stopped speaking. She looked up from her hands, which were clenched tightly together on her lap and met his eyes. Something special passed between them at that moment. She recognized from those eyes, which held hers like a magnet, that he understood what she had said, and that he too had been there himself. She also knew that they had taken their first step toward becoming friends instead of antagonists bent on bettering the other.

She broke the gaze that seemed to sear into her very soul and looked back to the fire before her.

What's happening to me? she thought anxiously. Her stomach and thighs felt tingly and her breasts started to ache as her heart beat wildly behind them.

From the corner of her eye she saw Ryan get up, and she silently cursed herself for losing the moment of companionship.

Soon a dainty cup and saucer appeared before her as Ryan said kindly, "You never had your coffee."

Taking it from him, she smiled her thanks and watched as he reseated himself beside her. For a short time neither of them spoke. They both sat and watched the flames lick the charred wood, each with their own thoughts about what had just transpired between them.

As though the break in their conversation had never occurred, Ryan suddenly spoke. "My mother wasn't as strong as yours. If yours tried not to cry, mine never stopped, not for a long time. I can remember listening to her sobbing late into the night and praying to God to make her stop. The very sound of it tore at my heart, and I was beyond frustration because there was nothing I could do to comfort her. Over and over she would say my father's name, and nothing I did or said would stop the crying."

He breathed deeply. "When she finally did stop, more than just the tears dried up—it seemed all emotion was drained from her. She would just sit and stare off into space, waiting . . ."

And so Ryan finally emptied his heart of all the bitter helplessness that had defeated him as a child. He talked for over an hour, telling her more about his younger life than he had ever told another person.

When he stood up to put another log onto the fire, Brianne wanted to rise with him and put her arms around him. He needed someone, or something, tonight.

What a tragic life he had led. And she had felt sorry for herself? The man had met his problems head on, even as a child, and Brianne now could better understand Catherine's admiration for him. She too had to admire his courage. Never once, throughout the telling of his story, had he asked for sympathy. It was more as if he were trying to create a common bond between them. She

214

marveled that in the past two nights he had learned more about her personal life than any of her friends. She had confided, drunk and sober, things that were buried deep inside her.

Suddenly she mentally shook herself. What was she thinking? This was not someone that she loved or wanted to build a life with. This was just temporary—a means of staying off the streets, as he put it last night.

He is handsome, Brianne thought wistfully. Dear God, he pulls at some undefinable strings deep within me, and he can be kind and giving of himself, but he's not for me. I belong a hundred years into the future to some unknown man who wears three-piece suits instead of riding britches and boots, and drives a car home each night, not a huge four-legged animal. And truthfully, he belonged to someone before I ever met him—the woman in Virginia, Stephan's cousin.

Foolishly, the last reason bothered her more than the others, and Brianne stood abruptly, placing the empty cup on the silver tray.

Smoothing the material of her gown, she smiled brightly and said, "Well, if I'm to see Briarfawn early tomorrow I think I should say goodnight. I enjoyed talking with you, Ryan. Thank you for this evening."

He looked puzzled, but quickly recovered, and Brianne regretted her abruptness when she saw the insolent grin come back onto his face.

"By all means, Madam. I myself am going to have a brandy. Are you sure you won't join me?"

Grinning as he watched her gulp and shake her head, he continued, "Ah yes, I'm sorry I brought up the subject of alcohol. You run along, I'll follow you up shortly."

"Follow me up?"

"Yes. Follow you up, meaning I'll join you when I've finished my drink." He turned away from her and went to

215

the decanter of liquor, and she used the opportunity to quickly slip away from him.

Grasping the hem of her wide skirt with both hands, she hurried up the stairs to her bedroom. There, sitting up asleep in one of the chairs, was Rena waiting for her.

"Rena, please wake up!" Touching the girl's shoulder, Brianne whispered frantically. "I'm not sure whether Ryan is coming up to this room, but I want to be in bed and asleep if he does!"

Rena's face showed her confusion as she tried to make sense out of her friend's ranting. "Of course he's coming into this bedroom. It's his too, you know. Remember what he said about keeping up appearances?"

Standing up, she said, "Now turn around and I'll unhook you."

Brianne picked out her most modest nightgown and pulled it over her shoulders herself.

Literally jumping under the covers, she hurried Rena. "Just leave those things until tomorrow morning. You can put them away then. Turn down the lamp and leave quickly before he comes up!"

"Brianne, what's wrong with you? You're acting silly!"

"Nothing is wrong with me! I would just like to go to sleep. Please, Rena, just go."

Shaking her head, Rena draped the gown over the back of the sofa and left the room muttering something about how it was time for some people to grow up and make the best out of what life dished out to them.

When the door was finally shut and the room quiet, Brianne tried different positions in the bed, trying to look as if she were asleep. Turning her back to the door, she decided, would only make him suspect she was faking, so she lay on her side facing it, believing it would look more natural.

Brianne hadn't felt the need to do this since she was a child, but if she'd been able to fool her mother on

216

countless occasions, then she should be able to pull it off once more and appear sound asleep if Ryan came into her room. It was a childish action, and maybe Rena was right about growing up—but not tonight.

Soon she became exceedingly uncomfortable from watching her breathing and holding the same position. When was he coming? It must be over half an hour by now, but she was afraid to move in case the door opened and he caught her awake.

Deciding to risk a deep breath, she inhaled deeply and just then heard footsteps outside the door. They hesitated briefly, and Brianne's breath left her body in a quick rush as she listened to the door opening.

Snapping her eyes shut and keeping her breathing even, she soon sensed him come over to the bed and stand beside it. Her heart pounded furiously against her chest and she thought that if anything, it would be that which would give her away.

After a few prolonged moments, Brianne heard him leave her and move about the room. Daring to open the eye nearest the mattress, she saw him standing by the lamp.

Dear God! He was beginning to undress!

She closed her one eye tightly and concentrated on her breathing. What if he meant to take her tonight? she thought in a panic. Even though he had said he wasn't going to force her, he *was* removing his clothes and coming into *this* bed!

First she heard one loud thud of his boot coming off and hitting the floor, and then another.

Boldly, she peeked again and cursed herself for doing so when she saw him unbuttoning his shirt. As he pulled his arms out of it she saw, by the faint glow of the lamp, the curling hair on his broad chest. There wasn't a great deal of it, but what there was trailed down to a V below his belt.

She had never watched a man undress before. But

when Ryan reached down to unbutton his pants, Brianne knew that she could not close her eyes to him.

She was mesmerized by the very sight of the man. He turned his back to her as he placed the trousers and drawers over a nearby chair, and Brianne swallowed a gasp as she marveled at the perfect symmetry of his body.

He really *was* beautiful! She had never thought of a nude man as exquisite, but he was magnificent, reminding her of statues of Greek athletes . . . and that same feeling of electricity passed through her as it had downstairs.

She wanted him, and cursed her own desire. No matter that she would inevitably be disappointed in the end, she still wanted to feel those arms around her, yearned for his hard body next to her own, wanted so much at this moment to experience those feelings he had evoked once before.

She felt foolish at becoming so totally aroused by the sight of him, but deep within her heart she knew that if he made a move toward her in bed, she would pretend to awaken—and let him.

As he extinguished the light, Brianne closed her eyes and tried to resume her normal breathing, although it was difficult after what she had just witnessed.

Ryan came into bed quietly, as though not to rouse her, and turned on his side away from her.

She waited for him to make a move and . . . nothing! He just lay there!

Her entire body felt as if it were burning up and she was contemplating moving closer to him when suddenly she heard him say in almost a parental voice, "Goodnight, Brianne!"

She felt as though someone had thrown cold water on her as she opened her eyes and stared at his back.

He knew! He undressed right in front of her, and all the time he knew . . . !

Chapter 15

The urge to do him bodily harm was overwhelming. He had humiliated her by revealing his knowledge that she was awake, and she wanted to punch that superior back that faced her! She lay still for a long time, staring through the darkness at him, trying to bring her rage under control. But when she finally did, something far worse entered her mind.

As she changed positions, she could see him once again. From a memory that was burned into her brain, she recalled the way the dim lighting had only accentuated his firm muscles and made him seem more than he really was. In the harsh reality of daylight, she knew he would look just like one more average man— with strong, broad shoulders, small waist and trim hips.

Damn! She tossed and turned again.

All right! So he was better than average, and his face almost classical, but his hair! Now that was something else—it would never stay combed, always falling onto his forehead. Many times since they had met she had resisted the urge to brush it back into place.

Dear God, she thought. Listen to me!

He knew just what he was doing, undressing in front of her like that, and she didn't know who to be more angry with—herself, for reacting to the sight of him like a sex-starved old maid, or him, for flaunting himself and then ignoring her. Deciding on him, she again wanted to curl up her fist and punch his better-than-average back, disturbing his sleep the way he had destroyed all hope of her finding slumber that night.

No more than ten minutes could have passed, and after countless times she tossed again. As she expelled her breath in frustration, Ryan turned and his arm shot out across the bed, encircling her waist. He pulled her over to him so that her back was against his chest, and spoke impatiently above her head.

"Look, we both have to get up early tomorrow and neither one of us will be able to get a decent night's rest with you tossing and turning. So just lie still and go to sleep."

As she instinctively stiffened against him, he said firmly, "Now good night!"

After the initial shock wore off, she found that lying like that, with his arm around her, was indeed very comforting and she eventually relaxed. Surprisingly, her eyelids began to close and her last thoughts, before sleep finally claimed her, were how nice and secure she felt lying next to him, and that it really didn't matter whose idea it was or how she got there . . . it just felt right.

She was faintly aware of a light, citrusy fragrance as someone brushed her hair back from her cheek.

"Time to get up, sleeping beauty."

"Umm . . ." She heard the whispered words, but refused to open her eyes and break the spell. Instead, she burrowed deeper into the pillow.

Moments later, an annoyed groan escaped her lips while she tightly clenched her eyelids together against the sudden glare of sunlight.

She distinctly heard Ryan's voice announce, "If you still intend to tour Briarfawn this morning, I suggest you start moving. I've already rung for Rena, so I'll meet you downstairs for breakfast in half an hour."

Pushing the hair away from her face, Brianne sat up, propped against the pillows. She saw Ryan standing at the foot of the bed, fully dressed, grinning and looking chipper, as though he'd been up for hours. Having never been a morning person, she found it irritating that others were so cheerful and gung-ho when all she wanted was to turn over and go back to sleep.

"What time is it?" she pouted.

Walking away, he hesitated, then turned and smiled. "Why, it must be six-thirty by now. Don't look so shocked. Plantation life starts early, so it's important to get a good night's rest."

He did it again! And her eyes narrowed as she picked up the pillow, ready to throw it at him.

"I'll remember that. Perhaps I *should* have had that brandy last night, then I too would have slept easily."

Ryan winked at her. "Not a bad idea—if you think you could've handled it."

That did it! She flung the pillow, which he easily deflected with his arm, and shouted at him to get out.

It only added to her annoyance to hear him still laughing in the hallway.

As she waited until Rena came and forced her out of the bed, Brianne renewed the anger she had felt. How like him not to do the gentlemanly thing and make no references to last night. Instead, he had to wake her with inferred insults, knowing she would feel like a fool.

It dawned on her suddenly that he actually enjoyed baiting her, knowing that like the mindless fish she would come back time after time to swallow the lure.

Jumping out of bed, she decided not to give him the opportunity again. She would be on time if it killed her.

She would show the high-and-mighty Ryan Barrington that two could play this game.

Ryan sat down at the dining room table to his first cup of coffee. Good God, he needed it. What a night!

When he had come into their bedroom the previous evening, the thought occurred to him to take Brianne then and there, and to hell with his plans for patience. He would have thought better of her if she had just stated her refusal rather than obviously faking sleep. But halfway through undressing he heard her expelled breath, and knowing she was watching him, he changed his mind. He would stick to his original plan and slowly bring her around.

The evidence of her discomfort was all the tossing and turning and numerous sighs. When he had had enough, he had brought her over to him and pinned her down, speaking impatiently with her.

He wasn't as upset with her as with himself, for this damned self-imposed celibacy. He knew he could have had her if he had gone along with her charade, instead of showing he knew she was awake. But he wanted to teach her something about honesty in a relationship between a man and woman. He also knew that it was too soon for them, and she would have regretted it this morning. When it did happen, he wanted no regrets, then or later.

If she was upset this morning because of what had happened, or hadn't, then he too had been punished for his part in it. It had been nothing less than pure agony holding her close to him throughout the night. Even when she had finally slept and he brought his hand up from her waist, she had moved in her sleep against him and it had taken all his willpower not to go further. Several times during the night she had snuggled closer to him for warmth, and he was surprised she didn't waken when evidence of his arousal pushed against her in return.

God, what a night! And the effort it took when he woke her to look refreshed, as though he'd had a peaceful night's sleep, was almost too much. He had wanted nothing more, after one look at her, than to slide back into bed, make love, and get some much needed sleep. Instead they'd traded insults until she had shown just how angry she was and thrown the pillow at him. From the look in her eyes he was lucky she was still abed, or something more substantial would have been aimed in his direction.

Not really looking forward to chauffeuring an angry wife about all morning, he sighed and stood to pour himself another cup of coffee.

As he was doing so, Brianne came hurriedly into the room. She practically slid to a stop at the sight of him and composed herself before giving him a dazzling smile.

"I hope I haven't kept you waiting," she said as she walked sedately over to the table.

Ryan hurried to pull her chair out for her. "Not at all. In fact, I was about to pour myself another cup of coffee. May I get you one?"

When she nodded, he returned to the sideboard and poured the stimulant for them both. They would need it, he thought, just to keep up with each other. Before returning to the table, he paused to look at her.

She was certainly full of surprises. One minute pouting because she had to rise early, then almost the next moment acting nearly eager to begin the day. He didn't understand her or what she was up to, but his instincts told him she had some plan. And he mentally made a note to watch her more closely today to see if he could figure it out.

Looking at her profile, he supposed all women were complex, beautiful or not, and his new wife was no

223

exception. As he walked over to her he fought the surging desire to kiss the nape of her neck that was exposed so enticingly to him. She had pulled her hair up into a bun on top of her head, and away from the high collar of the white lacy blouse she wore. He was happy to see that under the hem of her deep green skirt were the tips of boots.

She must have had them made in New Orleans, and he was grateful that Catherine had thought of them. Nothing annoyed him more than a woman attempting to get around outside in those little slippers they insisted on wearing.

"Here's your coffee, Brianne," he said, placing the fine porcelain china in front of her. "Now, would you please ring for breakfast so we can begin our little excursion, and hopefully be back before noon?"

He didn't know if it was what he said, or how he said it, but he could see her making a visible effort to control her temper. Puzzled, Ryan watched as she proceeded to ring the fragile crystal bell as though she were the town cryer, not stopping until a startled Lizzie peeked around the door.

With the cook's appearance, Brianne calmly replaced the bell on the white damask tablecloth and turned to face the older woman.

"Lizzie dear. I'm sorry for ringing so loud and long, but your master wishes his breakfast now, so he can then hurry and indulge me by showing me my new home."

Lizzie looked at her new mistress and then at Ryan, who caught the corner of his lower lip between his teeth and was studying the ceiling with a strained patience.

No how was she going to meddle in whatever was going on between them folks. Nodding her head, she quickly returned to the kitchen to hurry the three young girls who were training with her.

Brianne finally took her eyes from the closed door and

smiling sweetly at Ryan, took the matching snowy napkin from the table and placed it on her lap.

So much for marital bliss! she thought heatedly.

Later, as they made their way into the fields, Brianne thought back to the incident at breakfast and wondered what had made her react to his every remark. Ryan had the uncanny ability to pull the right strings, provoking her to lose her composure even when she was making a conscious effort not to do so.

From the corner of her eye, she looked at the profile of the man seated next to her. *What was it about him?*

Hoping to present a picture of self-assurance, Brianne lifted her head to the horizon and proceeded to ask questions concerning the growing of sugar cane, the seasons for its maturity, and most important to her, the hours the slaves spent in the fields.

Despite last night's embarrassment and this morning's insults, she found herself warming to Ryan as he described his home and the land that made up Briarfawn.

His land. To make a point, he stopped the small carriage and assisted her out. As she stood watching, he bent and scooped up a handful of dirt.

Staring at it for a few seconds, he let it sift slowly through his fingers, saying earnestly, "This is where our future lies, Brianne, in the land. I know it. They know it," he pointed to the black people beginning to start their day's work. "Someday you'll know it too."

He looked out at the rows of young plants. "So aptly named Mother Earth, she is like a woman. She can take a lot, but once abused she rebels, and only gentle coaxing will bring her back. Cultivate her, groom her, lavish care upon her, and she'll again open to you, giving back more than she received."

He brushed his hands together abruptly and turned back to the carriage. "Come. We're close enough to the eastern boundary so that I can show you where Briarfawn begins, and the road that leads to Mosshaven, Stephan's home."

He handed a very quiet Brianne up into the carriage and as they drove off in silence, she looked around her. Seeing it through Ryan's eyes, it did seem to be alive, and she thought back to his words.

From the look on his face and the sound of his voice, it was as though he were talking about a real woman. Stephan's cousin from Virginia didn't know how fortunate she was in not marrying him. For here was Ryan Barrington's one true love—his land.

Unexplicably depressed by that thought, Brianne still made an effort to remember everything Ryan had told her as they made their way back from the road. He promised to take her through the slave quarters before completing the tour, and that was what most interested her.

As they came upon them Ryan turned to her, explaining, "Every family has their own cabin. Single women without families have a cabin, and so do single men; never more than four in one cabin. All children born on Briarfawn are automatically free when their parents buy their own papers.

"I know you have strong views on slavery, Brianne, but I'd appreciate it if you would keep them to yourself until we can discuss them in private. I'm sure you'll see that everyone is treated well here, and any opinions or ideas you have for improvement I'd be happy to hear about when we return to the house. Agreed?"

Brianne nodded and eagerly took his hand as a group of children started to gather around them. She watched in amazement as Ryan greeted each by name. It must be a gift, she thought. The ability to retain names had always eluded her, but Ryan had no such problem as he lifted a tiny girl off the wheel of the wagon.

"Isabel, where are your manners?" he asked in mock severity. "Here I've brought this pretty lady to meet you and all you can think about is if there's a surprise hidden in the carriage."

The child turned large, innocent brown eyes up to Ryan and said saucily, "Oh, we knows who she is. That's Miz Brianne. My momma says she's as pretty as the summer flowers, so's I know she's your brand-new wife. And Misser Barrington, you always bring us a treat, and it's always hidden in the wagon."

"You and your momma are both right," Ryan laughed as he put the young girl back on the ground next to the other children.

There must have been around thirty of them, and three older black women, who Brianne assumed watched over the young ones.

Ryan introduced her to the children first, then confirmed her assumption, saying the turbanned women stayed with the children while their parents worked elsewhere. They were shy and averted their eyes, but the children were like children anywhere, anytime. Happy, curious about her, and very excited at the prospect of receiving a surprise.

After they were introduced they made proper little bows, which Brianne returned to each of them. They giggled at a grown-up acting like one of them, and Brianne asked Ryan if she might distribute whatever he had brought.

Ryan himself was smiling along with the children and gladly agreed with her, saying aloud, "Now, I wonder if Lizzie put that package into the carriage, or if she forgot? I don't recall seeing anything, do you, Miss Brianne?"

She played right along as she masked her face with concern. "Now that you mention it, I don't remember a package."

However, as their little faces fell she announced, "But I'll search every inch, to be sure we didn't miss it!"

She hurriedly walked toward the carriage, with the children following in her wake like baby ducks. After making a feeble attempt at examining the wagon, she held up the cloth-covered package like booty, and the children accurately responded with loud, whooping cheers. Even the older women lost their shyness and clapped their hands.

Laughing, Brianne returned to their midst and untied the cloth to reveal candies of some sort. Young James, tallest of the children, proclaimed them to be pralines, and they cheered once again.

After handing one to each child and each of the three women, she offered one to Ryan, who accepted and asked if she had ever tasted them.

Shaking her head, she bit into the sweet confection and was surprised as it literally melted in her mouth. It was very sweet, and all that remained to be chewed were the soft pecans.

She looked at Ryan with appreciation. "Another recipe I'll have to get Lizzie to share. This is delicious!"

The couple reluctantly returned to the carriage and waved goodbye to the children as they continued down the dirt road that led to the rest of the cabins. Instinctively Brianne put her hand on Ryan's arm as he directed the horse.

"Thank you for that," she said lightly. "It was fun. I had almost forgotten how being around children could brighten my day."

Ryan looked sideways at her and pronounced, "They liked you too. It would appear that you've captured just about everyone's heart here at Briarfawn."

Her own heart reacted strangely to his words and she tore her eyes away from him, stammering, "These . . .

these are their homes, aren't they? Would you mind if I looked around?"

Nodding his head once, he pulled the horse to a stop and helped her to the ground. Ryan stayed behind her as she walked through the rows of whitewashed cabins. Each had its own vegetable garden and some had porches, with rockers and chairs waiting to be used after a hard day in the fields. It wasn't as bad as she had expected, but it certainly wasn't as good as she wanted it to be.

Walking up the steps of a random cabin, she knocked on its wooden door. Receiving no answer, she hesitantly opened it and walked into a square room that filled the small house. Two beds covered with muslin lined the walls, and a table and four crude chairs sat in front of the fireplace, taking up the remaining space. It was clean, but nevertheless depressing.

Shaking her head, she left to join Ryan, who waited for her outside. When he asked if she wanted to explore further, Brianne shook her head, indicating that she'd seen enough, and they returned in silence to that glorious house at the end of the road.

It was all too much. Far too much grandeur beside such abject poverty. She felt guilty for the clothing she wore, realizing that the cost of one of her gowns would have bought decent clothes for all the laughing children she had just met.

From riding high on her jubilant acceptance by the young ones, she plummeted into depression from the inequality and her own guilt.

Later, as Ryan sat across from her, he noticed that she was once again toying with her food. He swore that since he had met her he'd never seen the woman eat a decent meal.

The look on her face was troubled, and he immediately

compared it to her earlier cheerful one. Whatever she had seen inside the cabin had changed her mood, making her pensive. They were to have tea in his study and there, in the privacy of closed doors, she would tell him what had happened—of that he had no doubt.

She clearly had no intention of eating, and since he was becoming increasingly aggravated with her changing mood, he too lost his appetite.

Throwing his napkin onto the table, he rose from his chair and walked to her side. "Since neither one of us is hungry, let's conclude this meal and go into the library."

It was more of a command than a suggestion, but Brianne nodded and allowed him to pull back her chair before she preceded him from the room.

He indicated that she should sit in one of the wing chairs, and walking behind his desk, he sat down. When she looked up to him he raised a finger, suggesting that she wait before any discussion. His reason walked through the door seconds later—Mary, carrying a silver tea service, entered the room.

Placing it on a high butler's table, she looked at Ryan expectantly.

"Thank you, Mary," he said, standing up. "That will be all."

The young girl executed a decent curtsey before closing the door behind her as she proudly left. Smiling after her, Ryan said, "She did that for your benefit, you know. I suppose she thought it would impress you."

When Brianne didn't respond, his voice lost its warmth as he asked, "Would you care for tea? I'm going to fortify myself for the coming discussion with a brandy."

He walked to the nearby cabinet and proceeded to do just that.

"Do you always drink when you know something unpleasant is about to happen?"

He startled her by slamming the crystal glass back onto the cabinet. "No! I don't *always* do that! I happen to hate tea, but from your attitude at lunch, I assume that this will be unpleasant. What the hell happened to you in that cabin? You were fine up until that point. In fact, I had the impression you were enjoying yourself. What did you see that changed you?"

Brianne gripped the arms of her chair and leaned forward, saying quietly, "It isn't so much what I saw, but how I felt. Look at us! Sitting here in this beautiful house—I'll grant you that, Ryan, it is exquisite—we're wearing elegant clothes and drinking from crystal and silver, while the people who made it all possible are sweating out in your fields, breaking their backs on your land . . . only to return to a shack and begin the same thing the next day. Ryan, don't you ever feel guilty? Doesn't your conscience ever bother you by the drastic unfairness of it all?"

He stood listening to her in silence, the only sign of his anger the muscle in his cheek moving as he ground his teeth together. Coming to stand in front of her, he swallowed the remainder of his drink and sighed, as though trying to control himself.

"I want to be patient with you," he said in a clipped voice, "but you're making it very difficult.

"You've come down here from the North with preconceived notions about *all* plantations and their owners. I too have read Mrs. Stowe's book. Do I act like Simon Legree? Is Isabel your version of Little Eva? Who are *you* to come here making judgments about my way of life, after reading some book or listening to political talk? You don't know a damn thing about those people, or what I've tried to do for them!"

With a frightening loss of self-control, he took the glass and slammed it against the heavy oak cabinet. Standing with his back to her, he stared at the shards of glass littering the carpet.

Suddenly he turned around and angrily pointed a finger at her. "That cabin—and I resent you calling it a *shack*, obviously you've never seen one—that cabin belongs to two unmarried men. They rarely eat there, preferring to take their meals with some of the others. They visit with the others and socialize with other families. But even if that were where they spent all their time, I would still be proud of it. They, and all the people here, take care of those cabins—those are their homes."

He regarded her for a few tense moments before continuing, "I will tell you this one time, and then never again, because I have no need to justify myself to anyone. The negroes here are well cared for. And do you know who does that? They care for themselves. I have never robbed a person, black or white, of their dignity. They are paid wages, a practice that has made me very unpopular among the other plantation owners, and from those wages comes the opportunity for freedom. No one on this plantation ever has to go hungry or poorly clothed. Because those who want to, work very hard, knowing they have a stake in the running of this place. If it goes under, then so do they. And they want it to succeed almost as much as I do. In the beginning I worked hard, sometimes sixteen hours a day, right next to them. It took me longer because my profits were shared, but we all did it for Briarfawn.

"Now I don't need to work as hard, but I still continue, because to slow down production would delay their freedom. I don't approve of slavery, and there are, unfortunately, many cases where your accusations would be justified, but not here. Not here!"

He ran a hand through his hair and uncurled his fist. "I'm doing the best I can, and it's working. Next time you're out take a look around, a really hard look, and tell me if it's not. I feel no guilt for living as I do. I've worked

232

too hard and too long, and I cannot change the law—only try to do what's best for everyone while working within it. So don't criticize me until you know what the hell you're talking about."

Brianne listened to his impassioned speech. But there was over a century of human-rights conditioning separating them, and she couldn't back down now.

"All that is irrelevant, since this way of life, as you know it, will be short-lived."

His brows came together. "What are you saying?"

She unconsciously cleared her throat, only now realizing that with her last statement she had opened the lid of Pandora's Box.

Rising, she went to the table to pour herself a cup of cooled tea.

From behind her she heard Ryan say with mounting anger, "I asked you what you meant by that!"

Forgetting the tea, she instead picked up a napkin and walked over to the broken glass. As she was about to bend, Ryan grabbed the cloth from her hands.

"Give that to me, *I* broke the glass."

As she watched him carefully pick up the tiny pieces of crystal, Brianne hoped that she had diverted his attention away from her hasty statement.

She felt her stomach tighten, though, when he said, "I asked you a question, Brianne. Why do you think my way of life will be short-lived?"

She looked at him, regretting before she uttered them the words she would have to say. "There will be a war. After it, all slaves will be free." She quickly added, "I'm sorry. But you should be prepared, and so should you prepare the blacks for what's to come."

Straightening up from the floor, Ryan waved a hand, as though dismissing her statements. "There's been talk of war for years now, and although I agree the talk of secession is alarming, I can't believe either side will go as far as war."

Now that the lid was opened, Brianne knew the rest would have to come out. "Would you please sit down with me? I want you to listen very carefully to what I have to say."

This time it was Brianne who indicated the matching wing chair for Ryan. As though indulging an insistent child, he shook his head and joined her.

Nervously, Brianne folded her hands together and took a deep breath, fully aware that the remainder of their conversation would be difficult for them both. For once it would not be she who sustained a shock to her security, but this man, to his whole future.

"I know you're confused about my background," she began hesitantly. "And I know you don't believe me when I've told you where I really belong."

Ryan expelled his breath in a rush as he interrupted her. "Please, not again! I admit you have a highly developed imagination, but why don't you write all these fascinating little stories down on paper? That way, if the time ever comes when we're bored with each other, you could pull them out and entertain us both. Think of it, Brianne! You could be another Mrs. Stowe, a woman you greatly admire."

She lost all patience. "Shut up! Harriet Beecher Stowe was born well over a hundred years before me, you idiot! I hope you can still laugh when I'm finished. As you said earlier that you would explain only once about yourself, well, I'll tell you this one time, and if you dismiss it as nonsense, you'll have only yourself to blame in the next few years."

Ryan made an effort to compose himself. "Will this take long?" he asked. "If you don't object, I really wouldn't mind having a cigar. I do so enjoy one with a good story."

"Go right ahead. I'm just going to give you a few

facts—but I might make a suggestion. Now would be a good time for you to have that drink. I think you'll find that you're going to need it."

Waiting for him to return, she ran her hand across her forehead, trying to recollect her thoughts. How do you tell someone about a holocaust? How could she not destroy him by telling him that this land he loves more than any woman will never be the same?

When he settled back in his chair with cigar in one hand and, following her suggestion, a drink in the other, she began while silently praying for guidance.

"When I was in high school, I had a history teacher who was obsessed with the War between the States. We would fill pages of notebooks with names, dates, anything he deemed pertinent. I was only an average history student, and it has been ten years, but I'll try to give you as much information as I can remember. It all starts in a place called Fort Sumter—it's outside of Charleston, I think, in South Carolina—in 1861. By that time the South had already seceded and formed the Confederate States, with Jefferson Davis as president. It was April 12, 1861," she said, surprising herself when the date suddenly sprang into her mind. She could almost see those notes in front of her, hastily written as her teacher droned on.

"The Confederacy shells Fort Sumter. The United States forces surrender and Lincoln, Abraham Lincoln, president of the United States at the time, calls out the militia and orders a blockade of Southern ports." The vision of her high school notebook vanished and she looked at Ryan, whose face reflected his shock. Sitting with his mouth open, he stared at her as though mesmerized.

Although she felt sympathy for him, Brianne nevertheless continued. "A man by the name of Robert E. Lee led the Southern army and Jefferson Davis was the president of the Confederacy until it fell."

"I know him," Ryan whispered.

"I can't remember what took place next," Brianne admitted. "But you *must* believe me when I tell you there will be a war. We studied it as the Civil War. It was terrible, Ryan, lasting for four years. Richmond was lost, Atlanta burned, New Orleans under martial law.

"It didn't end until 1865, when the South surrendered at a place called Appomattox, in Virginia, I think." Brianne noticed that Ryan had not touched his cigar or drink since she began to speak. Seeing the long ash about to fall, she reached over and took the cigar from him.

Grinding it out, she said emotionally, "So many people died. Men—and young boys. It was all fought, Ryan, because of slavery and the South's secession from the Union. The South never thought it would last that long, and they weren't prepared for a long struggle with the North. They were outmanned, and while the North had industrialized, the South was still farming. I remember reading that in a census taken before the war, only one out of ten Southerners actually owned slaves, and I didn't know why the others continued to fight."

He wasn't looking at her, and Brianne wondered if he even heard her anymore. "The loss of life was in the hundreds of thousands. The South was in financial ruin and remained like that for years. People like you, Ryan, would be no better off than those out in your fields now. Bitterness between the North and South remained for decades. There was a period of Reconstruction so corrupt that many of those who had managed to keep their homes during the war, lost them for back taxes.

"I wish I could explain it better, but it's going to happen, Ryan, and in less than five years! Nothing you or I can do will change history, but you can be prepared and help those people out there. They'll be free, and they won't be able to handle their freedom in the South. Isn't there some way we could educate them, give them a start? I could try teaching—it would be a beginning."

Ryan sat on the edge of his chair. His elbows were on his knees and he held his head with one hand, while dangling his glass between his legs with the other.

He appeared to be totally absorbed in the pattern of the carpet and Brianne asked softly, "Ryan?"

Never looking up, he said in a cracked voice, "Not now, Brianne. Just leave me for awhile."

Standing, she put a sympathetic hand on his shoulder. "I'm sorry. There's a lot I can't remember right now; maybe it will come back to me. What I have told you is the truth . . . I swear it."

"Just leave—please!"

Sadly, looking at a man whose life was crumbling from the tale she had told, Brianne closed the door to give him his privacy.

Ryan brought his head up as he heard the soft click of the door being shut. He rose slowly and walked across the room. As he stood before the window, looking out at his beloved home, he knew with a cold sense of dread that she was telling the truth, and instinctively he tightened the muscles on his face to prevent his eyes from watering.

Brianne left the house and took refuge on the wide, deserted porch. Knowing what Ryan was going through, she felt a surge of guilt. Did she have to be so blunt with him? Could she have told him in a gentler way, or had she been responding to his anger with her?

Looking out at the plantation, she had to admit he was right. It was working. There just wasn't the time needed to complete the work.

Brianne began to worry at dusk. Before dinner she had

237

asked Aaron to check on Ryan, and the servant had returned to tell her Mr. Barrington had asked her not to wait, but to proceed without him.

With real concern she stood outside his study, looking at the closed door. What was he doing in there? She brought her hand up to knock, but caught herself. Perhaps he blamed her as the bearer of ill tidings, resenting her for shattering his dreams. Deciding to let him be, she proceeded into the dining room to eat a solitary dinner.

Afterwards, she thought about asking Lizzie if she needed help cleaning up after dinner, but knew the cook would be scandalized if she did, so she thanked her and left to find Mattie.

Locating the housekeeper in the drawing room, she watched for a few seconds, as the woman examined the underleaves of a huge plant, before interrupting her. "Mattie, I have a favor to ask," she said coming into the room.

Forgetting the pesky insects she was searching for, Mattie wiped her hands on her apron and smiled. "Sure enough. What can I get for you, Miz Brianne?"

Brianne jammed her hands into the pockets of her skirt. "Mattie, Mr. Barrington has had some disturbing news this afternoon and has closeted himself in the study ever since. I know you care about him, and that's why I'm telling you this. Could you see if you can get him to at least eat dinner? He might listen to you."

In any other servant's eyes she would have been demeaning her role as wife, but she was almost sure that Mattie knew the truth about the relationship between her and Ryan. Besides, she knew Mattie would have more influence with him anyway.

"I'll do what I can, Miz Brianne, but that man sure can be stubborn sometimes. It's like my momma used to say—you gots to have more patience with the good ones 'cause theys the only kind worth it.''

She gave her mistress an understanding smile and left the room. Brianne followed Mattie but turned and headed for the staircase, not even waiting to see if the woman was successful.

Entering her own bedroom, she resumed her pacing. Her nerves were on edge from the prolonged wait for Ryan to appear, and she found that without him she was bored.

All the things she would normally have done on such an evening in Philadelphia were denied her. Forget going out—there was nowhere to go. Housecleaning was taboo. What she would have dearly loved to do was take a good book into the tub and soak leisurely, until the tension left her body. Scratch the books—they were with Ryan behind the unopened door, and it would only be selfish to ask the servants to carry the water upstairs again.

Suddenly it came to her—Rena!

Arriving at Rena's door in no time at all, Brianne knocked lightly. Softly calling her friend's name, she opened it to find the usually energetic redhead fast asleep in her chair, with the gown she was sewing abandoned on her lap.

Coming fast upon her disappointment was the realization that if she woke her, Rena would be embarrassed and insist upon waiting on her again to prove her worth. Knowing she was not to have any companionship this night, Brianne turned down the wick of Rena's lamp and left.

Sooner than she hoped she was back in her own room, and giving up the night as lost, she undressed and sat in front of her dressing table, brushing her hair.

How long was he going to stay down there? she asked herself for the hundredth time. Granted, what she had told him was shocking, but she would have thought he'd have wanted to question her in detail. He probably had continued to drink, and while she sat here worrying he had most likely passed out in the study hours ago.

Brushing her hair more vigorously, she became lost in thought and was surprised to hear the door open.

Ryan stood in its doorway looking at her, and Brianne was truly shocked by his appearance. Always so meticulous, he now looked as if he had been through the proverbial wringer.

Never taking his eyes off her, he walked into the room and dropped his jacket onto a chair. Making his way over to the bed, he finally turned away from her and sat down heavily on it.

His voice, when it came, was low and whispery, almost hoarse. "I never really believed you, you know. So many things didn't add up. I tried to dismiss the watch and your keys, but in the back of my mind—I knew you were different. I just couldn't accept it."

Slowly, as though forcing himself to do so, he turned his head and looked at her.

"How could it have happened, Brianne? How could you have come from the future?"

She stood up, automatically dropping her brush to the floor.

"You *believe* me?" she asked, stunned by his words.

Chapter 16

"How can I not? From the very first, you were shocked by your surroundings—and you knew too much, Brianne."

He ran a hand through his hair. "I've listened to your accounts of the future and marveled at your imagination—women in politics, running businesses, equal with men—how very hard my lifestyle must seem to you now. Such fantastic inventions! Self-powered carriages, giant metal birds that carry passengers above the clouds. God, that must be something!

"But it was the war that convinced me. You had the facts, Brianne, and I could see it happening as you talked." He shook his head as though still disbelieving. "The South will never let Washington dictate to it. Freeing all the slaves now would mean financial ruin. You are right, they will secede from the Union before knuckling under. God help us then," he said in a hushed voice.

Brianne came to Ryan, sitting on the bed next to him. Without thought she put her hand on his arm as a gesture of comfort and asked, "What will you do?"

He looked at her with anguished eyes. "I can't change history. I can't stop what's going to happen, but I can protect those I care for, and I can advise others to do as I will."

Smiling wryly, he added, "After you left me this afternoon I spent some time indulging in self-pity. Then I realized you hadn't mentioned that New Orleans was destroyed. That's right, isn't it?"

Brianne nodded. "As best I can remember. But I don't know about outside the city. Ryan, so many Southerners lost their homes."

"All right, going on the assumption that Briarfawn will remain intact, I've formed some plans. First, I'll draw up the necessary documents freeing all those who haven't bought their papers yet, and hold them in my safe until the time is right. Then, when this Confederacy forms, I'll offer those who wish to leave passage aboard the *Irish Lady* for Canada, away from the fighting."

Brianne was confused and held up her hand to stop him. "The *Irish Lady?* I take it that's a boat?"

"Not a boat, my dear. A ship. She's my largest. I named her for my mother."

Astounded, she asked, "How many do you own?"

Absently, as if it had no bearing on the conversation, he replied, "Four. They're all commercial vessels, but I can refit the *Lady* when it's time. That's not important, though," he exclaimed as he gathered steam.

"What is important is how we make it through this war. I can foresee a problem with money. All bills are federal notes that won't be worth the paper they're printed on in the South, so I intend to slowly convert to gold and I'll try to convince others to do likewise. Transferring certain major accounts to a foreign country now will guarantee the money to bring Briarfawn back into production later. I can't avert a war, but I can insure the continuance of my home."

His eyes changed once again, this time blazing with a ferocity that frightened her. In a deceptively soft voice he added, "My life's blood is in this land, and *nobody* is going to take it away. Not while I have a breath left in me!"

The hairs at the back of her neck rose and she knew with a terrible foreboding what he was saying.

"You can't mean you're going to fight?" she pleaded, hoping she had misunderstood his meaning.

He rose abruptly and walked to the fireplace, staring into the small flames. "You wondered what made those other nine Southerners who never owned a slave join the war? It was honor, something you can't understand unless it's inbred. Their homes were threatened, and no honorable man would not stand up and fight to protect his home. I don't approve of slavery, nor secession, but the answer is years away, and should have been gradual. However, you say in five years there will be a war. And because of my home, and the way I feel about it, I will take part in that war. I can't fight to prolong the institution of slavery, but I *will* use my ships to run the blockades you spoke of. Bringing in supplies is the only way I can honestly contribute to the South."

Aghast, Brianne stared at him. "That's madness! You *know* the South is going to lose. I've told you about the terrible loss of life both sides suffered, and now you're telling me you're going to risk yours for something you don't believe in? My God, Ryan! You could be killed! What will become of your precious home then?"

Ryan crossed the distance between them in a sure stride. When he came to the bed, he pulled Brianne up to stand in front of him. With one arm remaining around her back, he placed his other hand under her chin and slowly lifted it until their eyes met.

Holding her in his relentless gaze, he answered in a husky voice, "Then you, my beautiful wife, will continue in my place."

As his eyes continued to bore into hers, Brianne tried

to read the emotion in them, but the trembling that had started when he touched her only increased as he persisted in staring. She couldn't seem to concentrate on anything but his face and the solid force of his body as it pressed against her own quivering form.

Still holding her eyes captive, he lowered his face to kiss her. She knew she could never tear her eyes away from his and felt her heart begin to pound wildly as their lips met in a soft caress that never quite ended in a kiss.

It wasn't exactly a kiss, nor was it like anything else Brianne had ever experienced. It was more like a touching of senses. Both of their mouths were partially opened, and when Ryan moved his head, ever so slightly, his lips stroked hers. Their breaths mingled for a moment, and Brianne gasped with the sweet pleasure he aroused within her.

She almost cried out in dismay when he gently put her from him and said in a low voice, "You are my wife, and a part of Briarfawn. It's your home, and you'll preserve it, should you ever need to."

Never minding that she had no intention of being there that long, Brianne nodded stupidly. All she could think about was Ryan's mouth, and how much she wanted him to kiss her again.

So great was this unreasonable need within her that she had to concentrate when he again spoke.

"I don't think you'll have to do it alone, though. You did say your sister was married to a Charles Barrington?"

Not trusting herself to speak, she again nodded.

"Since Gavin has been here only once and expressed no great love for this climate, I seriously doubt that your brother-in-law is a descendant of his. Therefore, it stands to reason I will most likely live through this war. Hopefully, to see my great-grandchildren, one of whom, no doubt, will name a grandson Charles."

244

Her expression was incredulous. "I never thought of that!

"All this time I've been so concerned about myself that I never made the connection. Morganna once told me that the Barrington family was old, pre-Civil War, and had always lived in New Orleans."

Ryan's face erupted into a brilliant smile. "Then I must be right!"

He grabbed her to him and gave her an enormous bear hug that threatened to crush her ribs.

Thankfully for Brianne, it was brief. He held her away from him as he asked in a serious voice, "Can you cook?"

Surprised by his change of mood, she hesitantly replied, "Some—why?"

His smile nearly dazzled her. "Because, my fantastic time-traveler, I find I'm positively famished."

Taking hold of her wrist, he led her from the room. "Let's see if together we can discover any of Lizzie's treasures."

Much later, as she lay in bed, Brianne thought back on the pleasant two hours she had spent with Ryan in the kitchen.

Finding the leftovers, they had snacked on cold ham and biscuits and afterwards, drinking the orange tea Brianne had brewed, they spent well over an hour in easy conversation. Ryan's thirst for knowledge about the future seemed unquenchable, and Brianne's laughter echoed throughout the room as she watched his expressions.

They ranged from childish wonder at television to outright disbelief that America succeeded in putting a man on the moon. Once again she experienced frustration when she couldn't explain the technical reasons why

245

these things were possible. But Ryan wasn't disappointed by her failure, and continued to eagerly interrogate her.

When the conversation turned to her own incredible experience, Brianne could find no answers. Whatever had happened to her that night in the woods remained a mystery, for the only possibility was too frightening to accept.

Seeing her shudder, Ryan had suggested that they put Lizzie's kitchen back in order and retire to their bed. For a few moments when they had returned and confronted the large bed it had been awkward, and she had been grateful when Ryan excused himself and went into the dressing room. When he returned she was already in bed, and she whispered a silent prayer of thanks when she saw he intended to sleep in his underwear.

Now, as she lay with him only inches away from her, Brianne wanted to break the weighty silence that hung between them. He seemed to be waiting for her to make the first move.

Shyly she looked at him in the dark, and gathering up her courage, whispered his name.

"Ryan?"

Without looking at her, he answered under his breath with an expectant "Yes?"

Fearing rejection, she swallowed first before timidly speaking. "Ryan, I'm afraid of what's happened to me. One possibility is that whatever mistake took place will correct itself and I'll return. Or, more terrifying, there was *no* mistake, and I no longer exist in my time."

She could almost feel her cheeks burning as she asked, "Would you just hold me? I want to close my eyes knowing that for right now, I belong somewhere."

Without answering, Ryan raised his arms to encircle her and brought her head to rest on his chest. Smoothing her hair, he continued to play with it, saying, "It's best that we keep this to ourselves, without trying to question

246

the reasons it took place. It's important that we maintain a normal life and prepare quietly for the future. You're here now, and for the next few years life will be good. Try to be patient, and you'll see that. Don't fight so hard against what's happened; you can't change it, or it would have already taken place. Why not give in, Brianne, and enjoy *this* time?"

Lowering his head slightly, he gently kissed her forehead, saying, "Right now, as my wife, you're exactly where you belong," and tightened his arm about her.

Brianne breathed a sigh of contentment and snuggled closer to him, chastely kissing his bare chest with gratefulness.

"Thank you for understanding, Ryan. I can't begin to tell you what it means to know you finally believe me . . . and I'm beginning to see that by marrying you, I've also acquired a wise friend."

Ryan had to hold back from groaning aloud. The tormenting ache that had started when she came over to him, pressing her small body next to his, became an overwhelming need as she placed her head on his chest and then innocently kissed it.

Friend? It was anything but friendly thoughts that possessed him now! Battling the urge to take her completely in his arms, he concentrated on remaining absolutely still, praying she would not make any more moves to inflame his active imagination still further.

Tense with the effort, he kissed the top of her head and bade her a quick good night, hoping it would put an end to this evening. Trying to employ all his mental powers in controlling his body was a futile effort, for Ryan knew without a doubt it would be another long night. Dear God, he silently begged, let this be resolved soon—a man needs his sleep!

* * *

The next morning found Brianne waging her own battle to prolong the delicious moment of that half-dreaming state before complete alertness. She felt very sensual as she rubbed against Ryan's warm hardness, and brought her leg up to make closer intimate contact.

As the heat permeated through her lower body, she released her breath with heightened pleasure. The hardness moved slightly and she felt an overwhelming desire to clasp it tighter to her, as the churning in her legs and abdomen rose quickly to her breasts. Her nipples ached for the soft touch of a hand, even her own, and she moaned out loud in frustration.

Hearing the sound of her voice, Brianne opened her eyes and confronted reality. The source of her sexual ease was no dream, but a man's thigh!

Stiffening, she slowly brought her head up to see if the fates had been good to her and he might still be asleep.

Since luck had not been a frequent companion of late, she was more embarrassed than shocked to see Ryan's eyes open and a knowing grin on his face.

"Good morning, Brianne. Sleep well?"

Turning crimson, she answered in a muted voice, "Yes . . . thank you," as she attempted to untangle her legs from his.

His powerful thigh refused to release her one leg. She looked back up into his eyes and felt the need to fill her lungs with great gulps of calming air. The blue of his eyes had turned a deeper color, and even a novice could read the hot desire in their depths.

"Please don't thank me," he said huskily. "It was my pleasure . . . well, almost." The grin had left his face and was replaced by a more serious expression. His full lips were parted and he too seemed to be having trouble breathing. Very slowly he removed his leg and Brianne couldn't help shivering as the fine hairs on his leg grazed

248

her own smooth thigh.

Ryan admired his own restraint as he sat up. It was ludicrous, absurd. He could have taken her before she was completely awake, but he knew it wouldn't work. Her body was ready for him—but he still must battle her mind.

Laughing at himself, he threw back the cover and walked over to the washstand. Pouring water into the basin, he splashed his face and quipped, "I think, my dear wife, your body is trying to tell you something. You might try listening to it."

Sucking in her breath, Brianne was outraged. "Don't you dare say anything more!" she bristled. "I can't be held responsible when I'm sleeping, and no *gentleman* would ever make mention of something that was unconsciously done."

Drying his face, he looked over the towel at her. "But a husband would. Let's just say I'm confused with the roles I'm expected to play: gentleman in bed—husband out of it. Anyway, I was only teasing. Shall I get Rena? We can have breakfast together before I leave."

Deciding it was best to forget the entire episode, Brianne shook her head as she left the bed. "Don't bother her. I'll get dressed myself. I really don't see why I have to have help doing something I've managed to do alone, and quite well, up till now."

At his dresser, Ryan turned. "The mistress of a house this size needs all the help she can get. Remember where you are, and what we spoke of last night. It's expected."

Tying the sash on her robe, Brianne sighed. "I know, you're right. I'm just not accustomed to all this," she swept the room with her hand. "Give me time. I'll try to fit in with it. I promise, tomorrow I'll lie abed till Rena comes and pampers me like a helpless child."

Walking over, Ryan kissed her forehead. "Such an obedient wife," he said condescendingly.

Laughing while he sidestepped her half-hearted blow, he gathered up his clothes and walked to the dressing room, announcing over his shoulder, "I'll just bet Lizzie makes some remarks about strange creatures getting into her larder."

Coming to her wardrobe, Brianne giggled as she threw open the doors and once again marveled at the array of clothing available to her. Picking out a lovely blue sprigged gown, she started humming as she proceeded with her toilette.

Brianne felt young and pretty as she came down the stairs. Last night had been a turning point for her and Ryan. She had found a friend, and if she were totally honest with herself, she would also find a husband if she allowed it. Thoughts of what it would be like to be with him kept invading her mind. In another time she would have welcomed such a man into her life, but it would be foolish to involve herself deeply now when she didn't know what her future would bring.

As she stepped around the open door leading into the dining room, Ryan raised his head and smiled at her warmly.

The edges of his eyes crinkled as he looked at her in appreciation. His perfect white teeth showed in a wide smile, with no phoniness about it, making her feel he genuinely liked what he saw.

Ah well, she mused silently as he rose to seat her. She really should take his advice and enjoy it. She was, after all, living out a fantasy. Today, for the first time in a long while, she actually felt happy. Here she felt wanted, and possibly even needed.

Ryan touched her hand and she turned toward him. "You were off somewhere. I don't think you heard a word I said."

Brianne apologized for wandering. "I'm sorry. I was just thinking about my past and how much simpler life is now. What were you saying?"

He grinned at her. "Lizzie's been in and out of the room muttering about thieves. Do you think we should tell her and put her mind at ease?"

Brianne happily caught his mood and chided, "If we don't, she might start hiding everything, and that would be the end of our midnight raids."

"Although it was my idea, I think we should both tell her together," he said playfully. "She'd never yell at me with you present."

Brianne assumed a very somber face. "It's a deal. After all, the accomplice is just as guilty as the perpetrator. I promise to stand by you."

Ryan's eyes changed slightly with her last words. "What more could a husband ask?"

Guiltily, Brianne thought . . . Perhaps for a wife.

Chapter 17

"Ryan, I really don't want to do this," she complained as she looked away from him.

"Brianne, just hold it. C'mon."

She turned her face to his and grimaced. Hesitantly, she put her hand out and cringed as he placed a thick brown worm in her palm.

"There. That isn't so bad, is it?" Ryan asked, with a slight smile as he observed her face. He had brought her here to the shaded banks of the bayou to fish, having learned she had never done so.

Brianne looked at the worm curling in her hand and shivered with distaste. "Ugh! It looks like something Nature didn't finish. Take it back."

Ryan brought the fishing pole to her and said, "Why don't you bait it? You have to learn to do this sometime."

"Definitely not! I'd rather use bread, or cheese . . . anything but this." And she dropped the creature to the damp earth.

Stooping, Ryan picked it up and began to pierce it with a small hook. Brianne looked away and cried out with revulsion, "How can you do that? It's disgusting!"

Continuing with his task, he asked, "How do you think you eat? Besides, the worm can't feel it."

Brianne turned back to him. "I hate that! Everyone always said that. How do they know it can't feel anything?"

Finished with the worm, Ryan breathed deeply. "I don't know, but let's not fight over it, all right? I'll cast your line and then we can sit and talk."

Brianne gave in and nodded. She didn't want to argue with him either. He had surprised her when he asked if she wanted to go fishing with him, and she didn't want anything to ruin the afternoon. It was beautiful here, where the old oak trees seemed to bend down their moss-laden arms in a soft welcome, and she sat down Indian-style beside her husband. Grateful for the lightweight slit skirt that Rena had made for her, Brianne leaned her elbows on her knees and played with the grass in front of her.

"I'm sorry," she apologized. "If you want, I'll hold the pole." It wasn't much, but she wanted him to know she was trying.

Giving the wooden rod to her, Ryan smiled. "Just remember, if you catch anything . . . it's mine."

Brianne returned his smile and laughed slightly. "No problem with that. Though if I had my way, we wouldn't catch a single fish."

Ryan shook his head as he leaned back and lay down on the ground next to her. He put his arms behind his head and took a deep, relaxing breath. Brianne listened to his breathing and thought how nice it was that he would take time off from Briarfawn to spend with her this way. She was thinking about him more and more lately. She watched the way he worked with the people of Briarfawn, and the way they responded to him. Everyone loved him, or at least respected him, and she had to admit that she did too—respect him, that is. She glanced over to his leg that was so near to her own. She wanted to reach out and touch that muscled thigh, but didn't dare. She had the

254

feeling that she was fighting a losing battle with herself. More and more she wanted him to be near her. She found that she waited for him each afternoon, so they could share lunch together. He shared his morning's work with her and she questioned him about beginning her school. Even though he didn't quite approve of the idea, he listened to her and gave his opinions. At night she primped more than necessary, in order to make a good impression, and as she joined him downstairs she was rewarded by the way his blue eyes would light up at her appearance.

All right, she thought, as she absently played with the fishing rod in her hands. I want him to pay attention to me. What's wrong with that? He's entertaining, intelligent—and definitely easy on the eyes. In fact, she thought as she looked out over the water, he's gorgeous.

Ryan watched her hands caress the rod and groaned silently. The combination of the sun, the heat, and the lazy afternoon had started a curious feeling in his stomach that was intensified as he continued to be hypnotized by her slender fingers sliding up and down the shaft of wood. She couldn't know what she was doing to him by playing with the pole that way! He looked up at her profile and saw she was staring at the slow-moving water in front of her. Unwillingly, his gaze slid back to her hands. Her thumb and middle finger were gliding, ever so gently, up the pole. They would then hesitate for a second before sliding back down, pausing only to finger the grooves and bumps in the wood.

Ryan felt a sweat break out on his forehead that couldn't be attributed solely to the temperature, and his manhood began to respond to her tender ministrations to the fishing pole. Damn! It was too much. Humiliation, brought on by his celibate life, caused him to sit up and speak more sternly than he intended.

"You know you're spoiled, Brianne?"

Surprised by his words, she turned to him with a frown on her face. "I am not!" she said emphatically.

Thankfully, he saw that she now gripped the pole with a tight hand. "Yes, you are. You're spoiled," he insisted, with the beginning of a smile starting to emerge.

She looked at his mouth and her defensiveness began to fade. "Why, may I ask, do you consider me spoiled?"

Ryan glanced out at the bayou. "How did you manage? Before, I mean? You said you didn't have servants, yet you don't seem to have starved. How did you obtain your food, with no man around?"

Brianne laughed out loud. Shaking her head in amusement, she said, "I went to the supermarket. A store. The food, including fish and meats, is already packaged—prepared for you. All you have to do is cook it."

He turned to her and stared at her mouth. "I like to hear you laugh. You should do it more often."

Brianne wished he would stop it, and then again she prayed he wouldn't. Her lips began to tingle of their own accord. His hot gaze felt as though it were devouring them, and when she opened her mouth to speak her words came more slowly, as if concentrating and moving her lips at the same time were unnatural to her. "I . . . I never liked to think, even then, where the food came from. I guess you're right. I am spoiled."

He wouldn't stop looking at her mouth. "Then that's something we'll have to work on together, isn't it? I'm more than willing to teach you, Brianne. You know that, though, don't you?"

She stared at his mouth in return, saw his breath coming quickly. "Yes . . . I suppose I do," she said quietly. Where was this conversation going? And when had she stopped thinking about fishing and started imagining him teaching her other things, things that made her legs feel heavy with expectancy?

256

The space between them was magnetic with a charged tension and their bodies seemed to move together, ever so slightly, in response. She could feel her own bottom lip lowering as Ryan's had done, and swallowed in anxious anticipation of the kiss she knew was coming.

It happened so quickly, she almost lost the pole. The twine became taut as it tugged hard against her instinctive pulling. "I don't believe it! I think we've got something, Ryan!" she squealed in an excited voice.

Ryan breathed deeply and tried not to show his frustration with the untimely fish. "It certainly looks that way," he said with more patience than he felt. "Pull it in, or you're going to lose it."

Suddenly, Brianne handed him the pole. "No, I can't. You do it."

"Brianne, pull the thing in—or are you doing this on purpose?" He knelt behind her and put his arms around her, closing his hands over hers. Within less than a minute she and Ryan had pulled the fish to the bank, and she let go of the pole as Ryan wrapped the twine around his hand and lifted it out of the water.

She stood watching the fish fling its tail around in the air and pleaded, "Throw it back, Ryan? Please? We don't need it, and you know Lizzie's already planning something for dinner tonight. Please?"

He looked at her face, pity for the catfish clearly written on it, and then at her hands. Unconsciously she had brought them up to her chest in a silent plea, as if she were praying. Feeling the fight going out of the fish, he turned his attention back to it, unhooking it and throwing it back into the murky depths.

They both watched as it regained its strength and swam away from them. Ryan pondered the wisdom of giving in to her this time. This was supposed to be a lesson. With her attitude, she would never learn to take care of herself, and he was determined that she be able to fend for herself if the need should ever arise.

Holding the pole with one hand, he picked up the tin of earthworms and then reached for the worn blanket they had used for protection against the pesky red ants. He watched her turn her face to him and smile sheepishly.

"Are you angry?" she asked, as her eyes silently pleaded with him not to be.

Why was it, he thought with vexation, that she seemed to care more for a fish, and a lousy fishing pole, than she thought of him? "No. I'm not angry with you, Brianne," he said as he threw the blanket over one shoulder. "Not angry. Disappointed, maybe. You only thought of us. That fish would have gone to one of the cabins, where it would have been welcome. You have to start thinking about Briarfawn as a whole. It isn't just the main house, or even the cane plants or the mill. It's a responsibility for the people who live here. All of them."

When he saw her shame, he handed her the fishing pole and put his arm around her shoulders while he led her back to the house. "You've asked us to make changes for you, starting with the school. You've got to give a little too, you know."

When she nodded her head slowly, he continued, "We don't know what will happen when this war comes, not here. I won't be with you every day, to watch out for you. You have to learn to survive on your own—to provide for yourself. Next week I'm going to teach you how to use a gun."

"A gun?" She sharply turned her head up to his as she tried to read his face.

He looked down into her green eyes and saw the tension at the corners of her mouth. Instinct was telling him to lean down to her and wipe the worry from her lips with a gentle kiss, but he didn't want to scare her away. She felt right, cradled next to him, and he found that he liked the feeling. Instead he gave her a quick hug and said lightly, "Don't be worried. You probably won't have the chance to use it. It would just make both of us feel better knowing that you can."

Brianne didn't think it was such a great idea. The thought of using a gun was appalling, though she didn't dare voice her opinion on this matter, for she was still smarting from her selfish plea for the fish. She was determined to show him she could change, and made up her mind to start tomorrow.

"It was nice of you to come, Jimmie. I need an expert to help me with this."

"Miz Brianne, it don't take nothin' to learn how to fish," the young boy laughed as he looked up at her from under thick, dark lashes.

Brianne settled herself on the blanket and patted the space next to her for the boy. "Maybe not for you, my young friend. You see, where I grew up I liked to climb trees more than anything. I used to stick a book down my blouse and climb to the highest branch that would hold me. I thought there was nothing better than being suspended in air above everything, swaying in the breeze, and reading exciting stories about other people, other lands." She smiled in remembrance. "I didn't think there was anything that could beat that for spending a summer afternoon."

Jimmie nodded his sage understanding of a child's wish to spend an afternoon alone. As he handed her the tin of worms and dirt, Brianne asked, "Would you like to learn how to read?" Observing his shrug, she continued, "Once you learn, Jimmie, you can find out anything, go anywhere, without ever leaving. As long as you have a book, you'll never be alone."

"You gonna tell me 'bout other places? My momma says there's places where white powder comes outa the sky. Is that so?" he asked, as he took the lid off the tin and pushed it closer to her.

Brianne looked down into it and noticed the dark earth was moving ever so slightly. She glanced sideways at Jimmie. "You're not going to let me talk my way out of this, are you?" she asked.

"No mam. You said you gotta learn and I'm goin' ta teach you. You learn how to fish and I'll learn how to read. But you gotta fish first."

"Right." She looked back to the worms. Hesitantly she reached in and dug around with her fingers until she felt a slippery sensation pass over them. She closed her fingers and shivered as she brought one huge, fat creature into the air.

"Put it on this here hook, Miz Brianne," Jimmie said as he tried to hide the laugh that was beginning to creep up his throat.

Brianne took the hook and stared at both her hands. "What do I do? Can't I just wrap it around?"

Jimmie couldn't help it. His childish laughter escaped before he could control it. "You gotta stick it," he giggled. "Maybe, two—three times. That ole worm can't feel any . . ."

"Don't you dare say it," Brianne almost snarled as she brought the worm and hook together. She wanted to communicate with the creature and tell it she was sorry for doing this. She took a deep breath and pierced its soft skin with the sharp hook. "Ugh . . ." Her shoulders shook violently as she shuddered.

"Do it again. Hurry now, 'fore it gets off."

"What!" Brianne hadn't expected it to bleed, and she fought to keep her breakfast as she tried again.

"Want me to do it, Miz Brianne? You look funny."

Breathing deeply, she said through clenched teeth, "No. He said I have to learn, so I'll learn." And she brought the hook through the worm again.

"You done it! You done baited your own hook. Now stand up and throw your line out. Don't have to be far. Them catfish likes to bury in the mud, close to shore."

Jimmie stood with her as she cast the line into the dark bayou water. She felt almost weak with relief as she sat back down on the blanket, and she smiled at the child as he settled himself next to her. "I did do it, didn't I?" she asked with a pleased expression on her face as she wiped her hands on a rag.

"You sure did, Miz Brianne. Couldn't've hooked it better myself. Betcha' you did this before, huh?"

The corners of Brianne's lips curved in a knowing grin. "Nope. Couldn't have done it without you, Jimmie. Thanks."

She watched him shake off the compliment and square his shoulders as he nodded to the water. "Best you keep a watch on that line. Every once in a while, you best give it a little tug. Not hard like. Real gentle. Make them catfish think that worm is floatin' around like, waitin' for 'em."

Brianne did as he said and relaxed as the warm spring air blew softly over her arms. They sat together in silence and watched the water, each with their own thoughts. It was almost hypnotic, the way the sun was reflected off the bayou. Brianne listened to the sounds of the insects and birds and thought how proud Ryan was going to be when she told him she had caught a fish—all on her own. Of course, the fish had to cooperate, and she gave the line another short tug.

"Miz Brianne?"

She looked to her side and smiled lazily to the child.

"Is there really such a thing, like my momma says? You never did answer me."

She blinked at him for a few seconds before she remembered. "The snow? Of course. It comes every year. In the winter. I used to love playing in it when I was

261

a child, though when I grew up I looked on it as kind of a nuisance, annoying to get around in. When it first falls from the sky and settles on the ground, it's one of the most beautiful sights you'll ever see, Jimmie. Each snowflake has its own pretty pattern, but you have to look fast because the heat from your hand will melt it. When enough fell to cover the ground, we used to build snowmen from it, or slide down hills, or . . ."

She stopped as the memories came flooding back. It was still too painful to remember what she had left behind.

"You sure was lucky. I ain't never been nowheres but right here. How come you left?"

She looked out to the water again, trying to form some answer for him. When none came, she said a little too brightly, "We're going to catch a fish, right? But we didn't bring anything to carry it home in. Do me a favor, Jimmie? Run back and bring me another pail? We can put some water into it, and that way I won't have to kill the fish. I might let it go bad or something, but your momma, she would know just what to do. Get the pail and we'll give it to her."

Liking that idea, Jimmie nodded and stood up to leave. He could just imagine his mother's face when he told her he had caught the fish with Miz Brianne.

Sam Harkins stood not twenty feet away and watched the woman and darkie talk. He couldn't hear what they said, but he knew the small woman was the bitch that had ruined his face. He'd never forget the night she had clawed him in the French Market, and regretted letting her get away so easily. He'd thought never to catch up with her again until the meeting, not one week ago, that Abel Grimes and Pocker McCarthy had set up. Some rich bastard wanted to put the screws to another rich bastard and needed somebody to do his dirty work for him. It was no skin off his back, and he needed the money.

Abel had told him he'd already done a few jobs for the "Frenchie," and the man paid well. Not having had great luck lately, Sam was eager for the chance to make some money. He'd joined Abel, Pocker, and two others he'd never seen before in an abandoned warehouse to wait for the man who'd promised enough money to keep him in women and liquor for some time. Though lately the women had been fewer and fewer. It was the damn scratches on his face that refused to heal. Women were turned off by the oozing red welts on his cheek.

When Frenchie had finally arrived, he'd put Sam through a long series of questions. He could tell the other didn't take a great liking to him, but that was nothing new, or that bothered Sam Harkins. His friends, if you could call them that, numbered few.

He had got through the questions okay when Pocker, who got his moniker from the disease that had scarred his face, and whom Sam barely tolerated, had actually begun teasing him in front of the others about his cheek.

"Sam's still smartin', in more ways than one, from the little she-cat he tangled with down at the Market."

Harkins had seen the way the dark stranger looked at him with disgust, and needing the job more than his pride, had hurried to explain. "She might've been little, but she had the born instincts of a whore, all right—fought like one. From up North, she was, and dressed in some fine yeller gown that she probably lifted. Right off the boat, I'd say. Didn't seem to know where she was going."

Frenchie had interrupted him. "When was this?" he asked slowly in the accented voice.

Harkins had watched as the man's eyes lighted with interest. Grateful that the rich man's good graces had turned toward him, he said, "Three–four weeks ago, best

263

as I can remember. Late at night, it was. Pretty thing, with the damnedest green eyes I ever did see. Though if one of her own didn't come along, I'd of changed that face but good," he'd added for the benefit of the others.

Frenchie had looked at him for a long time before turning back to Pocker and the others. He concluded his business with them quickly, then asked Sam to stay behind. And it was then that Sam Harkins's luck began to change. Not only did he find out where the bitch was, but the stranger, who refused to use his real name, gave him the idea that stood to make him a great deal of money. Maybe then he'd see a real doctor about his face.

He turned his attention back to the woman. Real pretty, she was, dressed in a brown skirt and frilly white blouse. Sam could almost feel the way her full breasts were straining against the thin material. He couldn't believe his luck. He'd caught up with the bitch. Maybe she worked in that fancy house beyond the woods— didn't matter to him what she did. Frenchie had assured him he'd be paid plenty for her return. In fact, Frenchie's plan was foolproof. All he had to do was get the girl to the meeting place, and he'd be home free. It was worth the wait, and his patience paid off as he watched the kid run back to the house.

Brianne gave the pole another short tug, though silently she prayed that no fish would capture her worm until Jimmie returned. She smiled as she thought about the child. He was intelligent and curious. Both qualities were important if he was to be her first student. She really had no idea how to begin the school, and forced herself to relax as she let her mind roam free, wanting to be open to anything that might be of help.

Her first thought, when it happened, was that Jimmie was playing a trick on her, but instantly she knew the pressure of the hand clamped over her mouth was too strong. Instinct made her fight and her unknown assailant grabbed her by the waist and dragged her back into the woods. Kicking, grabbing at branches, anything to slow him down, she wasn't prepared for him to drop her.

Stunned by the fall, she looked up at the man towering over her and felt her heart stop beating as she saw a face straight out of a nightmare.

"Surprised? Didn't really think I'd let you get away now, did you?"

Brianne looked into his rheumy eyes and saw the hatred written there. She opened her mouth to scream but no sound emerged as Harkins shoved a filthy rag inside it. Her stomach reacted to her fear and she gagged as Harkins shoved her face down to the ground. Using one knee, he knelt on her back to keep her still, and Brianne thought her life would end at any second. She stared unseeing at the dirt, twigs, and broken shells that surrounded her face as she felt her hands being tied behind her back. Then her ankles were secured with a thick, rough rope. Terror such as she had never known made her heart resound in her ears as she heard him laugh.

"Ain't gettin' away this time, girlie. You and me, we got some unfinished business."

He turned her over and she stared at him. He was even more evil-looking than she remembered as he wiped his face on his stained shirt and looked back down at her. Greasy dark hair fell over a low forehead, and as she looked lower, avoiding his eyes, she was sickened again, this time by the three long, oozing cuts on his right cheek. She looked back to his eyes and saw they were fastened on her breasts. Forced to breathe through her

265

nose, she couldn't help breathing deeply, thus causing her breasts to rise and fall before his eyes.

"I ain't got time for that now, bitch," he said with regret as he came forward and picked her up as if she weighed no more than a sack of flour.

Slumped over his shoulder, Brianne thought she would pass out as his shoulder bone cut into her diaphragm. With each jarring bounce as he ran away from Briarfawn, she could feel herself growing weaker and as she fought the blackness, her mind screamed out to Ryan.

Chapter 18

"Tell me again, Jimmie—and stop crying. I know it's not your fault." Ryan managed to sound calm, although his mind continued to picture terrifying possibilities. He looked at young Jim and grabbed his arm. "Your mistress may be hurt. Now tell me—how long were you gone?"

With a small hand, Jimmie wiped his face and sniffled, "I jus' ran back to get a pail. Jus' like Miz Brianne said. When I come back, she was gone. I looked, but she wasn't here. I saw the bucket of worms all spilled, and I ran to get Nathen. He put me on the horse with Lucas, to find you, and he ran off this way. I don' know what happened, Misser Barrington! I swear!"

Ryan ran a tanned hand through his hair as he looked over the spot where Jimmie had left Brianne. The signs of a struggle were evident. He could see where she'd been dragged into the woods, and two sets of footprints, one larger than the other. The big ones were Nathen's, and glad that he would be so easy to track, he told Jimmie and Lucas to take Raven back to the house.

Before handing over the reins Ryan removed his rifle from the saddle and then turned to the woods. He kept his eyes glued to the ground as he followed Nathen's and the other's tracks, which were set deeper than before, as though he were carrying something heavy. Ryan swallowed his fear when he thought what it might be. My God! Why had she come back here without him? Jimmie said she wanted to learn to fish, and he cursed himself for a fool. Why had he lit into her yesterday about throwing the fish back? He knew she was stubborn. Didn't he know she would try and prove something? Damn, these questions weren't doing him any good. He pushed them from his mind, only to have them replaced by images of Brianne . . . her soft face smiling at him the afternoon they had agreed to be married . . . laughing with Lizzie in the kitchen . . . looking at him with tenderness the night he had told her about his mother. He pictured her angry, then sorrowful, when she told him what was to happen to his land. But the image he kept, and held, was the one of Brianne at night, in bed. Shy, hopeful, seductive, she was his woman—or she would be soon, and he would allow no one to harm her. No one!

He pushed deeper into the woods and his grip on the rifle tightened as he saw in what direction he was heading. It was away from the water and toward the old, abandoned shack. Few knew of its existence, since it was on the border of his land and in an area that wasn't worked. Whoever had taken Brianne knew exactly where he was going, and Ryan almost screamed in rage when he thought about the reason for her abduction. If she was harmed, he'd kill the bastard without any thought. She was his! he thought possessively. And in the terrifying possibility of losing Brianne, he freely admitted that he wanted her in his life. Ryan, who had given up on prayer over the years, found himself resorting to it as he broke into a run.

"Scream—go ahead—and I'll make your face a match

for mine." Harkins removed the rag from her mouth and watched with disinterest as Brianne gagged and took in great gulps of air. He sat on one of the overturned crates in front of her and smiled evilly. "Ain't so high and mighty now, are you, girlie? It's just you and me this time. Nobody's going to come and stop me this time."

Brianne looked at him with terror-filled eyes. "Please," she pleaded in a cracked voice. "Please, Mr. Harkins, I'm sorry if you . . ."

"*Mister*, is it?" he interrupted. "You learned some manners, girl, since the last time we met. Couldn't have nothin' to do with this here gun now, could it?" He held the revolver not six inches away from her face and grinned as he watched her eyes widen through the hair that had fallen on her face.

Still bound, Brianne sat slumped against one wall and watched in silent horror as Harkins reached out with one hand to the buttons on her blouse. "Such a fine thing," he said slowly, as saliva trickled out of the corner of his mouth. "Somethin' a real lady would wear. We both know you ain't got no rights to it."

Before she could speak, he ripped the thin cotton fabric down the front and revealed her breasts. She started to scream but he held the gun to her lips. "You give me a reason . . . I'd love it."

She barely breathed as she felt him place one hand on her left breast. Closing her eyes in horror and disgust, Brianne felt the gun taken away from her mouth and heard him say in a husky voice, "Don't care what he says. Waited too long for this already."

She couldn't help moaning out loud as Harkins grabbed her and slipped her breast out of the chemise. She felt his rancid breath and knew he was going to hurt her as she had hurt him. She couldn't look, couldn't even beg, for she knew her pleas would fall on deaf ears. The man wanted revenge. She closed her eyes even more tightly and whimpered as she waited for the pain. She heard a swift intake of breath and a long, agonized moan, but the degrading move didn't come.

Forcing herself to open her eyes, she viewed the astonished expression on Harkins's face just before he slumped onto her, knocking them both flat to the ground. Wildly, she looked about the abandoned house. It was dark and musty, the furniture overturned, but with the aid of the sun coming through the one window, she managed to make out the form of a huge man. As he walked over to her, she started to scream at him and the heavy body of the man on top of her.

"Miz Brianne, it's me—Nathen. I'm not going to hurt you." He rushed to her side and pulled her out from under the dead weight of Harkins. When he had settled her off to one side, he returned to the body and Brianne heard the sickening sound of a knife being withdrawn. She watched in a daze as Nathen wiped it on Harkins's pants before coming back to her. He cut the ropes at her hands and feet, asking if she could stand. She cried out as she tried to use her hands to cover her breast. The pins and needles in both her hands and legs were excruciating, but she forced herself to use them and stood up with the help of the large black man.

"Miz Brianne, you got to leave here right away. Think you can make it back alone?"

She looked at him in surprise. Pushing the hair out of her face, she said with a shaky voice, "Nathen, you come with me. Don't you stay here." She looked at the still form of Harkins and shivered.

"I can't do that," he said, shaking his head. "I can't stay here after this . . ."

Brianne could feel herself becoming hysterical again. "You saved me! He was going to kill me . . . I know it! You won't get in any trouble. I promise, Nathen. Please come with me?"

Nathen glanced over to the body. "He's a white man," he said quietly. "I won't wait around to . . ."

The door creaked open and both she and Nathen watched as the barrel of a rifle appeared. Nathen shoved her behind him with the hand that still held the knife. She grabbed at the rough cotton of his shirt and waited for something to identify the person holding the gun behind the door.

"Nathen! That you?" She and the black man breathed in unison with relief.

Impulsively, she grabbed the knife from Nathen's hand and ran toward her husband. Holding it in the folds of her skirt, she flung herself into his arms. "Ryan! Thank God!" she cried.

Holding her close, pressing her to his body, Ryan whispered her name in relief. "Brianne, Brianne . . . You're all right? I heard you scream and I thought . . ."

She nodded and turned her face up to his. "He took me from the river," she hurried to explain. "Jimmie and I were fishing and . . . and . . . I sent him back to the house. Harkins grabbed me and brought me here. Ryan— it was terrible. We struggled and I . . . I . . ."

She brought the knife away from her skirt and showed him. "Did I kill him? Is he d—dead?"

Ryan put her from him and slowly walked toward the body. He bent down and turned Harkins over. He felt for a pulse and looked up to the stricken face of his wife.

"No, Brianne, he's not dead. Not yet. We'll leave Nathen here to watch over him while you and I return to Briarfawn. Wait for me outside, Brianne. Hurry."

Relieved that he believed her, and wanting to leave the place of so much horror, she dropped the knife and ran out the door, only stopping to grab hold of a young tree trunk for support as she bent over at the waist and was sick. Had her stomach not rebelled at that moment, she might have seen the tall, well-dressed figure of a man

271

quickly leaving the scene.

Ryan picked up the knife and stared at it for agonizing seconds before holding its handle out to Nathen. He locked eyes with his overseer and said in a brutal voice, "Bury him . . . deep in the woods. No one's ever to know what took place here."

The proud ebony face never revealed a thing, and Ryan didn't expect anything less from the man. Nathen looked at the man he had willingly served for the last three years and merely nodded before taking his knife and going over to the body of the dead white man.

Ryan handed her the brandy and watched as she placed both her hands around the crystal to stop it from shaking. He'd brought her here to their room and had to shut Mattie and Rena out. Not wanting anyone to question her before he did, he waited until she finished the drink before he began.

Looking at her torn blouse, he tried to still his stomach as he asked, "Who was he, Brianne? What happened?"

She looked up at him with red-rimmed eyes and her mouth shook as she answered, "His name is Sam Harkins."

"You know him?!"

She nodded and stared at the carved knob of a nearby dresser. "The night I ran away—in New Orleans—he grabbed me down at the French Market. I was scared, Ryan, I didn't know what else to do. I scratched his face. He would have raped me, I know it, if Rena hadn't come along. She's the one who saved me. She took his attention away from me, and I ran. I never thought I would see him again. He . . . he must have been looking for me all this time."

He reached out and fingered the edge of her torn blouse. Very gently, he said her name. "Brianne?"

She pulled back from him and closed the remnants of the blouse over herself. Whimpering, she shook her head. "No. He didn't," she answered his unasked question. "There wasn't time."

Letting out his breath in relief, he touched her wrist. "He tied you?" he asked as he looked at the red welts.

She nodded. "He hated me. You could see it in his eyes."

Ryan leaned over, his face very close to hers. "Brianne, if you were tied, how did you stab him with the knife?"

She jerked her face up to his. "He untied me, of course. I . . . I told you we struggled and I reached the knife before him. Please, Ryan," she pleaded, as her face began to crumble in tears, "please. Don't make me go through it again."

He watched her and was torn between three emotions: anger, that he hadn't been the one to plunge the knife into the bastard's back; pity, for this woman who had come to mean more to him than he had thought possible; and pride, that she would take the blame for Nathen.

Knowing she must be honest with him, he sat next to her and said quietly, "I know what you're trying to do, Brianne, but it isn't necessary, and you can't carry this around inside of you. Don't you think I'd know Nathen's knife?"

Fearing what he would do, she grabbed his shirt. "He did it to save me! What difference does it make that he's black and Harkins is white? The man wanted to kill me! And he's not dead, Ryan, you said so yourself. Harkins never saw him. Please don't do anything to Nathen!"

Gathering her into his arms, he let her sob against his chest. "Shh . . ." He buried his face into her hair as he spoke. "I'll always be grateful that Nathen reached you in time. Never think that I would harm him. We owe him

273

your life. He's taking care of Harkins now. We'll never see the man again, nor shall we ever speak of this after today. He can't hurt you anymore."

Ryan softly began rubbing her back as he held her. "You must begin to trust me, Brianne," he whispered in a soothing voice. "If we're to build a life together, it must begin with trust."

Slowly, Brianne's arms slid around his waist and Ryan closed his eyes, knowing they had taken the first step.

The once-fragile relationship continued to strengthen during the next few weeks, and life at Briarfawn was peaceful. The incident with Harkins was never mentioned and gradually Brianne put it from her mind, wanting to shut it out completely. Ryan was planning a trip into New Orleans to see his lawyer and then his banker. He had carefully thought out his plans and decided it was time to act on them. He would be gone three days, and although he asked Brianne to join him, she declined.

The makeshift school she had started was just getting under way, and since she had enlisted Rena's help, she didn't think it would be fair to her friend to leave her alone. Both of them were floundering, not sure where to begin. They had decided to start with teaching the workers how to write their names, and in over a week they still had not accomplished that. Since it was voluntary for the adults, they had only seventeen pupils in the morning. Ryan had pushed back the work schedule, allowing the time for them to attend, and honestly, Brianne couldn't blame the others for wanting an extra hour's sleep. Those who made the sacrifice wanted to learn, even though they could all wind up in trouble for doing so.

The children were much easier. She and Rena made a

game out of the alphabet, and she was gratified to see how quickly they picked it up. Every afternoon as she dismissed them, she always reminded the children to go home and tell their parents what they had learned. Although pleased at doing something she considered important, she was still frustrated. Her ability to hold their attention would soon end without books and slates to write upon.

With that thought in mind, she found herself outside Ryan's study gathering up her courage to confront him. Knocking lightly, she almost wished he wouldn't hear her. Everything was going so smoothly between them that she was reluctant to cause a rift in their relationship.

Hearing him bid her to enter, Brianne swallowed her fear and crossed the threshold.

Ryan was seated behind his large desk, surrounded by papers. He never looked up but continued to write, and she remained silent, waiting for him to finish.

"What is it?" he impatiently demanded.

Startled, Brianne jumped and it was then he raised his head. "I'm sorry. I shouldn't have yelled like that," he said contritely. "I'm trying to make sure I have all the papers in order before I leave this afternoon."

Forgetting her reason for being there, she exclaimed, "This afternoon? I thought you were leaving tomorrow."

"I was. But if I catch the two-o'clock boat today, I can be in the city by late afternoon and catch Morrison in his office. Then I can finish my business tomorrow without losing half the day in travel. If all goes well, I should be back late tomorrow night."

Deflated, Brianne sat down in the chair opposite the mahogany desk.

Leaning across it, Ryan searched her troubled face. "Is something wrong? I meant to tell you earlier about my decision, but you were down with the children. Has something happened?"

She hastened to dispel any worries. "No, everything is fine. I came here to ask a favor of you, but it sounds as though you have a tight schedule and I wouldn't want to disrupt your plans."

Ryan smiled affectionately. "You've never asked for anything. If there's something you wish me to bring back for you, don't hesitate to ask now."

"It's not exactly for me," Brianne said, encouraged by his invitation. "Rena and I feel it would be very helpful to have books, and perhaps slates for the children to practice on. Paper is in short supply, and we've even taken to scratching in the dirt. We would only need about a dozen."

Seeing his mouth tighten, she quickly went on. "I know how you feel this, and I promise we'll do it quietly. I've already warned them not to say anything about it off the plantation."

In a show of exasperation, he rose from his chair and went to stand by the window. "You still don't understand. Something like this is bound to spread about the county. Landowners are afraid of an educated negro, and when word gets around that you intend to have a plantation full, there's going to be hell to pay. I know, I've gone up against them in the past."

She came to stand next to him and touched his arm. "Ryan, *you* know it's not wrong."

Continuing to gaze out into the distance, he remained silent. The only sign of his agitation was the familiar tightening of his cheek as he struggled to make a decision.

Finally he uttered the words she had prayed for. "Make your list."

So happy, she stood on tiptoe and kissed his smooth cheek, the one that had been clenched only moments before. "Oh, thank you, Ryan. I knew you'd do the right thing."

"Had I known what the reward was going to be, I'd

276

have done it a lot sooner," he chuckled.

About to leave, she paused at the door and turning back to him, asked something she had wondered about for weeks. "Ryan, are you very rich?" she inquired shyly.

Surprised and amused, he answered her. "I suppose you could say we don't have to worry about money. What is going through that beautiful head of yours?"

Pleased by his answer, she continued, "Then it wouldn't hurt if we supplied the material to make new curtains for the cabins, and a few other small things?"

Bursting into full-scale laughter, he pointed to the door. "Go make your list, woman, or I won't make the boat!"

Excited, Brianne shut the door and shouted for Mattie. When the housekeeper appeared, she quickly told her to bring something cool to drink for three people, and ran up the stairs to find Rena.

Her diligent friend was in her room, smoothing the lines of the lovely green gown she had just finished. Catching the young girl admiring herself in the mirror, Brianne exclaimed her approval. "Rena! You look positively radiant. I never guessed you had such skill. You should have trained to be a dressmaker, instead of a maid."

Brianne saw the patience of the last few weeks pay off, as Rena did a neat pirouette and primly answered in a most ladylike voice, "Why thank you, Brianne. I'm quite pleased with it myself."

They both burst into laughter at her transformation. Brianne grabbed her friend's wrist and hurried down the hall to her own room, renewed laughter her only answer to Rena's inquiries as to the cause of this unladylike display.

In fact, Brianne wouldn't say anything until Mattie appeared carrying the refreshment.

As she started to leave, Brianne asked her to stay. "I

need your help, Mattie. Come sit down with us and have some lemonade. Ryan has given permission to order supplies for the school, which Rena will help me with, and I'd like your help in supplying the cabins.''

The other two women's eyes met, and apprehension passed between them.

"Don't be silly!" Brianne admonished them, knowing what they were thinking. "No one will know what goes on in this room, and you both know how I feel about this servant–mistress barrier.''

"Now, Mattie, you sit here,'' she patted the seat next to her. "We have less than an hour to make up both lists if we want Ryan to take them into the city. And *I'm* going to serve the drinks—just to keep in practice. Now sit down, Mattie, and help me get organized.''

Looking scandalized, Mattie nervously complied.

Brianne handed each a tall glass. Glancing at them, she said with a devilish glint in her eyes, "Don't either of you dare tell Ryan. He thinks that I'm honestly trying to become the grand lady of the manor, waited on hand and foot and all that.''

Rena shook her head before turning her eyes to the ceiling. "Now that has to be the best-kept secret of Briarfawn! I suppose he just hasn't caught you scrubbing the laundry or polishing silver yet.''

Defending herself, Brianne cried, "Rena, that's not fair! I am trying. I just like to keep busy. I simply cannot sit around and watch other people work when I'm perfectly capable of helping.''

Dismissing that subject, she got back to the one at hand. "Now let's forget my shortcomings, shall we? And concentrate on these lists. Mattie, how many cabins do we have?''

Grateful for their help, she noted down their suggestions and was making one combined list when someone knocked on the door.

Mattie jumped up to answer it with the speed of a woman half her size and admitted Aaron, who announced he had come for Ryan's bags.

Brianne's heart sank as she realized the time had come for his departure, and hastily finished her writing. Thanking the women for their help, she hurried downstairs to find her husband.

She discovered Ryan in his study. Standing behind a cleared desk, he was locking a small black satchel. He looked up as she entered and smiled as though to melt her heart.

"There you are, little one," he said softly. "I was just going to send for you. Have you made your list?"

Irrationally, Brianne's heart started to beat faster when she heard his endearment. *Little one.* Strangely, she wasn't upset at being called that, and for a brief moment she wanted to ask him to wait while she ran upstairs and packed to go with him. Just the thought of being without him, even overnight, left her feeling empty.

She handed him the list of supplies, and without looking at it Ryan folded the paper and slipped it inside his coat. Picking up the bag, he came around the desk and put his arm around Brianne's shoulders, leading her into the foyer.

"Ah, here's Aaron." Both watched as the older man took the suitcase to the door.

Still holding her, he looked deeply into her eyes. "It's time I go. Everything should be all right here, but if you run into a problem, ask Nathen. You'll do fine, Brianne, don't worry so."

He lifted his hand to her face and eased the tension he saw at the corners of her eyes.

When Aaron opened the massive front door, Brianne impulsively said, "I'll walk out with you," wanting to prolong the protective feeling from being cradled within his arm.

Handing his smaller bag to Aaron, Ryan led her outside, pausing as they reached the steps. He withdrew his arm and turned to face her, his warm gaze burning into her.

"I'll miss you," he whispered as he placed both his hands on her upper arms.

Brianne memorized his face as if she might never see him again. Slowly she studied those clear blue eyes that seemed to be expecting something, and his full lips that were held slightly apart. As she looked upward, back into his eyes, she was distracted by the errant lock of hair that threatened to fall and block her view.

She finally gave into the urge and reaching up, brushed it softly back into place.

When she touched him, Ryan inhaled quickly and pulled her to him before she could bring her arm down.

They stood pressed against each other for a moment until Brianne, no longer able to fight it, instinctively placed her hand at the back of his neck.

Applying the slightest pressure, she lowered his face to hers.

Chapter 19

He kissed her slowly, savoring each moment. For him
it was made sweeter because this was her choice, and he
knew without a doubt his patience had been worth it.

Surprising both, a hot current of emotion seemed to
connect them, and when Ryan reluctantly raised his
head, Brianne felt stunned, shaken to the very core of her
being.

Dazed, she watched as his mouth formed the words,
"Until tomorrow night," and she could do no more than
breathe the same phrase to him as he released her.

Watching him ride away, she returned his wave until
he was out of sight, then hugged herself as a feeling of
loneliness assailed her.

Sitting in one of the large wicker chairs, Brianne tried
to sort out her feelings. She brought her fingers up to her
lips in wonderment. Why had she waited so long? Why
had she denied such pleasure? More importantly, why
was she so afraid to admit to the strong attraction she had
felt almost since the beginning?

She recalled over the past weeks the many times
Ryan's hand would hold hers a moment too long, or he
would accidentally brush against her body, sending
shivers across her skin. Though when she would look

into his face there would be no lecherous grin—in fact, he had looked as innocent as a child. She thought back over the past few nights. He had been acting decidedly uninterested, and she missed having him hold her. Oh, he was kind and catered to her during the day, but when they retired for the night, and she had indicated with her eyes and actions that she wouldn't object to resuming their closeness in bed, he had pretended not to understand, and made a show of how exhausted he was. Last night she had ached to feel his arms around her, and in bitter frustration she had turned on her side, away from him, and almost wept in her pillow. She had thought he didn't want her anymore, for he certainly had made no moves in that direction since their marriage.

Now, as she mentally felt his kiss once again, she knew she could put that fear to rest. He wanted her! She had enough experience to know that. Forgetting that she had once vowed he would never touch her, she was suddenly elated.

He wanted her! And she was honest enough with herself to admit she wanted him, but the intensity of her desire frightened her. Why now, when she was in this crazy position, had she found the one man who could make her feel like this? There had been no Ryan Barringtons in her old life, at least not in the circles she had moved in, but perhaps she hadn't looked hard enough, knowing subconsciously she was not meant to find him there.

She could call it predestination, a freak accident of time; whatever it was, it didn't matter—she *had* found him.

Excited, she began to plan her strategy. When Ryan came home, she would begin to show she wasn't averse to his attentions. She herself would be more affectionate, kissing him in the mornings, touching him when they spoke instead of being on guard at every move. Yes, she thought, exceedingly pleased with herself, within the week Ryan Barrington would have a consummated marriage.

Intruding into her thoughts was the sound of a horse coming up the drive. Forgetting he had left in a carriage, Brianne jumped up, thinking Ryan had changed his mind and returned.

"Afternoon, Brianne. Hope you don't mind me stopping in for a visit like this?"

Her face fell when she saw it was Stephan, not her husband. Recovering quickly, she said, "I'm sorry, Stephan. Of course I don't mind. You just missed Ryan, though—he's catching the boat for New Orleans."

Dismounting, Stephan came onto the porch. "I met Ryan at the foot of the drive and spoke with him for a few minutes. Thought I might come up here and see how you survived your first month of marriage."

Remembering the role Ryan wanted her to play, she smiled. "Very well, thank you. Although there's a lot I have yet to learn about being the mistress of such a large plantation, Ryan is being patient, giving me the time to adjust."

Thinking how true that really was, she invited Stephan to come into the house. "There we can have a cool drink and visit, out of the sun."

Instructing Mary, who was finally losing some of her shyness around her, to bring lemonade, Brianne ushered Stephan into the large drawing room, her favorite.

Once seated, Ryan's friend came right to the point. "I've been planning a party. Since your marriage, people around here have been very curious to meet you, but didn't want to intrude upon you and Ryan too soon. Being a close friend, and best man at your wedding, I didn't think it would be out of place for me to plan this reception—with both of you as guests of honor, of course. Before the invitations are delivered, I wanted to check with the two of you. I just talked to Ryan, and he said to seek your approval. How do you feel about it, Brianne?"

Smiling into his anxious face, she answered, "I think Ryan and I are fortunate to have you for a friend. Although I must admit to being a little nervous at the prospect of being on display, I am honored that you thought of us, and I gladly accept your kind invitation."

There! She surprised herself at how easily she was slipping into the formal speech of this era. After being here for over a month, it didn't seem quite so unnatural.

Stephan's eyes lit up at her acceptance, and she suddenly remembered his penchant for games.

Looking closely at him, she pursed her lips together and remarked, "Stephan, why do I think there's more behind this than an opportunity for me to meet the neighbors?"

Acting crushed, Stephan placed his hand over his heart. "You have wounded me, fair lady! Here I have come to you extending a sincere invitation, and you accuse me of ulterior motives. Hurry, pour me a cooling drink that it may put out the fires of indignation that threaten to consume me!"

Laughing, Brianne did as he asked. Handing him the drink, she lightly scolded him, "Here, you'll need it after that speech. Fires of indignation, hmm? Well, I'm still not convinced. You're up to something, Stephan. Now out with it—what is it you have planned?"

Dropping his facade, he became serious. "You're right. I see Ryan has told you too much about me. I suppose the price I must pay for my past conduct is the questioning of all future actions. This time you're correct, though. I didn't have a chance to tell Ryan before he left about the additions to my guest list."

Taking a deep breath, he continued, "This morning I received a letter from my uncle in Virginia stating that he and Caroline, my cousin, will be arriving within the week."

Brianne felt her heart stop for a moment. "This cousin, Stephan—is she the one Ryan was to have married?"

At his nod, her earlier feeling of happiness was shattered. He looked pained as he continued, "I'm afraid this is all my fault. You see, when your marriage took place, I was so elated with Ryan's change of plans that I hastily sent a letter to Virginia informing them, with relish I might add, of the beauty he had wed. Once she received this, my guess is Caroline browbeat her father into bringing her south to see for herself."

He looked at her earnestly. "I'm sorry about this, Brianne. I should have known she would never take this blow to her ego with a good grace."

"You really don't like her, do you, Stephan?"

Brianne saw him avert his eyes and almost hated herself as she asked, "What is she like?"

Stephan's eyebrows lifted. "You really want to know?"

When she nodded, he spoke with an intensity that shook her. "Did you ever seen a abandoned robin's egg? All pretty and fragile on the outside, it almost makes you want to cherish it as a prized gift? But if you hold it too long or examine it too closely it might crack, and what's inside turns out to be rotten and repugnant . . . that's Caroline. Beautiful on the outside, to be sure, but without a doubt spoiled and offensive within."

She couldn't imagine Ryan wanting to marry such a woman, and thought perhaps it was only a mutual dislike between the cousins. Disturbed by his words, she asked, "If this is so, then why are you so anxious for us to meet? Why the party, Stephan?"

Amusement once more lit his eyes. "The part about having it to introduce you was true. I'll even go so far as

285

to admit that I'm expecting to derive a certain amount of pleasure watching the reactions of some disappointed ladies and their parents when they see the woman who captured Ryan."

Putting his glass down, he continued in a lower voice that emphasized his dislike, "But as far as Caroline is concerned, I would have preferred that the two of you never set eyes on each other. However, she will be here in a few days and the meeting is inevitable. It would be much better, Brianne, if it took place at a social gathering rather than having her pop up unexpectedly for a visit. Caroline's surprise visits tend to leave one in need of medical attention. She likes to unsheathe her claws and rip one apart with her biting sarcasm. She's not going to take this lightly—she was certain Ryan was going north to propose marriage."

Brianne spoke with more assurance than she felt. "Thank you for your concern, Stephan. But you forget I'm a grown woman, not some young girl who has never experienced unpleasantness before. I'll deal with Caroline when the time comes—but I do appreciate your advance warning."

Smiling with a false calm, she changed the subject. "When is the exact date of this affair?"

Returning her smile, Stephan complied with her unspoken wish to end the unpleasant conversation. "One week from this Saturday. Beginning at seven, and lasting as long as the ladies' dancing slippers hold out. You'll experience your first Southern ball, Brianne, and they are something to behold. By the way, your cousin, Miss Ahearn, is also invited, of course. She's still with you, isn't she?"

Brianne barely hid a smirk as she nodded. He was so transparent. The alarm he had shown at the thought of Rena's absence made her wonder again at the possible reasons for this ball.

"She's right upstairs. Wait just a moment, Stephan, and I'll find her. I know she'd be disappointed if you left without saying hello."

"Of course." Stephan masked his pleasure under the disguise of manners, and rose as Brianne went seeking the woman whose red hair and blue eyes had left an indelible impression upon him.

Brianne knocked lightly on Rena's door. Receiving no answer, she opened it to find the room empty. Puzzled, she went in search of her missing friend.

She's probably playing maid again, Brianne thought with annoyance. They really must come to some kind of understanding. Shutting herself upstairs with her needlework, Rena refused even to join them for dinner. Not quite so frightened any longer of her threats to leave, Brianne made up her mind as she entered her own bedroom to have it out with her tonight, while they were alone.

Coming into the room, she stopped short at the sight in front of her. There was Rena, standing in front of her open drawers, holding her lingerie up to the light.

"Here you are!" she exclaimed. Placing one hand on her hip, she came to stand next to her friend. "What do you think you're doing now?"

Rena was undisturbed by Brianne's question. "I'm going through your things to see if they need repair. Is he gone?"

Brianne grabbed the nightgown out of the woman's hands. "This is ridiculous! I don't own a stitch of clothing over two months old, and some of them I've never worn, so how could they need repair? Will you please stop trying to be the world's greatest maid? Right now I have another role I need you to play."

Brianne threw the gown back into the drawer, but caught herself before slamming it shut. Turning around, she faced her friend.

287

"Stephan Daniels is downstairs and he expressly asked to see you—and you're going to meet him as my cousin, not my maid. Now come along, he's been waiting while I searched for you."

Brianne walked a few steps until she realized Rena was not following. Annoyed, she spun around and saw Rena staring at the distant wall.

"I'm not going," she stated quietly.

"What do you mean, you're not going? The man is waiting downstairs to invite you personally to a party he's giving for Ryan and me. Now don't be silly, come with me."

Brianne tried to take her hand, but Rena was adamant. "I'm not going downstairs, and I'm not going to his party. Tell him I don't feel well. Tell him anything, I don't care what, but I'm not going to see him."

Brianne came back to her. "Rena, what's wrong? You're frightened, aren't you? Why?" she asked softly.

Her younger friend looked pained as she shook her head. "What's the point? I met Stephan Daniels at your wedding, and he was very nice. But when he looks at me, I feel as though he can see right into my soul . . . and we both know the state of that. I can't face him, Brianne. I don't belong downstairs, my place is right here."

Brianne led her over to the bed, and they both sat on its edge.

Looking into bright blue eyes that were shining with unshed tears, she spoke earnestly. "Listen to me, Maureen Ahearn. I know for a fact that before my wedding you saw Father André and went to confession. What you did in the past is in the past. You have your future to think of now. Do you want to spend the rest of your life taking care of another woman's things, because you feel you have to punish yourself? How long will it be before you feel you have atoned for your sins? A year? Five years? Your entire life?"

Brianne held the girl's hands in her own. "You confessed your past life, and the priest forgave you. If you really believe that, then you must know that God has forgiven you too. Don't put yourself above him, Rena. He's already forgiven you . . . I think you must now learn to forgive yourself."

Seeing Rena's quivering chin, Brianne put her arms around the younger woman.

"You know you're a wonderful lady?" Rena whispered. "Everyone says so. The people here call you the *angel*, and they're right. You were sent here for a reason; look at all the lives you've changed for the better."

Rena's speech, meant as a compliment, only frightened her, bringing her own fear once again to the surface. If she had ceased to exist in the twentieth century, how could she ever hope to return to it? And who was she to talk about God and his forgiveness, when her own faith was on shaky ground?

She would never stop trying to reach Morganna and ease the pain she knew her sister was experiencing, but looking back, in the last few weeks she hadn't given her past much thought. She had almost, but not quite, resigned herself to this present life. She knew she was becoming too attached to the people around her, and if it were possible for her to return now, she would be desolate without them. She had never realized how isolated and lonely she had become, concentrating on her work, shutting herself off from other people and their problems. It was no way to live, she admitted now, and she had been the cause of her own unhappiness. She had been too frightened of being hurt to reach out to others.

Here, trapped in the past, she felt useful and her life *was* worthwhile. People really needed her, and the feeling was wonderful.

As she gently soothed Rena, Brianne stared off into

space, and it was like a fog slowly lifting. It came with such clarity that she sucked in her breath and held it.

I'm happy here! she thought in amazement. I'm happier here, now, than I've been for years. It isn't just because they need me—I need them far more. It was because for the first time since she had left her parents' home, she felt she belonged! She was part of this big family of people. Regardless of race, or the problems created by their differences, they all cared about each other. Ryan had achieved what he hoped for here.

Briarfawn wasn't ideal, but neither was it the horror she had expected. With everyone having a stake in the land, they all pulled together to see that it worked. From young Mary, trying so hard to please, to the fieldhand relentlessly toiling to gain his freedom, they each had a common goal—the success of Briarfawn. Everyone shared it, black or white.

And I'm a part of it! Brianne thought happily.

Pulling herself free from Rena, she stood up.

"This is our home," she said possessively. "And we've left a guest alone, waiting for us. Now, wash your face. You wouldn't want Stephan to know you've been crying."

Putting aside the towel, Rena asked nervously, "How do I look? Is this dress all right? Whatever will I say to him?"

Brianne laughed. "You look wonderful. And you know the dress is perfect for you or you wouldn't have made it, so stop worrying. We should hurry, before he gives up on us."

Before they entered the drawing room, Rena stopped and drew a deep breath. Catching her eye, Brianne winked reassuringly and they went in together.

With their entrance, Stephan stood up. "Miss Ahearn! It's a pleasure to see you again. I don't have to ask how you're enjoying your visit; the country agrees with you."

Brianne glanced at her friend in time to see her pale cheeks flush as she gave Stephan a shy smile.

He was completely captivated, and for once the man was at a loss for words.

Amused, Brianne stepped in to break the awkward silence. "Rena and I both love it here at Briarfawn. She's taken quite an interest in the plantation, and has been an immense help in the running of the house. I would have been lost without her."

Stephan looked embarrassed, and tried to compose himself as Rena sat next to Brianne on the sofa. "You are very fortunate, Brianne, to have your family with you."

Brianne loved it. He was really struggling. The attraction between them was obvious, and she decided to help these two friends with a little shove in the right direction.

"You're right, Stephan, I am. Although I have to confess that lately I've felt a little guilty occupying so much of Rena's time."

When the other woman protested, Brianne interrupted her by saying, "Now, Rena, you know it's the truth. Why, I've half expected you to burst into tears of boredom. But now Stephan's come to relieve that. Haven't you, Stephan?"

Happy that he could finally contribute something of intelligence to this conversation, he readily took his cue. The woman must think him an idiot, staring and mumbling as he was.

"I certainly hope so. Ah . . . Miss Ahearn, one week from Saturday I'll be giving a party in honor of Brianne and Ryan. I would feel honored if you would also agree to attend."

Rena looked into his hopeful face and knew that no matter what her own fears were, she couldn't disappoint him.

"I would be happy to come, Mr. Daniels. Thank you

291

for inviting me."

"Wonderful!" he exclaimed. Taking up his glass, he smiled at both women.

"Miss Ahearn, do you ride?" he asked suddenly. "Perhaps before next weekend I could show you our countryside. It's especially beautiful in late spring."

Brianne looked at her companion and silently prayed, *Please*, Rena, say yes. This is your chance. Don't sink back into your guilt. Please say yes, this could be a beginning for you.

Brianne and Stephan were both looking at Rena, both eagerly awaiting her answer.

When it came, it was in a timid whisper, "Thank you, I would enjoy that."

It was impossible to tell who was more pleased with her response—Stephan, whose face broke into a brilliant smile as he discussed a convenient date with her, or Brianne, who wanted to jump up and kiss her, so happy was she that her friend had made a positive decision.

Later, feeling pleased with the results of his visit, Stephan rose to leave, explaining he would be back the day after next.

Mounting his horse, he waved to both women as they stood on the veranda and made a mental note to arrive earlier on Thursday. He wanted to inform Ryan of Caroline's plans and warn him to be careful in dealing with her. He hoped this time Ryan would listen.

Halfway down the drive, he thought back to the afternoon. Brianne had surprised him with her calm acceptance. After the initial shock of learning Caroline would be present, she had impressed him with her assurance as Ryan's wife and mistress of Briarfawn. He liked that. It indicated not only that the marriage was going well, but that Brianne was confident in her role as Mrs. Ryan Barrington. He almost laughed aloud as he imagined his cousin's reaction when she met Ryan's wife.

Yes, it had turned out better than he had expected, and once again his thoughts turned to Maureen. Sweet, shy, beautiful Rena, whose soft blue eyes held a puzzling sadness that he wanted to erase.

And thinking of her, Stephan spurred his horse on, impatient for Thursday to arrive.

Chapter 20

Brianne was anything but confident as she watched Rena try on both her riding habits. The moment Stephan was out of view, Rena was instantly seized with anxiety and in answer to the question of what to wear, Brianne had taken her back upstairs and produced the two outfits.

"Which one do you like, Bri? Are you sure about this? I still don't feel right, borrowing your clothes."

Rena stood in front of her, wringing her hands together, and Brianne reached out with one of her own to still them.

"Will you please stop all this worrying? They both look well on you, so just choose one. And speaking of clothes, have you given any thought as to what we'll wear to this party? I think both of us will have to take a good look at the gowns and decide. I'll be depending on you to help me make the right choice."

She turned to sit on one of the striped chairs. "God, Rena, I don't know anything about a Southern ball, except what I've read. Then, it sounded so formal and lavish, but certainly romantic. Right now, it just seems frightening. What if I embarrass Ryan?"

Removing the blue riding habit, Rena said, "You'd never embarrass Mr. Barrington. Why don't you open your eyes? You must be the only one who can't read what's in his every time he looks at you. The man cares for you, and it's been growing over the past few weeks."

Brianne averted her eyes, and fastening the buttons on her own dress, Rena finished her thought. "If you're worried about how to behave, ask him. I'm sure he'd tutor you—or else do what I'm going to do, act very shy. They may not think you're very intelligent, but it cuts down the chances of making a mistake."

Sighing, Brianne rose from the chair. "I'm afraid I can't afford that luxury. Do you remember me telling you about the woman Ryan intended to marry? The one from Virginia?"

At Rena's nod she continued, "Then you also must remember she's Stephan's cousin. Before I came upstairs to find you Stephan told me she's coming south with her father to visit. He thinks it's because she's heard of our marriage. He doesn't have a very high opinion of her and wanted to warn me. He believes she's coming to cause trouble."

"What are you going to do?" Concern clearly showed on Rena's face.

Walking over to her dressing table, Brianne absently fingered the crystal bottles containing heady French perfumes. "I'm not quite sure. But one thing I am sure of: I must have my wits about me when I meet her. Stephan says she draws blood as she tears you apart verbally. Now maybe it's just something between the two of them, maybe they never got along, but I don't want to take any chances. A shy, retiring wife would be too easy a victim."

"Listen, Brianne, you're the only one who knows if he's worth fighting for."

"I hate that term—'fighting for a man.'"

"You might hate it, but that's what it sometimes comes down to. I've lived here for over a month, and one thing is clear; if Ryan Barrington truly wanted to marry this woman, no one would have stopped him. Not Catherine, not anyone. He married you, Brianne; that must tell you something."

Rena picked up the blue riding habit. "If it's all right with you, I'll take this one. The sleeves are a bit short, but if you don't mind, I'll alter and then rehem them before I return it."

Absently, Brianne said, "You can forget about returning it. I don't really need two habits. It's not as though I'm an accomplished horsewoman, is it?"

Throwing back her head, Rena laughed. "You only had one lesson. Be patient."

As Brianne shrugged her shoulders, Rena walked to the door but paused before it. She turned around, saying, "Thank you for the riding habit, and for prompting me to accompany Stephan. I only hope I'm doing the right thing. You know, Brianne, you help so many people it's a shame no one can help you now. You'll have to search your own heart and make your decision. Right now you need a little time to yourself. Let me know if there's anything I can do. I'm going to work on these sleeves in my room, and then I'll join you later for dinner if you like."

Brianne watched the door shut behind Rena with a solitary dread that comes with being forced to make a decision alone. She walked to the bed and picked up the rejected green riding habit. Selfishly, she was glad Rena had chosen the deep blue. Holding the other close to her, she ran her fingers over the material, remembering when she had worn it last week . . .

It was at breakfast that Ryan announced his decision. Before lunch Brianne was to have her first riding lesson. Ignoring all her excuses, he pointed out the practicality

297

of getting about on her own, and filled with a sense of impending mobility, she reluctantly agreed.

All went well as Ryan led her about like a child, holding the reins of the chestnut brown mare. When she finally relaxed Brianne felt secure enough to ask, "Ryan, I think I can take the reins now, don't you? This horse seems gentle enough."

Handing the thin leather straps up to her, he smiled. "Her name's Cloverleigh. And she's a mare, that's why she's gentle." Placing his hand on her thigh, he remarked quietly, "I don't want you to be hurt. I want to go slowly, let you get the feel of the animal under you. You'll let me know when you think you want something more powerful between the legs of this unusual skirt."

His implication was clear, and Brianne blushed deeply. She was at a loss for an answer, though Ryan didn't seem to expect one. He immediately started instructing her in turning and the pressure of the thighs, and spent a great deal of time lecturing her on the delicacy of the horse's mouth. Becoming bored with going in circles in the confined area in front of the stables, she ventured to ask if they might actually ride somewhere before she became dizzy.

Smiling, Ryan had agreed, cautioning her to take it slowly and remember everything she had learned. Ryan mounted his huge stallion and they took off at a slow trot down the drive. Her mare responded well to her commands, and halfway down she wanted to show off her newly acquired skill. Doing what she thought was right, she imitated what she had seen in the movies, picturing in her mind, as she urged the horse to a faster speed, the perfect image she would present to Ryan—a woman and horse acting as one, her cheeks flushed with excitement and her hair waving like a flag as the wind swept it up and off her shoulders.

Had she had the experience, perhaps she would have

succeeded in acting out the fantasy.

As she snapped the reins, the horse, startled by the sudden command, took off at a fast gallop. Shocked by the power under her, Brianne dropped the reins and Cloverleigh, confused by the action and lack of direction, veered off the drive and into the fields at full speed. Seizing the pommel, Brianne held on for dear life, and she knew absolute terror as the mare went careening through the cane plants and headed for the woods. There was no time to worry that every bone in her entire body was being tested as she bounced on the horse's back. She tried pulling on the coarse, dark hair of the mane, but nothing would stop the beast. She had a mind of her own.

Brianne didn't even hear the sound of the black stallion as it came abreast of her, for the air was reverberating with the deafening thunder of Cloverleigh's hooves and her own heart. From out of nowhere, Ryan's hand reached across and pulled the bridle, and mercifully the horse slowly came to a halt. The final picture she presented to Ryan *was* that of a woman and horse acting as one, though not the impressive image she had hoped for. Cloverleigh's sides were heaving and she was lathered and blowing loudly. On her back, Brianne reacted similarly. Trying to catch her breath, she gulped in large amounts of air in unison with the animal. To make it worse, once the danger had passed she broke out in a cold sweat and began to sob.

Ryan ignored her tears and yelled at her angrily, "What the hell did you think you were doing?"

Still crying, she shook her head. "I don't know . . . I . . . I thought I could handle her. It was stupid and—and childish. I'm sorry."

"You're right! It was stupid! You could have ruined a valuable animal—but more importantly, you could have been seriously hurt."

He was still upset when he brusquely handed the reins

back to her. She shook her head when she saw what he was offering and pleaded, "Please, Ryan . . . I learned my lesson. Let me walk back?"

Feeling more like a child than ever, she burst into fresh tears when he threw the reins into her lap and rode a few yards away remarking, "That horse is yours, Brianne. She belongs to you and will respond to your commands, if given correctly. Should you get off her now, you both will have lost a valuable lesson."

He waited patiently for her decision. More than anything, at that moment she wanted to please him and redeem herself in his eyes. Bending low, she patted Cloverleigh's long neck and whispered, "I'm sorry, girl. I don't know who was more frightened, you or me. What do you say we try it again?"

She stroked the horse a few more times, and gathering her courage, sat straight up and wiped her face on her sleeves. Clucking, Brianne pulled lightly on the left rein and Cloverleigh responded like a jewel. As they rode back, Ryan acted as though nothing out of the ordinary had taken place, and she was grateful.

Approaching the stables, he dismounted and walked over to her. Without a word, he took Cloverleigh's reins and led her and the horse into the dark recess of the barn. She waited patiently for him to say something, to reveal the extent of his anger, but he remained silent as he led the mare into her stall. When he raised his head to hers, she watched dark, shining hair give way to eyes that had lost their annoyance and turned soft with admiration.

"I'm proud of you," he said with an endearing smile, and she caught her breath as his hands encircled her waist. She waited just a moment, relishing the feel of his warm hands, before placing her palms to his shoulders. With his amazing strength, he lifted her off the horse and slowly, deliberately let her slide down the front of his body. It was excruciating pleasure. The tight bulge in his trousers transmitted an almost electrical charge when it came in contact with her womanhood and she knew that she moaned aloud as she fought the urge to wrap her legs around his waist. She knew that Ryan too felt the breathtaking surge as desire darkened his eyes and she heard his sharp intake of breath. He hesitated to lower her any further, but too soon her feet reached the ground. She felt the heat from his body beneath his thin cotton shirt, and for a sweet moment they just stared into each other's eyes. Slowly Ryan's hands left her waist and inched upward to the sides of her breasts. She felt wild signals going off throughout her, while at the same time her whole body seemed to ache with her need for him. They must have stood for a full minute without saying a word, before Ryan broke the mood by whispering her name.

"Brianne." She felt the breath leave her as he added, "I think you're about ready to move on to a different animal."

Confused by the thrilling emotions coursing through her aroused body, she didn't follow her instincts to press closer but gave him a quick, weak smile and retreated, leaving a safe distance between them.

I know I'm right! she thought ecstatically, as she lovingly hung up the garment that Rena did not choose. *He does want me!* She couldn't be wrong; too much depended on the accuracy of her instincts. And every single one of them was telling her to go to him. That was all he was waiting for—her. She had to be the one to make the first move. Realizing how patient he had been with her only increased the deepening desire and commitment she felt toward him.

Was this love? Was she feeling that mysterious emotion that had always eluded her? She only knew she wanted to be with him in any way that he chose. If the opportunity for her to return to the twentieth century had presented itself right then, she knew she couldn't have left him behind.

Very quietly he had crept into her heart and had claimed it for himself. He was a part of her now, and to lose him would mean returning to that dark emotional void that had been her past. She no longer cared how she had come to be here, nor would she waste any more time brooding about it. For some unexplainable reason she had been given this gift, this exchange of time, and had found the one person she was meant to love, to prize his happiness above her own.

Amazed and delighted with her new-found love, she vowed to keep it. She would allow nothing to destroy it, and that included Caroline Daniels. The woman may have thought she had some claim on Ryan, but he was Brianne's now—or he would be very soon. She would fight her with a determination born out of love, and that surely must be more powerful than revenge, which was what, perhaps, the Daniels woman would be seeking.

Picturing Ryan's face in front of her when they kissed goodbye, she could hear his rich, deep voice as he said tenderly, "Until tomorrow." Well, he didn't know just how right he was. When he returned tomorrow night, he would find a wife waiting for him.

A wife! For the first time, the reality of those words became clear to her. Dear God! How she wanted it to be right. She had left a time when commitments were taken lightly. Everywhere she had turned, couples were breaking up. People she would have sworn were happy together went their separate ways, destroying her faith in marriage. She had always wanted more than that for herself.

It amazed her that she and Ryan had been married for over a month, and yet today, on the front porch, was the first time they had responded to each other naturally, without worry of consequence. She smiled once again, thinking how Ryan had reacted to her boldness. When she had pulled his head down to hers, he had exploded with unrestrained passion. How tightly he must have kept those emotions under control over the past month! No wonder he had pleaded exhaustion and turned away from her in bed. Unknowingly, she had certainly put him through a bittersweet torture, and she giggled, thinking how relieved Ryan would be to know his patience had paid off and his agony was at an end.

Picturing Ryan in her arms, her thoughts returned unwittingly to the as yet faceless Caroline Daniels.

She walked slowly to the mirror. Stephan had said his cousin was beautiful, and moving closer she examined her reflection, wondering how she would compare.

Fighting down the self-doubts, she looked into her answering green eyes and touched her high cheekbones. Silently the glass responded with the only acknowledgment of any importance: Ryan liked what he saw, and that was all she needed to know.

Caroline might be a raving beauty, but Brianne was going to give her a run for her money. Now that she thought of it, Brianne was glad Stephan hadn't been able to tell Ryan about his cousin's arrival. She wanted to become his wife completely before he knew of it. Selfish though it might be, she wanted him first for herself, without the ghost of another woman looking on. Which meant that if Stephan was coming for Rena on Thursday, she would only have tomorrow night to make Ryan hers.

"You all right, Miz Brianne?" Mattie asked with concern. "I knocked, but you musta not heard me. Came to tell you dinner's ready when you are, but maybe you'd like to eat up here. Won't be a bit of trouble."

Walking over to the housekeeper, Brianne put her arm around the woman's wide shoulders as they walked from

303

the room. "I'm fine—just caught up in daydreaming. Besides, I'd really prefer to have dinner downstairs, with Rena. Do you realize this will be the first time she'll have used the dining room? I intend for this night to end her seclusion. And if she fights me on this, Mattie, I want you to back me up."

The two walked down the hallway to the bedroom Brianne had used when she first came to this house.

"I'll do like you say, Miz Brianne," Mattie whispered in a conspiring voice. "But you know Miz Rena, she can be stubborn."

"Well, she doesn't have any choice. If she gives us a hard time, we'll just say the mistress of Briarfawn requests her presence. That should do it," Brianne said quietly, and stifled a giggle.

"Why don't we take our coffee in the drawing room, Rena?"

Brianne was thankful dinner was at an end. Rena had picked her brain with questions about etiquette and tested her patience by watching her every move, observing the minutest detail, even down to the number of times Brianne chewed her food.

They settled themselves into the same wing chairs that she and Ryan always seemed to drift into after leaving the dining room each night. Here the two discussed the plantation, her school, and all their hopes and fears about what the future might bring.

Tonight, however, Brianne intended to fulfill a promise to herself.

Pouring the coffee, Brianne asked nonchalantly, "How do you feel about Thursday now?"

Rena's red head snapped up. "Nervous, of course. How else would I feel? Why?"

Brianne took her time, patiently handing Rena the

coffee. "Because I've been meaning to talk to you about your position here at Briarfawn."

When she saw Rena's eyes narrow, she held up her hand to forestall the inevitable threat to leave. "Let me finish, will you? Look, Rena, I'm living an incredible lie. I'm supposed to be a relative of the Murdocks, and you've seen how they live, how respected they are. Family connections are very important here. I've tried to act accordingly, but sometimes it hasn't been easy. So many things rub me the wrong way, seem cruel and unjust. Most I can't do anything about, but there is one problem whose solution is within easy reach."

"What are you getting at, Brianne? Do you want me to leave?" Rena asked with a wounded look in her eyes.

"You know I've never been happy that you devote all your time to fulfilling my wishes. When I met you that terrible night you helped me out of a nightmarish situation, then took me into your home. And when I had the opportunity, I tried to repay that kindness by bringing you with me to Briarfawn as my cousin and friend."

Brianne expelled a deep breath and said with finality, "I think it's time we said the debt is paid. We're both even."

Shakily, Rena placed her cup on the cherry table that separated them. "You're right, of course. It's time that I made a life of my own, instead of hiding out here. I'll always be grateful to you for showing me another way of life. We've been sort of isolated here this past month, but now people are going to be visiting, and you'll make friends who naturally would not expect your cousin to be your personal maid."

"Exactly!" She was surprised that Rena had given in so easily.

"If it's all right with you, I'll make plans to leave after Stephan's party."

Brianne's eyes widened, and she looked at Rena with a shocked expression. "I think we have our wires crossed, or else I'm not doing a very good job explaining this. I only meant that one month of servitude should amply repay your being brought here, especially since my motives were selfish in bringing you here with me. Let's just call an end to this debt you think you owe me. I don't want you to be my maid any longer, Rena. You're taking Mary's job away from her, and she's working for her freedom, something you already have."

Trying to make her understand, Brianne leaned closer to her friend. "I swept you along with my lies, and you're now stuck with being my cousin. And you're right, people would be shocked to hear of you working for me. Can't we just be friends? Can't you pretend to be my family? My sister was my closest friend, and you know how terribly I've missed her. Well, lately, the pain has lessened because I have you. But please, not as a maid, Rena. That puts us both in a difficult position."

She looked across at her imploringly. "I don't think I need a servant, but I'll put up with it for Mary. What I do need is a friend, and you've proved to be the very best. Please be happy with being just that—someone I can turn to in happiness or trouble, without fear of judgment. Would you be able to accept such a compromise, without threatening to leave?"

Rena's beautiful blue eyes filled with tears, but she smiled as she nodded. "This is twice in one day you've made me cry," she said in gentle reproach. "I still don't feel right about this new relationship, but you're the best thing that ever happened in my life, Brianne, and I'd do anything for you. Caring for you and being your friend only comes naturally."

"If you don't stop, you'll make me cry." Brianne was overjoyed and reached for Rena, hugging her as she said happily, "Thank God that's settled! And no more talk

306

about you leaving, either. How would I ever manage without you? Believe me, you pull your weight around here, and I'm not just talking about the school. I'd be like a fish out of water if I didn't have you to advise me."

The two spent the remainder of the evening in light conversation that somehow ended with a lengthy discussion of Stephan Daniels's attributes. As the grandfather clock in the foyer struck ten, both women mutually agreed to call it an evening, since school began so early.

After saying goodnight to the servants, Brianne accompanied Rena upstairs. Stopping in front of her friend's door, she kissed her lightly freckled cheek.

"I'm so glad we've settled everything, but I do have another question."

Rena looked at her skeptically. "Why do I find myself afraid to ask what it is? I thought we had covered everything, but obviously there's something up your sleeve, so out with it. What is it you've waited until now to ask?"

Brianne returned her look of speculation with one of innocence as she sweetly asked, "Do you think Ryan can possibly teach us to dance in only ten days?"

"Oh Brianne . . ." Rena laughed, and shaking her head she closed the bedroom door, leaving a happy woman alone in the hall, satisfied with the way the evening had turned out.

Closing the door to her own room behind her, Brianne looked at the large canopied bed and her smile slowly left her face. How strange it will be to spend the night alone in it, she thought.

Brianne took her time undressing, trying to enjoy the freedom this one night afforded, but failed miserably as she wandered about the huge room. Stopping in front of the liquor, which had remained permanently on a table for Ryan's convenience, she poured out a small portion of apricot brandy. Holding it up to the candlelight, she stared at the beautiful mixture of brandy and crystal. Knowing she would need all the help she could find in order to fall asleep tonight, she brought both drink and candle to the night table beside her bed, then slid under the covers.

Propped up against the pillows, she let her eyes roam the room as she sipped the sweet liquor, and they fell upon Ryan's brushes and the bottle of spicy cologne he always wore. Filled with a terrible longing, she glanced at the empty spot next to her.

I miss you, she thought. Strange that I should discover this love when you're not here. What are you doing now? Lying in bed, hopefully thinking about me . . . or has someone lured you elsewhere?

She knew Ryan was a healthy, virile man, and she prayed to God that she wasn't too late, that Ryan wouldn't succumb to another woman in the city.

Even at night there was no air moving, and those who ventured out into the hot, sticky evening were not rewarded for their efforts.

Ryan, walking the short distance from his hotel to Delphina's, mopped his forehead. Trying not to breathe in the dirt that was kicked up by passing vehicles, he again regretted accepting the invitation.

After a lengthy session this afternoon with his lawyer, Ryan had emerged from the stuffy office, only to run directly into Gregory Duville. The Creole must have learned quickly of his arrival in New Orleans, for he seemed to be lying in wait for him. Recovering smoothly, Ryan declined his invitation to dinner, explaining he had a previous engagement. Not to be put off, however, Duville had persisted and Ryan agreed, out of curiosity, to meet him for a drink over a friendly game of cards.

As Delphina's came into view, he again wondered about the point of this meeting. He and Duville had been involved in a few business dealings. Their encounters had been brief but satisfactory, if not downright profitable for them both. Yet there had been something in the man's eyes this afternoon when he'd asked about Brianne that automatically put Ryan on guard.

He knew Duville had met her on only two occasions, and he could only hope she had not let anything slip that might be difficult to explain.

Damn! He hated meetings where he was unprepared, and he realized now, as he entered the ornate foyer, that tonight he was at a definite disadvantage. His only recourse was to wait and see, and trust his own instincts.

Sighting him, Gregory Duville lifted one hand in greeting before rising to meet him. The first thing Ryan noted, as Duville crossed the polished oak floor, was that the man was dressed formally. So it wasn't business that the Creole had on his mind. All the more reason to be wary of him.

"Monsieur Barrington . . . Ryan," he amended in an effort to appear friendly. "So nice of you to meet me. I've reserved a table for us in the gaming room. Would you care to go to the bar first, or shall we have our drinks at the table?"

Ryan shook his head. "I'd rather not fight my way through that, if you don't mind."

He indicated the crowded mahogany bar, surrounded by finely tailored gentlemen, some of them highly respectable members of New Orleans society. Though that society's barriers were slowly beginning to crumble as more American money filtered into it, Ryan reflected. Five years ago the mix of Creole and American men gathered together at the bar would have been unheard of, but no longer. Money makes strange friends—always has.

The women who wove their way through them didn't

309

care what nationality they were, only if the pockets of their vests were full, and Ryan noted that they were dressed even more scantily than usual, probably due to the heat.

Duville eyed the women reluctantly. "Wise choice, I suppose, for a new bridegroom. Although I must admit Delphina's little protégées have made the most of this unusually warm night."

Feigning disinterest, Duville led the way to the gaming room.

As they approached it, a negro servant smiled broadly at Ryan in recognition, before opening the door to admit them. Once inside, they were struck by a wave of cigar smoke that the ceiling fans, operated by very young boys, did little to alleviate. Their table was, fortunately, near a window, and as Ryan slid into a chair he resisted the urge to remove his jacket. If Duville could stand being trussed up in that outfit, then so must he.

Drinks were ordered, and they were into their second game before Ryan's suspicions were confirmed.

"Tell me, Ryan," the man asked casually, "how does your beautiful wife like living in the country? It must be quite an adjustment after life in Philadelphia."

Ryan discarded one card, thinking the game they were about to play would require far more concentration than the poker before them. Two things were obvious: This meeting concerned his wife, and Duville knew more about her than he had suspected. Hopefully he was just fishing, and Ryan intended to make sure his line came up empty.

"Nice of you to remember her, Gregory. We both are enjoying life at Briarfawn."

"Remember her? She left an indelible impression upon me. Such coloring! Her unusual eyes . . . quite a beautiful woman you've married, Monsieur."

As Ryan's eyes narrowed at his effusive compliments,

310

Duville quickly added, "Forgive me, but I did assist her one night, and I'm afraid I've been haunted ever since by the confusion I saw in those eyes. She asked me the strangest question that night. She almost pleaded with me to tell her what year it was."

Ryan found it hard to remember the cards that were already played. Damn! He thought word must have reached Duville about Brianne's school, and pompous believer of the caste system that he was, the man was going to request the termination of it.

The Creole's last statement had sent him reeling. But he didn't blame Brianne, knowing at that point she hadn't accepted the transition of time.

Duville had asked him here with a purpose in mind. He *couldn't* know what had happened to his wife! Ryan himself would not have believed it coming from another. Forcing himself to concentrate, he threw in twenty dollars, calling Duville's hand.

The Creole overturned his cards: two pair, kings over nines.

Ryan's face was carefully masked, devoid of any emotion, as he showed the man his two queens, and waiting until the other's lips twitched in delight, he then turned over the remaining three cards: another queen and a pair of aces.

Duville's complexion took on an even darker cast. "My compliments, Ryan. But then, you always did have luck with the ladies, didn't you?"

Ryan decided to give him a little of his own. Besides, he didn't enjoy the game of cat and mouse, especially if he was thought to be the latter.

"I wouldn't call it solely luck. You see, Gregory, I've found that with women, as in poker, a little bit of skill only adds to the pleasure of the game."

Ryan appreciated the control Duville exerted. The most he did was inhale deeply and give him a tight smile.

Fifteen years ago, when the man was in his youth, one of the white gloves resting on the table would have been flung in his face for insulting in one breath the man's gaming ability and his manhood.

Duville signaled the liveried waiter for another round of drinks. "Speaking of ladies . . . your wife has fully recovered from her accident? I must say your marriage came as a shock, considering her aversion to you on the Court House steps. But then, women are fickle, aren't they? One can never be sure where their true feelings lie. A rejection can later turn into an enjoyable encounter . . . or the reverse."

Ryan wanted to knock him flat on his back, but he knew his anger was fanned more by his own insecurity with Brianne than by the implication of the double insult. The very thought of this man near his wife sickened him. Every muscle in his body was tight as a fiddler's bow, and he visibly controlled the urge to do violence.

"Brianne made a full recovery before our marriage," Ryan said in a calm voice, "while she was staying with Catherine and Samuel Murdock. The doctors assured us it was a fairly common reaction when someone sustains a traumatic head injury. I'm sure she would be embarrassed to be reminded of that period. And since she is very dear to me, I wouldn't want to distress her by discussing it further."

Duville's lips twitched slightly. "Very noble gesture, Ryan. Since the cards have deserted me this evening, I say we move on to a far more delightful entertainment."

Ryan wanted nothing more than to return to his hotel, but the wild gleam in the Creole's eyes told him he had planned this "entertainment," and that finally they had come to the real reason for his being here.

He gave his answer by standing and waving Duville forward, saying nonchalantly, "Lead on."

The other man was actually thrilled with Ryan's words, and only then did Ryan realize that Duville had feared a refusal. Whatever the lecher had planned, Ryan knew he was being set up.

They were met outside the gaming room by Delphina, who chided Ryan for his absence and told Duville in a much lower voice that everything was in readiness. Giving the younger of the two men a wicked wink of her painted eye, she motioned to the stairs and turned to greet another of her plentiful clientele.

Once upstairs, Ryan had his first misgiving when Duville stopped before a nondescript door and produced a large brass key. Ryan knew what was behind that door, as years ago Delphina had offered the key to him. For a certain amount of money, one could buy entrance into this dark room with a slit in one wall and observe the erotic behavior in the adjoining room. Not being a disciple of voyeurism, he had turned her down—after thanking her for the privilege, for few were asked or knew of its existence.

"Come!" Duville whispered excitedly, already in the room. "I think you'll find this *prostituée* of great interest. I've been intrigued from the moment I laid eyes on her."

Ryan shut the door behind him more loudly than he intended. He didn't need his instincts to tell him he wasn't going to like whatever was in the next room.

Duville gave way at the slit, excitedly urging Ryan on with his hands. Reluctantly Ryan approached the opening and was treated to a view of the banker Lawrence Halifax, short, fat, and lying quite naked atop a pink satin bed. His normally small greedy eyes were popping open at someone, or something, across the room beyond Ryan's line of vision.

He wondered what the purpose was of peeking into the man's private life. Duville was a stockholder of the bank, and it would not be in his interest to insult its president.

Moreover, Ryan wondered how he himself was ever going to conclude his own business with Halifax tomorrow, without picturing him thus.

He saw the woman's shadow moving before he ever caught sight of her. When she came into his range of vision, he was dumbstruck.

Clad only in a short, transparent wrap, she could have been Brianne. Long, heavy brown hair highlighted by the candlelight fell over her face, and from the side she bore a remarkable resemblance to his wife.

He didn't trust himself to do anything but attempt to breathe normally as his heart hammered inside his chest. He knew Duville was watching him, waiting for his reaction, but he ignored the man and continued to look into the room.

The woman walked over to the banker and removed her robe. Heavy white breasts hung like ripe melons, and she caressed them leisurely before coming to sit on the man's stomach. As his short little hands pawed her, she turned her face toward the narrow opening in the wall and Ryan breathed a sigh of relief as he saw the resemblance end. This woman was hard and calculating, her moves practiced for effect, and he felt no arousal in watching her. Looking away from the couple, he studied the flickering candle on the table by their bed.

Never in his life had he known such anger. Every instinct urged him to seize Duville and strangle him until the last wisp of corrupt breath had left his body. The insult to both him and Brianne was unbearable. He tried to think calmly.

Duville was a womanizer. His specialty was pursuing a woman who had not shown a great deal of interest in him. Ryan had heard stories about the man that sickened him. Once he had his victim under his control, he lost interest and usually left her broken, with a reputation in shreds. Ryan had often wondered if the man's misuse of women

314

stemmed from his widely publicized belief that the Creoles were a better breed than the usurpers, the Americans, for he never chose as his prey a woman of his own background.

Whatever his reason in the past, he had now singled out Ryan's wife, that much was painfully obvious, and Ryan knew that to beat him at his own game he must remain calm, and more important, confident.

Ryan stepped away from the opening and faced the man.

Reaching over, he brushed an imaginary speck from the Creole's shoulder. "Perhaps when Halifax is through, you should buy some of the woman's time for your own perverted pleasures. As for myself, it doesn't interest me. You see, Duville, I have the real thing, a *lady*, waiting for me, whereas you will always have to be satisfied with a shabby substitute."

The voice that answered him was tight with anger. "Now you see why your *wife* has intrigued me, Barrington. It isn't much of a resemblance, but it is there nonetheless."

Ignoring his last remark, Ryan opened the door to leave, saying in a low, menacing voice, "Be fair warned! Don't ever subject my wife to your fouling presence. Should you choose to disregard this warning, I'll not hesitate to end your miserable life."

Before slamming the door, he added his final insult. "You're a pathetic excuse for a man, Duville."

He was not ten feet away when he heard the same door open. "*Mon Dieu*, Barrington! You'll regret that! No one talks to me that way—no one! Remember this day, Barrington, when you lose what you hold in such high esteem!"

Ryan ignored him and the astonished stares of the men, most of whom he knew by name, as he walked straight through the gilded foyer and out the front door.

315

Reaching outside, he stood in the street and breathed deeply. Strangely, the air was no longer cloying and hot. In fact, compared to what was inside of that small room, it was downright refreshing.

How he hated the *Américain!* How he had always hated him, even when he was forced to do business with him. For three years, ever since Barrington had come to the city and bought his wife's family home, he had patiently waited for his revenge.

Duville refused to remember that his gaming debts had forced the sale. What he had kept fresh in his mind was that the arrogant American had taken over, renamed, and was making a success of Beau Rive, the plantation he had been barely able to keep running. He had waited all these years for the right opportunity to destroy the man. And it had fallen into his lap with the appearance of the beautiful and strange Brianne. Her marriage to Barrington was perfect. He could remember her glimmer of interest in him the night they had first met. It was all he needed. How much better that Barrington seemed to care for her. Duville hoped he was desperately in love; it would make his revenge that much sweeter.

Chapter 21

Brianne stretched, and luxuriated in a feeling of well-being. Some days were like that, waking up and feeling good about yourself and the world around you. At those special times in your life, you know nothing can go wrong.

Today was such a day. Ryan was coming home tonight.

Hurrying out of bed, Brianne ran to the window and pulled back the curtain. She looked up at the overcast sky and was disappointed. It should have been sunny, to fit her mood. Shaking off the momentary feeling of annoyance, she hurried to get ready for her morning class, having enough personal happiness to light up the entire world.

By lunchtime, though, she could no longer deny the small doubts that had been creeping up on her since her first session with the adults. She had found it difficult to concentrate as their gaze would leave hers to glance quickly at the ever-darkening sky, and when their eyes would again return she could read the worry in them. Since no one was getting much out of the instruction, she dismissed them early and returned to the house, only to find the same concern written there.

Over lunch Rena agreed that they should cancel the

children's class.

"I've seen this kind of storm before. It comes out of nowhere and builds up. The first year I came to New Orleans there was one, and I'll never forget how frightened I was, listening to that howling wind and watching buildings being blown away. It was a terrible sight."

Frightened by what Rena had said, Brianne left the table to seek out Nathen. She was told in the barn he could be found in the fields, and not wanting to wait for a carriage to be hitched, she instructed Luther to saddle Cloverleigh.

So anxious was she to reach the foreman that only as she cantered toward the workers did she realize what a sight she must make. Her wide skirt and petticoats were hitched up to her thighs and practically covered the entire body of the horse.

She had surmised accurately, the dark faces glancing up as she passed. If she hadn't been slowly sinking into depression, their open-mouthed expressions would have done much to lighten her mood.

Finding Nathen was easy because of his size. At first he had frightened her. Brianne had sensed an enormous power within his six-foot-seven frame, but had seen the giant of a man easily tamed by those not yet one-quarter of his size, the children of Briarfawn.

Walking over to where she had stopped Cloverleigh, he patted the mare's nose with one hand and touched the brim of his hat with the other. "Miz Barrington? Anythin' wrong?"

"That's what I'm here to find out, Nathen. What's your opinion of this coming storm? Do you think it's going to be bad?"

Nathen took off his hat and wiped his forehead with his sleeve. "Can't really be sure 'bout it, but the signs don't look good. Briarfawn's held out over them in the past and if it comes, the Gulf should take the worst of it."

"Mr. Barrington's supposed to come home tonight. Do you think he'll make it?"

"Mista Barrington's no fool, he's been through this before. If there's a bad one brewing, he'll stay put."

Brianne had a sinking feeling in her stomach, telling her Nathen was right. It would be foolish for Ryan to attempt to return. She looked at the bent backs of the plantation people and felt ashamed. Her only concern had been a selfish one. The storm had ruined all her plans for Ryan's homecoming, but she remembered her husband's words and the look in his eyes when he said, "You will carry on in my place."

"Nathen, supposing it is a hurricane that's coming. If the Gulf takes the brunt of it, that still means New Orleans gets hit pretty bad, doesn't it?"

Nathen shook his head. "Depends on when she turns, but the city stood in the path of many a bad one, that's for sure."

I'll worry about him later, Brianne thought. Pushing her fear for Ryan to the back of her mind, she asked, "What kind of damage can we expect here?"

"Mostly floodin' and wind damage. Trees bein' uprooted, cane floodin' out. But don't worry none 'bout the house, it'll take it. All them mimosas are kept trimmed so no branches'll come down on it."

Taking in everything he said, Brianne looked toward the sky and made a decision. "Nathan, I'd rather be safe than sorry. Call off this work and have everyone go home and prepare for the worst. I want you to check every cabin personally. If there's any you don't think will stand up against it, send the people to the big house and they can spend the night on pallets in the ballroom."

Nathen smiled broadly, and she felt she had gone up a notch in this quiet man's estimation. "Yes, mam. Don't think you'll be havin' to put nobody up, though. Mista

Barrington rebuilt most of them cabins 'cause of the storms."

Brianne nodded. "Thank you, Nathen, for your help," she said sincerely, and turned Cloverleigh toward home.

Nathen watched her struggle with the horse and allowed himself a rare smile. She was going to be all right, he thought with satisfaction. Ever since he was handed the tiny slip of a girl, unconscious and pale, he'd known it would be so. He'd felt she was special, and had been the least surprised of all to learn that the pretty stranger who had come from nowhere was to be the mistress of Briarfawn. A solitary man, he kept to himself but took in everything around him with a keen eye. She had changed over the last month. She was happy now, and Nathen was glad.

Riding back, Brianne heard the first rumbling of thunder and patted the horse's neck. They didn't make a pretty picture as yet, and she still felt uncomfortable on its back, but the horse had responded admirably to her awkward commands.

"You're a good girl," she said soothingly. "Just be patient with me. I'm trying . . . Lord knows how I'm trying to just fit in."

Raising her eyes to the dismal sky, she then began praying for Ryan's safety.

They left open a few shutters so the air could circulate within the house. All the potted plants and beautiful hanging flowers were taken off the galleries and placed inside the mature landscaping for protection. Brianne had ordered anything that was not bolted down to be removed. With her sleeves rolled up and wearing an apron of Lizzie's, she was carrying into the house one of the wicker chairs from the porch when Mattie stopped her.

"Lordy sakes, Miz Brianne! We've got men to do that."

"Please move out of my way, Mattie. I'm as capable of lifting this chair as any man, and besides, this is my home."

The housekeeper stepped to one side and Brianne continued into the ballroom, which was quickly becoming a storage area. Setting the chair down next to the others, she collapsed into it. Ruefully she glanced at the scratches made by moving objects across the beautiful oak floor. Was she doing the right thing? For the past two hours she'd had everyone scrambling about in every direction trying to carry out her frantic orders. Poor Mattie! She had only meant well, and Brianne supposed she hadn't seen too many white women lugging furniture around lately, especially when they had servants waiting to do it.

She glanced up from the floor to see Rena clearing the wide beveled glass doors that led into her glamorous warehouse. She and Mattie were bringing in the matching wicker couch, and quickly Brianne rose to help. When they had placed the sofa near the other grouping of outside furniture, the three women straightened and stared at each other.

Brianne was the first to burst into nervous laughter. "All right, I call a halt to this craziness," she said apologetically.

Sobering, she looked at Mattie. "I'm sorry I snapped at you. Put it down to inexperience, or that I'm worried about Ryan. I know it's best that he remain in the city, but I can't help wishing he were here."

Rena put an arm about her waist. "Of course you do. Ryan will be fine, and he'll appreciate all the work you've done to safeguard his home." She took the corner of her apron and wiped at a smudge on Brianne's face.

"That's right," Mattie added. "He'd be right proud of you. You done all that you could, chile. Why don't you go on upstairs, and I'll have a nice warm bath set up for you."

Brianne looked into their faces and smiled. "Thank you both. Anything that's not battened down now will just have to take its chances in the storm. I'll hold off on that bath, though, until later. Mattie, ask Lizzie to fix something light. I don't think anyone's in the mood for a big dinner. Tell her we'll eat on trays. Might as well make it as easy as possible."

As Mattie left, Rena and Brianne heard the sound of small pings against the heavily draped windows, and staring at the seven-foot shuttered casement, they listened to the rain that was beginning to fall so innocently.

Two hours later Brianne leaned back against the edge of the enameled tub and felt her weariness dissipate, along with the foaming bubbles that moments before had covered her body. Funny how such a minor thing as a bath can lighten one's spirits. And Brianne's spirits had been in dire need of an uplift as she'd watched the storm gather strength and grow in intensity.

Lifting one long leg out of the scented water, she again cursed the fates that would decree this rage of nature on the day of Ryan's return. Bringing the sponge up over her shoulder, she squeezed the silky water over her breasts and back, and as her hand returned to the water, she let it linger on her body.

Damn! So much for her plans! She had visualized her seduction of Ryan dozens of times, but seeing no point in torturing herself right then with fantasies that would only leave her empty, she stood and rinsed off the remaining soap with determination.

Donning the same exquisite robe, the one she hadn't worn since her first night at Briarfawn, Brianne rang for the servants to remove her bath and sat down to examine the tray Lizzie had sent up earlier. Knowing that her lack of appetite was a subject of concern downstairs, she bit into the cold chicken with a resolve to end the worry. Before she finished her dinner the tub had been emptied, and as Mary rolled it away, Brianne remarked to the housekeeper at her side, "You were right, Mattie, to suggest a long soak. It felt wonderful." And feeling she had done justice to the food, she stood up holding the tray.

Handing it over, she said, "Tell Lizzie it was delicious. I'm sorry all of you had to work so late, but tell everyone thank you, would you, Mattie? I'm not coming back down tonight. The sooner we all get to bed, the better. There's nothing more we can do now."

Once more alone, she walked to the fireplace and sat on the rug before it. Gazing into the blazing logs, she began to brush her thick hair. If she stared long enough, she could almost see Ryan's face in the dancing flames.

She had never assumed he loved her. Whatever he did feel for her was enough. She had waited so long and traveled such a bizarre distance to find this love that it no longer mattered. If love was there it would eventually surface, and perhaps he was a man uncomfortable with declarations, so she promised herself not to speak of that sentiment until he had.

As the rain beat incessantly against the windows, Brianne prayed for her husband's safety. If only the storm would stay out on the Gulf of Mexico and leave the city alone, she thought, and flinched as she heard another loud noise. Between the thunder and lightning and the strong winds, she expected to see a fair amount of damage tomorrow morning, but she no longer ran to the window every time she heard a frightening sound. The last time she had done so was to see a large branch separate from an ancient oak and narrowly miss the stables. Brianne knew she would pass the night better if she waited until morning to find the causes of the loud thumps and bangs.

Unbuttoning her robe, leaving only the buttons at her waist fastened, she stretched her legs out before the warming flames and ran her fingers through her slightly damp hair. Long curls traveled down her back and ringlets framed her face as the heat from the fire brought a rosy glow to her skin. She reached up and retrieved her glass of wine that remained half full from dinner. Earlier she had brought the pillows from the bed and carelessly dropped them to the floor. Now she stacked them up behind her and eased herself back against them.

Willing her body to relax, she sipped the wine and played with a curl that hung over one shoulder. As her eyes returned to the flames, she foolishly let herself slip back into her earlier teasing reverie, and thus did not hear the door open, nor the quick intake of breath at the picture she presented.

"Bri?"

At the sound of her whispered name her heart fluttered and she turned to the door.

"Ryan!"

Not really sure that she had not conjured him up, for he just stood staring at her, she got to her feet and ran toward him. She barely noticed him drop his valise to the floor as those strong arms she remembered so well enveloped her.

"My God, Ryan! You're soaked! However did you make it home? Never mind," she declared. "Come over to the fire and get out of those clothes."

"This is the homecoming I deserve, after braving miles of ungodly weather?" he teased, as Brianne led him by the arm to the warmth of the fireplace.

Helping him remove his long coat, she held the dripping garment away from them and impulsively stood on tiptoe to kiss his chilled face.

"Oh Ryan, I'm so glad you're here!" she breathed excitedly. "You are all right, aren't you? It must have been a nightmare on the river."

Shivering, he peeled off layers of clothing and explained his foolhardy journey. "I was all set to leave New Orleans by noon, as I had planned, when the first hints of the storm came. Word spread quickly on the docks, and the man I had hired for the return trip refused to make it."

Brianne stared at him incredulously. "What did you do?"

He gave her that rare little-boy smile. "Quite simple. I bought the boat."

"You bought . . . ?"

"The boat," he finished her sentence. "Actually, I had been meaning to purchase one long ago. This way we don't have to depend on the packets for supplies and transportation. However, I could have built two for the price that thief bargained for." He shook his head. "I suppose he could see how desperate I was to return."

"I'm glad you did."

Ryan looked up from the buttons of his clinging shirt. Smiling, he stopped trying to free them from the wet material.

Just then Aaron, followed by Mattie, came into the room carrying trays of food and steaming liquids. Brianne took that opportunity to rush into the dressing room and fetch Ryan's long velvet robe, remembering to grab a handful of towels before hurrying back.

Aaron had picked up the wet clothes by the time she returned, and glancing at Ryan's last remaining garment, she tossed the towels onto a chair and exchanged the robe for the sopping mass in Aaron's arms. Quick to catch on, the manservant did his job and held up the robe as a shield as Ryan shucked his drawers, while Brianne handed the wet garments to Mattie and led her to the door.

In a normal voice she gave instructions. "Hang these up in the kitchen to dry. Once you've done that, you and Aaron can go on to bed. We won't be needing you anymore tonight."

At the door, she smiled into Mattie's worried face and added, "I'm so thankful that he made it home safely. Don't worry, Mattie, I'll take good care of him, and if it isn't an emergency, don't let anyone disturb us in the morning."

The woman smiled her understanding and left. Brianne listened as Ryan dismissed Aaron and she smiled her thanks to the older man before closing the door, shutting the world out and leaving the two of them alone together.

Coming back into the room, she watched Ryan place the contents of his pockets on a table and noticed him shivering.

"Come here," she softly commanded.

He obeyed her quiet summons, meeting her in front of the fireplace.

"You're freezing," she gently reproached him. "Sit down in front of the fire while I get you a drink. I believe Aaron brought some hot brandy."

When he was settled in her place before the pillows, she handed him the steaming silver mug of liquor and watched as he took a few tentative sips. Satisfied that the alcohol would soon begin to warm his blood, she returned to the table and brought the tray of food to him.

She knelt down and placed it between them on the rug, and he looked over at her and smiled his thanks. His eyes roamed leisurely over her, taking in every feature and curve. When they settled on her chest, he remarked, "It seems I've ruined your robe. Perhaps you should change before you too are chilled."

326

Brianne knew the wet silky material was clinging to her, but it fit in perfectly with her plans. "Nonsense. I'll dry fast enough sitting here. Besides, before you came home I was practically toasted, lying here."

His eyes warmed. "I know. You looked like a beautiful painting come to life when I opened that door."

Smiling, she was nevertheless nervous now that he was really here with her, and she looked into the fire in an effort to calm down.

"Would you mind handing me a towel, Brianne?" he asked. "I'm afraid my hair is still dripping wet."

Gladly, she reached up and took one of the towels, only instead of handing it over to Ryan, she stood and slowly walked behind him. She looked down at his dark, shining hair and knew the time had come. Without saying a word, she began to gently dry his hair. She leaned slightly against his back and smiled as she felt his body stiffen. When she sensed him beginning to relax with her ministrations, Brianne stopped. Slowly, gathering up her courage, she walked around him until she stood facing him.

Aware that her robe gaped open at her chest and thighs, she stood in front of him daringly, leaving one leg exposed as she massaged his temples with the fluffy towel.

His face was level with her waist, the only part of the robe that was buttoned, and as she rubbed in circular motions, she slowly brought his head close to that secured section of her negligee.

Sweetly, her breasts began to ache above his damp head, and she was faintly aware that his hand had lowered the mug to the tray and was sliding it off to one side.

How she loved him. It was all new to her, this astonishing emotion, but it took little experience to recognize and feel the silent tension that was building up between them.

Just as she was bending to kiss his head, Ryan's hands suddenly reached up and caught her wrists, causing her to drop the towel.

"You realize, Madam, that if you do not stop this," he stated huskily, as he brought her down to kneel in front of him, "then before this night is over I will break our bargain and make love to you."

Amid the roaring in her ears she stared into his questioning blue eyes and quietly replied, "I give you full freedom to do so."

She removed her hands from his. Very slowly and deliberately she unfastened the remaining few buttons, and leaving the robe on and draped partially open, whispered in a shy voice, shaky with emotion, "Make me your wife, Ryan."

"Jesus!" His eyes darkened as he came to kneel in front of her. Holding her shoulders, he was surprised at the depth of emotion in his own voice as he answered, "I want you to know that after tonight we will no longer share a chaste bed, as before. There will be no going back, Brianne . . . not to anyone or anything. Once you're mine, I never intend to let you go. Be sure about this."

He waited for her to show she understood he meant to keep her with him. He would never let her return to the future, even if it were possible.

Brianne lowered her eyes and stared at his robe. Breathing deeply with anticipation, he was about to give up hope when her answer came as she reached out and timidly untied his belt. It fell to the floor and she looked up at him with what Ryan would have sworn was love, or something very close to that unknown emotion.

Lifting her tiny hands to his shoulders, she slipped them inside his robe and slid it off. Feeling as eager as a young, inexperienced boy, Ryan exerted a great deal of control as he reminded himself of his wife's previous lack of fulfillment, and resolved to move slowly.

Still holding her shoulders, he hooked his thumbs under the silky cream material at her neck and eased the gown down her arms.

They knelt before the firelight, facing each other, for exquisite, timeless seconds, each drinking in the sight of the other. She, with her hands on his chest, lightly touched the crisp, curling hair, and he, feeling the satiny smoothness of her skin, knew he had never wanted a woman more than the one before him.

Without saying a word, they remained transfixed but for their ever-deepening breathing, until Ryan applied the slightest pressure to her back and brought her body next to his. They both gasped at the naked contact and stared longingly at each other's mouth. Silently Brianne brought her chin up and Ryan covered her lips with his own in a light kiss that left both of them breathless and eager for more.

Sensations exploded throughout Brianne's body that left her almost dizzy from their intensity. Sensing this, Ryan deftly slipped an arm under her thighs and brought her gently to the rug, placing a pillow under her head.

Laying beside her, he leaned on an elbow. "My God, Brianne," he whispered in awe. "You're beautiful!"

She reached up and caressed his muscled shoulders, murmuring, "And you, Ryan," before bringing his head down to her.

This time the kiss was feverish, hot, inflamed by a passion kept too long under control, and Brianne wanted to drown in him, making her a part of him forever.

Raising his head, Ryan breathed heavily as he whispered, "Open your eyes, love. Watch me. See your body come alive through mine, and know you have nothing to fear."

Green stared into blue and remained fixed as hands became instruments of pleasure. Textures, scents, rhythm of breathing—all became familiar and touched off new delights.

When his mouth left hers to travel her neck, she prayed she wouldn't disappoint him, wanting so badly for it to be right this time, and his tongue left trails of burning skin as it freely roamed over her, breaking down her first defenses. He took his time, savoring each inch of skin, extracting for them both as much pleasure from kissing her palms, making her fingers stand straight up as his tongue teased each small digit, as when he slowly worked his way up her arm. Licking, nipping, his mouth devoured her. Everywhere he touched, her blood would rush to that spot, leaving her feverish, seething with awakened desire.

When his head left her waist and traveled downward, she was at first shocked as his mouth met and conquered that mysterious place between her thighs. Although frightened by what was happening to her body, she was helpless to voice an objection. Nor in her heart did she want to, as she rolled her head from side to side in exquisite rapture and wrapped her fingers through his hair, holding on as if it were her only anchor to earth as Ryan branded her as his.

When he left her she felt like some wild, frenzied creature, deprived of a primal craving, and she had to stop from crying out to him.

Kissing her mouth lightly, Ryan looked into her face and read her mind.

"It isn't over, little one. Not for me, and not for you . . . we're just beginning."

"Dear God, Ryan . . . I want you."

He smiled slightly at her words and kissed her temple briefly before whispering, "Do you know how long I've waited to hear you say those words?"

Ryan didn't enter her, but remained poised at the entrance to her body.

"Look at me, Brianne," he gently reminded her

when he saw the doubt begin to surface on her face. "Never take your eyes off mine," he whispered, and reaching between them, he caressed her already full, taut breast.

Mesmerized by his eyes, she unconsciously began moving against him, impatient to feel him inside her. But once again, he was her phantom lover of before. Slow and deliberate, he would give only fractions of himself as his manhood teased, inflamed, and finally, mercifully, seared her woman's flesh around him. It was done with such tenderness, Brianne wanted to cry. He moved very slowly within her, sometimes even stopping completely, wanting to let her become familiar with him. At one of these times his hand slipped between their bodies. Very softly he cherished her until Brianne moaned aloud as his fingers made loving contact with the core of her being. Only then did he resume movement within her.

She strained against him as the sweet pleasure returned and became almost pain, something only he could assuage. Not wanting it to end, but striving for just that, she could no longer endure his staring eyes, eyes that reached down inside her and took possession of her soul, leaving nothing unclaimed, and she kissed him with a wild passion. Lights danced behind closed lids, and she was cast wonderfully adrift in a sea of cascading emotions.

Dear God, don't let this end! she pleaded. But her whole body was seething, demanding that very release. Still, he persisted in his maddeningly slow pace, and it was only when he felt her fragile muscles begin to contract around him that he withdrew his hand, and together they moved in an ever-quickening ritual of love.

The storm raging outside was no less fierce than the one taking place in that sheltered room. Nature, in her most venerable form, was waging battle, intent upon victory. Ryan was an avid participant. Further kindling the rampant fire within Brianne, he whispered to her, urging her on, speaking of his own need.

There was no controlling it. The blood in her veins was like molten lava, swirling inside a volcano, begging to erupt, and Brianne's mind barely registered what was happening as her body was consumed by wave after wave of hot, unrelenting, intense pleasure. Thinking her joy complete, she was astonished to find new heights when Ryan tensed and cried out her name in a voice husky with passion. Holding him tighter, she brought him along with her, and together they accepted their destiny.

The room was now filled only with the tempestuous sounds from outside. The two lay quietly, save for their ragged breathing and pounding hearts, until Ryan lifted his head.

Gazing into her face, he cradled it tenderly within his palms, running his thumbs across her cheekbones.

"You were never a cold woman, Brianne, only one seeking." And kissing her mouth gently, he said, "Your search is over, love. You've come home . . . you're my wife."

Brianne didn't think such happiness was meant for mere mortals, and at his words her eyes began to fill. Holding him close, she freely wept into his shoulder and vowed never to leave this man. Never . . . she *was* home.

Chapter 22

Remembering last night, Brianne's lips curved in a secret smile as she leaned back against the warmth of her husband. Never would she have believed making love could be that exciting, and she blushed as flashes of the night before ran through her mind.

The second time they made love Ryan showed her what pleased him, and wanting his pleasure more than her own only added to the final joy. The last time, just before dawn, was the most surprising. She had never thought of making love as funny, but found it so as they laughed, talked, and teased, until the ultimate moments when laughter was the last thought on their minds. It was only sheer exhaustion that moved them to the bed. Pulling the comforter over their satiated bodies, Ryan had laughingly declared the marriage properly consummated. Giggling, she had agreed and snuggled against his chest. They had continued to talk quietly as they listened to the rain. As the storm outside had eased, so had the one in their bodies. It became gentle, soothing, and filled with a sense of wonder, she had drifted into a deep, contented sleep.

Brianne could tell from Ryan's breathing that he was still sleeping soundly, and she moved carefully as she left the bed. Taking the pitcher of water with her, she padded into the dressing room. There she washed quickly and changed into a fresh robe.

Tiptoeing back, Brianne thankfully heard Ryan's steady breathing and glanced at the domed clock resting on his dresser.

Twelve forty-five! Stephan was to arrive at two, if he still intended to come after last night's storm.

Hurrying to the mirror, she hastily brushed her hair and tied it back with a pale blue ribbon to match her robe. Looking at Ryan's sleeping reflection through the mirror, she smiled with happiness and pride. Catherine was right. He was quite a man, and she would fight to keep him, whether her antagonist was an old flame or the fates that had landed her here in the first place. She had no intention of giving him up.

Brianne carried the heavy tray across the room with aching arms. She had stubbornly refused any help downstairs when she had prepared this breakfast, and her resolve to accomplish this task alone was just as steadfast as she closed the distance between herself and the bed.

Placing her burden at the foot of the mattress, she climbed onto it and leaned carefully over her husband to softly kiss his cheek, one that was beginning to grow scratchy as the afternoon approached.

When his eyes finally opened and focused in on her, she smiled and whispered a gentle "Good morning."

He stared at her for a few seconds, then smiled. "I wasn't dreaming, was I?"

She returned his smile. "It was too beautiful to be anything but real."

Ryan reached out and traced the curve of her lips with his finger, and feeling herself begin to melt with his touch, she directed his attention elsewhere.

"Look," she said, pointing to the tray. "I took over Lizzie's kitchen and made breakfast for us."

His eyes held a devilish gleam. "I can think of a far more interesting task for you this morning."

It took every ounce of willpower to push his hand away. "Ah, but then you've never tasted my cooking," she said lightly, as she retrieved the food from the end of the bed.

"It wasn't breakfast I was thinking of tasting," he countered.

She lightly scolded him. "Stop it. Actually, it's more of a brunch, since it's after noon."

Resigned, Ryan stretched and sat up against the pillows. "So late! I should have been up hours ago to survey the damage from the storm."

Handing him a plate filled with her cheese omelets and Lizzie's hot croissants, she replied confidently, "You can relax. I've already talked to Mattie. She said Nathen came by earlier to report there was a minimal amount of repair work—clearing branches, replacing tiles, that sort of thing. Nathen seems to think the storm turned back into the Gulf before any major damage could be done."

"I really should have someone check on the boat, though," he muttered between bites of the soft, flaky roll. "I secured it the best I could, but there's no telling whether it still remains or floated back to New Orleans on its own."

Brianne poured him a cup of hot, steamy coffee, flavored with the chicory that even she was growing fond of. "I told Mattie about your wild purchase, and how you managed to get home last night. She said you were either a hero or a fool, and she wasn't sure which. Anyway, she'll have one of the men go down to the landing and report back to you later."

Giving her a playful grin, Ryan cocked one eyebrow. "Is there anything you haven't thought of?"

Brianne laughed. "As a matter of fact, yes. I don't know how we'll ever be ready by the time Stephan comes to pick up Rena."

"Rena?"

"Why are you surprised? Stephan invited her to go riding when he stopped in on Tuesday. I had to practically twist her arm just to get her to see him, but in the end she accepted his invitation on her own. Although after yesterday's weather, I doubt they'll do much riding."

Ryan wiped his mouth. "I'm not surprised that Stephan is attracted to her, Rena's a lovely woman. She just doesn't seem his type. In the past he always seemed drawn to a more flamboyant personality, hardly how I would describe our young guest."

Moving the tray back to the bottom of the bed, he continued, "I've been meaning to talk to you about her. Rena's position here is very confusing. I think you have to reach a decision. Which is she? Your cousin, or your maid?"

Brianne returned her own plate to the tray and came back to the top of the bed. "Strange that you should say that. Rena and I had it out, so to speak, about that very thing. She's a proud woman, Ryan, and she wants to feel that she's earning her keep, as she puts it. I told her that the time she puts in helping me with the school and around the house more than compensate, but I don't think she was convinced until Stephan came to visit. I believe it was the first time she was treated like a lady, and accepted for just being herself. She has a lot to forget, and I'm hoping Stephan might be the one to help her do that."

Ryan could no longer resist the impulse and reaching over, he pulled her into his arms. Holding his wife close, he breathed in the sweet fragrance of her hair and laughed in amusement. "All women are born matchmakers. Don't read too much into this," he advised gently. "They're only going riding."

Brianne slapped playfully at his chest. "That's not fair! I think when a woman is happy she naturally wants others to experience the same."

Loosening his hold, Ryan tilted her face up toward him. "And are you happy, Brianne?" he whispered softly.

She looked into his vivid blue eyes. God, how she loved him! She wanted to say the words, but knew she mustn't yet. Everything was too new, and the last thing she wanted to do was put pressure on him.

Instead of declaring herself, she quietly responded, "Happy is too common a word to describe how I feel. How about elated? Exhilarated? Joyous? No, joyful," she lightly exclaimed. "That describes it perfectly. Joyful . . . full of joy."

Ryan's eyes lit up momentarily with an emotion that excited her, and Brianne silently hoped it was true that the eyes were the windows to the soul. What she saw in Ryan's was like a flash of lightning. One moment it was there, demanding your attention with its unexpected brilliance, and in the next second it vanished, leaving in its wake a magnetism that compels you to search for its return. However fleeting, whatever had appeared in her husband's eyes was now gone and replaced by an expression of tenderness.

His probing eyes left hers to study her mouth. Finally he said carefully, "You're right, Brianne. That's a very good word."

As his mouth slowly descended to hers, she realized that was as close as he would come to revealing how he felt, and she gladly accepted what he offered by returning his kiss, thrilling once again at the contact when their lips met.

Moments later, she gently pushed him away from her. "If you continue, poor Rena will be left to greet Stephan alone, and I did promise to be with her when he arrived."

337

Continuing to hold her, Ryan protested, "He's not coming to see either of us, and I'm sure he'd understand if the newly married couple remained upstairs."

Brianne had been putting it off ever since he arrived last night. The time was now to inform him of her conversation with Stephan. Taking a deep breath, she sat up and began to gather the napkins they had used.

Ryan watched in amused silence. Obviously she had something to say but was having difficulty beginning. Hoping to help her, he asked, "Did Stephan speak to you about the party he's planning?"

She bit her bottom lip, finding it very disconcerting that he had shown, on more than one occasion, the uncanny ability to read her mind. Unconsciously, she threw the beautiful lace-edged napkins onto the tray.

Ryan took one look at her knitted brow and grabbing her arm, turned her around to look into her face. "Would you rather not go? It's all right, Brianne, we can always tell Stephan it's too soon."

Running his hand up her arm reassuringly, he added, "Perhaps later, when you feel better about it, we can have our own party and invite the entire parish."

"It isn't that. I've already told Stephan we'd be honored. I'll admit to being nervous about attending, but I was hoping you'd help me over the rough spots. You see, I've sort of volunteered you to be our dancing instructor and guide to the proper etiquette. Rena and I are in the dark when it comes to fancy balls and such."

Ryan laughed, and gathering her again into his arms, placed her upon his lap. "I've been many things in my life, but never an instructor of the finer arts." Puffing up his chest, he added decisively, "However, by the night of the party, both of you will look born to it. Of course, this means that Rena will have to come out of hiding. She positively disappears into the woodwork whenever I'm around."

Looking very pleased with himself, he stated, "Quite a delightful prospect—spending my evenings dancing with two lovely women."

Seeing her strained smile, he knew there was more. "What else is troubling you, little one?" he asked gently.

Brianne peered into his face and prayed it would remain the same after she told him. She began hesitantly, "Stephan . . . he didn't have time to tell you on Tuesday about the additions to his guest list."

She swallowed anxiously as Ryan urged her with his eyes to continue.

"Caroline Daniels and her father will be arriving any day, for a visit," she blurted out.

It wasn't the way she had intended to tell him, and Brianne cringed as she saw his eyes harden and felt his body tense under her.

"Stephan had received the letter only that morning, and he left the decision up to me whether to continue with his plans or not. I told him we were fortunate to have him for our friend and thanked him for thinking of us."

Looking into his face, which had returned to its former closed expression, her heart lurched and she quickly asked, "Was I correct, Ryan? Did I say the right thing?"

He placed a light kiss on her cheek and put her from him. Standing up, Brianne stared at his nude body as he grabbed his robe and smiled in a strained, polite way. "Of course you did. I'm happy you didn't disappoint Stephan."

Tying the belt, he then adjusted the collar of his robe and walked in the direction of his wardrobe.

Brianne couldn't believe he was going to leave it at that, not after last night, and she stopped him with her voice.

"Ryan . . . ?"

He turned and looked at her for a few tense seconds,

then, seeming to come to a decision, his face visibly relaxed and he came back.

Looking into her worried green eyes, he winked and said roguishly, "You are the only woman I have ever asked to marry me, Brianne. And judging from that breakfast you prepared, I made the right decision."

"Breakfast? What . . . !"

Ryan pulled her close to him and planted a light kiss on her forehead. "I'm teasing you," he laughed. "You have many fine qualities, my dear, and your culinary skills were a surprising addition."

His hands traveled lower on her back until they came to rest on her hips. Pulling her close, he whispered, "I can think of other newly acquired skills, though, that I find far more pleasing."

As he pressed her lower body still closer to his, Brianne wrapped her arms around him and laid her head on his chest. Even through the thick velvet she could hear the strong, steady beat of his heart and reveled in the security she felt. Here was a man to depend on.

Trying to understand, she bravely spoke. "Ryan, I don't want to pry, but I have to know . . . did she mean a great deal to you?"

She felt the breath leave his lungs as he exhaled deeply and Brianne waited with growing trepidation for his answer.

Tightening his hold, he dispelled her fears with his next words. "I apologize for putting you in this position. I should have explained Caroline to you long ago."

He stroked her hair and Brianne listened as his words reverberated within his chest. "I don't suppose I've been very fair with her. I let her assume that when the time came for me to marry, she would be my choice. Nothing was ever said, I never talked to her or her family about it, but I'm afraid by that omission a great deal was taken for granted.

"The two of you are as different as night and day," he said reflectively. "Caroline's a self-seeking woman, but I understood her, and she would have provided the family I wanted and the background I had once desired."

Brianne lifted her face to look at him. "I can't offer you a distinguished lineage, and I don't know if I will remain here long enough to give you the children you want. It doesn't look like you got the wife you envisioned, Ryan."

He cupped her face within his palms and looked deep into her eyes. "From what you've told me, your parents were fine people, a family to be proud of. Children will come, of that I have no doubt, but never let me hear you speak of leaving. I refuse to entertain the possibility. We can't understand what happened, but I will be forever grateful to whatever force brought you to me."

He kissed her lightly, then smiled wistfully. "You are correct, though. I did not get the wife I envisioned. I always thought the woman I married would more than likely be a silly, pampered belle, little more than a decoration. You, my love, have proved to be much more. You are my partner in this life, Brianne, and together we'll share the future."

He wiped away her tears and winked again at her solemn expression. "Come along, now. Soon the entire plantation will be speculating on what has kept us closeted within this room."

Brianne would always remember the next ten days with great fondness. The days were filled with hectic frenzy as the shipment of supplies arrived, and the nights swelled with happiness as Ryan directed them through the intricate paths of proper Southern etiquette. Laughter abounded as he assumed his position as dancing instructor, and the house servants clapped hands in time

341

to the animated strains that Tweed, a gifted field hand, brought forth from his fiddle. Used to modern dancing, Brianne found the Virginia Reel tame, with all that skipping and counting. But then there was the waltz . . . ah, it was storybook time again . . .

"Rena, keep your back straight when you curtsey. Don't bend from the waist. You're not a servant. Just lower yourself slightly. There . . . that's perfect." Ryan extended his hand to his "cousin" and gave her that famous Barrington grin—lips slightly parted and head held slightly to one side, as if in studied admiration.

"You're a natural, Rena," he said, as he walked her over to the side of the ballroom where Brianne was standing. "It's a part of your Irish heritage—the love of dancing."

Brianne thought back to her own lesson, not less than twenty minutes ago. Putting her fist to her hip, she said in a poor, exaggerated imitation of an accent, "And what about meself, sir? I'm as Irish as darlin' little Paddy's pig, I am."

Rena brought her hand up to her lips to cover a muffled laugh and Ryan chewed at the inside of his mouth as he reached for his wife's wrist. Bringing her back out to the center of the oak floor, he said with control, "You're about as skittish as Paddy's pig, that's for sure. Don't think I missed your performance while I was dancing with Rena—I didn't. Brianne, if you don't have a dance partner, don't dance alone."

At her offended look, he explained, "You stood there tapping your feet and swinging your . . . your . . ."

She brought her chin up and narrowed her eyes as she defied him to say it. "Swinging my what? Go ahead. What were you going to say?"

Ryan looked at the irises of her green eyes and noticed

that they had turned a deep emerald, almost the color they turned when Brianne was begging him in a husky voice to stop teasing and make love to her. He was constantly amazed by the depth of her passion. It was as if he had released a pressure valve, allowing years of pent-up emotions to rush forth, and he counted himself lucky, no, blessed, to be the one bathed by her desire.

He looked down at her defiant face, beginning to turn red in her anger, and smiled. "Never mind," he said, as he bent to kiss her pursed lips. "You can swing whatever you like," he whispered into her mouth, "when we're alone."

He watched as she fought back the smile that threatened to relax her lips. She took a quick breath to compose herself and straightened her shoulders. "I thought this was supposed to be a dancing lesson," she quipped.

She placed her small hand in his and reached up for his shoulder with the other. Turning to the group of servants by the door, Brianne said in a loud voice, "All right, Tweed, we're ready to try again." She waited until the slow, sweet sounds began before moving, but instead of gliding across the floor with her husband she stumbled, and Ryan's arms tightened around her.

Looking up to his face with confusion, Brianne heard him say, "*I* will lead. We're not going to continue until you relax. You have too much energy, Brianne. Just relax, and wait for me to guide you."

She thought of saying something, telling him he had no idea of what dancing was really like. So far he only had two to his repertoire. Why, she could think of six, seven dances that she could show him, and it would take days for him to master just one of them. And thinking of showing him modern dancing, she smiled and did indeed begin to relax.

Ryan felt the softening of her muscles and smiled. Nodding to Tweed, he waited for a few seconds, testing her, and when he found her to be still relaxed, he began leading her in a waltz. They glided across the polished oak floor, making a circle of the huge room. Dipping, swaying, Brianne had to admit it was wonderful. Waltzing was a dreamy style of dancing, one you could lose yourself in, and she thought it was a pity that it had lost its appeal in the late twentieth century. It was fun, yet so romantic, as the room whirled along with you. She looked up to her husband's face, saw he was pleased with her performance, and smiled at him seductively. "If you think I have energy now . . . you just wait until tonight, Mr. Barrington. You'll be amazed."

Ryan's mouth opened involuntarily. He knew she loved to shock him like that. Ever since he had come home from New Orleans, he had spent one incredible night after the other with her and knew, as he felt his pants become tighter across his hips, that tonight would be no exception.

Brianne bent over at the waist and let her hair fall toward the carpeted floor. With a hard-bristled brush she untangled the knots brought on from washing it earlier and thought about what Ryan had said about her dancing. Why, if he were with her now, instead of having been called away by Nathen, she would show him energy, just as she had promised during her lesson.

Straightening, she flung her head back and adjusted the Empire-waisted peach nightgown over her breasts. Of course she had energy, more than she'd ever had before, but it wasn't dancing that had given it to her. Smiling, she thought how perfect everything was. Everyone was happy, everyone, especially her.

She and Rena were working hard at the school and

slowly they were seeing progress. Stephan had come three times during the last week and managed to forget what he had come for and instead had sought out Rena. The two had long talks or went riding together, and Rena looked as if she too had more energy. She was just better at keeping it under control.

Brianne didn't want to control it. She wanted to reach out and embrace the world with her happiness. She wished everyone, at least once in their lifetime, could feel the way she felt right now. She couldn't wait for Ryan to return to their bedroom. She surprised herself by her wanton seductions of her husband. She couldn't help it. He'd fired a great need in her and she had reacted to that every night. She knew that he knew what she was doing, and most times he'd played along with her, but there were other times that he'd taken her without any pre- liminaries, without any games, just cravings and the desperate desires that, once assuaged, had left them both breathless and panting in the aftermath. Yes, she thought without the least bit of shame, she definitely had energy. And it wasn't from dancing.

Chuckling to herself, she thought back to the times in her life when she had loved to dance. You couldn't grow up so close to Philadelphia and not love it. Remembering herself as an adolescent, teenager, and young woman, Brianne found herself in front of the bed, and holding onto one of the tall posters, she pushed the draped material away from it. She and her sister had practiced dancing together, and if Morganna wasn't there and she had wanted to dance, she'd always found a sub- stitute . . . just like now.

She threw the brush onto the bed and searched her mind for a song. Before long, she could hear the drums in her head, like the pounding of a heart, growing louder and louder until a drawn-out strain from a synthesizer began the moving song. As she started to hum Huey

345

Lewis's "Heart of Rock n Roll," she reached out and used the poster as her dance partner. It was a fast dance, the kind she had loved to watch and imitate when she was a kid, watching Philadelphia's old Bandstand. They used to call it a jitterbug, and she would dance with her mother, her sister, anybody or anything that would provide a handle to hold onto. It didn't matter if it was a doorknob or a broom, she just wanted to move, like now.

Dipping her shoulders in time to the double beat, she would come to the poster and then push off as a phrase of the melody would come to mind.

"D.C., San Antone, and the Liberty Town, Boston and-a Baton Rouge . . ." Soon she was into it, back in a familiar pattern, brought about by years of living alone. The next time she stepped up to her wooden partner, she turned around, but instead of grabbing hold again she let go, forgetting the poster and dancing alone. She stayed in front of the bed, swinging her hips and moving her shoulders and arms in time to the beat of the song. "The old boy may be barely breathin', But the heart of Rock and Roll, the heart of Rock and Roll is still beatin'." She loved it. She knew she was a good dancer, and she closed her eyes as she gave herself over to it. Every once in a while she snapped her fingers as she mentally pictured herself out on a dance floor, not the one downstairs but a crowded one pulsating with bodies moving in rhythm with her own.

Ryan leaned against the door frame and watched his wife. The grin he had worn earlier when he opened the door and found her moving strangely around in a circle stayed frozen as she passed in front of the lamp. Her nightgown became almost transparent, outlining every luscious curve. She was a sorceress, singing about towns and weaving a spell over him, leaving him without a will of his own to resist. Knowing resistance wasn't what he wanted anyway, Ryan continued to watch, mesmerized by her movements. He felt a pang of disappointment when she opened her eyes and saw him staring at her. Whatever this Rock and Roll was that she was singing about, he wanted it to continue.

"Ryan!" Brianne could feel the blush creeping up from her neck as she watched her husband's grin spread even wider. Feeling she had to say something, explain her actions, she defended herself. *"That's* the dancing I'm familiar with," she said, trying to hide her embarrassment, "and it's quite permissible to do it alone, although it's better with a partner. Want to try?"

Shaking his head, Ryan closed the door behind him and said skeptically, "I don't think I could do it justice, Brianne. Not the way you do." He came closer to her and placed his hands at her shoulders, running his thumbs up her neck. "You were doing fine. Just continue."

She broke his gentle hold. "Oh no, you don't. I've had to learn your dances. You could at least try."

She smiled at him as he took off his shirt, and she tried to concentrate on anything but the crisp mat of curling hair that lightly covered his chest. When he reached down to unbutton his pants, Brianne quickly grabbed his hand. "Try it, Ryan. Please?"

He stood in front of her looking very uncomfortable, and she laughed. "It isn't like I'm asking you to do anything difficult. Besides, if I showed you some of the more popular dances, you'd think I should be put away in an asylum. We'll try something easy. Slow dancing. It's not like the waltz, Ryan . . . it's better."

She moved closer to him and brought her hand up to his shoulder. He put out his left and she placed her right one inside it. "It seems the same," he said as he looked down into her amused face.

She smiled at him slowly and said, "Closer. We have to be closer."

He obliged her by moving in half a step. She continued

347

to hold his eyes, saying lazily, "Closer."

"Brianne, any closer and we'd be . . ."

"That's the point, Ryan. Now move in closer." He was too tall to dance cheek to cheek, so she rested her head against his chest. "Take very small steps. Let me lead, just this once."

He obliged her, and soon they were dancing. Ryan felt it was another way for her to torture him. He could feel her breasts pressing against him and her soft breath was like exquisite pain as she breathed onto the hair on his chest. She was a minx, putting him through this when both of them knew how it was going to end.

She could feel the rumble of laughter as it came up his chest. "You're making this up, Brianne. I don't believe for a second that people dance like this. It's scandalous, and it's cruel of you to torture me this way."

"It's true. I swear I'm not making this up."

"Civilization could not have corroded that far. It isn't that I'm not enjoying it, but Brianne . . . it's like making love in public!"

She closed her eyes. Smiling, she said, "If we were in public, we'd have more clothes on. And speaking of clothes . . ." her right hand left his and trailed down to the buttons on his trousers.

Even though he groaned, he continued to hold her, and since they were in private, his suspicions as to the outcome of such behavior were accurate.

Two nights later, Brianne lay perfectly still. The perspiration glistened off her skin and was reflected in the moonlight. She didn't even turn her head to look at Ryan, just listened to his deep breaths matching her own as they tried to calm down in the aftermath of lovemaking. It had been perfection, and neither had minded, or even noticed, the humidity while the fire in

348

their bodies had been hot. Now the fire was peacefully beyond embers and they should have been relaxing in its afterglow instead of staying far apart, neither one wanting the touch of skin.

It was this damn humidity, Brianne thought irritably. Her blood was still Northern, too thick to withstand this torture of Nature. "Is it always this bad?" she whispered as her mind dwelt on the cool, air-conditioned rooms of her past.

Ryan let out his breath slowly and reached for her hand in the moonlight. "Promise you won't run away if I tell you it gets worse?" he asked, with a hint of laughter in his voice.

"You're kidding me. How does anyone live like this? If it gets much worse, I'm going to throw myself into the bayou—snakes and all!" She hated it. She knew she was whining, but couldn't stop the childish words. In the last five minutes not one single, tiny breeze had touched her through the mesquite netting that surrounded their bed. And if she heard another annoying buzz from the vicious insect as it tried to penetrate the fine gauze, she'd break down and start screaming. This must be how people went mad.

She took her hand away from his and sat up. Twisting her hair into a knot, she held the mass of tightened curls to the top of her head with one hand while shaking the netting with the other. "Get away, you horrible little bloodsuckers," she hissed, then blew down the front of her body in a futile effort to cool off.

Ryan chuckled at her scolding, then said, "You'll only be hotter if you move about so much."

She looked over to her husband in the darkness. "How can you stand this? Doesn't it even bother you?" she asked in a strained, frustrated voice. How could he have been so loving and concerned about her every desire less than ten minutes ago, and now ignore this furnace of a room?

Lightly, Ryan ran his fingers down her moist back. "You're miserable, aren't you?"

"Ryan, there is no *air* in here!"

Abruptly he pushed back the netting and stood up. "Get dressed," he said with authority.

Brianne hurried to close the netting. "What? Where are we going?" she asked in amazement, as she watched him put on his trousers. She strained her eyes in the darkness to see his face. Was the humidity driving him crazy too?

"Just get dressed, and hurry, before the mosquitoes attack. Put on your nightgown and a robe with long sleeves. Don't forget your slippers," he added as he buttoned the bottom of his shirt with one hand and pulled back the netting with the other. "Hurry up, Brianne!"

She dressed quickly. Her reasons were twofold: First, her naked body made too large a landing zone for the killer mosquitoes and second, her curiosity. Ryan refused to tell her where they were going, only that it was outside.

"Where outside? You can at least tell me that."

"Are you finished?" he asked. "Be very quiet. We don't want any company. Here, give me your hand. I'll lead you down the stairs."

She stayed behind him until they were out of the house. As she flicked away at the buzzing by her ear, she again asked, "Why don't you tell me where we're going?" She hurried to keep up with him and the pace was brisk until he slowed right in front of the stable.

"Oh no," she said with disappointment. "We're not going riding now, are we?" She could barely stay on a horse in the daylight, let alone stumbling around in the dark.

"Shh . . . you'll wake Luther," Ryan reprimanded, as

he felt for a bridle hanging against the wall. "Wait for me right here," he whispered as he disappeared into the darkness of the stable.

Brianne pulled at her sleeves to detach them from her sticky skin and shook her head each time she heard the insistent whine of mosquitoes, but it was little better than being in the bedroom. Worse, because now she was open to attack. Trying to distract herself as she waited for Ryan, she moved about and thought how unsuited she was for this climate. It must be something you are born tolerating. The North had its moments, but never like this. There really was no air moving.

She felt, rather than saw, Raven as Ryan led the huge black stallion up to her. Involuntarily she moved back a few feet away from the animal and watched as Ryan swung himself up and held out his hand to her. "Put your foot on top of mine and give me your hand. I'll bring you up."

She hesitated for a second, but knowing whatever he was doing was because of her complaining, she hitched up her nightgown and placed her slippered foot on his. She was surprised by his strength as she felt herself being whisked into the air, only to be held securely in front of him with both her legs off to one side of the horse. She put her arms around her husband and held tight.

He felt her shift uncomfortably and said apologetically, "It's too hot to saddle him. We won't be riding him that long anyway."

Brianne leaned against his chest and listened as Ryan spoke softly to the horse. Raven moved slowly away from the stable, and Ryan settled Brianne more comfortably in his arms.

"Better?" he asked, as he felt her relax.

"Mmn . . . yes. Thank you, Ryan." Just by moving, there was a slight breeze. And even though it was still a warm one, Brianne was grateful and forgot about the coarse hairs of the animal beneath her. "I'm sorry I complained so much," she said contritely. "I'm just not used to the weather yet."

Ryan bent his neck and kissed the top of her head. "Can you swim, Brianne?" he asked.

She brought her face up to his. "Yes! Are you telling me we're going swimming?" she asked in disbelief.

She could see the white of his teeth as he smiled down to her. "I've been keeping a secret from you. There's a small pool of water, drained from the bayou. It's formed on a small plateau, so the water is constantly moving and we just cleaned out the screening last week. The children use it in the summer. Nobody expected it to be this bad in late spring, but I'm sure they'll all be there tomorrow." He kissed the tip of her nose. "We'll just be the first ones to use it this year."

Brianne could barely contain her excitement. "I don't believe it! A pool! Hurry, Ryan!" she pleaded as she again tightened her arms about his waist.

They were far enough away from the house, so Ryan gently dug his heels into Raven's sides. The horse must have sensed their urgency, for he responded by lifting his head high and surging forth in a burst of unrestrained power.

Caught up in the magic moment, Brianne forget to be frightened. It *was* magical. The moon cast a silver glow to the forest and Brianne had to fight back the urge to reach out and gather the intricate, lacy Spanish moss that appeared to glisten with an eerie luminescence. Her nightgown fluttered about her legs like a soft, moving cloud, separating her, Ryan, and the horse from the dark earth below them, and it was a heady experience to feel the power under her and to press against the hard strength of her husband. She was breathtakingly embraced between the two, and felt for a brief, thrilling moment that all three were one.

She glanced up to Ryan and caught her breath. The air had pushed back his dark hair and by the moonlight she could see the almost boyish happiness in his face and the sharp definition of his cheekbones as his smile widened. This was his world. It was one of beauty and nature . . . one he wanted to share with her. As if in silent communication, he tightened his arms around her and brushed his lips against her forehead in a tender caress, conveying that he too felt enchanted.

Brianne had no idea where on Briarfawn this pool was located. She had stopped thinking about it as soon as Raven had transported them into this mystical forest. She only wished to concentrate on her senses . . . hearing nothing but the cadence of Raven's hooves as they crashed through the silent woods, smelling the sweet perfume of the late spring bougainvillea that acted as a fragrant aphrodisiac; seeing the shimmering luster of the woods as it blurred before her eyes; but mostly she was conscious of sharpened physical sensations. She reveled in the undulating movement of muscle and sinew beneath her, and basking in the powerful protective circle of Ryan's arms, Brianne feasted on the man she held close as she covered his chest with small, adoring kisses.

She was his, and Ryan felt almost primitive in the depth of his possession. Never had he imagined that any woman could stir such a powerful emotion within him. He felt invincible as he urged Raven through the night, his only thought to reach the pool and end the sweet torture that she had begun.

Ryan brought the horse to a sudden stop. Without a word, he dismounted and pulled Brianne down to him. Breathing heavily, he stared into her wide eyes as he unbuttoned his shirt.

"Now."

No further words were needed. Their eyes reflected

their wild need for each other. He watched as she stripped the robe and nightgown from her body, throwing her slippers on top of the small pile of clothing. She stood before him proudly, her nude body inches away from his. He had never wanted a woman so much, never wanted to make another so much a part of him, and his throat began to tighten from unspoken words.

He brought her close to him, wanting to feel her already hard nipples against his naked chest, her soft, satiny body as it molded itself to his. Almost growling, he reached down and grabbed her under her thighs, bringing her up to his waist. Instinctively she wrapped her arms about his shoulders and her legs around his hips, opening her velvety softness to him. Moaning, she held fast as he slowly walked them into the cool waters of the pool.

It caressed them as it inched its way up their bodies, its cooling properties having no effect on the fever raging inside them. The moon provided a phosphorescence, a beam of gray-white light that settled on the water, and Ryan brought his wife to its center. Bathed in night's ray and shoulder-deep in black satin, Brianne and Ryan clung to each other as one. It was their moment, chiseled out from eternity, their small piece of paradise.

Brianne could feel herself grow warm as she remembered that special night. She smiled in remembrance as she lay, attempting to rest for the party that night. Though how could she be expected to rest, when her stomach was in a knot and her hands became damp every time she thought about coming face to face with the formidable Caroline Daniels? She knew she was doing this to herself, for without wanting to, she had built a very strong mental picture of the woman in her mind. Even though Brianne had no idea what she actually looked like, Caroline was going to be spectacular, of that she had little doubt.

She had wanted to look beautiful for Ryan, and she and Rena must have tried on the ballgowns five times each before reaching a decision. Rena would wear the deep green, rather than the pink, because of her coloring. Rena's gown was of beautiful silk muslin, with flounces worn *à disposition*—woven embroidered bands of a tiny floral pattern that lay across the width of the skirt, with narrow frills showing the same pattern, on an even tinier scale, trimming the fitted bodice. Brianne's own gown was less busy, and that suited her, although she still thought the green might have highlighted her eyes.

She ran a hand over those eyes. Ah well, the green dress was Rena's. The red-haired woman could never have worn the pink gown, and Brianne would just have to make do with it. Again she pictured the Daniels woman, decked out and dressed to kill, and knew she would probably look like a little mouse next to her.

Brianne hated this insecurity, this questioning of her outward appearance, but then never before had she been in this position, about to meet a former paramour of the man she loved.

She must remember that whatever Caroline looked like, and no matter how she acted, she, Brianne, had what the woman wanted most . . . Ryan. She was sure enough of him now to know within her heart that he would stand by her and the two of them would face whatever the evening brought together.

A soft knock interrupted her wandering thoughts.

"Brianne?"

She turned and smiled at her husband as he peeked into the room.

"Come in," she said, happy for the interruption. "I'm not sleeping, I'm much too excited for that."

Sitting up, she pulled her hair up over her head and exhaled in an effort to release the tension that had been

355

building since morning.

Letting her hair fall about her shoulders, she asked with real concern, "Do you think we're ready for all this? I have visions of scandalizing all your friends by picking up the wrong fork, or something just as silly."

He squeezed her hand before coming to sit on the edge of the bed. "Stop worrying, love, you'll do just fine. What I really came in for was to ask what you planned to wear tonight. I expect you'll outshine every other woman there."

Brianne's shoulders slumped slightly at his words. "Don't expect too much. The gown I'm wearing is lovely, but it isn't overly fancy."

"Well, then, it will never do! You'll have to wear something else." He sounded positively pompous.

"It will have to do, Ryan," she stated with growing aggravation. "There isn't any other. But don't worry, it's suitable and I'll try not to embarrass you." What did he expect of her? Was she supposed to whip up another gown on the spot?

"I was never worried that you would be a cause for embarrassment, Brianne," and looking like the cat that swallowed the canary, he called out in a loud voice, "Mattie!"

The door swung open, and the housekeeper led in a parade of servants, each carrying an item of clothing.

Brianne sat on the bed, open-mouthed, as Mattie laid a fabulous creation before her. She reached out to touch the delicate material hesitantly, as though it were a work of art. It looked as if a thousand spiders had labored throughout as many nights to produce this masterpiece.

The gown was made of a silvery crepe material, a transparent silk with a crinkled surface. The crinkles made the silver thread that was woven throughout sparkle when a shaft of light came in contact with it. The bodice was fitted, with a long, pointed waistline in front and back. The neckline was very low, and she knew it would form a wide, deep curve over her shoulders, which would be softened by the delicate silk flowers, gardenias tipped in pale pink, that ornamented it. The sleeves were off the shoulder, short and wide, and would gather at her upper arms.

Brianne stared at the other articles, all made to match, right down to the layers and layers of crinolines.

Lifting her head, she looked in wonder to her husband. "How . . . ?"

Ryan beamed, and his face looked years younger. It was clear that he was very pleased with himself. "Remember, Stephan informed me about the party *before* I left for New Orleans. Once there, it was a simple matter of stopping in at Madame Fountaine's and threatening her very life if she didn't use this material to fashion a gown that would set New Orleans society on its heels. Knowing she was the only couturière in the city to have your measurements, she took advantage of her upper hand and held me up for a king's ransom. All worth it, though, by the look on your face."

Brianne was overwhelmed by his generosity. "It's exquisite! I don't know what to say . . . except thank you, Ryan. I was lying here feeling like a little field mouse when you came in."

Brianne carefully placed the gown out of her way as she came over to his side. Placing her arms about his waist, she rested her head on his chest and sat silently within the circle of his arms.

Ryan kissed the top of her head gently. "A field mouse? You certainly underestimate yourself. Brianne, you could walk into Stephan's home tonight clad in young Mary's apron, and you'd still create a stir. It's only fitting, however, that someone with your beauty should wear this gown."

"Oh Ryan . . ." She was about to tell him what was in

her heart, that she had come to love him, and his home, and never wanted to be separated from either, when Mattie cleared her throat.

"Ahem . . . it's not my place to say, but Miz Rena's already startin' to get dressed."

Brianne had forgotten about her presence in the room and stared at the housekeeper in confusion. Perhaps it was better this way, she thought. Tonight, when they were back in this room, she would reveal her true feelings and take the chance that he would respond the same. Dear God, she prayed. Please don't let me be wrong about this!

Kissing her forehead again, Ryan stood up. "Mattie's right. I'm using the room next door to dress, so I'll meet you downstairs later."

Taking her hands in his, he squeezed lightly. "Everyone will be too busy staring at the lovely picture you present to notice which fork you pick up. Stop worrying," he admonished. "The night will go well . . . you'll see."

She had asked Mattie to give her a few minutes alone. She needed this time to sort out the complex feelings that assailed her. Walking over to the mirror, Brianne viewed her completed costume. This night reminded her of her wedding day, when she had stood before another mirror and tried to come to grips with herself. That day she had been filled with fear, but tonight she felt a different kind of dread. All of it centering on one person—Caroline.

Well, she certainly was a match for her. Turning sideways, she peered at her reflection and felt like Cinderella. The woman who stared back at her could have jumped off the pages of the book.

The dress was perfection. She had Mattie lace her into the corset until its bodice was snug, but she refused to suffer any further discomfort to achieve a ridiculous eighteen-inch waist. Her own, which measured at twenty-two inches, was just fine. Eighteen inches! No wonder so many women passed out; they couldn't expand their lungs to get the air necessary to stay conscious. The vapors indeed! It was all this covered steel. The hoops, though, did provide a lightness and a buoyancy that she hoped wouldn't prove unmanageable.

Lifting the hem, she looked at the silver slippers that peeked back at her. Please, God, she prayed, let me remember the correct steps when they dance tonight. Glancing up, she moved closer to the mirror and scrutinized her face.

Rena had provided her with a pale rouge to blush her cheeks, and kohl, which she used to underline her eyes. A few months ago she wouldn't have gone to the store with so little makeup, but now it seemed natural. Pursing her lips, she judged the greasy substance Rena gave her as too much and blotted some off, leaving a pale, shiny color of pink on her mouth, almost the same shade as the soft gardenias at her breasts and hair.

Rena had done wonders with it. Pulling it up and back from her face, she had used a hot iron to achieve the cascading curls, and the whole was caught in a long silver netted snood that hung to the middle of her shoulders. Tiny miniature gardenias were attached to the band, and her face seemed to be framed by the delicate flowers.

Her green eyes sparkled and she straightened for a final overall inspection. Despite the warm, balmy air, she felt shivers run along her skin, and with a confident smile she whispered into the mirror, "Look out, Miss Daniels, I mean to keep him."

Brianne paused at the top of the staircase to gaze down at Ryan. He was standing in the foyer fingering a black leather case, which he placed on a small table, then, seeming to change his mind, quickly picked it up again. He looked so handsome, dressed in formal black, with a crisp white shirt and a complex cravat. Even from this distance, she could see the diamond stickpin nestled within its folds. For once he had forgone his high riding boots, and he looked almost modern with trousers reaching the floor instead of being stuffed into the tops of the ever-present boots. As always, there was an animal energy about him, and yet now he looked at ease, comfortable with his formal attire. She couldn't blame anyone, even Caroline, for wanting to be in her place next to him.

Seeming to sense her presence, he looked to the top of the stairs. Sucking in his breath, he stood for a moment and stared. She smiled at him shyly and began to descend while Ryan moved on unsteady legs to meet her. Dear God, he thought. She's more than beautiful! I'll have to remain by her side all evening, just to fight them off. A tremendous surge of pride and possessiveness passed through him then.

As she came eye-level with him, he extended his hand and returned her smile. "Brianne, you look absolutely beautiful! It was well worth the wait."

When her cheeks blushed a deeper pink, he lifted her hand to place a small kiss on the inside of her gloved palm and then led her down the remaining steps.

"Thank you, Ryan," she said breathlessly, more affected by his warm kiss than she had thought possible. "It would be hard not to look beautiful in this dress."

He held her at arm's length, looking her over from head to foot. "There seems to be something missing," he claimed with a puzzled look.

Suddenly his face lit once again and he declared, "I think I have just the thing." Presenting the leather case to her, he stated, "For you, Mrs. Barrington. The first of many."

Brianne opened the wide, thin box with trembling fingers, then, once she saw what it contained, looked into

Ryan's face with a shocked expression.

"Ryan?" Softly she whispered his name. "This is too much."

Smiling at her tenderly, he quietly exclaimed, "Nonsense! Quite the contrary. You've never asked for a single thing."

He reached over and picked up the delicate necklace. It was a fine chain worked in silver filigree, and hanging heavily from its center was the most perfect diamond, shaped like a teardrop.

He held it up between them, each of his hands holding an end. They gazed into each other's faces in silent communion for a few exquisite seconds until Ryan finally broke the spell.

"Brianne, if you don't turn around we'll miss Stephan's party, and I shall take you back upstairs and selfishly keep you all to myself tonight," he whispered huskily.

She continued to return his look, wanting nothing more than to give in to the urgings of her body. The electricity that passed between them was almost a viable thing, drawing her closer to its source, and it was with regret that she cast her eyes down and turned around.

Holding up her netted hair, she first shivered, then tensed, when Ryan's hands brushed her shoulders as he fastened the clasp. The diamond lay heavy and cold, but she knew her inflamed body would soon warm it.

Placing a light kiss upon her neck, Ryan whispered, "Come. Rena is waiting for us in the drawing room."

With an arm about her waist, he led her into the room and Brianne fought the impulse to take his hand and lead him upstairs, back into their room. She realized with horror that at that moment she really didn't care about Stephan, or his party, or even Rena. She only knew she *needed* Ryan to put an end to the throbbing of her heart. Shocked at how she had changed in the last few weeks, how totally enamored she was of her husband, Brianne made a valiant effort to compose herself as Rena turned around to them.

"Brianne!" Rena stared with admiration. "You leave me speechless!"

Brianne laughed self-consciously. "I know what you mean. I feel a little like the Snow Queen. I only hope people don't shiver when they come too close."

Ryan squeezed her waist affectionately. "Hardly. But then, I don't intend to let anyone get close enough to find out."

Brianne turned her attention back to her friend. "And you, Rena—you're beautiful!"

While Rena blushed prettily and fingered a lovely cameo attached to a black ribbon at her throat, Ryan left them to walk over to a table laden with liquor and fragile stemware.

Watching the two women, he was filled with pride. Brianne clearly was the most beautiful woman he had ever seen, at least she appeared that way to him. She would have the party buzzing within minutes of their arrival, and Stephan, who was obviously taken with young Rena, as evidenced by his frequent visits and lame excuses, would be completely overcome when he saw the lovely object of his attentions.

Brianne excitedly asked Rena, "Turn around. Let me get the full effect."

As Rena complied, she exclaimed, "Wonderful! Oh Rena, I'm so glad, and that cameo is perfect to offset the green."

Rena looked shyly toward Ryan and smiled. "Mr. Bar . . . I mean Ryan, presented it to me earlier. I told him he shouldn't have, but he insisted."

Brianne looked at her husband across the room and smiled her thanks. *God help me, but I do love him,* she thought desperately as he carried a tray containing three

362

glasses bubbling with champagne.

Coming to stand before the women, he offered each a glass. As they held the crystal before them, Ryan proposed a toast. "To the two most lovely ladies in the state of Louisiana, and my star pupils . . . let's give the rest of them a night to remember!"

Amid the laughter that followed, both Brianne and Rena exchanged looks. Each knew the other was praying Ryan was right.

Chapter 23

Mosshaven, Stephan's home, glittered in the distance. It was aptly named, Brianne thought, as they passed under the long columns of mature oaks dripping with Spanish moss. She glanced at Ryan and read the reassurance in his eyes, though Rena was continuing to wring the lace handkerchief between her fingers—visible evidence of the butterflies that must also be attacking her stomach.

She reached over and stilled Rena's hands. "Remember, *we* are the honored guests tonight, not the other way around. They're just people, Rena, and I'm sure they're as curious about us as we are of them. Neither of us has anything to be ashamed of—didn't Ryan pronounce us ready for this night?"

Easy words, Brianne thought. Now if only I could believe them.

She looked at her husband for confirmation, and he nodded. "I said by tonight you both would look born to this way of life, and when I set out to accomplish a goal, I give it my all. Happily, you ladies made the task a pleasure. Don't disappoint me now by getting the jitters. Both of you can hold your own with anyone there tonight."

Too quickly, the carriage stopped in front of the house and the door was opened by a liveried servant.

Before rising to descend, Ryan held the women's hands and gave them last-minute advice. "Now smile, and ladies . . . even before the lessons, I would have been just as proud to walk in with both of you. Be yourselves."

As Ryan stepped down, Brianne glanced at Rena, then quickly shut her eyes for a moment. Taking a deep breath, she snapped them open and plastered what she hoped would be interpreted as a friendly smile on her face as she took Ryan's hand.

Ryan stood between the women as the front door was opened to admit them, and Brianne's first impression was that of wealth. A gigantic chandelier sparkled overhead with hundreds of candles, and the walls were graced with portraits of the Daniels ancestors.

A young maid came and took Brianne's gossamer shawl as Stephan caught sight of them and exclaimed, "Finally! I was beginning to worry that my guests of honor would never arrive."

Although his words were directed toward the Barringtons, he only had eyes for the beautiful young woman who accompanied them.

Remembering himself, he quickly kissed Brianne's cheek. "You're a vision, my dear," he stated, and mischievously added, "If the women here tonight start to look green to you, it will only be because they're sick with jealousy."

Brianne laughed, and started to thank him for his silly compliment, but he had turned away from her to stare at the red-haired woman at her side.

"Rena!" He breathed her name in awe.

Seeing he was not capable of finding his voice, Rena surprised them all by saying smoothly, "Stephan, I'm so glad to be here. Mosshaven is more beautiful than you described. Might you show it to me later?"

Brianne did her best to hide the laughter that was threatening to escape her lips. Good for you, Rena, she silently cheered. She would be fine tonight, and Brianne was happy for her.

As Stephan hastily agreed to a tour later in the evening, Brianne saw a crowd of people forming at the entrance to the foyer. Placing her hand on his arm, Ryan steered her in that direction. Introductions were made all around, and throughout the next twenty minutes Brianne's mind was in a whirl. Never would she remember all the names, but the faces revealed a great deal. The men had shown open admiration and respect for her husband, thereby limiting more amorous expressions. The women were for the most part reserved, the younger ones waiting to pass judgment while those older were polite, though some seemed pleased to make her acquaintance and were almost warm in accepting her.

But she still had not met Caroline Daniels.

Sipping champagne, she looked around the room. No, she had met everyone in sight. She spied Rena on Stephan's arm and once again was surprised by her friend's aptitude. Rena looked natural and at ease as she smiled into the faces being presented to her. She was a much better student than I, Brianne thought miserably, as she felt her palms begin to perspire. Thank goodness for the long gloves!

Where was the woman?

Just then Stephan turned, and the crowd became hushed. Entering the ballroom was a woman too beautiful to be mistaken for anyone else.

Fair, with golden blond hair reaching the middle of her back, Caroline had chosen well when she dressed for this party. Her gown was made of a rich deep purple silk, and it contrasted sharply with her creamy skin, much of which was exposed by the deep neckline that drew attention to her ample breasts. Lying above them, hanging from her neck, was a magnificent necklace of diamonds and amethysts. She carried herself regally for her tall stature. Almost five feet nine inches, Caroline Daniels was always conscious of her height and loathed the smaller, petite versions of her sex that inevitably surrounded her, and whom she always towered over.

Throwing back her shoulders, she walked with a natural sensuality to her cousin and placed a perfunctory kiss on his cheek.

Stephan's eyes became jaded as he looked at her. "Always the one to make an entrance, eh, Caroline?" he stated sarcastically.

She ignored both his comment and the red-haired woman at his side. In seconds her mind had categorized the younger woman as no threat. She must be the bitch's cousin, the one that Stephan was so taken with.

Giving the young thing an insincere smile, she turned away from her to whisper to Stephan, "Where is she? That stupid Bessie told me Ryan had arrived."

Stephan's eyes narrowed. "Don't ever again use my servants to do your dirty work for you, Caroline."

Then, in a normal voice he continued, "I don't believe I have to point out Ryan's wife, if that is to whom you're referring. Just look for the most beautiful woman here tonight, and you'll easily find her. You can't miss her, Caro, she positively glows with happiness."

Her eyes became daggers, but seeing her father approaching, she only managed to say quickly, "You know, Stephan, even as a child I despised you!"

Stephan laughed as she walked away on her father's arm, and looking down at the confused woman standing next to him, he squeezed her hand. "I'm sorry for that, Rena. But you know, she's right. Even as a young boy I knew her for what she is."

Caroline was in a magnanimous mood, now that Ryan was near, and she graced everyone with her dazzling smile, even flirting occasionally with the more attractive younger men; but her eyes were continually searching the room until they finally came to rest on the only man who could hold her interest.

Damn him! she cursed inwardly. Even now, as she watched him bend his head to speak with someone whom he blocked from her vision, she felt her womanhood begin to throb.

He was meant to be hers! The only one who could dominate her and make her do his bidding, the only one she could not control; and no one, before or after him, was his equal.

Turning to her father, she said innocently, "We have yet to congratulate the guests of honor. Let us not forget our manners, Father."

The robust gray-haired man looked at his daughter anxiously but complied with her wishes, hoping, as they made their way through the other couples, that she would behave herself.

Hearing the woman's laughter as they approached, Brianne felt sick and was not in the least reassured when she felt Ryan's arm tense under her fingers.

From behind them they heard the rich, throaty drawl. "Why Ryan Barrington, you wicked man! Imagine our surprise when we heard you'd run off and gotten married . . . so quickly too!"

Ryan turned to face her, and Caroline's beautiful smile froze when he revealed the small woman he was shielding with his body.

He bowed slightly, acknowledging her. "Caroline."

Bringing the woman forward, he introduced them. "May I present my wife? Brianne, Miss Caroline Daniels from Richmond, Virginia."

Brianne disliked her on sight, and she knew instinctively the feeling was mutual. The woman's voice dripped with phoniness as she remarked, "Such a pleasure to meet you, Anne."

Ryan looked amused as he corrected her. "I'm afraid you misunderstood me. My wife's name is *Bri*anne, a fine Irish name. We've often wondered if our ancestors knew each other back on the old sod."

Caroline knew he was referring to the hasty remark she had once made implying that his only handicap in her eyes was his half-Irish ancestry.

Looking meaningfully into his eyes, she remarked, "How nice that you have *something* in common."

Ryan introduced her father, and Caroline used the time to examine the woman. She had not expected her to be *that* beautiful. It had been quite a shock when Ryan stepped aside, but she had quickly recovered, and in that moment had seen the dread in the woman's green eyes. So she knows about me, Caroline thought with satisfaction. All the better. In her mind, she was already scheming on the best way to use this information while her eyes lighted on Ryan's wife's dress. She had to admit it was exquisite, and must have cost a small fortune. She would bet it came straight from Worth, in Paris, and in all probability one of Ryan's vessels had carried it across. It should have been mine, she thought with vehemence.

While her father kissed the chit's hand, Caroline asked in a syrupy voice, "Why, Brianne, I simply must know where you found your gown. It's breathtaking. I'm afraid you put the rest of us poor ladies to shame."

Brianne recognized the insincerity in the woman's voice, but was able to answer with confidence, "Thank you, Caroline. It was a gift from my husband, and I do agree with you—it *is* breathtaking."

Brianne gazed up at Ryan, and the look they exchanged created actual pain for Caroline.

Never had he looked at *her* like that! Hatred for this woman who had stolen Ryan burned deep within her. I'll destroy her! Caroline vowed. And the sooner the better, she judged, looking at her former lover.

One last guest arrived, and it was Brianne who named him. "Ryan, look!" she exclaimed. "It's Monsieur Duville. I didn't know he was coming."

Ryan's head snapped up. His whole body tensed, while his face became a wooden mask, fixed in aversion. With his eyes never leaving the latecomer, who was chatting with Stephan, he uttered under his breath, "Nor did I."

Then, seeming to break himself away from the trance that held him, Ryan smiled at Brianne. "Please excuse me for a minute. I must speak with our host. I'm sure Arthur will safeguard you from the attentions of the more overly zealous guests."

Caroline's father nodded and assumed Ryan's position between the two women while Brianne watched in confusion as Ryan made his way across the room.

Whatever had made him react that way? she puzzled. And knowing how she must feel, why had he left her at the mercies of this blonde cat?

Brianne wasn't the only one to ponder those same questions. Caroline was quick to notice the drastic change in Ryan when the handsome Creole had appeared, and promised herself to find out the reason. This could prove to be a very interesting evening after all, she thought.

Ryan caught Duville's eye as he neared the doorway, and the man smoothly left his host to quickly mingle with the crowd.

Coming to Stephan, Ryan grabbed his arm roughly. "What the hell is Duville doing here? He wasn't mentioned as a guest. Or is this something else you forgot to tell me about?"

Stephan looked surprised by his friend's anger. "He wasn't on the original guest list I presented to you. Armand D'Arcy mentioned to me at the beginning of the week that Duville would like to attend. I believe he said something about Duville having already met Brianne, and wanting to congratulate her on her marriage."

Looking closer at the taller man, he was taken back by the animosity written on his face. "Ryan, what's wrong? You and Duville have done business together, so I naturally thought the request was sincere. I must admit, though, I was a little surprised by it. Imagine Gregory Duville lowering himself to attend an American's party!"

Both men looked in Duville's direction. Studying the Creole's back, Ryan watched as he made his way closer to his wife. Was the man foolish enough to disregard his warning?

Without looking at Stephan he said, "I'm sorry. Duville and I had a falling out when I was in New Orleans, and seeing him here must have shaken me up. Do me a favor, though, Stephan? Keep an eye on him. His presence here only proves he's planning something."

Stephan knitted his brow, but nodded without questioning further. As he watched Ryan return to Brianne's side, he pondered the wisdom of having such a gathering, considering that two of the guests wished anything but happiness for the couple.

Dinner was soon announced, and Brianne was relieved. If she had had to spend another minute with Caroline Daniels, she would have dropped this facade of gentility and told her off in no uncertain terms. Even the woman's own father was taken aback by Caroline's open hostility. All that, of course, disappeared like magic when Ryan returned to the strained trio.

A little miffed that Ryan had deserted her so soon after she had been introduced to the woman, Brianne hesitantly placed her hand on his arm. Walking into the dining room, she had no chance to ask him about it as she was struck with a wave of uncertainty.

She was not to sit next to Ryan but to Stephan's right, with an older, mustachioed man beside her. As Ryan seated her, he brushed her ear with a kiss and whispered the man's name. Wayne Courtland. Panic began as a small knot in her stomach as she looked around her.

There they were! She'd been to many formal dinners in the twentieth century, but this array of eating utensils, of infinite variety, was mind-boggling. Recalling her statement that afternoon to Ryan about embarrassing him, she smiled anxiously at her companion and looked again at the eight silver teaspoons to her right. Which one was the nut spoon? she thought in a panic. And why hadn't she paid better attention when Ryan was explaining, instead of making a joke of the lessons?

Dinner, it seemed to her, was prepared by a squad of black cooks and then served by a platoon of waiters in splendid livery. The food was displayed in a dazzling arrangement of silver, crystal, and fine bone china. Priceless chafing dishes, urns, and platters were presented.

As each waiter in turn offered his dish, Mr. Courtland took great pleasure in explaining the entrees to her as they were presented before her: Sweet, delicate white-and-gray-laced flesh of the spring roe, oysters, perch; lustrous red gleaming Smithfield hams from lean peanut-fed hogs, country hams; turkey, quail, venison, veal, and lamb; chestnuts, creamy dressings, stuffings, chutneys, and endless desserts. Among them was Mr. Courtland's favorite: brandied peaches, "buried in the groun'," he said, to age, and sometimes difficult to relocate. Brianne opted for the ice cream, a delightful link with her own past, and listened with interest as the man explained that the ice had been floated down the Mississippi for just this occasion.

Once Brianne ventured to glance down to the other end of the table, where Ryan was seated. Acting as hostess for her cousin, Caroline conveniently had Ryan beside her as she sat regally at the opposite head of the table. He looked to be concentrating on his food and listening to the woman's chatter with half an ear. Caroline, however, didn't seem to notice Ryan's lack of attention, but was quick to pick up Brianne's interest. Waiting for such a moment, she flashed the Northerner a smug smile and concentrated harder on her dinner companion.

Afterwards, Brianne made a point of ignoring that end of the table. Instead, she listened to the talk around her, which seemed to center on the belief that the South had an innate superiority over all other races and peoples. The males around her did not doubt that, man for man, they were braver, stronger, better than the troublesome Northerners. No one seemed to remember she was from the North, and Brianne had to bite her tongue more than once to hold back a retort.

In the end she realized that nothing she could say would make a difference. She could not change the history of these people, and they were to be pitied, for only the very strong would survive the next decade.

Caroline's lazy voice carried throughout the entire room. "I do believe, ladies, when the dinner conversation turns to politics it's time for us to leave the gentlemen to their cigars and brandy."

Rising to the polite laughter that followed her statement, Caroline led the women into Stephan's drawing room. Catching Ryan's smile, Brianne hurried to find Rena. The two stayed close together, prepared to band together if the need should arise, for both women knew that now would come the true test of their acceptance.

"How are you?" Brianne asked as they took possession of a lovely brocaded loveseat. "You seemed to be holding your own throughout dinner. I'm afraid I didn't fare as well. Stephan was sweet, of course, but . . ."

"Listen," Rena interrupted. "I've something to tell

you." She gave Brianne a false smile for the sake of the other women and whispered, "That horrible Daniels woman is out for you. Stephan's estimation of her wasn't off the mark. Why, you should have heard the two of them when she made her grand entrance!"

"Don't bother to tell me. I knew that before I came here. I didn't suppose she would take kindly to losing Ryan. I know I wouldn't."

"As long as you know, Bri, that witch is up to no good. I've seen her kind before. Oh, they weren't *ladies*, like she's supposed to be, but they were the same, if you know what I mean?"

Brianne tried to make her smile reassuring as she nodded her understanding.

The circle of women about them talked of fashions and children and the dreadful hot weather that was approaching, and Brianne joined in the conversation, all the while conscious of Caroline's eyes upon her.

Suddenly, from out of nowhere, the Daniels woman's voice rose above the others. "Tell us, Brianne, however did you capture the elusive Ryan Barrington? I'm sure there's quite a number of us here who are just dying to know."

Brianne smiled benignly back at her. Inwardly, she seethed. So she wants to do this publicly. Well, so be it. I'll stick to the truth, as much as possible, she thought, but she'll also regret asking this way.

Toying with her fan, Brianne managed to look properly embarrassed as she began her story. "Actually, Caroline, Ryan swept me off my feet the very day I met him. It was on Briarfawn, and so anxious was I to see it that I tripped and fell, injuring myself. My cousin, Catherine Murdock, attended me in Ryan's home, and I suppose you could say she was instrumental in bringing us together."

Brianne could see the mention of Catherine's name had gained her the approval of the other women.

Knowing that Catherine was considered a pillar in this tight aristocratic community, she continued, "Yes, I would have to say it was Catherine who showed us that we belonged together. Something that Ryan and I will always be grateful to her for doing."

Salena Grandeville, a regal matriarch who had been distantly polite up till then, spoke up. "It is obvious that you and Mr. Barrington are well suited. I must say it's good to see him happily settled at last."

The other women quickly agreed, and Brianne smiled her thanks as a black servant made the rounds of the room, offering more refreshments. When she came to Caroline, Brianne watched as the woman imperceptibly moved her foot in an effort to trip up the maid. The girl caught herself from falling, but not before she spilled some of the fruited punch on the beautiful oriental rug.

Caroline stood quickly as the poor thing looked at her master's relative with huge, frightened eyes.

Bringing back her hand in a flash, she hit the girl soundly on the face. "You clumsy fool!" she spat.

Chapter 24

Although the rest of the women gasped in surprise at Caroline's actions, Brianne's mouth opened, but no sound came out. Instead, a haze of red anger swam before her eyes. Rena grabbed her hand, transmitting a silent plea that she disregarded as she stared at the despicable woman across from her.

Who did she think she was? Who did any of them think they were? Their men, their *gentlemen*, were across the hall talking of war and rebellion, their grand, noble ideas leading only to destruction, while in here a *lady* showed her true colors. She was beginning to feel the South was a place of hidden violence. Underneath all the surface show of gentility and refinement, violence lay at its heart. Perhaps she was misjudging them, but too many here tonight, in this home, wanted a fight.

Feeling Brianne's eyes upon her, Caroline shot her a superior look before turning her head away. Brianne knew she would never forgive herself if she didn't speak up.

"How dare you strike that maid?" she coldly demanded. "You know as well as I do it was not her fault."

The room became deathly still with expectancy as all

eyes turned toward her, the outsider trying to gain admittance to their ranks.

Caroline looked shocked that Brianne would speak so accusingly in front of the others.

Seating herself once again, she smoothed her skirt and just as smoothly answered, "I keep forgetting you're from the North, my dear, and not used to our ways. Given the time here, you'll soon come around."

"I'll never come around to your way of thinking, Miss Daniels. I would be ashamed to have your thoughts in my mind."

From her side, Brianne heard a small groan and knew it was Rena's. She sensed the other woman's confusion, not knowing whether Brianne's remark had been an affront to the South, but she was too busy to worry about it as her eyes locked in battle with Caroline's.

Slowly Caroline rose from the chair and breathed in deeply. Seeing the fire in the Virginian's eyes, Salena Grandeville also stood.

Looking at Caroline, she said reprovingly, "Don't speak for all of us, Caroline. You have given the impression *our* ways are yours. That isn't so. However you handle things in Virginia, we in New Orleans never condone the mistreatment of those beneath us."

She looked at Brianne and said sternly, "I feel the need to refresh myself. Would you care to join me, Mrs. Barrington? Miss Ahearn?"

Grateful to the older woman for ending a potential cat fight, Brianne readily accepted and watched in surprise as the others followed in their wake, like so many pieces of flotsam coming into shore, leaving the startled and abandoned Caroline to sink alone.

With the added assurance that they had been accepted into this society, she and Rena descended the stairs with the others, who were greeted by their men and the strains of the musicians tuning up their instruments.

Brianne caught Ryan's eye halfway down, and he gazed at up her with open tenderness.

Her breath came quicker, and beside her she heard Salena quietly remark, "It is precisely that look which drives Caroline to distraction. Rejection causes people to react differently. Some brood for awhile, then pick up the pieces and go on, others are like Caroline and have a spiteful streak. Be aware, Brianne, what happened earlier was meant for you. She needed to vent her anger on someone, and the poor slave was just convenient. You would be wise to understand the way her mind works, rather than reacting emotionally."

Looking past her as they reached the last step, she smiled and said maternally, "Now run along to your husband. The dancing is about to begin and I'd like a comfortable chair to rest these aging bones in, while I watch the two of you leading it off."

Brianne told Ryan of the altercation as they walked into the ballroom. Handing her a cup of nonalcoholic fruit punch, Ryan stood in silence as the room filled.

As Brianne looked over the crowd of people, she heard him say thoughtfully, "It seems as though I've brought more than enough trouble to you. I'm sorry. But never think that I'd expect you to compromise your principles. The situation is difficult enough without adding that to it."

Frightened by his voice, she spoke up urgently. "No, Ryan, you're wrong. Happiness. That's what you've brought to me. It's taken me awhile to realize it, but I'm happy here. Certainly there's a lot wrong with this way of life, and I do feel obligated to fight those things, but being your wife isn't one of them."

He scrutinized her face. "Whoever would have believed, when we came to our agreement that day in the Murdocks' library, that it would have turned out so well?"

They didn't need words, as they smiled into each other's eyes in silent agreement.

Stephan, with Rena on his arm, interrupted them. "Excuse me. I'm happy to see the two of you enjoying yourselves, but until you dance with your wife, Ryan, you're denying the rest of us the same pleasure," and casting Rena a meaningful look he added, "and there just happens to be another lady I've been waiting to take into my arms."

Motioning toward the center of the room, Stephan lifted his eyebrows. "So if the two of you would proceed to the dance floor, we can continue the party."

Laughing slightly, Ryan inclined his head and led Brianne to the middle of the deserted parquet flooring. The conversation died down and the atmosphere was one of expectancy as Ryan held out his wife at arm's length.

Nervous to begin with, Brianne scanned the room, looking for the friendly face of her best friend. Unfortunately, her eyes lighted not upon Rena but Caroline, who looked quite friendly as she engaged in conversation with Monsieur Duville.

At least the woman wasn't looking at her, Brianne thought, and Ryan drew her attention back to himself as he softly said, "Look only at me . . . this night is yours."

He bent at the waist and gently kissed her hand as the orchestra began the soft melody of a waltz. Approval was heard throughout at his gesture, and Brianne found herself swept into his arms after the opening bars.

She was mesmerized by him as he once again seduced her with those words. They floated along the gleaming floor, oblivious of the surrounding crowd, never speaking, never noticing the envious glances from both sexes—from those young enough to hope to capture what they were viewing for themselves one day, or from those older, who looked on with the nostalgia of days gone by, knowing if they had not already experienced such a love, it might forever elude them.

Brianne wanted that moment to last forever. The steps came naturally, and she was able to give her full attention to studying Ryan's face.

His errant lock of hair fell slightly onto his forehead and she noticed once again the tiny lines of responsibility permanently etched there. So much had been placed upon him, from such an early age, that she wanted more than anything to help erase them. Eyes that could quickly flash with anger were now gentle and seductive as he made love to her with them, and his lips were curved in a captivating smile.

She had to fight not to move closer to him. This is it, she thought dreamily, that rare thing the poets had put to paper. Love. Such a small word to encompass so many emotions.

Looking beyond the handsome exterior, she saw many qualities to admire. Honesty, generosity, and a strong sense of responsibility . . . he truly cared about people, and she knew those things were what had brought about her change of heart. She had seen the man within and had come to respect him.

Suddenly applause assaulted her ears and she was abruptly brought back to the present. Consciously, they moved apart amid the cheering and Ryan brought her hand back up to his lips as they left the dance floor. Only then was Brianne embarrassed at being so publicly displayed, and she had one more reason to be grateful for Ryan. While they were the center of attention, he had made it seem as though they were the only two people in the room.

They were toasted and congratulated by the many well-wishers, and as the music began again, they watched as the floor gradually began to fill.

It was a sight she would always remember. Soft pastels mixed with deep, vibrant colors as the wide gowns swirled past her. This is truly elegance, she thought romantically. It seemed almost mythical to her, knowing it was lost forever, never to be seen again in modern times.

Rena and Stephan danced by and she merely smiled, not making any attempt to catch their attention. Those two had eyes only for each other, and she was pleased for them both. They were a good match, and fond as she was of Stephan, she knew Rena would be the perfect foil for him. Her practical nature would provide his life with a balance. Brianne chuckled inwardly. Ryan was right, she was turning into a matchmaker.

As she turned her attention back to the crowd around her, she realized, from the expectant look on their faces, that someone had obviously asked her a question. Looking to Ryan for help, she breathed a sigh of relief, for once happy he could pick up on her thoughts.

Amusement lit his eyes as he answered, "Of course, my dear, you have my permission to dance with the senator," and looking at the elder statesman's wife, asked, "provided that the favor is returned?"

Brianne watched as the older woman actually blushed, and as the senator guided her into the flow of dancers she thought with exasperation that no woman, no matter what her age, was immune to the Barrington charm.

So began the remainder of the evening. It appeared a trend had been set. Once Ryan had relinquished his wife, others stood in line to lead her around the floor.

Brianne found most to be charming and witty, intent on leaving her with a good impression, though occasionally she would be captured in the arms of a boor, one with very obvious intentions. Then she would look for Ryan's head above the dancers, all the while murmuring how protective her husband was toward her. It never failed to work, and gave further proof of the respect, almost the fear, they felt for him.

Although quite breathless when Stephan claimed his

dance, Brianne ignored her pounding heart and took his arm. As they moved effortlessly through the couples, she looked up into his face and sincerely commented, "It's a beautiful party, Stephan. Thank you, I'll remember this forever."

Smiling, he remarked, "Forever is a long time. There will be so many nights like this for you, Brianne—I think in time this one will be lost in the shuffle."

Swinging her widely, he looked pleased and smirked boyishly. "It is a good party, though, isn't it?"

As she nodded her approval, she laughed. "Yes, Stephan, it's a very good party indeed. I don't believe there's a single person here tonight who would argue with you on that."

"Oh, I don't think we'd have to look too hard to find at least one who's a little disappointed with the way this evening has turned out. Rena told me what took place earlier, and I must apologize for the behavior of my cousin. To think that creature is related to me!"

Shaking his head in dismay, he added, "I did warn you about her, though."

"Yes, you certainly did. If she weren't so vindictive, I could almost pity her."

Stephan threw back his head and laughed while they danced. "That would add fuel to the flame, should Caro know you pitied her. Don't waste your pity on the likes of her . . . save it for the Fullerton lad."

At Brianne's confused expression, he continued, "That young fool over there." And with his head he indicated across the dance floor a tall, handsome man who looked to be about Stephan's own age. The man was speaking in earnest to his dance partner . . . Rena.

"Look at the way he's holding her! I swear if he comes one inch closer to her, I'll break both his arms."

"Stephan?" Brianne brought his attention back to her. "I think Rena can handle him, although I don't see

383

anything unusual in the way he's holding her. Perhaps, my friend, you're a mite jealous?"

He looked taken back by her suggestion, then smiled sheepishly. "Perhaps," he admitted.

As though to change the subject, he twirled her around in a wide circle, and Brianne was duly impressed by his dancing. In fact, she was impressed by all the men. Here dancing was an important social accomplishment—one that she thoroughly enjoyed. At the music's end she accompanied Stephan as he purposefully made his way toward Rena and her partner. She returned the warm smiles of the other dancers while searching the room for Ryan. Usually he was easy to spot, his head visible above the rest. Not seeing him anywhere, she deduced he had left the room to smoke with the other men, and turned to Rena and her partner.

The young man seemed a bit nervous as Stephan continued to glare at him, while Rena glanced at both men with growing apprehension.

Thankfully, the orchestra announced the Virginia Reel, and squeals of pleasure were heard around them.

Almost forcefully, Stephan claimed Rena while young Fullerton looked embarrassingly in Brianne's direction. Following Stephan's advice, she did take pity on him, although not for the same reasons.

When he politely asked her to join him, she remembered how it felt to be alone, and readily accepted.

Standing in line, waiting for the music to begin, her eyes again sought out her husband. Ryan was nowhere to be seen and Brianne was disappointed, but had little time to indulge that feeling as the lively fiddles started and she was caught up in the dance.

Ryan was annoyed more than anything else, as he followed Caroline into the cool night. When she had threatened to cause a public scandal unless he spoke with her in private, he had made sure Brianne would be

384

occupied dancing, thus affording him the time to meet with Caroline outside.

It wasn't in his nature to operate behind someone's back, especially his wife's, but he knew Caroline would follow through with her threat, and he didn't want anything to ruin this night for Brianne.

As he walked out into the moonlit garden with Caroline, he couldn't help remembering the hours he had spent with this woman—this talented woman who knew how to use her body, and his, to extract every ounce of pleasure during their unions.

This time, at the conclusion of the reel, Brianne was truly breathless, and her feet were beginning to hurt. Realizing she hadn't missed a single dance, she asked Rafe Fullerton to excuse her, pretending to leave the ballroom for the room set aside for the women's convenience. Instead, she veered off at the last moment for the terrace. What she really needed was fresh air and time to cool down.

Quietly, without attracting attention, she went outside. Standing behind a large, feathery fern, she leaned back against the cooling bricks of the house and breathed deeply. Opening her eyes and ears, she took in the scene before her.

The still moonlit night was filled with its own sounds—the owl's lonely calling, the endless melody of crickets and the frogs by the pond; the distant barking of kenneled hounds. She smiled as she looked out into the garden. There the fireflies, like the winking lights of fairy lanterns, danced across the lawns. Again she breathed deeply, this time identifying the smells of jasmine, honeysuckle, magnolia, and the overwhelming sweet olive trees.

It was all there, the sounds and scents—a gentle

seduction of her senses, a subtle invasion that was as powerful as any drug. It was moments like this, she thought, that lingered in the memory . . . a glimpse at paradise.

Closing her eyes, she gave herself over to it, straining so she wouldn't miss a sound. It was then the hushed murmur of voices carried to her, and she grinned. This was a night for romance, and any couple that took advantage of it was fortunate.

Staying in the dark lest she embarrass the couple, she looked in the direction of their distant voices.

The smile that had softened her face froze, hardening her features with pain. There could be no mistaking Ryan's form, nor that of the tall woman standing so close to him.

Chapter 25

Ryan hardly had to lower his head when she demanded that he look at her. Caroline reminded him of a petulant child, refusing to believe that he wished to remain with his wife.

"Are you really happy? Can you so easily forget what we once had together? What we can have again?" Her soft voice almost purred when she added, "Don't tell me she can make you come alive the way I can. I'll never believe that."

Ryan knew he had hurt her pride, but never for a moment did he think she harbored any deeper feelings.

Not wanting to hurt her further with truthful answers, he said uneasily, "I'm sorry if I misled you, but don't do this, Caro. Don't embarrass either one of us. What we had is in the past. Let it remain there."

As she came closer, Ryan's body tensed. Running her hands up his arms, she encircled his neck, at the same time pressing her breasts against his chest.

"I don't believe you, Ryan," she murmured. "I don't believe you can leave me in the past."

"Caro . . ."

"What's wrong? Are you afraid to kiss me? I know you want to, I can feel it in your body. Kiss me, Ryan," she urged. "As you once did, before that woman came between us. Only then will I believe you."

Ryan stared at her ripe mouth, watching as she caught her bottom lip between her teeth, and unwittingly a montage of scenes picturing Caroline in bed flashed before him.

He was vaguely aware that the fast-paced music had ended and another waltz had begun as he grabbed her roughly by the waist and brought his mouth down on hers. He released her abruptly, feeling he had given her the proof she demanded, but he was mistaken.

Almost shaken by the force of the kiss, Caroline looked back at him with a satisfied expression. "Well . . . I wasn't wrong, was I?"

Wanting to end it as quickly as possible, Ryan said heartlessly, "I'm sorry to disappoint you, Caroline, but it seems I only come alive now for my wife."

Without waiting for an answer, he turned away from her and hurried back into the house to find Brianne.

Breathing as though she had run for miles, Brianne felt physically ill as she fought to control her ragged breath. Sweet Christ! Had she really seen that? Had she just witnessed the man she loved return to his mistress? Loved! By God, she had loved him, had been going to tell him this very night that she wanted nothing more than to stay with him forever!

Once again she leaned back against the house; now it seemed like her lifeline, the only thing keeping her vertical and squeezing her eyes closed, she saw the passionate scene before her and felt the bitter pain of betrayal. *How could he?* She hadn't wanted to believe what she saw and had almost shouted her denial, when Ryan had quickly pulled the woman to him and kissed her long and hard. Then, it was almost with regret that he had pushed her from him and turned away.

How could he have deceived her like this? Knowing

that they had made love every night for the past few weeks was unbearable, and Brianne cringed thinking about the night she seduced him. *She* had brought about the change in their relationship. It was *she* who had made the first intimate moves. God, how he must have laughed, knowing one more female had succumbed to his charms. And she had done just that. Lulled by his gentle behavior, she had fooled herself into thinking he might care for her.

He cared for no one but himself and his precious Briarfawn, she thought bitterly. Now that his mistress had shown up, he thought to put his wife off with presents. Humiliated, she wanted to tear at the dress she had worn with such false pride and rip the diamond, which hung like a mocking stone, from her neck.

She had actually deluded herself into thinking he loved her, and Brianne was mortified that she had stooped so low for any man—especially Ryan Barrington. Her first estimation of him had been correct. When would she ever learn? she silently fumed, while thoughts of the things she had done on those warm, languid nights brought tears of shame to her eyes.

Once more she felt alone, isolated from reality, and an emptiness took hold of her soul. She heard the terrace doors open, and wiping her eyes, she stared off into the night, fighting desperately for some semblance of control.

A young couple, Jedd Latimer and Therese Corday, stepped out onto the balcony. Brianne had instantly liked the soft-spoken woman, and as the two neared the railing, she attempted to pull herself together and repair her shattered pride. She would not ruin this night for the others, especially Stephan and Rena.

Breathing deeply, she could feel the transformation take over. Having felt almost immobilized by the painful emptiness of her heart, she was determined to fill that void. Two could play this game. Ryan Barrington would have to look hard to find the sweet, adoring wife he had brought tonight. In her place would emerge a different woman, finally grown up, and intent on giving an acting performance that would fool a pro.

Brianne heard a soft laugh that drew her attention back to the couple, and for a split second she watched with envy as Jedd touched the young woman's face and whispered to her. Young love. Rena had been right, those months ago, when she said it only existed in the minds of women. And this was one woman who had been rudely awakened to that truth.

Coughing lightly, to make her presence known, Brianne stepped from behind the plant.

Surprised, the couple parted abruptly.

"Mrs. Barrington!" Jedd exclaimed. "I'm afraid we didn't see you."

Brianne smiled at their discomfort, hoping to put them at ease. "And I'm afraid I didn't wish to be seen. I just stepped out for a breath of fresh air. I didn't want to insult anyone by leaving the party."

Looking out into the night, Therese said sincerely, "It is beautiful out here, isn't it?"

Brianne followed the younger woman's eyes, looking out at the scene she had earlier thought of as magical.

"Yes, I suppose it is," she murmured quietly.

"Are you all right, Mrs. Barrington? You seem distressed." Therese looked closely at the woman's face, seeing a sadness that she hadn't noticed earlier in the evening.

Brianne recovered quickly. "I'm fine. Just a little tired from all the dancing. You two enjoy the night—I'd better return before I'm missed."

Forcing herself to smile, she left them at the railing and rejoined the party.

As she looked around her, she knew it was of no use to

try to regain her earlier mood. The party seemed to have lost its glitter. The furnishings were too ornate, the costumes, including her own, now looked garish, and the room rang with a false gaiety. She supposed it was her own miserable mood that made her feel that way, but wanting nothing more than to be by herself, she couldn't help hoping that the evening would end soon.

Watching the happy faces as they danced by, she was startled when a long-stemmed glass was raised to her face.

Turning to look at the man offering the refreshment, she was surprised.

"Monsieur Duville! Thank you."

Taking the light wine, she smiled her thanks and looked out once again to the dancers.

"You look lost in thought, Madame. Not unhappy ones, I hope?"

Now is the time, she thought, to begin my performance. Smiling, she replied, "Who could be unhappy on such a night as this, Monsieur?"

Duville raised his eyebrows a fraction and raised his glass in a toast. "May I congratulate you, then, on your marriage? I hope you will always be as happy as you are tonight."

With his words, Brianne's face froze. It sounded like a death toll, reminding her of the odious position she was in.

"Mrs. Barrington? I sincerely hope I haven't said anything to upset you."

"No. Not at all." Brianne answered too quickly, and if she hadn't been so preoccupied she would have caught the gleam of satisfaction in the Creole's eyes.

"I was just remembering the last time I saw you," she lied. "I'm afraid you must have thought me quite unhinged. I should have apologized to you before."

"Nonsense. Your husband explained about your accident. Think nothing of it, I was glad to be of help."

He drew her attention and her dismay with his next words. "You know, Brianne, I have thought a great deal about you since our meeting."

She was unsettled by his deep, probing eyes, which seemed to look right through her. Was he actually making a play for her? If so, she knew how to dissuade him.

"Ryan . . ."

She hesitated as he continued to stare. Attempting again, she muttered, "My husband . . ."

Gregory Duville smiled lazily. "Sometimes husbands are the last of all men to understand a woman."

So, Brianne thought, he's not afraid of Ryan. She looked at him in a different light, and seeing the tall figure of her husband making his way through the crowd, she quickly looked up at the Creole and brazenly asked, "Will you dance with me, Monsieur?"

Gregory Duville's face mirrored his pleasure, and the two hastily joined the other couples swaying to the soft strains of a waltz.

From the corner of her eye Brianne watched Ryan stop in mid-stride and stare at them murderously.

I'll kill him! Ryan vowed silently. As surely as I stand here, someday I'll take that bastard's life and derive great pleasure from it. And what the hell does Brianne think *she's* doing?

He knew he had caught her eye in warning as he hurried to her side, but she had chosen to ignore him and race off with the devil himself. The muscles worked furiously in his cheeks as he watched his wife flirt shamelessly with the Creole.

I should beat *her* for making a fool of me in front of the others, especially Duville, he thought. But knowing he could never harm her, Ryan continued to watch the couple with a prejudiced eye.

She must have felt his eyes upon her, for she briefly

dragged her attention away from Duville, and as she returned his look, Ryan felt physically struck by the scornful force of it. Why should she look at him with loathing? Was it not she who was making a scene?

The episode with Caroline flashed through his mind, but he dismissed it. Brianne had been occupied with dancing. He had hurried back to find her, only to be waylaid upon reaching the house by Salena Grandeville. The grand dame obviously was taken with Brianne and detained him for a full five minutes, extolling his wife's virtues. When he had finally extricated himself he proceeded into the ballroom and found the object of the discussion staring into his enemy's eyes as though he had come up in her estimation. What had happened to her in the short time he was gone?

When the music ended Ryan watched Brianne speak with Duville, who then led her off the floor in the opposite direction from him, and for the rest of the evening she didn't refuse a dance, thus managing to stay clear of her husband.

At first he had thought to give her room, letting her work off whatever was troubling her, since she obviously didn't want him by her side, but after over an hour of watching his wife in the arms of other men, Ryan had had enough. He had watched her closely throughout that time, and only he could disconcern the strain in her smile, the tension in the way she held her head.

As another dance was announced, he saw Brianne accept the arm of one more man, the brother of Jedd Latimer. Determined, Ryan managed to interrupt them before they reached the dance floor.

"I'm sure you understand that I would like the company of my wife for this dance."

The Latimer boy reddened and held out his arm to Ryan, while Brianne watched with increased annoyance as her husband gingerly removed her hand and placed it on his own muscled arm. Her heart pounded furiously against her ribs, only this time it wasn't from naive rapture. Now that she fully understood his deceitful heart, she could be his match.

Ryan swung her into the waltz and remarked sarcastically, "I certainly don't have to ask if you enjoyed yourself tonight. You didn't sit out one dance. Don't you ever tire? Or do you enjoy making a spectacle of yourself with every man in the room?"

Brianne gloried in his jealousy, never minding that it was caused by no other reason than possessiveness.

Looking properly taken back, she replied sweetly, "Why, Ryan, wasn't it you who gave me over to them? And besides, I would hardly call you a wallflower tonight. I recall seeing you in the arms of several women, yet I haven't lost my composure over it, have I?"

"I have not lost my composure, Madam. If I had, you would not be standing before me, but tending a sore bottom. You deserve a thrashing for the way you've behaved."

Surreptitiously, even though she danced with others, she too had watched him. She saw the way his eyes followed her, then would slip to Caroline, who seemed to be spending a good deal of time with Gregory Duville. It was as if he couldn't make up his mind which woman he wanted. And now she was supposed to be grateful he'd picked her? And listen to him while he lectured her like a child? Well, she put an end to that.

"Kindly remember, sir, that you are speaking to an adult who is fully aware how she acted, and is just as fully aware of *your* actions tonight."

It did her heart a world of good to see her husband's mouth drop open and feel him stumble to a halt.

"Really, Ryan!" she said in exasperation. "Must you dance like a bumbling novice?" She looked him straight in the eye and said cuttingly, "You were such a good instructor, and as your star pupil, I learned my lessons well. *Especially* those tonight. It was quite an eye-opener, but I did learn . . . and I'll never forget, not ever."

"Brianne, I think we should talk."

"Talk? Why, Ryan, haven't I made myself clear? I'm through talking, through with being a naive fool. As a matter of fact, Ryan, I'm through with anything pertaining to you."

Seeing his eyes narrow, she flashed him a brilliantly false smile before adding, "Now, it was you who wished to dance, so shall we finish it and be done with this night? Or would you prefer to stand here in the middle of the floor for the remainder of it? Then we shall both be spectacles."

He didn't dance with her, he punished her. Tightening his hold on her waist, she was hard put to keep up with him as he swung her about like an abused rag doll.

When the music ended, Ryan kept a firm hold on her arm as he led her through the ballroom. Within a matter of minutes he produced her wrap and together they sought out Rena. They found her, flushed with happiness, standing next to Stephan in the foyer. Brianne couldn't hear what Ryan said to his friend, but she barely managed to get out her own thanks before her husband hustled her and Rena out the front door, leaving their startled host staring after them.

The air inside the carriage was so thick with tension, Rena felt she could cut it with a knife. She looked at the couple nervously, but took her cue from their brooding expressions and kept her silence. In fact, no one spoke for the entire trip, and all three were relieved when the lights of Briarfawn came into view.

Mattie stood waiting to greet them at the front door with a smile on her face, but seeing Ryan slam the carriage door shut, she wrung her massive hands. "Lordy, I shoulda' knowed it wasn't to last," she mumbled under her breath.

The somber trio headed straight for the stairs, and as they passed Rena's room, Ryan paused to wish her good night.

"It was a pleasure to have escorted you, Rena. You handled yourself well, and I received many compliments about my charming *cousin.* I can honestly say I'm proud to have you as a member of my family."

Brianne slammed the bedroom door closed. He possessed such a double-edged tongue. It was obvious what was meant as a compliment for Rena was also meant as a contrast to her own behavior. Well, what about him? What about his behavior? Or doesn't that count? Is it only the women in this house who must toe the line?

She ripped the dress from her body, not caring if she ruined it in the process. Throwing it on a chair, she grabbed the silver net in her hair and yanked it off just as she heard the bedroom door open. Ignoring him, she removed the hoops and constricting corset. Leaving them on the floor where they dropped, she walked over them to her closet clad only in her chemise.

Unbuttoning his shirt, Ryan asked quietly, "Are you ready to talk?"

"I believe I've already answered that," Brianne stated.

"You haven't said anything except to make some ridiculous remark that you're through with anything pertaining to me. I think you should at least listen to what I have to say."

Brianne picked out a nightgown and robe and walked slowly to the adjoining door. Before opening it, she said calmly, "Please don't label what I've said as ridiculous. I meant every word. I am through with you, Ryan, completely and totally."

She turned the knob and walked through the dressing room into the smaller bedroom beyond.

"What the hell do you mean by that?" he yelled

after her.

Not answering, she shut the door behind her and clung to the bed poster as she felt her composure begin to crumble.

The door splintered on its hinges as it crashed against the wall behind it. "I asked you a question, Madam! What do you mean by that statement?"

Brianne's nerves had been frayed to their limit for hours and were about to break. Fighting it, she walked to the top of the bed and began turning it down. "I should think it's self-explanatory," she said in an even, controlled voice.

Ryan looked at her with bitterness welling up in his eyes. "Am I to be condemned without a hearing? You would do as much for a stranger, but not your own husband?" Noticing for the first time what she was doing, he demanded, "And who is to sleep in this bed?"

Remain calm, she reasoned with herself. Don't let him know his temper is getting through to you.

Sighing, she said patiently, "I am, Ryan. I thought I made that clear."

"Like hell you are! Get back in your own room, where you belong. Damn it woman, but you're trying my patience."

Brianne lost all reason. "Patience! Don't dare speak to me like a child, or one of your servants to be ordered around. I *am* where I belong. I'll never share your bed again . . . never! Do you understand me? Can you get that through your thick, conceited head? I'm *not* your whore, and I won't be made to perform like one! Now *you* leave . . . get out!"

She screamed the last words, hoping the sheer volume of them would carry him beyond the room.

"Oh, I'll leave, Brianne," he said as his face turned a deep red, "but you're coming with me."

He moved toward her and Brianne backed up against

the wall. "Don't touch me, Ryan," she warned in a shrill voice.

But he was quicker than she was, and grabbed hold of her upper arm. Picking up her nightgown in his other hand, he literally dragged her back into the master bedroom.

"Since you insist on behaving like a child, you'll be treated like one," he said, as his breath came more quickly. He stopped once to pry her fingers from the door molding, which she had grasped in an effort to heed his progress. "Jesus, Brianne!" he swore, "you can be a real hellion!"

Upon reaching the bed, he flung her unceremoniously onto it. Throwing her the nightgown, he commanded, "Now put that on. You're going to listen to me, like it or not!"

Brianne threw the gown to the bottom of the mattress and said disgustedly, "You still don't believe me, do you? Nothing you can say will make the slightest difference."

Gulping for breath, she continued, "I'll repeat myself, so listen carefully. I will *not* share your bed, nor will I play whore to you when the Daniels woman is out of reach. Oh, it was a very touching scene, Ryan, I'll give you that, and you did meet with her away from the others, so you must have some shred of propriety, but you'll have to make do with *her*, because you'll never touch me again. I won't be your wife, nor will I be commanded when to dress and undress," she fumed, indicating the nightgown with an outstretched hand.

Now it was no longer the hurt that lay between them, but a matter of stronger wills. "Put it on, Brianne, and then you *will* listen to my explanation of what you think you saw between Caroline and me," he threatened slowly, as a cheek muscle moved in unison with his clenched teeth.

"You can go to hell! And don't ever mention that woman's name to me again. I may have been stupid enough to believe your lies before, but not after tonight. Whatever you feel the burning need to say, save it. Or better still, go to her with them—your words don't affect me any longer." She returned his expression with unwavering eyes. If she weren't already so upset, she would have trembled at the sight of his eyes turning a dark, threatening blue.

Without warning, he reached out and grabbed hold of her shoulder. As she forcibly pulled back from him, he tightened his grip and their combined pressure tore the fragile silk of her chemise.

She saw his surprised expression, but her fury was released by the rending of the material at her chest. She gave no thought to her own safety. All she could think about was to hurt him as he had hurt her. At that moment, she hated him.

"You bastard!" she spat, as she brought back her hand and slapped him soundly on the face. She watched as three thin rivulets of blood emerged on his cheek where her nails had scratched him. She had marred his perfect face, that face that had lied to her from the beginning, the one Caroline had kissed, the one she herself had loved. Loved, damn it! He had made her love him and then betrayed her as soon as the Virginian was near. Seeing the garden scene once more in her tortured mind, she shoved him aside and walked away from him.

Ryan's hand shot out and grasped her upper arm. "We're not leaving it like this. You're my wife," he said angrily, as he pushed her over to the bed.

She felt the mattress against the back of her thighs and was unable to keep her balance. As she lay half on the bed, Brianne stared into Ryan's set face. She could tell by his eyes what he intended to do.

"Don't."

She said the word as the two of them continued to stare, breathing together like animals in battle.

He leaned over her, trapping her with his body. As she pushed against his chest, he brought his mouth down on hers. The kiss was full of anger and Brianne moved her head, for she could not bear what had once been so beautiful being turned into this. He tried to become gentle with her, but she fought him with renewed strength. Suddenly, unnaturally, her body became deathly still and she breathed into his ear, "This time you're not drunk, and this time I'm no stranger. I'll hate you forever for this."

Ryan too became very still. The only sound to be heard in the room was the labored breathing coming from their bodies. He stayed frozen, staring at the mattress beside her head, then slowly he released her hands and removed himself. Turning over onto his back, he wiped his face on his arm and said quietly between breaths, "I'm sorry, Brianne . . . I am sorry." He watched as she slowly rose from the bed and said to her back, "I don't know what else to say to you. I should never have let you provoke me. If only you had listened to what I had to say . . ."

Brianne reached over and picked up her nightgown with a shaking hand. She turned her face down to him and said calmly, very quietly, "Don't ever touch me again. This body is mine, and I'll never allow it to be abused by a man again."

As if in slow motion, she dragged the nightgown off the bed and walked from the room that had once held such happiness.

Never would he forget the sight of Brianne's face, or her look of pure hatred when she spoke to him. As he watched her leave the room, Ryan knew she was also leaving him. She meant every word she had said. He closed his eyes as he heard her lock the door to the other bedroom, and realized they weren't just back at the beginning, full of distrust for one another. They were as far apart now as if Brianne had remained in the next century. And knowing that to be the truth, he squeezed his eyes tighter, feeling moisture on his face. He didn't need to open them to know its color would not be the bright red from the scratches but a clear, salty liquid . . . something he hadn't experienced since his mother's death, some twenty years ago.

In another bed, miles away at Mosshaven, Gregory Duville drove hard into the fair giant of a woman beneath him. He felt like a young man again. He knew it wasn't the woman who was moaning and scratching at his back who had renewed his vigor. It was the taste of victory, the sweet rendering of revenge.

Caroline gazed up at the dark man above her. He wasn't Ryan, nor did he possess Ryan's finesse in lovemaking, but he was there, and he surprised her with his ability to arouse her. Thinking of the way he had ripped her clothes from her proud body made her shift from under him until she was on top. She would be the director of this interlude. She took him deeply within her and began a slow rock, watching his distinguished face go slack with desire. She took his hands and brought them up to her full breasts and stared as his fingers worked their magic, making her nipples harden as his thumbs flicked over them. They never spoke a word as she took her hands away from his and placed them in back of her, on either side of his legs. As she leaned back against them, she threw back her head and concentrated as he thrust into her rapidly, again and again. No, he wasn't Ryan, but he would do until she got him back, and she lifted her head to look at the man who was stirring the white-hot fires within her. She and the Creole exchanged a knowing look. The knowledge that together they had begun the division of the Barringtons only added to their frenzied passion.

Chapter 26

In the next three weeks Ryan didn't see Brianne, except briefly. He left for the fields before she got up, and she kept to her room when he returned. He tried once, when they met accidentally in the hallway, to talk to her, but she kept her silence and quietly shut the bedroom door in his face.

How long must he pay? Nothing would be settled if she insisted on her solitude. It was driving him crazy, and it wasn't good for her either. Rena, his only dinner companion of late, had told him in the last week Brianne was pale, and often tired. She had been refusing breakfast lately, and had missed the last three days of school. In Brianne, that was cause for concern. The schooling of the negroes was the only meaningful thing in her life; it was, in fact, her only interest now.

Ryan would not punish himself any longer though, Brianne was doing a fine job of it alone. Last night Stephan had joined him and Rena for dinner, and as they lingered around the table afterwards Ryan confessed what had taken place in Stephan's garden the night of the party. He knew there was good cause for Brianne's anger if she had witnessed it without hearing his rejection of Caroline; however, he felt unjustly accused and swore the couple to secrecy, for when his wife was ready to hear the truth it would come from his lips.

Now, as he dressed for another day of losing himself in his work, he reflected on how lonely his life had become without her. Even the house had become subdued. For those few weeks after his return from New Orleans, it had come alive as it was meant to be. There had been laughter and quick smiles, and the servants had taken their cue from their mistress, but now they too were hushed, as though waiting for the return of happier times.

As Ryan left his room, too large now that it had been emptied of Brianne's clothing, he paused outside her door. Reaching out to turn the knob, he checked himself. He would give her a few more days, for in the back of his mind he admitted he was hesitant to confront her—not about Caroline, but what had happened later. The scratches on his face had healed and would leave no scars; he wasn't sure Brianne had been as lucky.

It was hot. It was always hot lately, even in the morning, when she felt the worst. Something was wrong with her. Staying in her room so much had made her listless and cranky, but this illness that attacked her as soon as she opened her eyes was frightening. She felt so weak, and no wonder—every time food was within sight or smell, she was sickened by it. Deprived of even sleeping on her stomach, because her breasts had suddenly become tender, she had light blue circles under her eyes from worry. What frightened her the most was the possibility that she might have contracted yellow fever or malaria or one of those dreadful diseases that led to epidemics, and for which there was no cure. Hadn't Rena told her of a yellow fever epidemic in 1853, and didn't she say thousands had died? Including Stephan's parents? What she wouldn't give for an antiseptic, kindly

404

old general practitioner, with an office decorated in Early American furniture and fluorescent lights over the examining table. There would be a locked cabinet filled with instruments, and such life-saving drugs as antibiotics.

What did she have now? Herbs! Hardly comforting when faced with a threatening disease.

She kept her eyes closed and willed her stomach to remain where it was. At least feeling so miserable had stopped her from agonizing over Ryan. That part of her life was done, over. It was almost as if they no longer lived together, for he had finally taken her seriously and left her alone. She refused to think about what took place following Stephan's party. The one thing she could not accept was her own loss of control. For the first time in her life, she had physically harmed another.

The week following the party she had existed in a trancelike state, robbed of all emotions. Then anger had begun to fill that void. She would not act on that anger, though. Rather, she ignored Ryan's existence and made her own plans. Once she was feeling better, she fully intended to leave here. She'd go north, maybe back to Philadelphia. There she might be able to find work. Although there was nothing waiting for her in 1856 Philadelphia, at least she'd be on more familiar ground.

As another wave of nausea overtook her, she tried to ignore it and imagine what types of job would be available to her.

The knock on the door was firm. Rena entered the room carrying a heavy tray and Brianne winced as the sickening aroma of eggs carried to her nostrils.

"Please take it away. I can't eat," she whispered.

"You'll try!"

Brianne opened her eyes slightly and groaned as she saw the impersonal expression on Rena's face. "Please . . ." she pleaded. "I'm really sick!"

"Oh?" Rena sneered. "Well, you'll never get better if you don't eat."

"Don't you understand? I *can't* eat! I can't even look at it. Now take it out and leave me. I could have something terrible, like yellow fever, and it would serve you right for bullying me if you caught it."

Brianne felt truly miserable, but their raised voices only made her stomach react violently. She closed her eyes tightly and concentrated on taking small breaths.

Startled by the slamming of the tray on her night table, Brianne's eyelids snapped open as Rena swore. "You know something? I used to look up to you, but now I find that you're turning into a childish pain in the ass!"

Brianne sighed and turned her face away. "My, how easily we forget our lessons. Whatever happened to being a lady?"

Rena refused to let her turn her off, and she walked around the bed to face her. "It looks like you bring out the very best in me."

Brianne smiled weakly. "Don't make me laugh, even that makes me sick." She looked at her friend with frightened eyes.

"What *are* the symptoms of yellow fever?" she asked hesitantly.

It was Rena's turn to laugh as she sat on the edge of the bed.

"Don't worry, you don't have yellow fever," she stated. "But for someone who's so smart about so many things, you certainly are stupid about your own body."

"What do you mean?" Brianne asked with interest. Rena sounded confident, and Brianne needed answers.

"When was the last time you had your monthlies?"

It was just a question, a few words gathered together, but it had enough impact to stun her.

Rena touched her shoulder. "Brianne?"

She blinked at her friend, then slowly replied,

"Around two weeks before Ryan's trip to New Orleans."

A slow smile spread across Rena's face. "Well, I think we can safely rule out any disease. Congratulations, Mrs. Barrington, I believe you're going to have a baby."

Brianne raced from the bed just in time to bend over the chamber pot. Violently ill, she stayed until the spasms had eased. Picking up a towel, she wiped her perspiring face and turned panic-filled eyes toward the other woman. "It can't be true," she croaked out. "It must be something else!"

Rena dampened a cloth and brought it over to her. "Would you rather it be yellow fever?" she asked in amusement.

Brianne roughly grabbed the towel from her hand and applied it to her throbbing head. "One's as bad as the other."

Reaching out to her friend, she pleaded, "It has to be something else. This couldn't happen to me. Not now!"

Rena put her arm around Brianne and led her over to the bed. Easing her back onto the pillows, she sat next to her and took her hand. "Think, Brianne," she said earnestly. "Even in the twentieth century women must still have the same signs—morning sickness, fatigue, tenderness, and most important . . . the absence of monthlies. From my own limited experience, I would say you're definitely pregnant but if you doubt me, call in Mattie. I'm sure she's been around enough pregnant women in her lifetime to confirm it."

Brianne closed her eyes and shook her head dejectedly. As much as she wanted to deny it, she knew with a sinking feeling that Rena was right. Her period was late and the nausea was erratic, coming in the mornings and sometimes disappearing until late afternoon.

How could this have happened? Stupid question, she thought disgustedly. But she had always thought it happened to other women, not to her, and especially not now.

Brianne opened her eyes and stared at the younger woman before her, who was older and wiser than her years.

"I'm pregnant!" she said in wonder.

Rena smiled. "I certainly think so, but how do you really feel about it?"

Brianne hugged herself and looked out the open window. "Frightened, mostly. And shocked. I never considered the possibility."

"Never?" Rena asked gently.

"Someday, yes. But this is all wrong. I had this fantasy of how my life would be when I made the decision to have a child, and it wasn't like this. I had hoped to love the father."

"You did that, Brianne. When this child was conceived, it was with love. Whatever your problems with Ryan are now, they certainly didn't exist then. I've never seen a woman so much in love, or happier. It was watching you that gave me the courage to seek the same thing."

Brianne shook her head. "You don't understand. And what about your belief that love only exists in the minds of foolish women?"

Rena smiled shyly as she poured the tea. "I believe I was the foolish woman, becoming so disillusioned by life that I was afraid to give it a chance. Don't let that happen to you. You have more than yourself to think about now. Think about the child."

"Promise me," Brianne pleaded, "that you'll tell no one about this. Give me your word this will be between us. I don't want anyone to know."

"Not even the father?"

"Especially not the father. This is all he ever wanted, Rena, a child to carry on his precious name. The timing is wrong now. Promise me you won't tell him?"

Rena sighed. She hated being placed in this position, keeper of secrets that could bring two people back together again. First Ryan, and now Brianne . . . if only they would be honest with each other. Pride! It wasn't worth it.

"Rena? Please . . ."

She shook her red curls. "I don't like it. It isn't right not to tell Ryan, but I'll respect your wishes."

Brianne breathed easier. "Thank you. I know I'm putting you in the middle and I'm sorry, but you know I wouldn't do it unless I thought it was important."

Rena nodded and handed Brianne the dark tea. "My mum said when she was pregnant it helped to sip tea and take little bites of biscuits before she rose. Try it, Brianne. You must eat for the child's sake."

Suddenly, Brianne had a purpose to her life again. A child! This time it was a part of *her*—someone who wouldn't leave, or be left behind . . . someone who truly belonged to her. She accepted the cup, and sipping the tea, held out her hand for the biscuits.

Brianne remained in bed after Rena left. Closing her eyes, she waited for the nausea to subside. How much more, she thought despondently, was she expected to endure? She had almost come to accept what had happened to her. She had deluded herself into thinking she was happier here, living in the past, and had even been stupid enough to make a complete fool of herself over Ryan.

Well, now she had to pay, just like so many women before her. She lightly touched her flat abdomen, running her fingers over it. It was always the woman who had to pay for foolishness, and she had certainly been a prize fool. Gingerly she attempted to rise and was surprised when her stomach didn't rebel. She slowly walked over to the window and pulled the light curtain aside. A subtle breeze cooled her as she looked out at Briarfawn.

It *is* beautiful, she thought wistfully. The grounds were still a spring green and in the distance, beyond the lawns, she could see new rows of sugar plants that would soon encircle the house, as far as the eye could see. It was an idyllic life here, but not for her.

She heard a horse approaching and looked over to see Ryan coming up to the house. Young Jeremy ran over to take the reins and Ryan spoke to the boy for a few seconds before the child threw back his head in laughter. Brianne smiled to herself at the pleasant sound and watched as the boy walked the horse away.

Unwillingly, her eyes devoured the man as he too watched Raven follow the child back to the stables. He looked tired and hot. The back of his shirt was clinging to the middle of his shoulders, and as if reading her thoughts he pulled out his handkerchief and wiped the back of his neck. Before he turned back to the house, Brianne saw Rena come up to him, carrying the slates for the afternoon class.

Pulling back from the window, she held her breath as the two engaged in conversation. Once Ryan glanced up toward her room, and her heart began to pound.

Rena *wouldn't* tell him, she thought with alarm. She wouldn't break her promise, made only a short while ago.

She quickly moved even farther back from the open window. Braced against the wall, she knew it wouldn't sit well with Rena to keep such an important thing as the future birth of a child from its father. Sooner or later something would slip, and then she would be a prisoner here forever.

I must get away now, she thought frantically. She looked about the room with wild eyes, not seeing much in the way of help before her. She did have the diamond. It brought such pain every time she looked at it that she wouldn't hesitate to sell it. Surely she would get enough money from it to buy passage to the North, hopefully with a sufficient amount left over to support herself until she found employment.

Going to the dresser, she tore open the drawer and held the jewelry up to the light. How ironic that it was in the shape of a teardrop. Prisms of blue and rose and purple shot out like rays, and she reluctantly recalled the night she received it. Remembering walking down the staircase, dressed in his gown, so in love with Ryan, so sure he felt the same, brought tears to her eyes. It *had* been lovely, though, and for a brief moment she had felt love. On her part, anyway. No matter the pain that followed, she had experienced love, but to be near him now was agony, and a constant reminder of his betrayal.

More than anything, she just wanted to go home . . .

She dropped the diamond and slowly walked to a chair. Sitting down, Brianne tucked her legs under her. The word kept repeating itself in her mind, like the steady rhythm of a train: home, home . . .

But this was no child's dream, and saying magic words wouldn't bring her back. She didn't know how to find the way.

"Dear God, help me," she whispered. Covering her face with her hands, she sat curled up in the corner of the large chair and wept . . . for herself, for the child, and for the loss of a love barely begun.

Suddenly her head snapped up and she stared across the room unseeing, as her skin broke out in chills. I've never really tried! she thought incredulously. She'd been right where it had all begun, and she'd never gone back, never even been to the woods where she woke up. If she went back to the same place, maybe it would happen again. Perhaps then she would be free of this nightmare at last. God knows she didn't belong here, and she was willing to try anything to return to where she did.

The fact that Brianne would be taking Ryan's child,

411

without his ever knowing, was only a fleeting thought. She'd leave tonight, at dusk. Mattie brought her dinner up to her around five, and she would make an attempt to eat while the housekeeper was still with her. It wouldn't be hard to convince anyone that her appetite had yet to return. Then she'd ask Mattie to take the food away, telling her she'd be retiring early and was not to be disturbed until morning. It would work. It had to!

Mattie's eyebrows came together as she looked closely at her mistress. "Ain't no good, you goin' on like this, Miz Brianne. You has to eat."

"I tried, Mattie, you saw me. But I just can't. Please do as I ask and take it away. Maybe tomorrow. Right now I just want to rest, so tell Miss Rena I don't want to be disturbed. I am exhausted, but I'm hoping a good night's sleep will give me the energy to fight this thing. So please, stop worrying over me."

As Mattie again shook her head, she picked up the tray and walked to the door. Just before she closed it Brianne called out to her, "Mattie?"

The woman looked back and Brianne's heart melted. She knew she would miss her.

"You never stopped taking care of me since the first time I laid eyes on you, all those months ago. I just wanted you to know I appreciate it."

Mattie looked her straight in the eye, and in doing so lost her subservient attitude. At that moment, they were just two women. "I knowed that, and that's why I keep on worryin' so. You were the best thing that ever happen to this place, and it ain't the same with you shut up in this here sick room. You best try harder, Miz Brianne. Your home needs you."

Mattie didn't wait for a reply, or to see how her words affected her mistress, she just shut the door and walked straight for the stairs, righteously knowing she had spoken the truth.

Brianne stared at the closed door. She couldn't let Mattie's words change her decision. Everyone would manage without her, just as they had done before she came. She would miss them all, they were a part of her, and she would continue to worry about their future, but Rena would continue with the schooling, she was sure Ryan would permit that. Now she had to be selfish. If she didn't leave this place, it would remain an unhappy home. She no longer had the ability, or even the desire, to change it.

Waiting until she knew Ryan and Rena would be in the dining room, she left the bed. Remembering the biscuits from that morning, she took them from their hiding place and broke off a small piece. Chewing slowly, she wrapped the remainder in a scarf to bring with her. Having already picked out her riding habit as the most suitable clothes to wear, she quickly lifted it down from her wardrobe.

Once dressed, she tied back her hair and surveyed the room. She'd have to do something about the bed, and feeling like a child, took the pillows and laid them vertically, then covered them with the quilt. She stood back and looked at her work. Not very convincing, but it might pass inspection in the dark. Knowing she had no time to lose, she pocketed the diamond and tiptoed to the door, listening to the sounds of the house.

It was easier than she expected. Moving very slowly, she managed to reach the front door without being seen, and hearing voices in the dining room and the clatter of the dishes, she knew everyone was where they should be.

Brianne turned and looked around the foyer.

She quickly said her goodbyes to the beautiful house, then, as her eyes became misty, she reached out and turning the gold knob, made her exit.

Her one problem, she reasoned as she kept to the bushes, would be in the stables. Coming closer, she saw the door was open and knew Luther would be there, tending the horses that he loved.

Deciding that aggressiveness would be the best way to handle it, she squared her shoulders and strode into the building, calling out, "Luther? Are you in here?"

From a distant stall, she heard him answer in surprise, "Yes'm, I'm here."

Waiting until he appeared and began to walk over to her, Brianne asked casually, "Luther, please saddle Cloverleigh for me. I'm going to take her out."

"Cloverleigh?"

"Yes, Luther, my horse. Now, would you please see to it?" Brianne held her breath as she watched uncertainty cross his face.

"Luther?"

Coming to a decision, the man nodded and walked back to the stalls. In a few tortuously long minutes, he returned leading the mare.

With his help Brianne mounted, and thanking the confused stablehand, she slowly left the barn. She held the horse to a very slow walk until they were away from the house and then, hoping she was far enough away not to attract attention, urged the mare on.

It was not hard to find, being at the end of the south field, and coming upon the water, Brianne looked about her. It was just the way she remembered, except now it was getting dark and the foliage was blending into the night.

Nervous and a little frightened, Brianne tied Cloverleigh to a branch and patted the horse. "I'm glad you're here, girl. As much as I want to do this, I don't want to do it alone."

Sitting on an overturned log, she looked out into the

woods and waited.

Dusk gave way to night and nothing happened, except Brianne's nerves became frayed from listening to the strange sounds of the forest. The same noises that had enchanted her the night of the party now sounded ominous. And yet, nothing . . .

Every time Cloverleigh snorted, Brianne's heart jumped and she had the sinking feeling nothing was going to happen at all. She was cold, tired, and frightened, and looking about her with impatience she said aloud, "Well, *I'm* here, God. Where are you?"

Nothing . . .

She waited and waited for something, anything.

As the woods started to close in on her, she hugged herself in fear and started to cry. Nothing was going to happen. She was never going to escape back to where she belonged. She was being punished, just as she'd been taught in school. She had grown up fearing God from the time she was a small child. Her schooling had taught her about a God of vengeance, who doled out punishments for wrongdoing. It wasn't until she had left and begun to think on her own that she realized they were wrong. Her God was a God of love and forgiveness, not retaliation. But now, after everything that had happened since she had come to this spot, months ago, she began to doubt her beliefs.

She blinked back her tears and whispered into the night, "Why? I tried, I really did, but it's no good. I don't belong here. Please . . . please let me go back?"

The horse sniggered and Brianne laughed nervously. "You're right, girl. They say women act strange when . . . well, I must be crazy, sitting out here waiting for miracles. But you know, I thought it might happen."

Looking up through the trees to the sky beyond, she said in an anguished voice, "You're supposed to know everything. If you really do, then you know how

415

unhappy I am. I can't stay here! I won't!"

Shaking her head, she held it in her hands as she wiped the tears away. "I'm in pain," she whispered hoarsely. "Every time I see him, it's worse. I can't stand to be near him, I feel so betrayed. I have to leave. Take me back . . . please. Don't force me to make my own way here."

Hugging herself, she wiped her face on her shoulder and cried, "I'm alone, and frightened about the future. I've lost control over my life, and now I have no control over my body. His child is growing inside me and there's nothing I can do about it, there's no way to stop what's happening."

Jesus! She must be losing her mind, sitting out here, talking to the night. Nobody was going to answer her. If only there would be some sort of sign. She didn't expect a burning bush or anything so dramatic, just something that would help her to know the right thing to do. But it wasn't to be, she thought harshly. She'd been abandoned by the very God who had placed her here, and this time the pain of betrayal thrust even more deeply, slicing away at her soul. Completely defeated, she stared off into the night and wept tears of bitterness.

Ryan stood silently, not five feet away, and was unable to move. Late for dinner, he had seen her leave the house from his study window and decided to follow at a safe distance.

At first he was annoyed that she had tricked the household into thinking she was too ill to leave her room, then quickly he became concerned when he saw in what direction she was heading. Leaving Raven nibbling on grass at the edge of the woods, he had carefully walked up to the levee. There he had seen Brianne sitting before it, looking about her expectantly, as though she intended to

416

meet someone. Jealous visions of his wife with another flashed through his mind, but he had quickly dismissed them when she startled him by speaking aloud.

Initially he had feared for her sanity when she called out to God, but slowly he realized she was pouring out her hurt and misery to the only one she thought would hear her. It had cut into his heart to listen and know he was the cause of her pain. She wanted to leave him and he knew she would do it, sooner or later, if he didn't make her see reason.

He wanted to reach out and stop her anguish but found himself frozen when he heard her say she was carrying his child. He had been exultant, thrilled that she was to give him a child. His happiness was fleeting, though, as Brianne burst into fresh tears.

Not wanting to frighten her, he moved very slowly. Passing the mare, he caressed her nose before coming to stand behind his wife.

"Brianne?" Very softly he called to her.

Her head spun around and she looked at him with terror in her eyes. "No!"

"Brianne, it's all right."

She stared at him wildly. "How long have you been there?"

"Long enough," he tried to smile, "to know we're going to have a child."

Brianne expelled her breath and her chest looked caved in. She appeared on the verge of collapse, and Ryan instinctively reached out to her.

"Don't touch me!" she shrilly yelled at him. Moving further away, she cried, "I don't care what you heard, I'm not coming back with you."

Sitting on the log, Ryan calmly asked, "Where do you intend to go?"

"Anywhere . . . away from you!"

Ryan refused to let her anger him. "Well, if you think

417

coming here will transport you back to the future, then I'll wait with you but I'd suggest you come away from the trees. This area is known for the cottonmouths that inhabit it."

Brianne jerked herself away from them and looked at the branches surrounding her. He couldn't make out her face in the dark, but he knew she was terrified of the snakes. She came to stand closer to him, and after a few moments of silence joined him on the log, with a respectable distance between them.

From the corner of his eye, he saw her rub her arms. "Are you cold?" he asked with concern.

Ceasing her actions, she shook her head.

Ryan looked out into the night and said slowly, "We have to talk, Brianne. I've let this go on too long."

"I thought you understood there's nothing you could say that would make any difference in the way I feel. Save your breath, Ryan, I told you your words don't work on me any longer." Brianne was beginning to feel more than foolish for coming out here.

Ryan tried again. "Brianne, I thought we had come to an understanding between us. I thought . . ."

He said exactly the wrong thing. "How dare you speak of that time?" she interrupted. "I'm not the same girl. I grew up very fast. Let me tell you something: it's better like this. If you don't care, you can't be hurt. And believe me, Ryan, I *don't* care."

She said it calmly, dispassionately, and it took every ounce of control to bring it off. Never did she want him to know the heartache she experienced by his nearness.

He knew it was now or never. She must listen to him. "You have every reason to be angry. But you never bothered to find out what led up to the scene you witnessed. Caroline . . ."

"Shut up! Do you hear me? Just shut up! I don't want to know, not now, not ever!"

418

"Brianne, you're being irrational. It isn't what you think."

They both stood when she started shouting again, and unconsciously, she rolled her fingers into fists, bringing them up before his face. As if suddenly realizing what she was about to do, she quickly dropped her hands and walked past him.

"I can't be around you without losing control. You're no good for me, and I've got something more important to worry about than you. I'm leaving," she stated, while attempting to mount Cloverleigh.

Too weak to lift herself up, she brought the horse over to the log and used it to boost herself into the saddle. Before she could take up the reins, Ryan grabbed them.

"You're not going anywhere tonight. You're coming home with me and spending the night there. You'd be lost in five minutes if you took off now."

Brianne didn't say anything. She kept her silence as Ryan led her out of the woods to where Raven waited. Never would she admit she was grateful he had insisted she return for the night. She knew he was right. She'd had no plans, and most certainly would have gotten lost. She'd figure everything out later. Right then, all she could think about was the welcome sight of Briarfawn.

Chapter 27

"A baby! Why, no wonder you been feelin' poorly." Mattie's grin was so infectious, Brianne smiled.

If possible, Mattie fussed over her mistress even more than before. Tucking Brianne into bed, she remarked, "Don't you worry none. I'm gonna take care of you myself."

Brianne hated to admit just how good it felt to be back in her own room, and after Mattie and Rena left, Brianne stared into the darkness and let her mind wander. Alone, in the quiet of the night, honesty came easier and she realized how much trouble she had recently caused. Without meaning to, she had made others miserable, along with herself. Now that she knew her *illness* was natural and she was not suffering from anything else, she could begin to put her life in order.

She had asked God for a sign, and Ryan had come. Not what she was hoping for, but at least she knew that she was meant to remain here. Whether *here* meant Briarfawn, she wasn't sure.

It was too much to think about, and in truth her head was filled with too many confusing thoughts. Right then, sleep was uppermost in her mind. The loss of energy that accompanied being pregnant was annoying, but for tonight, she'd gladly give into it. Snuggling down under the satin quilt, Brianne closed her eyes, putting her misadventure out of her mind.

She willed her body to relax and could feel the peacefulness of sleep coming over her when suddenly she heard the locked door of the dressing room open. Immediately her room was flooded with a pale yellow light.

Ryan stood in the doorway, holding a candelabra.

"Brianne," he softly called her name. "Are you awake?"

"How did you get in here?" she demanded, startled that he could gain entry without her knowledge.

He came closer, placing the heavy candle holder on a round table. Pulling a chair up next to it, he sat down heavily and smiled a little sadly. "The same way I've come in every night, after you've fallen asleep, and every morning before you wake."

He held up a large brass key to show her before placing it on the table. "Did you really think anyone could keep me out of this room?"

She didn't answer him, uneasy that he had come in while she was sleeping to check on her.

Ryan hadn't really expected a reaction. He had come to her for a purpose and he would get on with it. "You made it very clear how unhappy you are here. I attribute that to my presence. Since learning that you are *enceinte,* I've done quite a bit of thinking on how to improve the situation. You cannot leave, Brianne, not carrying our child. It's very important that you take care of yourself, and the best place to do that is here, where there are people who will care for you. More than anything, I want my child born on Briarfawn. *This* will be his home, his heritage. Therefore, I've come to a decision. *I* will be the one to leave, not you."

She stared at him, her eyes wide with disbelief. "This is

your home! I can't allow you to do that."

Ryan looked at her sadly, saying in a quiet voice, "This is *our* home, Brianne. I had hoped you'd realized that. Besides, it's already done. I've sent a letter to Gayle Sawyer, captain of the *Lady*, telling him to sail with the morning tide. I'll join him early tomorrow, and we'll set sail for England at dawn."

She was shocked. "Ryan . . ."

He held up his hand. "I have already written to Stephan, asking him to check on Briarfawn weekly, although with Rena here I'm sure it'll be more often than that. Nathen is more than competent and can handle everything until my return. I expect that to be in early October, before the cane is cut."

"Early October!" She couldn't believe this was happening. "That's . . . that's over four months away!"

Ryan rose and picked up his candle. "I am aware of that." Bowing slightly, his eyes held hers when he lifted his head. "I wish you well, Madam, during my absence. If there is anything you need, look to my study. Money has been set aside for you. Anything else that arises, rely on Nathen's and Stephan's judgment. They'll not fail you."

Taking a deep breath, he added, "All I ask is you take care of yourself and the child, Brianne. No matter what we've let happen, that's the one good thing in our lives right now. Now if you'll excuse me, I've quite a bit of packing to attend to."

He turned and walked away from her, and she was too stunned to stop him. Before he left the room, he stopped and looked at the dresser. Reaching out slowly, he picked up the discarded diamond and held it in the palm of his hand. For a moment he stared at the necklace before gingerly replacing it, and she had to strain to hear him whisper goodbye before going through the door and shutting it behind him.

Her first reaction was to run after him, telling him it

423

wasn't necessary. He loved this place and now, because of her, he was leaving it.

Going to England!

But she couldn't bring herself to plead with him. Anyway, it was the child he was concerned with, not her. He had told her more than once how important an heir was, and now he was willing to go to any lengths to insure its safe arrival.

Pulling back the mosquito netting, she left the bed and lit her own candle. When she came to the table she picked up the key and was foolishly moved to find it still warm from his hand.

Damn it! She couldn't change what had happened, any more than he could. It created a barrier between them as strong as if it were made of steel. Dropping the key, she went back to bed, already knowing that sleep would elude her this night.

She heard them carrying his heavy trunk down the hall and fought with herself to keep from opening the door to stop him. But she knew he had made up his mind, and he would go. The only thing that would keep him here was if she could forgive him and resume being his wife . . . and that was the one thing she could not do.

She glanced at the ornate porcelain clock by her bed. Four o'clock in the morning. It was still dark, and he'd have to make New Orleans before dawn. She almost resented that he now owned his own boat, making travel on the river so convenient. If he had had to wait for the packet, maybe he would have changed his mind.

Voices, low and muffled, came from beneath her window and she walked over to it. In the courtyard below her, she watched the small group say their goodbyes. With lantern held high, Aaron also watched as Ryan hugged Mattie. Nathen, atop his own horse, held

Raven's reins while waiting for his employer, and Brianne watched as Ryan extracted himself from Mattie and turned to kiss Rena's cheek. He said something to both women, and they nodded.

Satisfied, he walked over to the prancing Raven and mounted. Slowly bringing his head up, he looked at the house with longing, as if he'd already been away, and she watched as he turned his head toward her.

Forgetting that the candle highlighted her in the darkness, she wiped her eyes with one hand while touching the window with the other, as though in doing so she could stop him from leaving. He stared at her for a brief measureless span, then quickly turned, digging his heels into the stallion, and she watched as he raced away from Briarfawn . . . away from her.

As the ship pulled up to the dock, Ryan stood at her rail and looked out to the city of London. From the past he knew the squalid living conditions didn't end at the wharves, but continued into the city itself. Once inside, though, there were more than a few sections that were beautiful, places Ryan had known intimately in years past, and he had seen enough of the world to know this town teemed with a vitality known only to the great capital of the British Empire.

For more than the hundredth time during the voyage, Ryan imagined Brianne's reaction if she had been at his side. The first time was inside his cabin, back in New Orleans, when he was getting settled. He had looked around and envisioned Brianne on the bed, or sitting in the chair, or even looking out the paned window, excited by the coming trip.

Since then, at every sunset he had pictured her next to him gazing out over the ocean, glorying in the breathtaking spectacle before them. He had even told the captain that on this sailing he would be working, and would take his turn at watch—anything to take his mind off her. But she crept up on him always. Even when he would climb the rigging and concentrate all his powers on the task before him, he would see her face, flushed with happiness because a young negro child had learned to write his name. At night sheer exhaustion couldn't banish her, and she remained an unwelcome companion in his now solitary life. It was bad enough to be constantly worried about the situation between them, but must she also haunt him these long months away from Briarfawn?

Loud cries and coarse remarks, shouted in jest, brought his attention back to the present as London's own welcomed the *Lady* back to its shores. There was a contagious excitement spreading among his men, for they knew that after unloading the *Lady*'s holds, they would find a full belly, ale, and willing women to warm their sailor's lives.

Ryan didn't have the heart for it. He knew his wife would be in attendance wherever he ventured. Better to stay aboard and do his drinking alone, he decided.

He threw himself into his work, laboring side by side with the men he paid to unload the ship. By dusk all had left, save Ryan and the first mate, one Jamie Hollander.

Jamie had sailed with Ryan years ago, and his fondness for his old captain, plus all the adventures and misadventures they had shared, he felt gave him the right to speak his mind.

"And you'll be tellin' me with all them taverns and wenches out there, you're goin'ta spend the night in here? *I'll* be tellin' you, Cap'n, you spent too long on that plantation of yours."

With a sly wink he added, "Why, all them fine ladies up in London Town would welcome you back with more than open arms, if they was to know you'd be here.

426

Remember, Cap'n?"

Ryan smiled at the goading of his old mate. "Jamie, you old sea dog, if *I* remember correctly it was you who made out quite well with the lady's maids. Could it be that your concern for me tonight is based on *your* memories, not mine?"

Jamie's eyes quickly averted and he smiled sheepishly as Ryan laughed at his attempt to play the innocent.

"Just do as I ask, Jamie, and bring me back a bottle. And not that rotgut they sell down here, either. I don't want my insides ripped apart." Reaching across the table, Ryan picked up a small leather pouch and tossed it to the first mate. "I'll trust you, Jamie, to bring me back what I need."

Jamie caught the pouch agilely in mid-air and the tinkle of coins could be heard. Weighing the pouch in the palm of his hand and judging its worth, he nodded. "Aye, Cap'n, you can depend on me to get you what you want."

Touching the top of his cap, he left quickly, plans already forming in his mind as to the best use of this money.

Ryan happened to be looking over the ship's log in Gayle Sawyer's cabin when Jamie returned. After knocking at the door, the first mate announced, "I got everything you need, Cap'n. Put it in your cabin."

Ryan wasn't finished reading, so he answered absent-mindedly, "Fine, thanks, Jamie. Now, don't let me spoil your first night in port. Go ahead." And without looking up, he waved his old sea mate out.

Within minutes, Ryan replaced the log in Gayle's desk and looked around the cabin. It had been his for three years and hadn't changed much since that time. A few personal additions from the *Lady*'s new captain could be seen, but it still remained just as he remembered.

He ran his hand with appreciation over the polished teak and the gleaming brass fittings. Gayle had done a fine job of commanding his ship, and although there were times when he longed to be at her helm himself, Ryan knew his place was at Briarfawn.

The *Lady* had provided the means, and the rest had been up to him. Up until a month ago, he had thought he'd almost reached the fulfillment of those dreams, the ones he would lay awake at night, in this very cabin, fantasizing about. Years ago, in the compact bunk across from him, he had come up with the name for his future home after spending a weekend at the lodge of a country squire who had three eligible daughters. He had met the man at a London club and agreed to accompany the large party for a hunting weekend, anticipating the respite from the hectic life of the city before once again sailing out.

Knowing the good squire's intentions of unloading one of his daughters, Ryan spent most of the weekend outdoors. It was on his last day that he had come upon the beautiful doe. Glad that he was alone, he had stalked her through the woods, waiting and watching as she made her way through the growth. There was a moment when she stood stock-still before slowly surveying the forest, and although Ryan's rifle was in his hand, he could not sight her with it. Having made sure he was downwind of her, he had remained unnoticed and his attention was suddenly caught by a movement to her side. There, surrounded on three sides by wild, thorny briars, was a newborn fawn, and he watched as the doe carefully picked her way through the camouflage.

He had felt a sudden peace as he looked on, seeing the interplay between them as the mother cared for her young, waiting patiently as thin, spindly legs made uncertain attempts to stand. Finally upright, the fawn suckled hungrily as the doe continued her vigilant watch.

It had been a beautiful sight to witness, and as he turned away, Ryan remembered losing his taste for the hunt, wanting at that time nothing more than to be aboard ship once again.

Days later, lying here in this very bed after his turn at watch, Ryan had known what he would name his future home. What he had seen in that forest was what he wanted to recreate for himself, and those who came after him. A place where all who lived would be protected; someplace secure, where happiness and love could be nurtured.

Briarfawn . . . God, how he missed it.

Feeling that he was becoming melancholy, with nothing better to do than reminisce about the past, Ryan left his old cabin and made his way to the smaller one he had insisted upon using. There, thanks to Jamie, he would find the remedy for the haunting memories that plagued him.

Anticipating the liquor, Ryan became frozen to the floor as he stood in the doorway to his cabin. Lying seductively on his bunk was a beautiful young woman, apparently nude under the sheet pulled up to her barely covered breasts.

"What are you doing here?" Ryan demanded, annoyed but also taking in her lush curves.

She looked confused. Pulling the sheet higher, she replied in a hesitant, small voice, "I was told to come here. A man named Jamie showed me into this cabin."

Ryan closed his eyes briefly in exasperation. He should have known Jamie would be behind this. Going to where the man had placed his bottle, he poured himself a stiff drink and threw back his head as the brandy slid smoothly down his throat. At least Jamie had done something right, Ryan thought, as he turned his attention back to the woman.

"The man was mistaken. Please get dressed."

Her mouth opened in astonishment, but she quickly recovered. Wrapping the sheet around her as she rose from the bed, she held his gaze with her soft blue eyes. As she slowly walked over to him, she threw back her head, causing her dark blond hair to fall down her back.

She was tall, and by the time she stopped in front of him her mouth was only inches away from his own. He continued to stare at her as she opened the sheet and held each corner in her hands, lightly touching his shoulders.

Looking at him proudly, she asked quietly, "Are you sure, love, that your friend was mistaken?"

Dispassionately, Ryan looked down at the woman. She was fair—peaches and cream, she would have been described at home. Her full breasts thrust out at him invitingly and her long legs were posed seductively before him. She was a beauty all right, and Jamie had chosen well. His lack of interest was as much of a surprise to him as it apparently was to the woman.

"Don't I please you?" she asked, shocked at the suggestion.

Ryan reached out and touched her face. "At any other time you'd have pleased me well; a man would be a liar to say otherwise. But tonight your hair would have to be darker, with golden lights shining upon it from the candle, and your beautiful blue eyes would have to be green, turning as deep as emeralds when we made love."

"Close your eyes, then, and pretend I'm this woman. I don't mind."

Ryan's face broke into an amused grin. "I'm afraid you'd also have to shrink about five inches."

She laughed lightly before looking back into his eyes. "There's not much point, is there, love?" she asked seriously.

Ryan smiled at her kindly, but shook his head.

With regret showing in her eyes, she turned away from him and dropping the sheet, began to dress.

He watched with detached interest as the woman clothed herself. He was sure she was no ordinary

430

prostitute that plied her wares on the docks. Jamie must have had to do some fast work to find her, and thinking of his mate, he asked, "Have you been paid?"

She pulled her dress over her head, and when her face appeared she looked at him skeptically. "I'm *always* paid first, and there's never before been a refund, so don't expect one now."

"A very sound business practice," Ryan declared lightly. "You should be paid for your time, however used. I wanted to make sure, that's all."

He poured himself another drink and asked, "Do you mind telling me your name?"

She looked at the tall man for a few seconds, as though reassessing him, before answering, "Cassie Hamilton."

"Well, Cassie Hamilton, would you care to join me for a drink?" Ryan held up the French brandy for her to see.

Cassie inclined her head once and started to pin her hair back into place as she walked over to him. "You're Ryan Barrington, aren't you?"

Ryan handed her the drink, then bowed slightly. "At your service. Jamie mentioned my name?"

"Jamie? That little man? No, all afternoon I've been hearing talk about a Captain Ryan Barrington that's come back to London. Seems you're famous in certain circles. I was curious to see this man who's been causing such a stir among some very high-placed ladies."

Ryan looked amused. "So word has spread already, no doubt helped along by my friend Jamie. Well, Cassie, has your curiosity been satisfied?"

"Not quite, as well you should know, Captain." Cassie sipped her drink and gazed at the tall, handsome stranger before her with a twinge of disappointment. Who would have thought the Ryan Barrington of the tall tales this afternoon would turn her down flat tonight? But Cassie was pragmatic, and the facts presented to her were that of a man in love, truly in love. For if she could not tempt

431

him, nobody would.

She finished her drink and placed the glass back on the wooden table. Picking up her shawl, she walked over to him.

"Have you told her?" she asked out of the blue.

"Who?" Ryan was genuinely confused by the turn of the conversation. But Cassie was a tough lady—at least, she had been a lady before her husband was killed. Now she supplemented her late husband's pathetic estate revenues with a very select clientele. She had learned not to mince words or waste time, and being here was now a waste of time. She had two children to support and boarding school tuitions to pay.

"The woman with the darker hair and the green eyes that change. Have you told her?"

Ryan laughed. "Ah . . . that woman. Have I told her what? Are you always this puzzling?"

She was becoming annoyed at his evasion of her question. "I'm not the puzzle, Captain Barrington, you are. I merely wanted to know, after being turned down for the first time because of another woman, if you have told this lady that you love her."

Ryan's grin froze as he stared at her in shock.

It was Cassie's turn to laugh. "Well, by that expression I gather you haven't. Let me tell you something. I haven't always been in this business and I remember what it was like to be in love . . . and Captain, you're in love. Your face told me when you spoke of her, and your body convinced me. I'll give you a piece of advice, free of charge. A woman needs the words."

Wrapping her shawl about her shoulders, she reached up and ran the palm of her hand across his cheek. "I know if I had a man like you I'd want to be told, and often."

She kissed him lightly where her hand had been and turned to leave, saying, "The night is still young and I have bills to pay . . . just like the so-called upstanding citizens I shall meet with tonight."

"Cassie, wait!" Ryan called out to her as he reached into his desk and took out several gold coins. Walking to the doorway, he placed them into her hands. "Thank you for your advice," he said sincerely. "You're quite a lady."

Cassie looked into her palms and stared at the coins lying within. A small fortune. Enough that she could go home tonight and skip her appointments. Her eyes started to water as she realized with relief that the pressure was off, for a little while at least.

Raising her eyes, she conveyed her thanks by saying, "And you're quite a man Ryan Barrington. It was a pleasure to have met you."

Turning quickly, she fled the corridor, eager to be away from him less he observe her crying. Imagine Cassie Hamilton reduced to tears? she thought in bemusement. She would have sworn she'd buried them along with her dead husband.

Chapter 28

Across the ocean, Brianne and Rena reluctantly left the small shop in New Orleans. Both women had been fascinated with the huge selection of material. Bolts of silks, satins, batistes—fine, handkerchief-thin cottons—from all over the world dazzled their eyes and made selections difficult.

It had been Rena's idea to travel into the city for the day, the purpose of the trip being to purchase material for the baby's layette. Confining their purchases to the delicate cottons, they each carried a package as they stepped onto the busy street.

"Brianne, I know of a coffee shop not far from here. Why don't we rest for a bit? You look tired." Rena gazed into her friend's face with concern.

Brianne returned her look with one of affection. What would she have done the past few weeks without Rena? What was once a friendship had grown into love. Over the months they had laughed, cried, learned, and grown stronger together. Rena was more than a friend, more than a "cousin." She was her surrogate sister, and Brianne loved her as one.

Hooking her free arm through Rena's, she briefly leaned her head against the taller woman's shoulder.

435

"That's a great idea," she said. "But no coffee shop. We're going to the St. Charles Hotel."

Rena stopped walking. "Brianne, do you think we're dressed for that?"

Brianne looked over their gowns with assurance. Rena was costumed to perfection in pale blue and white, while her own wide gown of tiny mauve and cream stripes complemented the elaborate hat she balanced on her head. "Rena, we're dressed to the hilt, as we used to say. I thought we might be overdressed this morning, but looking around the city I can safely say we're fine. In fact," she arched one thin eyebrow, "I think even Madame Fountaine would approve."

Rena smiled at her reference to the haughty French couturière. "If you think so," she said uncertainly, as they walked to the hired coach that had been patiently waiting for them.

Before reaching it, Brianne said, "Well, I do think so. Know what else I think?" Rena looked down at her as she continued, "I also think we're two fine-looking ladies. Foxes, in fact."

Rena laughed. "Thank you for your first compliment, but *foxes?*"

As the driver helped her into the coach, Brianne said over her shoulder, "That too is something we used to say. But don't worry. It means everything is put together just right." There, she thought. That should put an end to Rena's insecurity.

Rena joined her on the wide leather seat and took her hand. She looked into Brianne's eyes and said, "Then we're definitely two foxes."

Brianne laughed. "Now you have it." It felt good to release some of the heartache that had formed around her soul, and with a lighter heart she informed the driver to take them to the St. Charles Hotel as if it were an everyday occurrence.

436

Neither woman was prepared for the St. Charles. It was a huge, beautiful building with twenty white columns in front. It reminded Brianne of the classic Grecian architecture that dotted the country's capital. Stately, enormous, it seemed to take up an entire city block.

Standing in front of it, both women were in awe. Sensing the hesitancy returning to Rena, Brianne opened her mouth to speak while never taking her eyes away from the hotel. "Let's not get intimidated just by the size of it. Remember last week when Salena Grandeville and Maybelle whats-her-name said they came here at least twice a week, sometimes more when they stayed in the city? If you remember correctly, they were shocked that we've never been here." And putting her gloved hand on Rena's arm, she gave her friend a gentle push before they both entered the grand St. Charles Hotel.

It was the classiest place Brianne had ever seen, boasting a thousand guest accommodations, an enormous barroom, cigar stores, a telegraph station, a steam bath, various confectioneries, a barber shop, a bakery, a laundry, a ladies' "ordinary" and one for the gentlemen, plus a large dining room that could seat four hundred people.

Just walking through the lobby into the rotunda was a staggering feat. Brianne compared the noise and confusion to that of the New York Stock Exchange. She had no idea what she and Rena had wandered into until she stood on tiptoe and raised her head to see over the crowd.

Mounted on a platform, the shouts of an auctioneer rose above the frenzied chatter of the onlookers. Brianne couldn't believe her eyes! Right here, in the grandiose St. Charles rotunda, a slave auction was taking place! Bile rose in her throat and she clutched at her chest as a great wave of pity assailed her. It was too far to see the eyes of the poor people being sold, but she could feel their apprehension clearly as a young child stood behind a resigned black woman and an older man straightened his shoulders in an attempt to look younger, stronger.

Brianne couldn't stand to see any others and turned her head away. As she looked through the throng of people, she noticed it was almost a jovial atmosphere. Men were engaged in business transactions about her and she caught the shouts of cotton, sugar, and commissions from the traders and merchants as they conducted their business. She wanted to scream at them. Hadn't they any decency? What about those unfortunates on the platform? How could they let this happen?

"Brianne . . . *please!* Don't do anything," Rena pleaded in a nervous voice. "These people don't see it as being wrong. Let's just get out of here." She tried to bring Brianne away by pulling her upper arm, but the smaller woman didn't budge. Her eyes were riveted on a man not twenty feet away.

Rena followed her line of vision and gasped. Gregory Duville was standing with a group of well-dressed men whose attentions were centered on the wooden platform.

"Please, Brianne, let's leave this," Rena again pleaded, then groaned as one of the men noticed them staring and informed the others.

Duville lazily turned toward them and Rena could see an instant transformation come over him when she and Brianne were recognized. Excusing himself, Duville made his way through the crowd. As he stopped in front of them, he smiled as he removed his hat. "Madame Barrington, what a pleasant surprise. Have you and Miss Ahearn come to enjoy the dining room? If so, I'd be pleased if you'd both be my guests."

His smile was meant to be disarming, but Brianne found herself unable to return it. She was still too upset to play Southern belle for him.

Rena caught a look almost of fear in the Creole's eyes

as Brianne continued to stare at the man. "Mrs. Barrington isn't feeling well," Rena volunteered. "I'm afraid we weren't prepared for this," and she indicated the continuous confusion with her eyes.

She sensed his immediate relief as the taut skin around his dark eyes relaxed. "Then perhaps I could escort both of you ladies outside?"

Yes, Brianne thought, outside, where the air was less charged, less oppressive, less shameful.

"Thank you, Monsieur, I would appreciate that." Gratefully, Brianne placed her hand through his arm as he took her package. Rena stayed close to her side, and the three of them left the noisy rotunda.

"I've heard your husband is abroad, Madame. Have you any idea when he'll return?"

Brianne tried not to tense with his question, but gave him the pat answer that she had already passed on to numerous neighbors. "It was unfortunate that Ryan was called away on business. We expect him to return from England by early October."

They were already nearing the doors when Duville bent his head and whispered, "It must have pained him to leave you so soon after your marriage. I, Madame, could not have borne such a separation."

She should have been shocked, but found she needed this balm for her injured ego. Her husband had left her alone to face everyone with his abrupt departure, and she enjoyed this unexpected male attention.

"Madame Duville is a very fortunate woman, Monsieur," Brianne murmured. Let him think his words referred to being separated from his own wife.

As he signaled for a carriage, the dark Creole flashed her a look that said he had read through her words.

Rena was the first to enter the carriage, and Brianne noticed that she was almost disdainful of Duville's hand as he helped her up. Mentally shrugging off her friend's annoyance, Brianne smiled as he next extended his hand to her. His fingers covered hers as he brought her hand up to his lips. Even through the cotton of her glove, she could feel his warm lips. He lifted his eyes to hers and said in a muted tone, "If I can be of any assistance while your husband is away, please feel free to contact me. I would consider it an honor."

Brianne found she couldn't respond to his obvious flirtation, but Rena had no such problem. She leaned forward and said in her prim, newly cultured voice, "Thank you for your offer, but Mr. Daniels pays us daily visits. We're very fortunate to have him for a close neighbor. He's been so kind and helpful."

Duville inclined his head and Brianne smiled apologetically as he handed her up into the carriage. As he closed its half-wooden door, Brianne felt obliged to bid him a friendly farewell. "Again, I must thank you for rescuing me. I hope the rest of your day is free from weary, overtired females, but Miss Ahearn and I both thank you for your help."

He raised a single finger to the tip of his black hat, held her eyes with his dark, probing ones, and replied, "You, Madame, could never be a bother. It was my pleasure."

Rena instructed the driver to the wharf where a boat was waiting to take them back to Briarfawn. Noticing that her friend sat back stiffly, she observed, "Why are you so upset? The man's a harmless flatterer of women, that's all."

"Hmph!" Rena knew Brianne's intelligence but couldn't understand why she refused to see through the man. How could she fail to see the evil lurking behind those dark eyes? It was becoming harder and harder to be caught in the middle of Ryan and Brianne's difficulties. And now that Stephan too had confided in her, she didn't know how much longer she could control her tongue.

Looking straight ahead, she said abruptly, "That man's heart is colder than ice!"

Gregory Duville watched the carriage pull away and ground his teeth together in frustration. Barrington didn't deserve the woman. He felt certain if the Ahearn woman had not been present today, he'd be well on his way to seducing Barrington's lovely young wife.

Nothing had gone as planned . . . That stupid *canaille* Harkins had botched up an opportunity to get his hands on the green-eyed temptress. He never should have expected the imbecile to follow instructions, but at least he himself couldn't be implicated in the kidnapping. The ugly bastard was probably lying at the bottom of a bayou—a fit ending for such scum.

Then, to make matters worse, the hot-blooded Caroline had suddenly turned cold, refusing to acknowledge even his card. But they had succeeded in driving a wedge between the Barringtons. The upstart, Ryan Barrington, had been miserable enough to leave, and from that Duville could derive a great deal of satisfaction.

As his lips started to curl upward, he turned back to the hotel. And if a certain red-haired woman could have seen his truly evil smile, she would have shuddered and crossed herself for protection.

Chapter 29

Swallowing hard, Rena almost regretted her decision when she saw Brianne's face—almost.

Dropping the material on her lap, Brianne stared at the younger woman. "You what?" she asked in a shocked, disbelieving voice.

Rena squared her shoulders before repeating her statement. "I asked Stephan to bring Caroline with him when he comes tonight."

"Why? You know I've been trying to avoid her since I've begun to show! I can't believe you did that, Rena." Brianne's fingers began to rub her temples. In the four months that Ryan had been gone she had done her best to maintain a normal life at Briarfawn. Her mornings were taken up in receiving calls from her neighbors, but the remainder of the time was spent caring for her home. Thankfully, Nathen was a thoroughly competent manager and the few problems that did arise were minor. Besides the house and the school, she had taken over the bookkeeping for the plantation, just to keep a hand in the running of the complex operation. Though when she was honest with herself, she would admit it was also a way to fill the lonely nights and take her mind off her personal problems. It was bad enough to know that despite everything, she missed Ryan and wanted him home; now she had once again to accept Caroline's presence at Briarfawn.

Looking up, she said in a determined voice, "Since it was your idea, you'll have to entertain them alone. I won't subject myself to Caroline's innuendoes or snide remarks again."

Rena returned her gaze, breathing deeply and barely containing her impatience. Coming further into the drawing room, she sat opposite Brianne. "It's time you put a stop to her, and before Ryan returns. Caroline's been coming here for months now, uninvited, acting as though *you* were a temporary trespasser on her domain. I thought you should let her see you and the positive proof that you are the only mistress Briarfawn will have. Once she sees you're carrying Ryan's child, she'll have to accept you as his wife."

Brianne folded the tiny cambric gown she had been sewing. Looking at her bulging abdomen, she doubted the wisdom of Rena's words.

"Even this," she said, placing her hands on her stomach, "will not stop that woman. Why do you think she's remained here, instead of returning to Virginia? She doesn't believe that it was urgent business in Europe that took Ryan away so suddenly. You saw her face when she came the week after he left . . . she could barely hide her laughter. I've put up with her all these months because maybe she does have a legitimate claim, Rena. Even though she and Ryan weren't officially engaged, both expected it to happen until I came into the picture."

Rena shook her head vehemently. "Don't be absurd! We both know Ryan wouldn't have married you if he were committed elsewhere."

Brianne put the half-finished gown aside, saying, "You don't understand. There's more to it than that."

"Oh, I understand, all right, more than you think. Did

444

you really believe everyone in this house had suddenly gone deaf after we returned from the party?" Rena watched her closely, judging her reaction, and Brianne blushed deeply, averting her eyes.

"I'd rather not discuss that night, if you don't mind."

Snatching the sewing kit away from Brianne, Rena startled her. "Don't continue being a fool! The time is long overdue for you to discuss it. If you had mentioned it just once, maybe then I could have stopped this before it got out of hand."

"Before what got out of hand? What are you talking about?" Brianne observed Rena as she seemed to struggle within herself for the right words.

Looking at her with sympathy, Rena softly said, "You were wrong, Brianne. Ryan never deceived you with Caroline."

When Brianne started to protest, she quickly added, "I know what you saw. Ryan told Stephan and myself about it soon after. What both of you don't know is that you were set up. It was planned . . . by Caroline and that Creole, Duville. She was to get Ryan outside and Duville was to make sure you saw what took place."

Stunned, Brianne tried to argue against the logic of her disclosure. "Gregory Duville never took me outside. It was my own idea to slip out to the terrace."

Rena nodded. "They planned it for after the reel. Everyone is a little breathless following that dance, and it would only seem natural to leave for a breath of fresh air. Actually, you played right into their hands by doing it of your own accord."

Brianne felt sick to her stomach as she asked fearfully, "How do you know all this? Surely not from Caroline?"

Rena laughed with derision. "From none other. It appears Caroline made a major mistake the night of the party. After we left the party was soon over, and those guests who had traveled a distance were invited to stay

445

the night at Mosshaven. Well, early in the morning hours, before dawn, Stephan happened to observe our friend Duville leaving his cousin's rooms. Unfortunately he didn't say anything to them at the time, not until Ryan told us of his encounter with Caroline in the gardens. It was then Stephan confronted her and threatened to reveal her behavior to her father, promising a scandal that would carry all the way back to Virginia if she didn't come clean. I suppose she knew Stephan would love to humiliate her, so she told him everything, including the fact that it was *she* who insisted Ryan kiss her to prove he could put her out of his life, which is exactly what Ryan told us. Don't you see, Brianne, she *knew* you were out on that balcony. It was all planned, to separate the two of you."

Holding her stomach, Brianne cried out, "But why? Oh, I know Caroline's motives, but why Duville? He was always kind to me." Though as she described the man, she remembered his lack of respect for Ryan the night of the party and his flirtatious overtures at the St. Charles.

Rena shook her head. "From what Stephan's told me, and even he's not sure, I don't think it concerns you so much. As far as we can figure, you're just a means of getting to Ryan. Duville owned this plantation, Brianne. It was from him Ryan bought it. Perhaps he resents Ryan's making a success from his failure. All we know is Duville has some personal vendetta he wants to settle. Stephan says Ryan will make sense of it when he returns. For on the night of the party, and in his letter before he sailed, Ryan asked Stephan to keep an eye on the Creole."

Stricken, Brianne demanded, "Why didn't you tell me this before? How could you have let me go on thinking it was Ryan's fault?"

"If you remember correctly, Brianne, you wouldn't listen to anyone, not even your husband. I've broken a promise to him by telling you it was Caroline who forced herself on him. She practically blackmailed Ryan to get him outside, threatening to make a scene and embarrass you both right there in the ballroom. I kept his secret for as long as I could; he said when you were ready to hear the truth, he wanted it to come from him. It's just a shame that he sailed before hearing about Caroline's confession and Duville's part in it."

Brianne could picture in her mind her husband as he left that June morning. She could still see his face staring up at her and her own hand raised in a silent farewell. She thought about the night of the party. If he had ever come close to loving her, it had been then. Incredibly, it was later that very night that she had killed all hope for them.

The baby kicked in protest at her wistful daydreaming, reminding her of the present. With determination she rose from the chair and smiled at her friend. "Rena, come help me choose a gown. We're having guests tonight, and it's very important that I look my best."

Red curls flying, Rena threw back her head and laughed. "With pleasure! I've been waiting months for this very night."

Brianne joined her and together they ascended the stairs. Halfway up Rena slipped her arm about Brianne's increasing waist and murmured, "It's good to have you back. We've all missed you."

One advantage of being pregnant, Brianne reflected, was that she was no longer forced to wear the wider hoops and the hated corset. She turned sideways and looked at herself in the mirror. Grimacing at her reflection, she ran her hands over the emerald green velvet at her stomach, pulling the material in underneath it to see her silhouette. Dear Lord, she was big for five months! Any weight she had gained was right up front.

Mattie had said she just looked big because of her size, but Brianne had seen smaller women who had become pregnant and hadn't even begun to show until now. She maintained her own schedule, watched what she ate and walked daily around the plantation, but she still thought the baby was too big.

Turning forward, she adjusted the deep neckline. Thank heavens her breasts hadn't increased yet. She felt guilty enough every time poor Carla had to adjust a waistline. The woman had done a marvelous job on the gown and despite her growing body, Brianne still managed to feel pretty, thanks to the clever seamstress. The gown hung in soft folds and the deep rich color enhanced her eyes. She felt she needed something at her breasts, though—there was too much cleavage and nothing to relieve it.

Walking over to her dresser, she opened the top drawer and searching beneath the fine lace handkerchiefs, withdrew the diamond. Banished were its sad memories, and she fastened it around her neck before returning to the mirror. Bringing her hand up, she touched it lovingly; then, almost of their own volition, her fingers traveled to her breast.

Ryan . . . she wanted him now, not next month, and she silently cursed that there was no way to reach him before that. Were it possible, she would go straight to him and beg his forgiveness. But she would think about all that tonight; right then there was a certain woman waiting for her to make an appearance, and she had a score to settle.

As Brianne approached the drawing room, she could hear Rena's soft voice and Caroline's thick drawl as the woman answered. Thrusting her stomach out even farther, she entered the room with confidence. All heads turned at her entrance, and she had to bite her bottom lip to keep from laughing aloud as Stephan's and Caroline's eyes widened with shock.

Stephan was the first to recover, and his face changed quickly to ill-concealed pleasure. Rising, he came to meet her. "Brianne, you look radiant! Congratulations! Does Ryan know?"

Brianne managed to look suitably embarrassed. "Yes, he was told right before he left."

She came to sit in one of the chairs before the fireplace and looked directly at Caroline. Brianne had to admit that the woman sitting opposite her was striking, her beauty only slightly marred as her usually flawless complexion became mottled with an inner rage as she returned her hostess's look.

Glancing at Brianne's stomach in disbelief, she reflected bitterly, "Knowing Ryan as I do, I find it strange that he would leave you in your condition."

"It isn't a condition, Caroline," Brianne said quietly, and smiled. "I happen to be pregnant. It's a very natural state. Ryan knows I'm a healthy woman and there is no need for me to be pampered. I wouldn't think of keeping him from his business, although his last words to me expressed his concern that I take care of myself. A very easy request to grant, I'm afraid, since the entire household—and everyone on Briarfawn, it seems— watches over me."

Stephan handed her a glass of white wine. Bending, he placed a kiss on her cheek. "I'm so pleased for the both of you. Ryan has waited a long time for this."

Looking at Rena, he exclaimed, "How did you ever keep this a secret? I was suspicious that something was up, since Brianne had kept to her room whenever I called lately, but I thought she was getting tired of my constant visits."

Rena smiled sweetly at the man she now knew she loved with a hopeless intensity. "It wasn't easy, Stephan, believe me. Many times it was on the tip of my tongue, but I had to honor my promise to Brianne." And giving her friend a knowing look, she said smoothly, "I think she wanted to wait for Ryan's return in a few weeks, so they could make the announcement together, but I convinced her to join us tonight."

Brianne smiled her thanks and added, "I'm glad she did. It really makes little sense to try and hide this until Ryan comes home. And I'm sure he'd want you both to know."

Caroline's eyes became slits that couldn't hide her jealousy. How she wanted to knock Brianne off her pedestal! She was forming a scathing remark with that intention in mind when Aaron announced dinner.

Politely, Stephan offered his arm to his hostess and they followed the two single women into the dining room. Just before seating her, he squeezed Brianne's hand and whispered, "Perhaps now the state of Virginia will look more appealing."

Brianne suppressed a chuckle as she took Ryan's place at the head of the table and watched as Stephan tenderly seated Rena before holding out a chair for his cousin. Throughout dinner the conversation centered on Ryan's expected return next month and the baby's arrival in early February, less than four months away. Brianne thought Stephan very sweet to seem so interested in her plans for a nursery, but she had the distinct impression that his interest was just one more way to infuriate Caroline, who made no effort to disguise her boredom.

Once more gathered in the drawing room, the women were seated by the fire and Stephan was pouring himself a brandy when Brianne made the suggestion to him.

"Stephan, why not take Rena outside? She's spent the entire afternoon sewing baby clothes with me. And although she's been wonderful about it, I'm sure she'd like the chance to escape for a short while."

Stephan looked uncertainly at her, but Brianne smiled, nodding her silent assurance that she'd be fine alone with Caroline. Both she and Caroline watched the couple as they left, obviously eager to be by themselves.

When she heard the front door open, Brianne said, "I think they're well suited for each other, don't you?"

Caroline shrugged. "I've never really thought about it. Your cousin appears to be what Stephan wants, but then Stephan is an easy man to please when it comes to women."

"Unlike Ryan?"

Caroline seemed surprised. "As a matter of fact, yes. Ryan is more discriminating. His woman should complement him. Besides being beautiful, she should also be intelligent, witty, and charming. And most important, know how to please him."

Brianne smiled wryly. "Why thank you, Caroline, for the compliment. And all this time I thought you disliked me."

"You weren't mistaken," Caroline haughtily returned her smile. "Is this to be a showdown, then?" she asked, hoping to intimidate the small woman across from her.

"I think it's time. Don't you?" Brianne rose from the chair and walked to the crystal decanters filled with various liqueurs. "Would you care for something to drink? It might not be a bad idea to fortify yourself."

"I have no need to fortify myself against anything you might have to say. But you might want to pour yourself one."

Smiling, Brianne walked back to her. "Because I'm pregnant, I've restricted myself to an occasional glass of wine, which I've already had, so I don't think I'll be drinking."

Caroline's expression hardened. "You're very sure of yourself now that you're breeding, aren't you?"

"What a way to put it!" Brianne said in surprise and laughed. "I've always associated breeding with animals—hardly how I would describe carrying the child of the man I love."

"Ah, but where is this man? If he felt the same, wouldn't he be with you at this important time? Hardly how *I* would describe a devoted husband."

Brianne cast her a pitying glance. "You gave it a good try, Caroline, but it didn't work. Ryan rejected you—not me. When I found out what you had done I'll admit I wanted revenge, but watching you during dinner, I surprised myself by beginning to pity you. It must be very hard to accept the fact that you've lost him."

Caroline indignantly straightened her shoulders. "Save your pity, Brianne, you'll soon need it for yourself. When Ryan comes back and sees you, it won't take him long to look elsewhere. You forget, he hasn't been here to watch your belly grow. I know Ryan, and the shock of your appearance will turn to distaste. Why don't you just let him remember you the way you were? Leave here before he sends you away."

"You are desperate, aren't you, Caroline? But I don't think you know Ryan at all. If you did, then you'd know how much this child means to him. I'm not apprehensive about Ryan's return—I'm counting the days until we can be together again."

Leaning forward, she looked directly into the woman's eyes. "Don't fool yourself any longer into thinking you have a chance to get him back. You don't."

Caroline bristled at her words. "Who are you to tell me what to do?"

"I'm his wife," Brianne replied softly.

Caroline laughed bitterly. "Wife? You have no idea what he needs. He was mine! This home should have been mine! If it weren't for you showing up here, they both would've been mine by now. Oh, I'll admit you have the upper hand now," she challenged, "but soon that will change."

Blithely ignoring the implied threat, Brianne answered, "I have the *only* hand, Caroline. I suggest you

452

look elsewhere for a man—there's none for you on Briarfawn."

The room rang with Caroline's derisive laughter. "Let's stop parrying with words, shall we? You saw Ryan kiss me. He hasn't forgotten how it was between us, any more than I have. Something like that, something so powerful between a man and a woman, cannot be easily extinguished. There's always a residue of embers just waiting to be rekindled. I intend to be here to ensure that."

Her words gnawed at Brianne's insides. Caroline was obviously determined—but then so was she. "That was certainly candid, so let me be equally honest with you," she replied in a deceptively calm voice. "You and I, Caroline, we can never be friends, but neither did I want us to be enemies. I realize you feel jilted, but Ryan himself has told me he never actually proposed to you— he said he never even mentioned the word marriage to you or your family. As far as his kissing you the night of the party, again Ryan has told several people, besides Stephan, how you blackmailed him into it. He left with you because of *me*. He knew you were spoiled enough to ruin my evening. Does that sound like a man waiting to begin an illicit affair? I think not. How do you imagine Stephan first learned of your little plot, if not from Ryan?"

Lifting her chin, she added, "Stay, if you feel the need, but I wouldn't want to be in your position when Ryan learns of your accomplice."

Brianne rose from her chair, then added her parting shot. "You must know Ryan would never touch the discards of Gregory Duville."

Caroline jumped to her feet, and Brianne feared the blonde might attack her as the woman's fingers curled into her palms.

"How dare you!" she shrieked to Brianne's retreating back, all the more enraged because Brianne's last remark had hit home—her involvement with the Creole having been disastrous from the beginning.

Brianne swung around just before she left the room. "I'll dare *anything!*" she shot back at her. "Anything at all . . . I just wanted you to know that. I'm not afraid of you, Caroline, and I have no intention of losing Ryan. I'm prepared to fight you with every dirty trick in the book if need be, but I don't see that happening." Placing a small, delicate hand on her stomach, she said carefully, "Save yourself the pain of being thrice rejected and leave, go back to Virginia. However, should you decide to stay on at Mosshaven, please keep in mind that you're not welcome in my home uninvited."

Raising her head even higher, Brianne coldly added, "Perhaps, for our child's christening, Ryan and I might allow you back on Briarfawn."

Even across the room, Brianne read the fear in Caroline's eyes, and she turned and left before the woman could recover and form a reply.

Surprised, she saw Stephan and Rena standing by the front door and realized they had never gone outside, wanting to be near should she need them. So upset by her scene with Caroline she could no longer trust her voice to thank them, she forced a tight smile and headed for the stairs.

A loud crash came from the drawing room and Brianne paused briefly on the steps. She contemplated returning to learn the cause, but thankfully heard Stephan running in that direction. Brianne's hand tightened on the polished banister and pulled herself up another step. All she wanted to think about was the soft bed that waited for her, and not in the room she had exiled herself to. Tonight she was returning to the bedroom she had shared with Ryan . . . and it would take more than Caroline Daniels to make her leave it again.

Chapter 30

"Mattie, where did we put the liners for the drawers? I can't seem to find them here."

Ryan was standing in the foyer, and a shock ran through him to hear her voice.

The vast expanse of the Atlantic Ocean couldn't diminish his need, and when he had reached New Orleans he had left all business at docking for the ship's captain in order to return with haste to his home. It seemed to him he had been like a man waking from a dream when the levee of Briarfawn had come into view. Not wanting to wait any longer, he had left all his luggage there by the water, and had walked to his home. Each tree that he had passed welcomed him back. The stalks of cane, swaying in the breeze, waved to him and the dirt beneath his feet crunched out its own distinct greeting. When the columns of Briarfawn had been sighted in the distance, his chest filled and his eyes began to burn.

Home . . . never did he wish to leave it again. He didn't know what the time apart had done for Brianne, but it had made him realize just how important this life was.

He would tell her everything. Please God, he silently prayed, don't let her turn away again. He had to face her with the truth . . . the truth about their senseless fight and his deplorable behavior, but most important, the true extent of his feelings. Feelings? He loved her! Why had it been so hard to admit that before?

Since London, he had been obsessed with finishing their business and returning to Louisiana in record time. Urging Gayle Sawyer on, he had worked like ten men himself to make their home port two weeks earlier than expected.

Turning around in the large entry hall, he placed a finger to his lips, silencing Mattie's impending squeal of pleasure upon sighting him. "Shh, don't give me away, Mattie," he whispered. "Let me surprise your mistress."

The housekeeper flashed him a huge smile, silently pointing to the stairs, and Ryan reached over and planted a kiss on her round cheek before taking the steps two at a time.

Brianne wiped away the perspiration on her forehead with her apron and looked about the room. It was coming along nicely and she knew she'd be pleased with the end results. Converting the bedroom she had once used into a nursery was just the thing she had needed after her confrontation with Caroline. It took her mind off the woman and let her concentrate on happier things, such as the practicality of using yellow as the main color of her baby's room.

Their baby, she corrected herself. Hers and Ryan's. She looked down at herself and smiled. Within the past few weeks, since learning just how wrong she had been and how shamefully little trust she had placed in her husband, Brianne talked constantly to the growing life inside her.

I wonder what your father will think of all this? she silently mused. He had said she could use the money in his study for anything, but she wasn't sure how he would react to the house being changed. She hoped he would be pleased, for it seemed the obvious room to redecorate, with its close proximity to their bedroom. Everyone had been generous with their time and talents. Nathen had enlisted the help of two field workers to cover the pale green walls with the soft, sunny color and offset that with the glossy white of the trim. Carla and Rena had combined their sewing expertise and produced heavy white priscilla curtains with frills of cotton eyelet. The same pattern was duplicated on the skirt for the large wicker bassinet Stephan had found for her in New Orleans. Altogether, it was a cheerful room, done with love.

Running one hand across the polished chest of drawers that Jesse, Briarfawn's carpenter, had proudly presented to her, Brianne opened another button on her blouse with the other in a feeble attempt to cool off a bit. The unexpected late fall heat was bad enough, but Louisiana's humidity was unbearable when one was pregnant. Looking toward the door, she called even louder, "Mattie? Did you get them?"

Not hearing an answer, she impatiently left the room to find the liners herself. Purposefully rounding the doorway, she stopped dead in her tracks and stared at the apparition before her.

"Ryan?" she breathed his name, hoping he was really standing there and was not something seen only through the powers of her imagination.

He took in her appearance, and smiling appreciatively, softly greeted her, "Hello, Brianne."

Without thinking, giving no thought as to how they had parted months before, or whether he even wanted her, Brianne let out a cry of happiness and ran down the hallway.

Surprised at her reaction, he instinctively caught her as she leaped into his arms, throwing her own about his neck. Holding her, he felt her warm breath against his neck as she buried her face against his shoulder and held on to him tightly.

"Oh Ryan, I'm so glad you're home," she whispered happily.

Just as quickly her mood changed and she said contritely, "I'm sorry I didn't trust you, or even listen when you tried to explain. Please say you forgive me?"

Ryan closed his eyes and breathed in the sweet fragrance of her hair. "Shh . . . we'll talk later, and then I'll beg your forgiveness. Right now, let me look at you."

He put her down in front of him and gazed tenderly into her face.

Brianne, realizing what she must look like, whipped the kerchief off her head and ran a hand through her hair. "What a way to greet you! I must look a sight!" she exclaimed, sniffling back tears of happiness.

Ryan took her chin between his finger and thumb. "You are a sight. One I've imagined a thousand times while I was away from you. I missed you, Brianne."

"And I you." She looked deeply into his eyes and silently breathed a sigh of relief. What she saw was not bitterness, or even resentfulness, but something that made her heart beat faster, turning her blood to liquid fire.

Confused by those renewed yearnings, she sought control. "Come," she said as she took his hand. "I have something to show you."

She led him to the redecorated room and saw the surprise on his face give way to pleasure as he walked into the nursery. He gave the bassinet a gentle swing and watched as it slowly swayed.

He turned around, his face shining with pride. "You did this?" he asked incredulously.

Smiling, she nodded and tried to hide her own pride with words. "Someone had to give some thought as to where our son was to sleep."

Ryan viewed her enlarged girth and smiled affectionately. "Are you so sure it will be a son?"

"Don't ask me how I know, but I do. The next time we'll have our daughter. This, Ryan," she said, touching her stomach, "is your son."

He stared at her abdomen for the longest time as a range of emotions played across his face. Finally he seemed to shake himself free and walked over to her. Without speaking, he bent, and taking her unawares, picked up his wife in his arms.

As he carried her into the master bedroom she gladly held him around the neck, placing her head on his shoulder as he spoke at last. "You know I wouldn't be disappointed to have a daughter, not in the least."

"I know," Brianne murmured. "Neither would I."

He kissed her forehead as he gently placed her upon the bed. Sitting up, she watched him shut the dressing-room door and greedily drank in the sight of him. If possible, he was more handsome than before. Deeply tanned from his months at sea, his skin shone like that of some bronzed god. His shirt was opened almost to the waist, and the crisp mat of hair that lay between the linen was bleached by the sun. His hair also was lighter and the curl, which at times had infuriated her, was once again falling onto his forehead. She could barely wait to push it tenderly back in a caress.

Coming to sit next to her, he brushed her own hair back from her face as he said in a husky voice, "God help me, but I want you, Brianne."

She turned away from him to stare at the bed, her heart pounding a staccato against her chest, and Ryan touched her shoulder compassionately. "I know. I've hurt you, and I'll spend the rest of my life trying to make up for that."

Brianne shook her head. "I don't want you to. No one person is at fault. I share as much blame as you, probably more."

"What then? The baby? Do you fear for the child? I just want to hold you, feel you lying next to me. I can wait until after the child is born," he lied, as the ache continued in his groin.

Brianne laughed timidly. "You may be able to, but I can't. I know it's silly, Ryan, but I had planned your homecoming so differently. I wanted to look just right, not like this," she said disgustedly, picking at her skirt, "all sweaty, and dressed like a charwoman."

Ryan chuckled as he stared at her back and bent head. "Don't you know, silly lady, I would want you just as much if I'd found you cleaning out Raven's stall? Although I might suggest we bathe together first," he laughingly added as an afterthought.

Brianne joined in his laughter for a moment, until she felt him lift her hair away from her neck and place a kiss behind her ear. Closing her eyes, she leaned back against his chest and felt the heat from his body through the light material at the back of her blouse.

"I don't want to hurt you," he breathed into her ear.

Brianne shivered in delight as familiar sensations ran from her ear down to her legs. "You won't. I happen to know for a fact that it's all right up until the last months. I'm not quite sure when that is, Ryan, but I just know it isn't now . . . not now," she sighed as his hands slid from behind her to encircle her stomach.

Slowly, very slowly, he caressed their child in ever-widening circles. He raised his thumbs, brushing the undersides of her breasts fleetingly, and teased unmercifully by making her wait until he completed each circumference of her stomach.

Leaning her head all the way back against his chest, she took his hands and placed them directly on her breasts, too impatient for each stroke of his fingers to reach them. "Oh Ryan . . . I have missed you."

Over the material he gently cupped each mound,

bringing her nipples to excited peaks. Again he kissed the back of her neck, only this time with more fervor, and lightly ran his tongue down the sloping plane of her shoulder.

"I want to see you," he breathed. "I've waited far too long already."

She turned and looked into his eyes. "I'm not the same, Ryan. I've changed in the last few months. You may be disappointed."

Without answering, he turned her completely around and held her eyes while slowly unbuttoning her blouse. Without once taking his eyes away from hers, he stood her up and slowly, deliberately undressed her. When she stood, clad only in her thin, unbuttoned chemise and despaired that he would find her unattractive, he smiled tenderly and removed his own shirt. She wanted to look at his chest, but couldn't break the spell he held her in. When he finally bent to take off his trousers, then Brianne buried her hand in his thick, curling mane.

Nude, he knelt in front of her and deliberately kissed her distended stomach. "My God! You're beautiful," he said quietly. "How else would the mother of my child look to me?"

Sitting on the bed, he brought her with him to stand between his legs. He ran his hands down her flanks while Brianne fingered the sculptured planes of his face. Moaning, he buried his lips between her soft breasts as he tightened his arms around her and lying back, brought her with him onto the bed.

Brianne placed her hands on the mattress on either side of his face, and raising her head, she let her hair fall around them, making a lustrous copper tent.

"Have you any idea how much I want you, Brianne?" he asked, running his palms against the tips of her breasts. The callouses, developed from months of climbing rigging, scratched lightly against their buds and

461

they bloomed provocatively into his hands.

"As much as I want you," she murmured, watching the color of his eyes turn a deep, warm blue. The tips of his lashes matched the gold flecks in his eyes, and Brianne hoped their child would be blessed with their beauty.

Each stared into the other's face for long, soul-stirring moments until neither could take much more, and by mutual agreement their heads moved toward each other quickly. It was their first real kiss since their misunderstanding months ago, and they feverishly clung to each other as they poured out their loneliness and hurt.

Flushed, Brianne whispered against his mouth, "Never again leave without me! I couldn't bear to be separated from you."

"Never, little one," he promised, claiming her once again.

Her mouth was as eager and hot as his own, avidly devouring, tasting the salt that remained on his lips, and breathing in the clean scent of the ocean that still clung to him.

Ryan swept her onto her back. His tongue went on an uncharted course down her body, lingering for seconds to alternately kiss her palms, the inside of her elbow, the tender sides of her breasts . . . always avoiding the obvious points of arousal. Taking his time, he adored her completely, finally pausing to partake of her sweetness where he knew she wanted him most.

Inflamed beyond belief by his skill, she writhed in total abandon beneath him and felt the delicious tension coil within her, begging for release.

Grasping his hair, she brought him up to face her. "Please, Ryan," she pleaded, "I want you inside me."

Confusion crossed his face. "The child?" he asked uncertainly.

Brianne lightly ran her fingernails down his chest, pausing briefly to excite him as he had done to her.

Letting her hands trail farther, she heard his sharp intake of breath as she encircled his throbbing manhood. "The child will be fine. You and I are suffering . . . it's a sweet torture, Ryan, but there's no need."

She smiled at the first hint of doubt surfacing on her husband's face as he hesitantly placed himself before her. She waited patiently and watched with tenderness as he treated her as if she were a fragile piece of glass.

Placing her hands on either side of his face, she captured his gaze. "I won't break, Ryan," she whispered. "Please . . ."

Ryan's arms formed a brace, holding himself above her as he stared into her pleading eyes. "If anything ever happened to you," he despaired in a tortured voice, "I'd never forgive myself."

Seeing that she would have to take matters into her own hands, Brianne's idled down his sides to grasp his hips. "You are mine, Ryan Barrington, and I've waited a lifetime for you," she whispered bewitchingly. "I'll not wait any longer."

Slowly she dug her trembling fingers into his hips and enveloped him completely. An agonized moan escaped her lips as she tilted her head back in overwhelming pleasure, for he filled her aching loneliness and replaced it with a hot, scalding sweetness.

Ryan's face showed his surprise. There was a roaring in his ears, a dryness to his mouth, and a surge of blood that filled his manhood, hardening it until it was inflamed, ignited by exquisite fire.

Brianne . . . Brianne . . . he repeated her name in his mind as blue eyes hypnotically locked into green. She was his goddess, his woman, his wife, and he cried out almost savagely as he finally, really came home to her . . . at long last.

Later, brushing the hair back from her face, he gently

blew on her forehead, for their bodies were lightly covered with a glistening dew from their astonishing exertions. Ryan could never remember being so totally moved by a woman. This small creature held his heart, his very life, in her hands—for he could not foresee an existence without her.

"I love you, Brianne," he whispered huskily. "I wanted to wait to tell you, so you wouldn't think it was said in the heat of passion. I mean it with every fiber of my being. I'll love you now, while you're beautiful and young . . . and I'll love you more when you're beautiful and have grown old with me. All I ask is that we're honest with each other. Never let something unsaid come between us."

Feeling wet tears on his chest, he tightened his hold around her shoulders. "Shh . . . it's all right," he said into her hair. "You don't have to feel as strongly as I do. It will come in time. It's frightening at first, I know. I tried to avoid facing it, but when it was shoved under my nose by a very wise lady in London, I found it to be comforting, reassuring, and downright exhilarating."

"Really?" Brianne wiped her face and turned her head to see him better. "Since we're always going to be honest . . . I have a confession to make."

Slipping a leg across his, she fitted herself comfortably next to him. "Do you remember that night when we raided Lizzie's kitchen?"

When he smiled, she brushed back the defiant curl and continued, "Well, it was that night that I started to fall in love with you."

Ryan's face underwent an extraordinary change, registering astonishment that quickly turned to elation. "All this time, and you never . . ."

"You weren't the only one to be frightened. I too had never experienced love, but that night, when you held me, I knew I was where I belonged."

He kissed the tip of her nose. "You'll never know how difficult that was. I was so afraid I'd lose the battle with my body and scare you further away. I'm glad now . . ."

Suddenly he sat straight up and moved quickly away from her. "My God, Brianne! What was that?"

She too had felt it, as her abdomen lay against his side. Looking at him with exaggerated patience, she giggled. "That, Ryan, was your son. I think he's filing his first complaint. By the force of that kick, I would say he doesn't find love quite as *downright exhilarating* as we do."

"Does it hurt?" he asked with naive concern, looking at her as though afraid to come near.

"Of course not! Come here," she directed. He came back hesitantly, and Brianne thought it ridiculous that this huge man was afraid of his own child. Realizing how much he had missed, and wanting to acquaint them as soon as possible, she asked Ryan to sit back against the pillows with his knees bent. Using them as a backrest, she lay sideways and took his wrist.

Placing his tanned hand firmly on her rounded belly, she then demanded in mock indignation, "Now . . . just who is this very wise lady in London, to whom I owe a debt of gratitude?"

Chapter 31

Once again, Brianne found herself back in the baby's room. Over the past three months she had found herself haunting it frequently—staring at the empty bassinet, opening the chest of drawers to inspect the perfect tiny clothes, waiting . . . always waiting.

It wasn't in her nature to be overly patient, and she felt months overdue, instead of only a week. She knew now how Morganna had felt the night she had called her in Philadelphia. As the birth of her own child became imminent, her thoughts were filled, more often than not, with her sister. Poor Morganna! How had her disappearance affected her? She knew if their positions were reversed she would never stop searching, never give up hope of her sister's return.

Brianne thought about Morganna's baby, the niece or nephew that she'd never see, and she was thankful her sister had the child to comfort her.

She knew why Morganna had wanted her with her for the birth of her child. It was fear . . . the unspoken fear of every new mother. Although secretly frightened by the enormous task awaiting her, Brianne knew she was as ready as she'd ever be. Everyone except her husband and Rena thought her to be a little eccentric when she laid her own rules for the delivery. The chance of having a doctor present was slim, so she would have to entrust herself to Lucas's wife, Tessa. The older woman was an experienced midwife and Mattie had insisted on being her assistant.

Although Tessa at times spoke "patois," a mixture of French and English that sometimes was difficult to understand, she seemed intelligent and knowledgeable about childbirth, but more important, Brianne knew dear Mattie would watch out for her and the child, doing everything humanly possible to ensure a safe delivery.

She picked up her candle and walked over to the window. It was still there, just as she had known it would be. Like a beacon in the night, the constant fire in the sugar mill illuminated the building where the cane was processed. Her husband was there, just as he had been almost every night, along with most of the men on the plantation. From doing the bookkeeping, she knew there was over $85,000 invested in machinery to crush the cane, while fires burned night and day to boil the syrup into sugar and molasses. Everyone worked fourteen to sixteen hours a day, and Ryan encouraged them by abundant rations of food, presents of tobacco, and draughts of the sweet syrup.

She knew now that the peaceful way of life she had known on Briarfawn had all been leading up to these frantic last three months. Brianne remembered in early October, when the cane had reached maturity, coming into the fields to watch as the cutters severed each stalk close to the ground, cutting off the top, which Ryan said contained "injurious" juices. Behind the cutters came broad-tread carts on which the cane was piled and carried to the mill. Months passed, Christmas came and went, and they still worked in shifts to make sure the precious blaze continued.

More often than she wished she was alone, and Brianne kept the memory of the week following Ryan's return close to her, to bring out on long nights such as this. As reunited lovers she and Ryan had been greedy . . . always touching, as if to be reassured that the overpowering emotions were real. Needing no one but themselves, they guarded their privacy with ferocity.

Then had come a series of turmoils that forced them to relinquish their precious solitude. First Stephan had arrived to welcome Ryan home and tell him of Caroline's and Duville's duplicity. Enraged, Ryan accompanied his friend back to Mosshaven, returning hours later to calmly inform Brianne that Arthur Daniels would be taking his daughter on an extended holiday to Europe. Ryan said that after throwing an impressive temper tantrum, Caroline had finally consented to her enforced exile when Stephan pointed out it was conceivable she'd be in the right place to capture a titled husband. Grateful that the woman would be out of their lives, Brianne didn't even press him for more details. It had been enough to know she would be gone.

Ryan had remained very quiet as he resumed his life on Briarfawn. She had sensed him seething inwardly as he supervised the harvest, and felt he was silently plotting his revenge on the Creole. In the months that followed, as word slowly drifted back to them of Duville's impending financial ruin from mismanagement and the sudden calling in of his gambling debts, Brianne had watched her husband's face for some clue as to his involvement. Finding none, she had finally confronted him.

She remembered Ryan sitting behind his desk busily entering figures in his ledger. Knowing how hard he had worked to produce the three hundred twenty hogsheads to be shipped that year, she had been hesitant to disturb him. Not surprisingly, when she reminded him of their pact never to let anything unsaid come between them, he had hastily cleared the papers and demanded to know what was bothering her. As she told him, she had seen his face relax and he leaned back in his chair, lazily propping his feet up onto the desk.

"Come here, Brianne," he had softly commanded. When she stood next to him, Ryan had reached for her hand and lovingly kissed the delicate skin of her wrist.

"I vowed once to kill Gregory Duville, before he ever met Caroline," he had said matter-of-factly. "He promised that I would lose that which I valued above all else. After finding out he too had been the cause of our separation, and just how close I had come to being deprived of a life with you, I'll admit I wanted him to pay dearly. When I calmed down, I gave up the idea of ending his miserable life. He wasn't worth another separation from you . . . because it would have been murder if I had come in contact with him, nothing else would have satisfied me. Instead, I decided to do to him what he pledged to me. I have taken that which he valued above all else—his self-esteem, his social position—and made him an outcast among his own kind."

He had lit a thin cheroot and exhaled heavily, surrounding his head in a thick blue smoke. "It matters little that he has no positive proof I'm behind his misfortunes . . . he and I both know I have been revenged," he had declared in an unemotional voice.

Brianne remembered staring at her husband and knowing why he was accorded such respect by his peers. Ryan Barrington was, very quietly, an extremely powerful man . . . and Gregory Duville had been a fool not to recognize it.

Rubbing her back, Brianne walked out of her child's room and returned to her own. Although constantly tired during the day, sleep eluded her at night, and without Ryan to hold she prowled the large bedroom instead of climbing back into bed. And it would have been climbing too, so hard was it to get in and out of now. She avoided

470

looking into the mirror when she passed; her body was so distorted she would only be depressed to see her reflection. Ignoring the nagging ache in her back, she again took out the cream. Every time she applied it to her now rock-hard abdomen, she thought of Rena laughingly telling her that nothing would stop the dreaded stretch marks. Well, she only had two silvery thin lines, and she'd just bet when it was Rena's turn she'd beg for the cocoa butter recipe.

That was another problem that was finally resolved. Rena had at last agreed to marry Stephan. When he had first proposed in November, she was prepared to run away rather than face him with the truth of her past. It had taken the combined efforts of both herself and Ryan to convince Rena to trust Stephan's understanding nature. She finally told him, and Brianne's heart went out to her when Stephan sped away from her, punishing his horse in his need to put distance between them. But to his credit, it had taken him less than a week to digest her story and come back to Briarfawn, insisting that Maureen Ahearn was the only woman he wanted. He surprised her with a stunning engagement ring at Christmas, and Rena set the date for April, insisting she would stay with Brianne until after the baby was born and she was back to normal.

Brianne sincerely hoped she would be back to normal before then. She replaced the cream and stopped short as another cramp began. In the last month she'd had so many twinges and aches, as the baby moved and positioned himself, that she no longer thought, *Is this it? Is this labor?* Mattie said when it happened there would be no doubt in her mind as to whether it was or not. She had tried to remember everything she had read or heard about labor and childbirth, and knew the term was meant literally—it would probably be the hardest work she had ever done in her life.

She glanced over at the bed with longing. How sh
wished Ryan could be there with her. Never mind that h
dissolved into much-needed sleep soon after his head h
the pillow; she still enjoyed holding him and watching hi
face as she tenderly brushed the hair back from hi
calmed brow.

Deciding it was time to rest as the heaviness continue
in her back, she put one foot on the bed stool, preparin
to make the awkward climb.

A frightened cry escaped her lips and she stood stil
looking at the carpet beneath her. Eyes widening at he
ruined gown and the soaked circle upon the rug, sh
screamed for Rena.

Within a matter of seconds, the bedroom door swun
open and Rena, clad in her nightgown, quickly surveye
the situation and Brianne's panicked face.

"Mattie!" The scream coming from her throa
matched Brianne's for sheer volume and alarm. Rushin
to her friend's side, she put her arm around Brianne'
waist and let her lean against her.

"I'll send for Ryan," Rena said soothingly.

Brianne shook her head. "Don't. Help me get into
fresh nightgown. I was just shocked when it happene
without any warning."

Rena quickly pulled out a clean gown and after helpin
Brianne out of her soiled one, completely startled th
smaller woman by screaming a second time at the top o
her lungs.

"Mattie! Get the hell up here!"

Coming into the bedroom, the housekeeper replie
sleepily, "Ain't no baby gonna be born in the time it take
to walk up them stairs. You jus' calm down, Miz Rena
Miz Brianne's the one havin' the baby." Looking at he
mistress, she asked with a motherly concern, "You al
right, chile? I see your water broke. Any pains yet?"

Brianne adjusted the nightgown over her tigh

abdomen. "No. Nothing I would call pain. Just discomfort."

Mattie walked over to the bed and turned it down completely. "Well, you best get into bed. They'll soon be comin'. I've already sent for Tessa."

Brianne again shook her head. "Not yet, Mattie. I don't intend to lie down until it's necessary. First labors are usually long, and they say walking and keeping busy helps to shorten them."

"Ain't never heard of that," the housekeeper said in a disapproving voice. "You do what you wants, but when Tessa says to get into bed, you're gettin'." After cleaning the rug Mattie left, saying she would meet Tessa and tell Lizzie to start the fires going.

Vaguely Brianne realized that Mattie was fulfilling her instructions to have plenty of boiling water available. She had insisted that anything that came in contact with her during delivery must first be sterilized. Her major concern, the one that plagued her the most, was the high risk of infection that claimed the lives of many women during childbirth.

"Brianne? Are you all right?" Rena asked, peering into her face. "You're just staring off into space."

Brianne tried to clear her head. "I'm fine. Really. I'm just a little awed by what's happening. I've waited so long, and now that it's finally here, it doesn't seem real."

Walking gingerly to Ryan's dresser, she opened the drawer and pulled out a small leather envelope. Tossing it to Rena, she said lightly, "C'mon, let's play cards. You didn't think I taught you how to play gin rummy for nothing, did you?"

"You can't be serious! You want to play cards now? You're having a baby, damn it!" Rena stared at her as if she had lost her mind.

"You know, you're really going to have to do something about that habit of yours. Do you know you curse hysterically every time you're upset? I understand, Rena, but Stephan's never seen that side of you that's lurking just beneath the surface. I think I'd try and be more careful around him, if I were you."

Standing in front of her, she reached for her friend's hand. "You want the truth, Rena? I'm scared to death. I'm fighting down my own panic with every swallow. I'm about to give birth, at home, without the benefit of a doctor. I don't know that much about what I'm supposed to do, or what will happen if there's a complication. I can only pray, just as I have for months, that God will look after me and that my child is born healthy. Now will you *please* deal the cards? I need something to take my mind off those things."

When Mattie, accompanied by Tessa, came into the bedroom, neither could believe her eyes or ears. Their mistress was bent over the bed in the throes of her first real labor pain. Clutching the sheet in her white-knuckled fist, she gasped out, "You're too easy . . . don't always go after the aces."

Miz Rena, standing next to her, looked about ready to fall apart. Helpless to be of any comfort, she replied, "I don't give a good damn about the aces, or this stupid game . . . just tell me what to do!"

Mattie, the first to recover, rushed to her mistress's side. "Miz Brianne, you can't be playin' no cards. You're about to have a baby! It ain't natural for you to be out of bed now. It jus' ain't natural!"

Brianne regained her breath as the contraction subsided and looked at the three determined faces that circled her. Reluctantly she gave in, muttering as she let them help her into bed, "I'll tell you what's not natural . . . lying on your back when a baby comes down and out. I may not know much about it, but I do know that."

Four hours later, Brianne was soaked from her

exertions. Hours ago she had lost control of her labor. It was nothing at all like she had read or heard about. She had tried taking short, deep breaths, but that had only helped in the beginning, now it seemed nothing could free her from the agony that was forced on her.

Two steel hands gripped her lower back, then invisibly worked their way around to meet on top of her abdomen, creating such pain and pressure that she had bit through her lip twice. No sooner would it end, and Brianne gratefully collapse back against the pillows, then it seemed another would begin.

After she had injured her lip, Tessa had given her a thin piece of wood to bite on, and through a haze of raw anguish she watched the anxious faces and heard the comforting voices meant to reassure her. Dimly, she wondered why modern times was overpopulated—how anyone, knowing what this was like, would make the conscious decision to go through it again was beyond her. And as another contraction began, she tightened her hold on Rena's hand and tried desperately to control it.

Impossible.

As Rena wiped her face, she looked up at her dear friend and finally conceded, "Get Ryan," she said weakly. "Tell him to hurry . . . I . . . I need him!"

She watched Rena's face change from almost pain, as though she too were feeling each spasm, to relief.

Bathing her face with cool water, Mattie stopped and nodded to her mistress. "Thank God! 'Bout time too. Not right for a man not even knowin' he's 'bout to be a father," she proclaimed. "You stay, Miz Rena, I'll send somebody to fetch him real fast."

Brianne closed her eyes when the door shut behind Mattie. She knew she was silently crying, feeling sorry for herself. She had wanted to do this alone, present him with his child with he returned from the mill, but she was defeated. She had no reserve of strength to draw upon.

She needed Ryan; he would provide her with his. He had to, for she couldn't go on like this much longer.

She knew she should work with the pain, that every contraction meant her baby was that much sooner to being born, but she couldn't. She thought of it as her enemy, something to fight against, and it was quickly vanquishing her. As the hands she imagined rubbed together in anticipation at her back, she once again began the assent of torment that would cease only for a brief moment after she had reached the peak of her misery.

Ryan was wide awake after hearing Mattie's worried explanation in the hallway.

"She's jus' too tired, Misser Barrington. She's been at this for hours and now she don't have the strength to push that baby out. You have to make her push, Misser Barrington . . . or we gonna lose 'em both!"

He stared at the woman for a few unbelievable seconds. It couldn't be true. He couldn't lose Brianne, not now! Grabbing Mattie's fleshy arms, he said fiercely, "No matter what—you save Brianne! You tell that to Tessa. Brianne comes first!"

He flung open the door and surveyed the scene before him. Sucking in his breath at the sight of his wife, he rushed to her side and placed a soft kiss on her pale cheek.

"You should have called me sooner," he said gently. "Didn't you know, little one, I would have wanted to be with you through this?"

Brianne felt the tears slide down her cheeks, but she didn't possess the strength to wipe them away.

"Ryan," she barely breathed his name. "Thank God you're here." No sooner had she addressed him than another pain pulled her back into its unrelenting agony.

Ryan watched in frustration as the most precious gift

of his wife slipped further away from him. She was too small for this child, and she needed immediate help.

As soon as the contraction was over, Ryan assumed command of the room as though it were the deck of the *Lady*. In his booming captain's voice, he shouted out his orders.

"Bring me two lengths of rope and all the extra pillows we have! I want everybody moving—and I want everything here in less than two minutes! Now get going!"

He cleared the room of the startled women and turned to his wife. Brushing back her hair from her forehead, he gently whispered to her, "We're going to do this together. Please don't give up . . . I love you, Bri . . . *please* try. The two of us can beat anything."

Why couldn't she see him clearly? Why was his face surrounded by a haze, almost a fog her vision couldn't penetrate? But she clearly heard his voice, his beautiful voice, and it was like the first drops of rain on a parched desert, giving her sustenance and renewal.

When she started to moan again, he talked her through it, not bothering to make her push, knowing she'd need every ounce of strength she had left once the women returned.

He tied each length of rope to a poster at the bottom of the bed and gently lifted Brianne down to the lower part of the mattress. She looked at him with the eyes of a trusting child, believing he was going to fix everything, and he silently prayed that he wouldn't let her down. He and Rena stacked pillows behind her and at her sides to support her back, then he positioned her into a half-sitting position.

Tenderly he placed her feet against the footboard and brought the ropes up to her hands. Wrapping one around each of her wrists, he explained what she must do.

"I saw this in the Islands, years ago, and it worked

477

then. When the next pain comes, Brianne, I want you to brace your feet against the footboard and pull up with the ropes, all right?"

She smiled weakly and nodded to him. Ryan stood at the bottom of the bed and called to her as the contraction came, "Look at me, Brianne. Block out everything but my face. Remember when we were dancing together at Stephan's party for the first time? I loved you then. You were the most beautiful woman I had ever seen, and you were mine. Neither of us needed anyone else then . . . we weren't even aware that there was anyone else in the room. There's no one but us now, little one. Pull on the ropes, let them help you."

He held her feet against the bed and she did as he asked. Concentrating on his soothing voice, she let the ropes take some of the pressure and before she realized, he was telling her to ease up as Rena chafed her hands to get the circulation back into them from pulling so tightly.

It was over! She had barely been conscious of the pain now that she had him to help her. He was smiling at her, telling her she was terrific, before calling the three women before him, and Brianne relaxed against the pillows, not even bothering to listen to the discussion. She just wished Ryan would come closer so she could tell him how grateful she was that he had found something to give her relief. Blessed relief.

Ryan looked at the three pairs of hands before him. "All right, Tessa, we're lucky yours are the smallest. You're going to have to help her. Before the next contraction, feel for the baby's head. When she starts to push, you steadily pull. You've done this before?"

As the wizened midwife nodded her understanding, everyone came back into position.

Ryan brought his wife back into his control as Tessa worked between her legs. When she looked like she was about to panic, he started to cheer her on. "Push,

Brianne!" he commanded. "You can do it. The baby's coming . . . I can see its head! C'mon, you can do it!"

The other women joined him, encouraging Brianne to bring forth her baby. Behind her, supporting her neck, Rena whispered into her ear, "Push, damn it! You can do this!"

They were telling her of their confidence in her, and she drew from them, feeling for the first time that she possibly *could* do it.

First came the head, with a mop of dark hair, surprising everybody, then in a flash the body rushed from its warm cocoon into Tessa's capable hands. Everyone started laughing with relief as Ryan picked up the slippery child and Tessa continued to work on Brianne.

Piercing screams filled the room as the baby wailed at being so rudely disturbed, and taking a cloth from Mattie, Ryan gently wiped the blood from his child.

In amazement, Brianne weakly watched the flailing arms and legs and listened to the healthy screams emanating from the tiny red body.

She whispered her husband's name as another contraction began.

"Ryan . . . ?"

As Tessa separated the child and mother, she finally nodded to Ryan, and wrapping a soft blanket around the child, he brought the bundle to Brianne.

Placing the child on her lap, he looked at her with eyes that spoke of love without the need of words.

"I'm so proud of you, Brianne," he whispered. "Thank you for our son."

Brianne looked down at the child squirming in her arms, then back at her husband. "A boy?" she asked, surprised, although she had said it would be.

As Ryan happily nodded, he watched her unwrap the baby and examine him. "He's beautiful!" she proclaimed in wonder, holding the tiny fingers up for a closer inspection.

When the crying continued, Brianne looked helplessly at Mattie.

The housekeeper came over to her young mistress and looked with pride at the new member of the family. "My guess is this chile's hungry. Takes after his daddy, I'd say . . . no patience when it comes to bein' fed. If you still intend to nurse him yourself, Miz Brianne, I 'spect now's the time to get started."

Suddenly Brianne was filled with an unexpected energy. She felt as though she had just won the gold medal at the Olympics, finished first in the Boston Marathon . . . she had just done something absolutely tremendous! Even knowing millions of women before her had done the same thing couldn't take away from her elation.

She looked up at the faces before her and smiled brilliantly. "Thank you so much . . . all of you. Each of you holds a special place in our son's life."

She unbuttoned her gown without the slightest hesitancy and placed the baby to her breast. All watched with interest as the tiny mouth rooted for a few seconds before abruptly latching onto his mother. Brianne jerked in surprise when he began to suck so vigorously, and the three women began to laugh.

"Comme il faut! Ain't nothin' shy 'bout that boy," Tessa chuckled. "He's gonna be jus' fine, Miz Brianne."

Rena placed an arm about Mattie's shoulders and joined her in shedding grateful tears. Sniffling, she looked over at Brianne and said roughly, "I hope you realize that after everything you put me through tonight, I claim the right to be his godmother."

As Ryan watched Brianne cup their son's head in her palm while she nursed him, he felt an acrid burning in his own throat from his unshed tears. Should he live to be a

480

hundred, never again would a single moment mean as much to him as this one. Afraid of embarrassing himself, he left his wife enraptured by their son and eased unnoticed from the room.

Hurrying to his study, he poured himself a stiff drink and throwing back his head, finished it in one gulp. He slowly walked over to his desk and sat down heavily. He had come so close to losing them both! Overcome by both relief and gratitude, he freely let the tears come as he laid his head back against the soft leather of the chair . . . so thankful for the two precious lives upstairs.

Later, coming into the room, he saw the women had been busy in his absence. Gone was any sign of childbirth; Brianne was shining in a pale yellow gown with a matching ribbon holding back her hair. It was hard to believe she had just gone through such an ordeal.

As he came closer he saw her eyes were closed, and he looked to her side. Lying next to her, clad in a white embroidered gown, was his son, sleeping on his stomach with his fist close to his mouth. As though sensing Ryan's presence, Brianne slowly opened her eyes and smiled up at him lovingly.

"Where have you been?" she asked softly.

"Truthfully? I've been downstairs trying to pull myself together. I was so frightened at the thought of something happening to you that I needed the time to myself."

Holding out her hand to him, she brought him to sit next to her on the bed. "I don't think I would have made it without you, Ryan. You were my strength, my lifeline. I'll always be grateful to you for bringing me through."

Looking uncomfortable, Ryan patted her hand. "I've come to a decision . . . I don't think there should be any more children, Brianne. I never want to see you suffer like that again."

"Tessa says the first time is the worst. After that, it's supposed to be easier. I have to admit I felt like that myself—no more children. But that was before I held him."

Reaching over, she gently touched her son's smooth cheek. "Nothing worthwhile comes easy, Ryan. Hard work only makes you appreciate it more."

His voice became hoarse when he spoke. "I love you, Brianne. Probably from that first moment I woke you by the levee, I knew you'd have to be mine. You've completed my life in a way I didn't think possible."

She placed her arms around his neck and breathed in the masculine scent of him. "Ryan . . . I don't know what I'd do without you. I never want to be anywhere but right here, within your arms."

Pulling back from him, she looked into his eyes. "If it's agreeable with you, I'd like to name our son Travis Morgan Barrington, after your father and my sister Morganna."

Ryan looked over at the sleeping form of his infant son. "I'd like that. Travis Morgan Barrington," he said the name over again, liking the sound of it. "Thank you, Brianne, it means a lot to me to have my son carry my father's name."

Reaching inside his jacket, he pulled out a velvet box. "I almost forgot," he lied. "I bought this in England, and was waiting for today to present it to you."

Brianne opened the box and gasped. Attached to a very long gold chain was a heavy gold disc with the words *Never Fear Awakening* engraved in an ornate scroll.

"I thought it was time you had a watch of your own," he said, pleased by her reaction. "Open it and read the inscription."

She did as he asked and stared at the watch for a very long time. Lifting her head, she wiped away her tears and softly commanded him. "Come here," she said gently, opening her arms. "Come lie with us."

Positioning himself next to her, he lay against her breast, within the crook of her arm.

Brianne broke the silence when she brushed his funny curl back from his forehead and placed a light kiss on his brow.

"You're right," she said softly, as she thought about the astonishing inscription, and placing her hand on her son's back, she felt it gently rise and fall with his sweet breath as she continued to stroke her husband's head.

Closing her own eyes, she let the precious calm overtake her. Timeless . . . joy such as this had no earthly bounds.

Epilogue

Morganna Barrington was more than a little weary as she made her way up the old stairs leading into the attic. She knew this last effort of Charles's was another attempt to dispel the gloom that had seemed to settle on the old house during the last month. Coming into the musty room, she brushed away the cobwebs and looked about her with disgust. Old furniture, long discarded, intermingled with chests of clothes and memorabilia left behind by generations of Barringtons.

At least they had something to remember them by, she thought selfishly. She, on the other hand, had very little to take out and hold close as the anniversary marking her sister's death drew near.

It still seemed as if she were living a nightmare. How could her vibrant older sister be gone forever? The unfairness of it hit her squarely between the eyes every time she thought of it.

What should have been the happiest time in her life, the birth of her own sweet daughter, had turned into a horror movie that refused to end, never flashing the closing credits, never letting the light come back into her life, never letting her breathe a sigh of relief that it was all fiction, the product of someone else's imagination.

Lifting the lid of one old crate, she browsed through the contents but her heart wasn't in it. She supposed it was for a good cause, and that Charles had the best of intentions when he had announced last week that their home was to be a part of the tour sponsored by the Christian Women's Exchange. What she really resented was that as a member of the organization, and owner of the house, she was requested to dress in a period costume, preferably pre-Civil War, and guide the tour through her home.

Just what she needed, she thought sarcastically, a group of strangers tramping through her home, expecting her to regale them with some tale about her ancestors. Well, they weren't her ancestors. Charles's mother should be doing this, not her.

She slammed the lid in anger, creating a storm of dust that flew about the room. Coughing, she looked to another chest, hoping to find the correct period and leave the room to the ghosts whose lives were contained in the many boxes. She had always hated it up here and never came, unless accompanied by her husband. Charles, however, had been working late so often, and with his busy schedule she had thought to get this over with while the baby was napping.

Thinking of her sunny child, she smiled with a mother's pride. How she loved her . . . named for her aunt who ironically had died the night she was born, she magically looked like Morganna's sister. In the last year Morganna had watched in fascination as her daughter's blonde hair gradually turned a darker brown that caught the sunlight and shone a beautiful copper, like her sister's. When Brianne was six months old her eyes looked to be hazel, but now Morganna was sure they would be a deep green, as lovely as her namesake's.

She was doing it to herself again, and she knew she should let it go. The memories, all painful, flooded back to her and she wanted, for her family's sake, to be done with them. They didn't deserve this. What they did need was a wife and mother . . . not this shadow of the person she used to be. Sitting down on an old rocker, she let it wash over her, knowing somehow that this time it was important for her to remember . . .

She blamed herself for Brianne's death. *She* was the one who had called, feeling sorry for herself and dropping so many hints that Brianne had felt obliged to drive down to be with her. Why had Brianne insisted on driving? she asked herself for the thousandth time.

Her grief when she was told of her sister's accident had been overwhelming. She didn't care what the coroner's report said: cerebral hemorrhage, caused by the sharp blow to the head, death occurring minutes later after she had somehow fallen down the ravine . . . Morganna Barrington *knew* it was her fault. Never would she forget the sight of her sister's coffin being interred in the Barrington vault—Morganna had insisted on that, wanting her sister close to her, and Charles had readily agreed. Strange that in almost a year, she'd never gone to the cemetery. She couldn't believe Brianne was there.

Angry with herself, and wanting to be done with this present task, she jumped up to rummage through more boxes.

Not finding what she wanted, she wiped her forehead on her sleeve and looked about unhappily. This junk should be stored at Briarfawn, the family compound across the Mississippi, not here. There was more room there and everyone in the family could go through it and keep what was valuable or meaningful, discarding the rest.

Shaking her head at the clutter, Morganna spied an ornately carved leather trunk under three old chests. Going toward the back of the attic, she came upon it. She struggled for a good five minutes to remove the ones on

top before she was able to see the faded leatherwork. I
was quite beautiful, and showed the expert craftsman
ship someone had employed years ago. It was too bad th
leather was cracking; she wouldn't have minded having
downstairs.

Taking an old cloth, she rubbed at the tarnished bras
clasp. Initials had been engraved. *B O B* . . . obviousl
some old Barrington ancestor. Dampening the cloth wit
her tongue, she rubbed harder. *B Q B*

Intrigued, Morganna fought with the lock until th
leather, aged by decades of neglect, broke under he
hands.

Opening the trunk, she removed layers of tissue pape
that threatened to fall apart until she came upon a dress
Picking it up gently by the sleeves, she let out a lov
whistle.

It was still beautiful. Fabulous material, which looke
to be silver beneath the yellow of age, was fashioned int
an elegant ballgown. Faded silk flowers were attached to
deep neckline. It really must have been extraordinary i
its time, and she could imagine herself wearing it if i
could be cleaned without damage. Laying the dress on th
discarded tissue, she burrowed further and found unde
the dress a silver netted snood and small slippers sh
knew would never fit her.

Wanting to know something about the woman wh
had worn this creation years ago, she dug deeper into th
chest and came up with an old photograph, probably on
of the first taken with a camera.

Morganna smiled. He was certainly handsome, thi
Barrington, although he looked uncomfortable and
little unsure of the gadget he was looking into. Morganna
turned it over and read the fluid, fancy script. "To m
beautiful wife. Remember, this was your idea. Forever
R."

Putting the picture aside to show Charles, sh

searched further, finding an embroidered infant's gown and some larger ones, as the child grew. Picking one out, she put it on top of the ballgown to dress her daughter in . . . might as well go all the way and have them both in costume.

Morganna's hand felt the leather portfolio and she pulled it out, anxious for any information as to the owner of the trunk.

Kneeling before the chest, she gingerly untied the faded brown ribbons and opened the pigskin folder. The first thing she saw was a paper, or parchment, with writing on it.

Taking it out carefully, she unfolded the thin paper and stared as her name swam before her unbelieving eyes!

Falling back on her heels, she tried desperately to control her hands as she read the letter addressed to her:

For my dearest sister,
Morganna Quinlan Barrington
"Don't be frightened when you read this, as I know in my heart this letter will one day reach you. How I came to be here, a hundred and thirty years into the past, I don't know. Perhaps you can figure it out, knowing what's become of me. I've thought about time travel, perhaps an accident of time, and I know there is a theory that people simultaneously lead many lives. I've even entertained the possibility that I might have died . . . to me it no longer matters.

I could write you volumes about what has happened to me over the years, but just let me say . . . I *am* happy, happier than I ever thought possible. As I write this it's hard for me to believe that I'm thirty-nine now (I still think of myself as being young), and we've just bought this home from dear friends of ours, Carl and Emily Howard. (Some will never get over the tragedy brought by the Civil War.)

I know someday you will live here, share the same rooms as I, watch your children grow here, as I will. That's why I wanted to store a little of my life away for you.

You were the best part of my old life, Morganna, the only part I miss. It was a joy to me, having a sister like you. You played the part of adoring younger sister with a sincerity I knew was real. You never knew that I envied you. Bright, always cheerful, you succeeded in finding love and happiness while I struggled just to find myself. Perhaps I wasn't able to in your time because it waited for me here.

I am happy, Morganna, never doubt that. I'm loved by a man, Ryan Barrington, whose description I cannot put down on paper. Suffice it to say he is my life, along with my children. I'm enclosing a picture, recently taken, of my family. Along with Ryan and me are my sons, Travis Morgan, named for Ryan's father from Virginia and for you, and Edward Patrick, in memory of our own father. Both are a source of constant pride and show promise of being fine men.

The young blonde, with the inquisitive eyes that you can't tell are a piercing blue, is my daughter Katherine Anne. I'm afraid she's more like me than I would have hoped, but she makes me laugh, and I hold a very special place for her in my heart.

After Travis was born, I started keeping a journal for you. I wanted you to know that whatever happened to me isn't frightening, although in the beginning I too thought I was losing my mind. God willing, this will reach you and one day you will know that peace too.

Be happy, Morganna. Take joy in your family, for they are a part of me. We'll always be together, never ever doubt that . . . each of us carries the other within her heart.

Love,
Bri

Morganna slumped back onto the dusty wooden floor. It *was* Brianne's handwriting! What kind of morbid trick was this? Who would do such a thing? Deep within her heart, she knew the answer . . .

She reread the letter, concentrating on every word. At its conclusion, she waited a few seconds, building up her nerve, before taking out the picture. She watched her own hand shakily bring forth a photograph in sepia tones, approximately 5 × 7 size.

"My God!" Morganna clenched her fist to her mouth to keep from screaming. *There she was!* Surrounded by her family, Brianne was seated on a bench outside this very home. Older, even more beautiful, she had a serene smile on her face and held a young, laughing girl of about seven or eight around the waist. Behind her was the handsome man she had viewed earlier, only this time he was relaxed and proud as he stood between two teenaged boys, an arm around the shoulder of each. Unlike in most old photographs, everyone was smiling, and Morganna felt the photographer had captured the true essence of a happy family.

After studying each face closely, Morganna held the picture to her chest as she emptied the portfolio. Falling onto her lap, unbelievably, was the watch she had given Brianne for her twenty-fourth birthday. Picking it up, she stupidly pushed the time button, half expecting to see a readout. Along with the watch was her set of keys, the name of the Philadelphia insurance company Brianne had worked for clearly visible on the pewter disc. Everyone had assumed they had been lost the night of the accident.

The last item was a piece of antique jewelry, about the size of a silver dollar, a round gold fob watch, attached to a long, braided chain, with the words *Never Fear Awakening* engraved on it.

She opened the cover, and holding it up to the thin shaft of light coming through the attic window, read the inscription:

Ryan Jonathan Barrington—Brianne Quinlan Barrington
United by more than marriage—
bound by more than love
1856–1986–INFINITY

Morganna held the watch in the palm of one hand and brought the picture back into view with the other. Looking at her sister wearing this very watch in the photograph, she stared at the face smiling back at her.

"You were a very fortunate woman, Brianne," she whispered between sobs. "Very few women know that kind of love."

Miraculously Morganna's heart was once again light. She wanted her own daughter now, needed to touch base with her own reality. Her family had waited patiently until she worked her way through this grief. Now it was done, and she knew her sister had given her the most precious gift of all . . . her own life back.

She closed the empty trunk and placed the chests back on top of it. Wearing the watch around her neck, she carefully picked up the diary, the dress, and the personal belongings of her sister. When she left the attic it was no longer a sinister place for her, and she knew she would come back.

In her bedroom she left the gown on her bed and

opened her bureau drawer. Lovingly she placed Brianne's things in the back, for she wasn't ready yet to share this with anyone. It was enough right now for her to know what had happened.

Hearing her daughter's funny giggle across the hall, she ached to hold her in her arms.

Standing in the doorway, she watched the child playing with the dust motes that fell in a sunlit ray across her playpen. Sensing her mother's presence, she looked around at her and smiled brilliantly.

Morganna felt rooted to the spot. Moving on stiff legs, she came closer and bent to pick up her child as small hands grabbed for the watch dangling invitingly before her eyes. Turning it over and over in her hands, a sweet, beautiful face turned up to her mother's and smiled once again, her face lit by emerald eyes, eyes that her mother had loved throughout her lifetime.

Clasping the child closer to her chest, Morganna cried out her name.

"Brianne . . ."

As God was her witness, for that brief infinitesimal moment, that suspended second in time, Morganna didn't know whether she held her own child, or perhaps her own sister.

And in the end it mattered little. Brianne was right . . . They would always be together, each carried within the other's heart and mind.

Afterword

"Don't be afraid . . . it's only falling asleep in one world and waking up in another."
>   —Francis Edward Aloysius Xavier O'Day
>   (1907–1962)